The Black Rook

Davey Cobb

Science Fiction and Fantasy Publications

The Black Rook

Davey Cobb

Science Fiction and Fantasy Publications

Science Fiction and Fantasy Publications
HTTPS://SCIFICANTASYPUBLICATIONS.COM
An imprint of DAOwen Publications
Copyright © 2022 by Davey Cobb
All rights reserved

The Black Rook / Davey Cobb

ISBN: 978-1-928094-87-6
EISBN: 978-1-928094-88-3

Edited by Douglas Owen
Coverart by MMT Productions

10 9 8 7 6 5 4 3 2 1

For mum and dad. Without your love and support, this book would not exist.

PLA

NURSADE

GORRANT

DELLËS

THE
NÖRTS

NÖRTISH
SEA

ULMAR

WOLTLAND

NORNMAR

BURGENBAR

BRON

MAYSTONE

WEST
FORGIA

MILFOR

SCOTBRANT
SEA

MENCIA

GORDEMIA

SYLVIAN
EMPIRE

ROOKS LAN

GOLMAR

CRAMDOR

MLUKOT
LAND

ALGE

SYLVIA

EMERNI

THELIA

SPICE
SEA

NOCRYNAS

OSS

SEA OF SOULS

KLEÄM

Continent of Nortavia

CARTHANE

NORTHERN
SEA

MYRAKÄSS

T

MARLIN BAY

TYLDAR

GADENS
LAND

SHIELD
OF
LANYS

VRESTALONIA

THE MARRIDAN

DRAGON'S
TOOTH

DRAGON'S
EYE

THE
WORLD'S
HAND

VAAK

KRÄMISE

UNIC
WILDS

ARTHENSHOLD

KARHOLD

CUSPEN
SEA

ARM OF ANDERS

DELSOLM

RHYNËST

LERTHIAN REPUBLIC

THE
DRAVES

Tossed Overboard

1452 - HMS Temper - Northern Sea

The ship creaked like old bones as it rocked with the current. *And they might well build it of bone and flesh,* Hanzus mused, for the Temper was as brittle and bothersome as any living being he'd ever encountered.

The biting breeze harassed his desk candle, threatening to extinguish the flame and plummet his wooden tomb into deeper darkness. The wick fought in a valiant effort to remain alight, the dancing flame casting erratic shadows across the wall. But the waves hitting the starboard side were too soothing to close the window.

For a moment, all was calm.

And then he remembered.

Wherever Hanzus's mind wandered – summer mornings courting the beautiful Edrianna Lametzer, evenings spent losing at cards to Arwel Nate – it rarely roamed from the moment he'd witnessed true madness.

He'd fought in countless battles, participated in a handful of tourneys, traversed the Feleric peaks and even swallowed poison. Everything paled in comparison to the look in Tamara Lockett's eyes on the day of her husband's sentencing. Sir Henry's trial had been a mere formality, of course. He was guilty of aiding the traitor Jesmond in a plot to murder the King. Worst of all, Henry and Jesmond had calculated every detail of the aftermath. Plans to reorder government and a list of nobles to be assassinated in due course were discovered in Henry's manor. Treason and treachery were inked in every book and scroll.

Tamara had shrieked like a banshee when the judge confirmed her husband was to be hung, drawn, and quartered. Her screams resonated in Hanzus's skull. Seven years had passed and still he could hear her.

A tear formed in his eye. *Ridiculous. Pull yourself together.* Goose bumps rippled across his arms. A chill flashed down his spine. He wasn't sure why her reaction had affected him so much. After all, she was the wife of a traitor, fortunate to be spared from the hangman's noose.

Her face, as it had been then, flashed before him like a spectre. She was beautiful, even with makeup dribbling down her face, her eyes painted with malice and sorrow.

Snap out of it. Henry deserved his punishment. If his schemes had come to fruition, you'd be the one drawn and quartered. He studied his memory of Tamara's features, searching her maddened pupils. *Did you know, Tamara? Did you know all that your husband had planned for our kingdom? The misery he sought to inflict? You were his confidant, weren't you? Perhaps you even helped him construct his list of condemned men. Was I among them?*

Hanzus had never learned of the names Jesmond and Henry marked for execution. He hadn't wanted to. After hearing Tamara's inhuman cry, he'd wanted to forget the whole affair ever took place.

Pity he never had.

Hanzus swallowed the lump in his throat and reached for his goblet. The cool pewter soothed his aching fingers, the plum wine caressed his dry throat. *The taste of the Sylvian coast.* Familiarity. *The first thing I'll do when I'm home is sample a few favourites from the cellar.* Thelian red, Emernian blue, cheese from every corner of Gadensland.

His gut contracted. He couldn't remember the last time he'd eaten real food. He blew out the candle, slid out of his chair, and approached the window.

The honey-coloured moon watched over a calm sea. The sky was otherwise black, its multitude of stars hidden.

All was quiet. A blissful reprieve following the crew's singing and dancing, which had dragged on for much of the night. They were heathens all, making merry while the Goddess was upon them. But it was to be expected, he supposed. He'd seen Lerthians and Burgens among the crew – Goddessless folk if ever there were any.

Hanzus breathed in the silence, welcoming the salt that tickled his nostrils. He was thankful to be homeward, relieved to have escaped Carthane alive.

The thought had barely sunk in when a knock came at the door.

He turned to face the narrow plank of wood, wondering who it could be. It was well past midnight. Who aboard had the audacity to stir him? His servants' quarters were on the other side of the ship, well below deck.

A second knock came, a soft rapping.

"Yes?" Hanzus croaked, meeker than he'd intended.

The door creaked inward. The intruder had taken his word to mean *come on in*. A dark figure crept through the crack, then the long, benign face of Edgar Morske came into view, illuminated by the moon. The captain of the ship slithered in, closing the door behind him, his features unreadable.

"My lord," Morske said, inclining his head. "Forgive me for disturbing you at such a holy hour."

Hanzus waited for the captain to explain his intrusion, but when it was clear the skinny wretch was going to just stand there eyeing him through the darkness, he asked, "Do we have sight of land?"

Morske opened his mouth, then hesitated, perhaps realising the sarcasm in the baron's tone. "Alas, no." He gestured at the stool next to Hanzus's desk. "May I?"

"You may not." Hanzus sank into his chair on the far side of the desk. He owed Morske a great deal of gratitude for agreeing to ferry him back to Dyllet at such short notice. Still, there was no excuse for disturbing a man when the moon was present.

"Ah," Morske said, unsmiling. The stool was his, of course, it was all his. This cabin was his largest guestroom. Its furniture was not cheap. All the same, there were some places in the world where the crime of disturbing a man during a full moon was punishable by death. "Were this no pressing matter, my lord, I would have waited till the morrow. As it is..." He cut himself off and blinked around the room.

Hanzus sighed. "Sit down, captain."

Morske slinked over to the stool. "Obliged, my lord. Truly obliged." He crossed his legs, tapping his elevated knee with one bony hand. A ruby ring glowed in the moonlight.

The ceiling lamp illuminated half of Morske's face. His visible eye, a dull grey orb, blinked at Hanzus.

"Well?" Hanzus poured himself more wine. Morske's eye scanned over the goblet, but he didn't ask for a cup. "What is this pressing matter, Captain Morske?"

"Please, my lord, call me Edgar." Morske ceased his tapping. "We're a day from port. Were I willing and able to placate you with untruths, I would be inclined to assure you that the journey's discomfort was nearing its end."

Hanzus raised his eyebrows. *Now that is an odd thing to say.*

Morske continued: "I bring news, as it happens. Word from the capital."

Hanzus feigned disinterest, sipping from his goblet. Was King Halmond dead? *Has Prince Perryn finally got his wish?* Perhaps the Sylvians had invaded, or the peasants of Vinerheim had revolted once again.

"A pigeon arrived just now," Morske said, caressing his knee. "A pigeon sent from the palace." He drew a sharp breath, reached into his coat, and retrieved a small roll of parchment. "The pigeon has been kept aboard, my lord. It awaits your reply."

Hanzus set down his goblet. *This crook's testing me.* He must have taken leave of his senses. *Does he know who I am?*

"Alas, my lord, you'll have to forgive me. I misread the lettering underneath the mark... Thought it was addressed to me. I assure you, I stopped reading the moment I realised my mistake." He placed the curled parchment on the desk and slid it over to Hanzus. "I've old eyes, my lord. My wife tells me to wear spectacles, but... I don't think they'd suit me. Do you?"

Hanzus snatched the parchment and unrolled it, squinting at the tiny writing. The lettering was wild, clearly rushed. The mark, he realised, as he flipped it over, was not the Verstecian coat-of-arms but the small sigil of an owl. *Arwel.* How did the Baron of the Tyldar know he was aboard the Temper? *And what on earth is he doing in the palace?* He turned it over in his hand, reading the scruffy text over and over.

Hans. Hope this finds you. Beware. The Despot is everywhere.

He read it again and again. *Gelmosh curse you, Arwel. How could you be so clumsy?* Morske had intercepted the letter. And he was smiling smugly. Evidently, he understood its meaning.

"Curious," Morske said, inspecting his fingernails. "I deliberated for some time after reading our good friend's message. What could the Tyldar baron be referring to? Who is this supposed *despot*, and how is he everywhere? The most curious thing, for me at least, lay in the baron's decision to reach you *here*. Was he threatened? An attempt made on his life? I pondered, for a while." He exhaled, glancing out the window. "Arwel Nate is a formidable man. To imagine him spooked... frightened..."

Hanzus didn't like where this was going. Edgar Morske was a trusted captain in King Halmond's fleet, a veteran of the seas. The very sight of him made Hanzus's skin crawl, but he was a man worthy of respect. And fear. Morske hadn't won every one of his naval battles on some whim. He was a shrewd tactician, a master swordsman, a chief negotiator. *And now he's here accusing me of something.*

Hanzus considered Arwel's message. *Beware... The Despot is everywhere... Despot... everywhere...* The hurried writing, the speed of its arrival. *It's an immediate warning about...*

Morske picked at his fingernails, removing dirt and flicking it toward the window. "Who might *despot* refer to, my lord? I hoped you might provide me with an answer. To ease a troubled mind, you understand?"

Morske didn't appear very troubled. Hanzus was still considering his next words when the captain added, "It couldn't refer to the King now, could it?"

Hanzus presented the captain with a smile. "Does Halmond strike you as a despot?"

The words sliced through the air like a hot blade through butter.

Morske's eyes widened a fraction, then he returned his attention to his nails. "You are clever, my lord. Perhaps *too* clever. But Arwel Nate... well, he is different. He's no fool, I'll give him that. He'd have known there was a good chance his message would be intercepted. If Despot referred to the King, then... well, I'd have misjudged him terribly."

Did the captain seriously believe Hanzus would interpret the message for him? The meaning of it was clear: Arwel was warning him about Morske.

Morske serves the Despot. Goddess above, I knew there was something amiss. Ever since Hanzus boarded the Temper, Morske had been sniffing about his business. Hanzus ran his fingers down his breeches, praying that his scabbard remained under the desk.

Fuck.

The sword was gone.

"Arwel's message is of no real concern to me. You see, my lord, I face a dilemma of my own. A terrible, terrible dilemma." Morske blew on his nails, satisfied they were clean. Then he met the baron with a dead stare. "For your friend's pigeon did not arrive alone. No. There was a second pigeon, as it happens, carrying a message addressed to Edgar Morske. A message bearing the royal mark."

A shiver rippled across Hanzus's body. This had to have been what Arwel was warning him about. *The captain's received an order from the Despot.*

"Aren't you a little old for the intrigues of court, captain?"

Morske giggled at that. "True enough, my lord. For too long have I endured the machinations of Vinerheim. Do you want to know what I learned during my tenure as the King's naval advisor? I learned to dance and make merry like a royal. I mastered the ability to triumph at cards... how to detect if a man is lying by the way he moves his eyes." He paused for impact, a glimmer of emotion cracking his face. His eyes creased in revulsion, his bottom lip quivered a fraction. "I enjoyed court life, as long as I was on the right side. The winning side. But then my fortunes changed, and old allies became wretched foes. So, I tired of the court. Begged to be relieved of my position, demoting myself, once more, to a life on the seas." He sighed, stretching out his back. "The bridge is my court now, my lord. The deck filled with my courtiers. I may have angered the King when I resigned from my post, but no matter how far I stray from the Motherland, the Diamond Banner flies over my bridge. And it always shall."

"If the ship is your court, you must loathe the thought of reaching Dyllet."

Morske hummed in reply, whispering some melody that Hanzus had never heard before.

Hanzus fidgeted in his seat. He would've preferred silence.

"I trust you have enjoyed a comfortable journey so far, my lord,"

Morske said, finally ending his bizarre song. "The Temper might be an old girl, built in an era when comfort was far from essential, but she's as reliable now as the day she was conceived."

When are you going to get to the point, you senile bastard? You're here to kill me, aren't you? Well? Go on then. Make your move.

"Sure, the ship's no palace, but she offers some comfort. I like to think of her as a tavern of the seas."

"I thought you said the ship was your *court?*"

"Aha! No, my lord. I said that the *bridge* was my court. I had taken you for an attentive man."

Morske uncrossed his legs, and Hanzus caught a flash of steel hiding under his coat. The captain's purpose was finally revealed: his orders were to slit the baron's throat before they reached Dyllet.

That had been the contents of his royal letter. *The Baron of the Krämise is aboard your ship. Kill him.* The reason didn't matter. In all probability, Hanzus's body would soon drift to the bottom of the Northern Sea.

But not while I've still air in my lungs. Hanzus scanned the room, aiming to be as discreet as possible. Where had he put that sword? Or that Dulenmeake dagger?

"Have you lost something, my lord?"

"Is our business here concluded?" Hanzus asked, playing the fool. "My eyes grow heavy. I'd much like to rest now. I don't suppose I'll have much of an opportunity after we land."

"Ah, yes. I don't suppose you will. Dyllet never sleeps, as they say. The workers labour all through the night, and I've found, no matter how far from the quay I rent a room, I can still hear the dockworkers grunting and yelling."

Hanzus reached for the decanter. Perhaps he could distract the fool long enough to remember where his weapons were. "Care for wine, captain?"

Morske's thin lips curled. "I'd be honoured, my lord."

Honoured by your own mediocre wine? Hanzus poured into both goblets, handing Morske the one he hadn't been drinking from. *Now think... where in Hektor's name did you put it?*

"Exquisite," Morske said after his second sip. "Thelian, is it?"

It's quite clearly Sylvian, you old fool. Is this one of your tricks, or has the salt air numbed your tongue? "I'm not sure."

"My lord... may I call you Hans?"

"My friends call me Hans."

The captain's mask cracked. With every dry comment the baron made, Morske's eye twitched, the corners of his mouth pinched. Hanzus parried the man's flowery statements, but he was never aggressive. All he needed was enough time to... Then it came to him. *The bed. When you unclasped your cloak, you dropped your sword down the side of the bed.*

He peered at the four-poster, squinting through the gloom. Grey sheets, muddy curtains.

It must be over there.

But Morske wouldn't let him trot over there and retrieve it. He would have to pass the captain to reach the bed. *What are you going to do? Think. Decide.* The dagger was likely somewhere near the sword...

Then he remembered.

Hanzus finished his drink and loosed a sigh. "Captain Morske, why are you really here?"

The words cut like a knife, eviscerating the captain's mask of calm. The face underneath was a contortion of features – his eyes glowered, his nose scrunched up to his brow, his lips quivered agape, revealing stained teeth.

"You are right, Hans," Morske said, his temper subsiding. "I have tarried for long enough. I take no great pleasure in my purpose this evening." He placed his goblet on the desk. "You see, I am quite familiar with the *despot* Arwel refers to." He leaned on the table with one hand. "For it is that very despot that sends me to your chamber."

The clock's methodical hands were ticking, pounding away like a mad drum.

Edgar Morske was a fine tactician. As captain upon these seas, he'd bested every enemy foolish enough to engage him. Under his captaincy, the Temper had overcome Carthanian pirates and Nortish raiders. It had defeated Baron Tealbank's fleet. He had overcome great odds, helping to besiege ports, capturing vessels twice the size of his own. Only now, for the first time in his life, he had underestimated his foe.

Morske reached for his sword as he leapt from the stool. His coat brushed his goblet to the edge of the table, sending it crashing to the floor, spilling dark liquid over the table.

Clumsy old fool.

Before Morske could unsheathe his blade, Hanzus retrieved the dagger that, he realised, he had slipped into the desk's top drawer. The blade was already out of its scabbard. He swiped at the captain's reaching hands.

Morske staggered backward, clutching his fresh wound with his offhand. But he didn't drop his sword. Dark liquid oozed from his wrist, trickled down his hilt, painting his blade with his own blood.

"Blackguard!" the word rasped from Morske like the howl of a beaten dog.

"Who sent you?" Hanzus demanded. He could have reached across the table there and then, but he had to be sure...

"Bah!" Morske spat, his spittle landing on Hanzus's doublet.

Hanzus wiped his dagger clean of blood. "The Lord of the Seas, reduced to a petty cut-throat. Tell me who bought you, Morske. Tell me how much you sold your honour for."

Morske snarled. "You make me sick to my fucking stomach, the lot of you. You know where I come from, boy? Where I had to scrape myself out of before I stowed away on my first ship? The Pig District in Vinerheim. The fucking *Pig District*. I came from nothing. Less than nothing. Don't even know who my father is. Men like me have to *earn* their rank, Lord Irvaye. All the while, men like you remain at the top of the heap, smiling down at the shit-stained rabble below. A gilded cunt like you couldn't possibly know..."

"Enough!" Hanzus pounded his fist onto the desk. Morske spoke as if he was the first person to experience poverty. He wasn't the first common lout to look up at the nobility with envy. He'd heard it all a hundred times, and a hundred times it had sounded more convincing than Morske. *But it's not the reason you're here to kill me.*

"I asked who bought you, you spineless cur!"

Morske grew paler by the second. He was swaying on the spot. He dropped his sword. Its clatter made him jump. Then he laughed, a low rattle from the pit of his stomach. He stopped holding his wrist, and blood oozed from the gaping slit, dripping onto the floor.

If the captain died now, Hanzus would never learn the truth.

"The Despot, as you call him... he isn't your real enemy..." Morske collapsed, and as he fell, his face smacked against the table.

Hanzus shifted around the table, clutching his dagger. Blood leaked from the captain's wrist. An indistinct whisper hissed from his lips. His eyelids flickered slower with every beat.

Hanzus knelt beside him, pressing his ear to the man's shaking lips.

"They won't... stop... until you're..." The words dissipated into a whisper and then silence.

Morske was dead.

Hanzus's mind raced. The Despot had ordered Morske to finish him, but why now? And why use Edgar Morske, a once venerated man, a hero of the high seas?

As he looked down at this bloody, withered, empty vessel, Hanzus shuddered at the speed at which the man had left the world. *All that renown, all that success, and with a slice of my blade, it all came undone.* He moved over to the door. *Will my fate be the same? Will someone slit my throat the moment I land in Dyllet?*

The Despot is everywhere. Those were Arwel's words. If he commanded agents on the high seas, where would Hanzus ever be safe?

Hanzus opened the door a crack and peered down the corridor, swallowing bile. The coast was clear. *Amazing.* Morske hadn't even trusted his own men to kick down the door and murder Hanzus. The captain had likely hoped for a quick, silent death before tossing the baron overboard.

Well, he thought, looking back at the captain. *Someone is getting tossed overboard tonight.*

A Deplorable Task

Barrett almost tripped over a cat as he escaped through the front door. A bloody stray. His eyes stung, greeting the morning sun. Oh, how he wished mornings were something written in fables.

He'd spent the previous night writing again. At dusk, he'd read a few chapters of Gregor Murret's *Temptation of a Hound* before reaching for his quill.

He couldn't escape it, not even at home. The Harvest preparations were all he could think of. The Baroness's demands were excessive: organising a marching band, planting a flower garden, paying the kingdom's greatest actors to perform a half-dozen plays, importing enough food and wine and ale to drown a dozen armies.

If Barrett failed to intervene, the Baroness would cripple her husband's finances. Conversely, if Barrett challenged her, he would consign himself to the dungeons. Or the river.

"Morning, Barrett," Mrs Russet croaked, looking up from the hedge she was trimming.

Like Mother, the Russet matriarch followed a strict daily routine of harassing her neighbours and profusely watering her garden. Not that he faulted her for the latter – her garden was a sight to behold for its variety of sunflowers, pansies, and marigolds. *As loud and excessive as Harvest will be.*

"Good morning." Barrett smiled without meeting her eyes as he jogged down the garden path.

The walk to work was the best part of his day. It was the only time Barrett was left alone, providing he chose his path carefully, avoiding the leafy stretch inhabited by the gentry and the high streets infested with pickpockets and street-merchants. The diversion took him through Balenmeade's poorest district.

He turned onto Slop Row as workers emerged from their shacks, grimacing at the grey sky as they plodded toward their torturous fields and factories. Barrett had never understood why those poor buggers bothered to turn up for work. If he was as unfortunate as them, he'd leave Balenmeade for good and seek work out in the country. The thought of deserting this dark town was appealing, and perhaps it would have been possible if Father had not left him with a mother and brother to care for.

The houses of Slop Row – for want of a better word – were shacks of rotting wood and damp straw. How people could live in such dire conditions was beyond Barrett. *They're no better than rats.*

He scurried along the backstreets that ran parallel to Factory Lane, escaping the poor district.

"Barrett, me lad!" Fester Gace boomed as Barrett turned onto Mercantile Alley. The enormous butcher stood outside his shop, grinning like a deranged pig as he waved a meaty hand at Barrett. "Fine thing it is to be seeing you this morn." He stepped into the street, blocking Barrett's path. "Don't suppose you've had time to consider me little proposition?"

Proposition? It took Barrett a moment, then he remembered. *Shit.*

"Not yet, I'm afraid, Mister Gace." Barrett eyed the thin gap between Gace and the wall to his left – he could just about slip through if he hurried. "But thank you for reminding me. I must be off. I... I'm running late for work."

The butcher grinned. Barrett couldn't stop thinking about how much his face looked like a stuffed hog. "Please, call me Fester. And take your time, lad. Think hard and think well. After all, your future depends on it." He waggled a meaty finger in Barrett's face. His breath reeked of eggs. "Come back to me with an answer. That's all I ask."

Barrett's forced smile was waning. "I will do that, Mister... Fester. I'll let you know... soon, I hope."

Fester relaxed his stance, exhaling in a drawn-out sigh. Barrett saw the opportunity and seized it, squeezing past the gap Fester left and pacing off down the alley.

"Though not *too* soon!" Fester shouted after him. "Take your time, lad!"

The fat oaf would never catch up to him, but he'd never cease his pursuit either. The butcher was determined to wed his daughter to Barrett, drooling over his one chance for social advancement.

Barrett had nothing against the trade of butchery, and he couldn't fault Fester for seeking a better life for his daughter. No doubt an accountant for a son-in-law sounded better than a pig farmer or a goatherd. Barrett had no intention of marrying the poor girl, though. He didn't intend on marrying anyone, for that matter. *See where marriage got Father. And the Baron.*

The path between Huckback Lane and the Balenmanor was an obstacle course of eager tradesmen, winking girls, and their grinning parents. Avoiding the hands that sought to strip him of coin was an arduous task, but he relished the challenge.

"Barrett Barrett," Old Drodger barked with his raspy voice. The professional drunk's extensive portfolio included every inn, alehouse, and brothel in Balenmeade. He stood with his back to the door of the Dancing Buck, waiting for their doors to open. "When you gonna let me buy you a pint? Tonight? Here, what say we snatch ourselves a cheeky one before the crows come home to roost?" He stood there gawking at Barrett like a dog, anticipating its meal. What he referred to as crows, Barrett realised, was his wife and children. The Goddess had blessed him with five daughters. It had been this abundance of women that had driven him to the bottle. How Drodger had maintained a marriage for all these years was a mystery to all.

"I'm late for work," Barrett said, edging his way past the tavern. *Will anyone let me be?*

"Boys'll be over soon!" Drodger shouted after him. "Got a pack of cards if you ever up for a game of royals!"

"I'll have to pass!" Barrett called back. "But thank you!"

"Be here if you change your mind!"

Yes, and you'll be here tomorrow and the next day and the day after that...

Barrett slammed the door shut, then he breathed a sigh of relief. Once he'd regained his composure, he hung up his coat and undid the top button of his shirt. It wasn't until his neck was free that he turned to face the room. Two pairs of eyes were blinking at him, one amused, the other agitated.

"Rough night?" Reymond inquired. His slanted eyes and wrinkled lips appeared sly and goading – to the unfamiliar. The steward was a few months younger than Barrett, but his attitude was inferior by some years. He had grey eyes, a mop of oily brown hair and large, droopy ears. If one ignored the latter trait, Reymond was a rather handsome Krämisen. Not as attractive as Barrett, but good enough to land him a half-decent bride.

"Rough morning," Barrett amended him, edging away from the door, his gaze locked on the second pair of eyes that were evaluating him. Their owner, Norben, was another whose appearance deceived, for if looks defined the man, he would have been the meekest, gentlest being in Balenmeade.

"Late to work, I see," Norben hissed, his crooked nose slicing through the air like a rogue's dagger. He shifted away from Reymond's desk, shuffling toward Barrett. "And I *do* see, Mister Barrett, I do. Don't think these ancient balls can't see for what you really are." And he pointed, much to Barrett's relief, at his eyeballs. "'Tis becoming something habitual, Mister Barrett. I'm sure the Chamberlain would be keen to hear of your indiscretions. Your lack of punctuality." He looked Barrett up and down. "Your *lack* of presentation."

Reymond exaggerated a groan. "Leave it be, you old coot. He's what, five... no, six-and-a-half minutes late? My, the scandal."

Norben swivelled his head toward Reymond. "Oh, you mock while you can, boy. In my day, punctuality weren't a thing to be scoffed at." He turned back to Barrett and grimaced at his open collar. "Neither was pride in one's appearance. Mere words to the likes of you." He then started muttering under his breath. The only words Barrett made out were *fuck* and *fucking*.

Barrett walked over to his desk and sank into his leather chair. The seat was in disrepair, for much of the seam-work had come apart, and the stuffing was poking out through the gaps. But it was still comfier than his bed.

"Anything new?" Barrett asked Reymond, who'd returned to studying his book.

"Hmmm?" Reymond lifted his head, peering over his circular spectacles. "Oh, the numbers are just as dire as our last review. See for yourself." He reached across the table and planted a hefty volume on Barrett's desk, causing a cloud of dust to bounce off the surface.

"Look at the state of this place," Norben snapped, aiming an accusing finger at Reymond. "Pigs, the lot of you. When I were your age, we spent every morning polishing the tables. Scrubbing the book covers clean. Not a quill were lifted before the place was spotless."

Reymond frowned. "Shouldn't you be doing something productive yourself?"

Barrett couldn't for the life of him pinpoint what Norben actually did around the manor. All he did was wander around, moaning at others for shirking their duties.

Norben seemed not to hear Reymond's jibe. "Lazy, the lot of you. 'Tis in your bones. Sign of the Times you were raised in. When I were your age, men were starving." He muttered something under his breath, then returned his gaze to Barrett. "Food weren't plentiful back then. Wars were waging. Every man worked the fields, low and high. Few had time for the idle trade of writing."

"My, your day sounds far superior to our own," Reymond groaned, then he lifted his pocket-watch and tapped the glass. "Almost half-eight, Norben. Time for your medicine, isn't it? Or whatever it is you do with your mornings."

"Now folk would rather sleep at their desks than commit to a day's work," Norben continued, undeterred or deaf, to Reymond's insult. Funnily enough, Barrett felt like falling asleep in his chair. "Only medicine I need's a good brew," Norben then muttered.

"Yes, I'm sure in your day it was all a man needed." Reymond stood, placed a hand on Norben's back, and ushered him toward the door. "Come now, Mister Norben. I'm sure the maids await your presence as we speak. *Where oh where is that lovely Mister Norben,* they'll be saying. You wouldn't want them to shirk from their duties now, would you, Mister Norben?"

"Suppose not," the old man croaked, somehow placated. "Course, I could do with a brew first." He then struggled against the young man's hand, turning back toward the desks.

"Come, your tea is not in here, Mister Norben," Reymond said, chewing on his cheeks to hold back the laughter. "It's outside the door. I'll show you."

"Right, right," Norben grumbled. "Outside. Yes. Maids'll be shirking from the task at hand. Halls won't polish themselves."

"Certainly not," Reymond agreed, and he gave Norben a gentle push through the door and shut it behind him. He stood with his back against it and groaned a sigh of relief. They had avoided an entire morning of Norben, for now.

"Thank the Goddess you showed up, Barrett. Thought I'd be stuck with him all bloody day."

"I simply couldn't stay away," Barrett groaned.

He flicked through the book Reymond had placed on his desk: a logbook containing the weekly earnings of every official business in Balenmeade. When he neared the end of the book, he found what he'd been looking for: every transaction relating to the Balenmanor in the preparations for Harvest.

"Look at this," Barrett said, running his finger down the list. "Thirteen barrels of black grapes. Eighty-eight boxes of Cutter Isle mackerel."

Next to the total value of each product, the same initials written in bold blue ink. *H. W-W.* Though the initials themselves threw him off, the handwriting was unmistakable.

"The same signature every time," Barrett said, scratching his chin. "H. W-W. Heatha Wurtz-Worley. Shit on me, she's going by her maiden name."

"Think nothing of it." Reymond sank into his seat. "How long has the Baron been gone for now? Nine months? You know what she's like. She's livid, no doubt, for he *left me alone with these Goddess-forsaken children.*" Reymond's impression of the Baroness was lamentable.

"Her attitude toward her husband is the least of our concerns," Barrett said, as he continued to pour down the list. "It's her relationship with coin that frightens me."

He noticed, in the few places the Baroness's signature didn't reside, the thick, simplistic writing of the Chamberlain, denoting some of the more extravagant purchases.

"Four pheasants from Marland. Nine-hundred gold crowns. Bouquets arranged by the Faire Lane Florist. Two-hundred-and-twenty-five gold crowns. Where do they expect these crowns to come from?" The numbers were sickening. "These expenses have to be plugged, or there won't be a Balenmanor come winter."

"They will be," Reymond stated. "Our baron has reached Marbow, so say the reports. That brings his estimated arrival to within the fortnight. Hanzus won't stand for this nonsense. These planned frivolities will fall under his ire." With an accomplished smile, he licked a finger and delved into a logbook plaguing his desk.

"And where then does that leave *us*?" Barrett asked him. "*We* are his bookkeepers. Our purpose is to scrutinise every expense, every transaction, every minor change of the accounts. And yet, faced with this gross overspending, what can we do to stop it? Stroll up to Heatha and politely ask her to slow down?"

It was that very dilemma that caused Barrett so many sleepless nights.

Reymond's smile was undiminished. "If anyone's going to take the blame, it'll be Old Chamber Pot."

Unlikely. The Chamberlain was a master of squirming his way out of hopeless situations. Servants took the blame for his indiscretions and failures. It was the way things had always been.

Barrett squinted up and down the list of purchases. "The Krämise has produced a good harvest, so say the reports. But if the Chamberlain has his way, he'll squander the crowns generated from agriculture on the very thing that celebrates it. Is one brief celebration worth *this* much?"

Reymond flashed a grin. "For brigands such as you and I? It's worth every copper." The shift in topic was enough for him to shut the book he'd just opened. "Rumour has it Maisie Taverner has accepted an invitation to the dance."

Barrett shook his head in disbelief. "Don't believe it, Reymond. Maisie Taverner is a tease and a prude. How many men has she turned down in the past year alone? Twelve? Twelve hundred?"

"Oh, but just wait till you hear who the lucky sod is," Reymond said.

Barrett waved him away. "Spare me. You know I loathe gossip. Besides..." He loosed a sigh. "We have work to be getting on with."

Reymond groaned and shrugged his arms. "Oh, the work will get done, whether or not, we will it so." He drew out a sigh, staring at the ceiling for inspiration. Then he leaned on his desk, his hands within grabbing distance of Barrett's book-pile. "So, I was talking to Maisie Taverner yesterday evening. I was trying to get to the bottom of this rumour regarding her date to the dance, but she wouldn't reveal a thing. She did, however, tell me she saw *you* in her father's tavern the other night, romancing some buxom bit of fancy."

Barrett rolled his eyes at Reymond. Those words were not worthy of reply.

"So, did you do it?"

Barrett leaned both elbows on his desk. At last, he satisfied Reymond with his full attention. "Did I do *what?*"

Reymond scoffed at him. "You take me for a fool, don't you? Everyone knows you've never laid with a woman, or rather... *hadn't*. So, did you do it? *How* did you do it? Did you, you know, play around with..."

Barrett cut through his words with a sharp wave of the hand. "Pull your mind out of the gutter, Rey. The woman you're talking about was Layla Brewman, and..."

"*Brewman?*" Reymond yelped. "The wife of his, truly?"

"Yes," Barrett groaned. "Layla, wife of Nipp Brewman."

Reymond slapped the table, howling with laughter. "Nipp's a class bugger if ever I saw one. Man don't know his wife from his shoelaces. Truly. He wouldn't have caught you fucking her, even if he saw it with his own eyes. Deary me, Barrett, *deary me*. Missed a golden opportunity there, my friend. Could have stolen the queen's jewels right in the middle of the throne room, and the king, Goddess bless him, would never have known you were there."

Reymond laughed to himself for a few minutes, repeating the same crude jokes about Nipp's foolishness and his wife's adultery.

"Ah, that Nipp," Reymond said, grinning like a maniac. "He's the gift that keeps on giving."

When Reymond's jokes subsided, he returned to his logbook.

Reymond was a fool. Although Barrett considered him a friend, he was a friend that was forced upon him daily, like a cake enjoyed so many times. It had become the least appetising thing imaginable.

As the morning dragged on, so too did Reymond's gossiping. And three cups of tea had his lips moving all the more fervent. He spoke of his love for huckberry wine, his visual ratings of Balenmeade's *wenches*, and noted all the mountains he'd climb before he reached thirty.

They broke their fast in the servant's mess at quarter-to-eleven. Stewards boasted a pride of place in the mess. Their table was situated farthest from the door, next to the window. Colourful pavilions would soon fill the grey-green field outside the Balenmanor, playing host to mummers, musicians, jesters, and sword-swallowers.

"You know, I've always wondered," Modger Yarris said as they dined. "Why'd your pa name you Barrett Barrett? Did he possess an odd sense of humour, or did he just lack an imagination? Thank the Goddess my pa didn't name me Yarris Yarris."

Barrett found it ironic that the son of a farmhand teased about his father. "I guess he had a sense of humour," he said as he watched a leaf fall from a tree bordering the field.

Luncheon was a generous portion of rye bread, buttery sweet potato, strips of venison and honeyed parsnips. All watered down with goblets of wine and mugs of brown tea.

The maids and grooms weren't as fortunate as the stewards: their rations comprised of colourless stew and a thin slice of yesterday's bread. Still, no one complained as they wolfed down their servings. And though some shot unfriendly glances toward the table by the window, the majority clung to the idea that they would one day sit at the stewards' table.

Or so Barrett imagined.

"Strange summer we've had," the Baroness's lawyer, Marc Kest, said, picking at his venison. "Too warm for my liking. Hot summers welcome the coldest winters. I pray you all remember that the next time you sip vodka under the sun."

Edvard Linn dropped his fork, chuckling as he folded his arms. "Ever the shining optimistic, Kest." Linn was a steward from the east wing. Thus, meals were the only time Barrett encountered him. His role, if memory served, had something to do with choosing curtains or purchasing bedding.

"Marc's right," Reymond said, grinning. *"Bad omen is the clear sky."* He mimicked Kest's tone, puffing out his chest and narrowing his eyes in mockery.

Kest waved a dirty fork in Reymond's direction, undeterred or oblivious to his jest. "You're a well-read man, my friend. And as sure as Gaam writes, the autumn will be harsh. The winter greater so."

The gaggle of stewards nodded in unison. None smiled now. They were all much older than Barrett and Reymond, and as such, preferred complaining to bantering.

"I'm reminded of a poem I read just the other evening," Kest continued. "An old wives' tale re-imagined by the genius that is Herandina Wardsmoor."

The old stewards hummed their appreciation of the name. Barrett was relieved and quite surprised that Kest returned to his food then, sparing them from Wardsmoorian poetry. Barrett would sooner listen to Mother rant about the leaky roof than endure Herandina Wardsmoor. The old bat's emotional pieces had been the basis of his early wordsmith studies, for which he possessed scant fondness.

Barrett turned his attention to the scenery outside the window. Amber leaves fell from the trees, adding to the patchwork of varying shades of red and brown littering the footpath. The clouds were moving quickly, pale swirls of grey forming the shapes of mountains.

Somewhere in the background, the stewards were droning on about inconsistencies in the weather, their physical wears, and the vast overspending of their baroness. The latter caught Barrett's attention.

"It's going to be the biggest celebration to date," Kest said. "Hundreds flock to Balenmeade as we speak, and thousands more will come."

"And they'll all need feeding," Edgar Vassel buzzed in a monotone, one of the Chamberlain's personal scribes. "They bring crowns, sure, but our warehouses can only stock so much."

"I fear their coin will not be enough to compensate for our

expenditures," Modger Yarris chipped in. He turned to Reymond then. "How *do* the figures look? Have we any hope for the winter?"

Reymond wore a nervous grin, directing their collective attention toward Barrett.

Warmth flushed Barrett's skin as every eye scrutinised him.

"Well?" someone croaked.

"I..." A lump caught in Barrett's throat, a swell that prevented the words from reaching his lips. *Goddess curse you, Reymond.* He hadn't a clue what to say. One word of contempt toward the Baroness and the stewards would be queuing up to inform the Chamberlain of his treachery.

"The coffers will hold," Reymond said at last, dragging the stewards' eyes toward him.

Relief swept over Barrett. There was something about people looking at him that filled his stomach with sick. Made him want to smash through the window and retreat across the field. He liked to think it was the Goddess's way of telling him he was no speaker.

Barrett sipped his bitter tea. Then, without warning, the hall doors burst open, filling the room with silence.

Barrett spilled tea over his hand, shocking himself with lukewarm liquid. When he looked up, he noticed the Chamberlain had entered the hall with two grim-faced men by his side.

"Fuck me," Reymond whispered in Barrett's ear. "What's Old Chamber Pot doing here?"

Barrett swallowed the lump in his throat. "Shouldn't he be dining with the Baroness?"

The Chamberlain paused in front of the mess as the doors thumped shut behind him. He wore a golden doublet and cravat like someone poised for an audience with King Halmond.

No one was eating now. Some took a few furtive sips from their mugs.

The Chamberlain whispered to the man on his right, then picked up the nearest goblet and tapped it with a spoon, seeming unaware that the mess was already silent.

"Gentlemen." The Chamberlain nodded toward the stewards, who inclined their heads. "And *servants*." To the rest of the hall, he bit down on his lip as if the sight he beheld was a steaming pile of shit. "There is a matter for which your utmost attention is required." He looked around, searching for a particular face. Then, after taking a deep breath, he announced, "The Harvest Festival has been postponed by a week!"

The hall filled with whispers. Some servants frowned and groaned, but the vast majority seemed perplexed.

Barrett sipped the last of his tea, bitterness scraping down his throat.

The Chamberlain continued, "And an additional week means more time to prepare an even greater festival! You will, I assure you, be compensated for your supplementary labour." The groans persisted. "I have drawn up a list of tasks for each and every one of you. Whether you are the longest serving steward" –he gestured toward the appropriate table– "or the maid who empties my chamber pot, you will all be expected to undertake additional tasks. These tasks will not, I'm afraid, necessarily correspond to your station. After all, we are a family, are we not?" And he forced an excruciating smile that seemed as unnatural as the sun beaming down on the Krämise moors. "And what good is family if they cannot band together?" He inhaled a sharp breath. "Now, I bid you all a good day, and may the Goddess watch over you." He was holding back a grin – it was the last thing Barrett noticed before the Chamberlain spun on his heel and left the hall.

The room became a theatre of protest as the stewards lunged out of their chairs and hurled abuse at the two assistants the Chamberlain had left behind.

Reymond sat back in his chair and sighed. "Well, it's not as bad as the end of the world."

"Why would they postpone the festival?" Barrett asked.

Reymond shrugged. "Perhaps the Baron got lost on his way back to Balenmeade."

Barrett couldn't tell if Reymond was joking, and he didn't want to find out.

On the other side of the table, Old Norben was yelling at the Chamberlain's assistants, "I've been serving the Barons of the Krämise since your mums were babes!"

Edvard Linn stood with one foot resting on his chair. "The Baron won't stand for this! Just you wait till this reaches him!"

When the anger died down, one of the assistants unrolled a sheet of parchment and cleared his throat. "Chambermaids! In addition to your expected duties, you will wait on tables during the feast."

Stone silence. Not a single chambermaid stirred.

"Stewards of the interior, Francis Becken and Edvard Linn, you will aid the planners in all aspects of their decision making."

Becken and Linn seemed somewhat subdued by the prospect. Becken folded his arms and smiled to himself.

"Stewards of bookkeeping, Reymond Morgen and Barrett... uh... Barrett." He conferred with his partner, no doubt wondering whether the double-name was a sleight of hand, or some audacious fool had indeed named their son Barrett Barrett.

Barrett's pulse pounded like a furious drumbeat in his ears. Every servant in proximity stared at the pair in question.

"No, this can't be right," the assistant muttered just loud enough to hear, reading the parchment over again. The second assistant whispered in his ear, and they nodded together. He repeated, "Bookkeepers, Reymond Morgen and Barrett Barrett will aid in the endeavour of cleaning and maintaining the Baron's stables."

Barrett could hear his own breath, but the hall was otherwise devoid of sound. He could detect laughter on the faces of his peers. He didn't dare turn and face Reymond.

As the assistant continued down the list, not one of the tasks handed to the other stewards was as demeaning... as *humiliating* as that allocated to Barrett and Reymond.

The Chamberlain was punishing them for what crime he was unsure. He disliked the young bookkeepers – he'd made it quite obvious in the past – but Barrett had reasoned the man treated all his servants that way.

The assistant's lamentation rattled on for what seemed like an hour. Barrett sank into his chair and played with his fork. All the while, Reymond pounded the table with his fist.

Reymond slammed his logbook against the table.

"Cleaning the fucking *stables*? Who does he think he is? The Baron of the Krämise?" He fell into his chair and slapped a hand across his face. "*How* did the Baroness agree to this? And why now have the festival planners discovered they need additional labour?"

"He's doing it to spite us," Barrett concluded. "If the stables needed maintenance, he'd have hired some hand from the city."

They had been going over the subject all afternoon, getting absolutely no paperwork finished. Soon after they arrived back from luncheon, a letter signed by the Chamberlain was deposited through their office door, which stated that their stable duties would begin that very evening. They would contribute an hour every morning and two hours every evening.

"He'll run us ragged," Reymond groaned, scraping a hand through his hair.

Maybe that's the point. Exhaust us, so we have no energy left to enjoy the festival.

The stables were in a dire state. The stable hands had taken the horses, pigs and cows into the field so the stewards could clean the space without interference, but the stench of animal had seeped into the very walls and floorboards.

Reymond was sombre, which was as unusual as the sun refusing to set – which it did, quite suddenly, as they picked up their shovels and got to work.

Stable Master Egan, a portly man with the biggest hands Barrett had ever seen, had given Barrett and Reymond the task of removing all the excrement and dirt and replacing the hay with the fresh stockpile in the yard. They both covered the bottom half of their faces with scraps of linen, but it did nothing to shield them from the stench.

Servants and soldiers alike stopped to chuckle at the hapless bookkeepers as they passed the stables. If there was one thing they could agree to revel in, it was a steward being cut down to their size. Some even hurled jeers their way, but none dared linger more than a few seconds, lest the Baroness or Chamberlain spot them from their windows above.

As Barrett shovelled a large pile of cow-or-horse shit into the wheelbarrow, he felt burning in his right shoulder. The grim feeling he was being watched. He assumed that someone was invigilating his performance from a nearby window, but he didn't dare turn around to investigate. The feeling continued for as long as he was shovelling until, finally, the brown piles abated.

"Well, that's most of the shit sorted," Reymond said, panting, his forehead gleaming with sweat. "Now for the hay, I guess." His voice contained neither mirth nor anger. He'd worked like a common dolt, and now he was speaking like one.

"This is ridiculous," Barrett said, leaning his shovel against the barn door. "Why are we being punished this way?"

Reymond shrugged. "You know what Old Chamberpot's like. The only good part of this is the fact I'll sleep well tonight." He placed his hands on his hips and, biting his lip, he surveyed the vast wooden barn.

Holes and gaping tears spotted the roof. Barrett felt sorry for the animals that resided under it when the rain came down and for the fact that three species had to share the same abode. Though the stables were large, there were no partitions or separate barns. Horses, pigs, and cows forced to exist in disharmony.

Barrett supposed it wasn't much different from when the servants ate their meals together in the mess.

"You take that side," Reymond said, gesturing towards the right of the barn. "Though I suppose it makes no difference, really."

Barrett started toward the far wall. A thick accumulation of hay lined every wall. They had consciously neglected to search those piles for animal shit, and Barrett saw no reason to stray from that strategy now. When they levelled the new hay into the barn, they would be able to mix it with the old hay skirting the walls. After removing any noticeable strings of excrement, the stable master would be none the wiser.

And so, shovel in hand, Barrett began scooping up the main body of hay.

The braziers that scattered the yard outside had been lit, and their warm hues pulsated through the cracks in the wall.

As the evening turned to night, Barrett could only see the vague outline of his surroundings. But still, the stable master had not returned to relieve them from their duties.

"Two hours, they said," Reymond groaned. "Two *fucking* hours. How long's it been? *Four?*"

Barrett didn't possess the energy to respond. He trundled on with his job, fearing that if he stopped, he might not have the strength to start again.

Then something aroused his senses. He heard a rustling in the corner of the barn, close to a particularly large gathering of hay. His head surged with energy, willing his senses into motion.

He waited, holding his breath, a shovel gripped tight. To his astonishment, the sound came again – louder this time, a snapping sound, like boots crunching on a pile of branches.

Was his mind playing tricks on him? Was this true exhaustion? He turned back to Reymond, but he seemed blissfully unaware of the sound as he brought in the new hay.

Barrett turned back and squinted in the direction of the sound. Perhaps it was a mouse? A spider?

The rustling came again, only this time it continued for a few seconds before fading into silence once more. Barrett could feel sweat dappling his forehead. If it was a mouse, he prayed it hadn't contributed to the excrement piles.

He pointed the end of his shovel towards the sound, proceeding with caution, expecting a rodent to pop out at any moment.

"Who's there?" he hissed at the hay.

The rustling announced its surprise, but it abated as soon as it had started. With the tip of the shovel, he prodded the pile. Then, to his horror, the pile responded, not with a mouse's squeal but with words.

"Oi! Watch it!"

Barrett threw his shovel aside. His hands were shaking, his breathing fast and laboured. Despite the tremor coursing through his body, despite every fibre of his being shouting at him to turn and run away, he leaned forward and peeled back the top layer of hay.

The first thing he made out was a face: dark, bulbous eyes blinking up at him. The skin was pale, even in the brazier's warming glow. Shaggy, hay-infested hair framing tiny, flared nostrils and a set of dirty teeth.

"Who are you?" was all Barrett could manage.

Without a sound, the face cracked a smile.

Mavrian

Eplin's hand was cold as ice and just as numbing. Mavrian's stomach lurched as he investigated the curve of her back, the plumpness of her buttocks, his eyes and hands working as one.

Mavrian resisted the urge to recoil and vomit. Everyone knew the price of defying Eplin Garr.

"Perfection," he said, informing an invisible observer. His breath was warm against her cheek, stale as old ale.

Mavrian offered him a smile, turning onto her side. "The storm has abated," she pointed out, gesturing toward the window.

Eplin's eyes widened as they beheld her chest. He traced a finger over the curve of one breast, teasing her hard nipple.

"Yes," he sighed, seeming disinterested as he gazed over at the window. "The Twins relent." He seemed irritated, as if the calm sky was something to lament. It meant, of course, that he had no further excuse to loiter in her chamber. The sea could ferry him away now.

He could finally leave.

"The vassmirs laboured day and night," he said. "At *night*, would you believe? I heard them from the balustrade outside my own quarters, chanting in the moonlight. The Twins have been appeased, it would seem. But at what cost?"

Mavrian shuddered at the thought. Communication with the Twins was impossible at night – everyone knew that – so who had the vassmirs been speaking with? She pushed the possibilities out of her head. "I bled three times," she lied. She'd only done so once. "The first was for Vässa, the second..."

Eplin's forced a sigh, silencing her. "The destination of your blood is not for you to decide." He sprang from the bed, padded over to the window, and poured himself wine from the jug.

He stood there, illuminated by the brazier, skin touched with pink, sipping from his goblet.

His nude form was glorious, from taut buttocks to powerful biceps, but the sight made her sick. He had the build of a warrior, a body most women craved. *Women that don't know him.* Mavrian rubbed her hand up and down her torso in an attempt to warm herself. *It's curious how he maintains such a figure.* She rarely saw him swimming nor sparring with the other lords. What she garnered from the whispering servants and chattering ladies was that he spent most of his days meeting with the Loress Meels or otherwise locked up in his chamber.

Not much of a chance to work the body... unless he's fucking that old bat Meels or ordering his servants to join him in bed.

Whenever he visited Mavrian – and his visits were few and far between – he remained as vigorous as ever. His stamina could have him last for hours. Part of her wished he was fat and lazy. That way, he'd have spent more time filling his belly and less time filling her. Certainly, the fucking would be dull, but it would be over quickly. *And fat men are easier to manipulate.* She'd heard it said.

"You're perfect," he said suddenly, turning back to her, his eyes glowing scarlet in the brazier.

Mavrian found herself blushing. He wasn't complimenting her for her own sake, she realised, he was thinking aloud. Eplin always spoke his mind in her presence, believing her trustworthy or so benign that she posed no threat to him. And she wasn't sure which possibility frightened her more.

"Will you leave on the morrow?" she asked him. He had docked his ship for over a week now, arriving just before the storm started.

His eyes narrowed over his goblet. "You'd like that, wouldn't you?" He glared at her as he sipped, drinking his fill. His face softened. "I grow tired of these fruitless gatherings in the Capital. Nothing is resolved, and yet I am summoned *constantly*. The under-lords bicker like unruly children, and that's *all* they do. They echo the Overlord's words to curry his favour, ingratiating themselves, licking his arse like well-dressed harlots. I doubt anyone truly believes or even comprehends that which they spew. And they call that counsel. *Counsel*, would you believe?"

"I'm sure the Overlord values *your* counsel, my lord," Mavrian said, the words slipping off her tongue. Thankfully, his mind was too distant to detect the sarcasm.

Eplin turned back to gaze at the Gateway fading into the horizon, its warm hues bleeding into a pale sky. Soon, the treacherous moon would be upon them, its great eye unblinking, watching them in their beds.

"Still," Eplin said. "For once, there will be *something* to discuss. The negotiations in Carthane, I'm told, proved to be a shambles. I know no details as of yet, but *apparently,* it was a tremendous waste of time. Moreover, a waste of resources. Lorr Byss and Loress Lömas attended. Can you imagine the expenses? Thank the Twins, I was never chosen. I cannot fathom an attempt at diplomacy with those creatures. I'd rather milk into my hand than be forced to sit and speak with Humans. Let alone treat with them."

"*Humans?*" Mavrian echoed, not recognising the term.

He craned his neck towards her and smiled, the condescending grin of an adult laughing at a foolish child. "Yes, that's what they call themselves, the Kinsmeer. That great stain upon this world." He sighed. "Peace can never exist between our two races. The sooner our

Overlord and his cock-kissing underlings realise it, the sooner we can all realise our destiny."

"*Destiny?*" she thought aloud, scolding herself for doing so. He was beginning to sound like one of the vassmirs, speaking of grandeur and *chosen paths*. Was he mocking her, playing with the naivety he believed she possessed?

Eplin scoffed at her, surprised or disgusted, then poured himself more wine. "The purity of our people can only be realised when the world is *governed* by our people." He sniffed at the air, suspecting something foul. "I don't like the look of some of the under-lords. The mud in their eyes... subtle in some, overt in others. Degenerates. Kin of mixed blood. And yet it is *their* unclean minds that corrupt our Overlord." He loosed a sighed. "He grows old, Mavrian. Complacent, blind to their meddling. He might not... *appear* old, but his soul is waning. The tether between body and spirit disintegrating." He laughed a hollow chuckle. "And they say he can't die. Gods, can you think of anything worse?"

Mavrian could think of many worse things: Eplin's penetrating eyes, for one, his long fingernails scraping across her body, his hands seeking entry into every crevice.

Despite his lingering gaze, she didn't dare cover herself. She would have to wait for him to leave before she could dress.

"Strösten purged most of the Kinsmeer... *Humans,*" she corrected herself, eager to appear to be listening.

"Aha!" Eplin cried, his eyes burning deep crimson. "You are right, my dear. Most *were* purged. *Most*. Not all!" He returned his gaze to the windowpane, exhaling through his nose. "I fear there are few in Sela'Fundor that share our vision, my love. How can they not see? The purity of the realm is *all* that matters." He waved his free hand as if to dismiss her. "This war with the Kinsmeers' empire is nothing more than a distraction. A means to keep the rabble preoccupied, to keep them from rebelling against their weak leaders. It's true, the Kinsmeer started this war, but the task should be ours to finish it."

Mavrian pondered at the contradiction. *If the war is a distraction, why should we finish it? Why not walk just away and agree to a peace?*

"There is much purity in this realm," Eplin said, sadness seeping into his words. "But it has become sullied as of late. And no greater example exists than upon this very island. The Lady Meels has grown complacent. Too indolent to sniff out the Kinsmeer lurking in the gutter. It's of little consequence, however. Kleäm is a meritless backwater. Always has and always shall be."

Backwater? Eplin made many sweeping statements. Most of the time he aimed to shock her, but now he was being flippant just for the sake of it.

"Our Overlord regards Kleäm with disdain," Eplin continued. "This island was a Kinsmeer stronghold once, you know. If it were possible, I'd consign it to the bottom of the ocean before I populated it with members of the pure race." He stopped to catch his breath. "As it stands, Kleäm remains with Plargross. Our defences here must be strengthened, our garrison more than doubled. If the Sylvians attack, and attack they will, Kleäm will be one of the first."

"Kleäm is impenetrable," Mavrian reminded him. Much of the perimeter was cliff. The small stretch of beach the island did have was protected by three layers of wall. Meelian Castle would rain fire down upon any creature foolish enough to land there.

Mavrian was no military expert, but an assault upon Kleäm would require thousands. The loss of life would be immeasurable.

There was only one real entrance into Kleäm, and that was through the harbour, but the seawall's aquatic gate prevented unauthorised access. And even if the wall was somehow breached, there were dozens of watchtowers and ballista surrounding the harbour.

Kleäm is impenetrable, was the island's motto for a reason. Then she remembered Eplin's usual quip to those words: *Everything is penetrable, and everyone is pregnable.*

Oddly, he did not utter that phrase now, saying instead, "I do not fear an attack from the sea." He padded over to the bed and seated himself beside her, lingering on the edge. "I fear one from within."

His hand landed near her ankle, brushing up to her thigh before resting at the entrance to her passage. She wanted to slap him away, to mount a protest. *Gods, have you not had enough for today?* But his fingers were already inside her.

"Kleäm is loyal to the Overlord," she said, stifling the urge to cry out. She looked him dead in the eye, hoping to make her disinterest plain. "Every Bloodkin is loyal to the Overlord."

"Oh, dear, dear, dear..." He shook his head, pursing his lips. "The loyalty of our kin is unquestionable. But there are other things... *wretched* things..." His words trailed off, his eyes widening as they stared into the depths of her pupils. He removed his hand with a jerk, then wiped her wetness across her thigh. "You are the only thing that matters, you know. That which you symbolise... your pure blood... your unspoiled nature."

Her stomach lurched at that. *But you have spoiled me, Lorr Garr.*

He placed his damp fingers under her chin, lifting her face to his level. "And you *are* pure, Mavrian. Your fire is strong, your blood thick. You are worth a thousand times more than the others. You are invaluable."

The scarlet around his pupils was aglow – *passion*, she realised – but not any kind of passion for her beauty. His passion would drain her until she was an empty shell. He wanted all that she was. He wanted to consume her.

It was at that moment that she realised he would be her downfall. She was his possession now, his slave. And no matter what happened, even if she escaped, his was the last face she would see before closing her eyes forever.

She gasped, clawing at the bedsheets. *Vässa... Vällas... save me from this man.*

He let go of her, expelling the air from his lungs. He closed his eyes, muttering under his breath, then he snapped them open and smiled at her.

"Bleed for the Twins," he said, running a hand over the smoothness of her stomach. "Pray that my seed grows in your belly." And with that, he stormed over to the wardrobe, threw on a robe, then turned to the door. "When next we meet, my dear, you will be carrying my child."

Vagrant

The cellar was lit by a single oil lamp perched on the edge of a table. Barrett could only make out the girl's prominent features: chapped lips, little round chin. Her muddy-blonde hair brushed her shoulders. Her eyes were a shade of chocolate – an uncommon sight in Balenmeade.

The cellar reeked of spilled ale and lingering damp. The low ceiling allowed Barrett just enough space to stand, though he ducked more out of fear of touching the mould than for hitting his head. The ceiling was higher on the other side of the room, and it was from there, high on the wall, that a strip of moonlight slithered through a window, casting a beam of blue-grey across the table. Dust encircled the light before the girl's face.

Barrett swallowed. The walls of his throat were tight and coarse, squeezed of all moisture. His saliva was warm, like a soothing beverage.

"Who are you?" he asked. *More importantly, how did you come to find yourself in the stables of Baron Hanzus Irvaye of the Krämise?* She was nothing special if looks were any indication, but she had to have sneaked past the Chamberlain's eagle-eyed guards, and that alone was no small feat.

As she fidgeted on her stool, her twisting neck revealed the contours of her bones. Thin, chalky skin stretched across a brittle frame. She was short – as Barrett and Reymond had discovered when they led her into the cellar – a child or a dwarf. It was hard to tell when there was scant light, and she offered no words. Whatever the case, she was ghoulish, wraithlike. She had hard cheekbones and eyes set deep into her skull. She reminded him of one of the Gutterfolk – those wretched souls that lingered outside the walls of Balenmeade, begging to be let inside and given a free meal.

Perhaps she is one of them. But then that would mean she sneaked past the city watchmen and *the Baron's guard.* And she didn't look *that* clever.

"Who are you?" he tried again. "How did you come to be sleeping in the stables? You'd do well to answer me." *Hektor knows the Chamberlain won't ask so nicely.*

There was something odd about her face, her impassive manner. She blinked at him like an innocent animal, unsure what she was looking at. She'd offered no resistance after he'd lifted her up from the stable hay and guided her to the cellar. She'd said nothing. She made no sound at all.

All he had been her vacant stare, following his every movement like a curious cat.

His hands were trembling, cool sweat trickled down the middle of his face. She posed no threat, displayed not a drop of intellect, and yet her vigilance made him nervous. *You're being irrational.* He knew she could speak, that she wasn't altogether simple, for he'd heard her utter words in the stables. Though, come to think of it, he couldn't remember what she'd said. Perhaps she'd grunted or sighed, and he'd misinterpreted the sound. Perhaps she was a half-witted mute. *But she could still be dangerous.* She'd found solace in the shit-infested hay of the stables. She was desperate.

And a desperate girl could do anything.

Pull yourself together. You're a steward of the Balenmanor. The keeper of Hanzus Irvaye's books. You're in control here.

Suddenly, the girl lifted her head and looked him dead in the eye. "Where am I?" Her voice was raspy, shaky. She spluttered into her hand. "All I can smell is shite."

Barrett hid his surprise at her accent. She formed her words different from what he was used to, placing emphasis on words where a normal person wouldn't.

He bit down on his lip. He wasn't sure whether he should chastise her for cursing or comfort her to stop her shaking.

"You are inside the Balenmanor, the home of Hanzus Irvaye, Baron of the Krämise. But you knew that, surely?"

She shrugged, blinking around at the dark bare-brick walls. "*This* is a manor? Don't look like much."

Barrett resisted the urge to shout. *Don't test me, girl.* She was trying to provoke him. That was it.

"My colleague has gone to fetch the Chamberlain," he said, allowing her remark to slide. "Now, how did you come to find yourself sleeping in the stables?"

She shrugged again. "Didn't *find* myself. I put myself there."

Barrett ground his teeth. "Why were you sleeping among horses and... and cows?"

"And pigs," she added, as if they were of the highest importance.

"And pigs," Barrett accepted. "How did you come to be there?"

"It were the first warm spot I found, really."

"So, you just happened upon the stables of Hanzus Irvaye, the Baron of the Krämise?"

She gazed at him with suspicion. "Well, no. The first place were the stables of some fat innkeeper, but he weren't too fond of me. So I tried to sleep in a pile of shite behind some sweet shop, but it were claimed by a horrid old man, and he chased me away."

Barrett shook his head. "The streets of Balenmeade are no place for a young girl."

He guessed she was sixteen or seventeen, but her irregular accent made the maturity in her voice difficult to place. Equally, she could have been a whelp plagued with a dry throat or an older woman cursed with stunted growth.

She folded her bony arms. "Streets ain't a place for no one."

Barrett bit away at his lip. He'd already sacrificed completing the stable work for this girl. Learning of a vagrant stowing away with the animals would enrage the Chamberlain, especially once he realised her appearance had distracted Barrett from his labour.

Barrett took the seat opposite the girl, breathing through his mouth. The wine-taster used the lavish high-backed chair as he ensured the Baron's collection was up to standard. A duty he was known to abuse.

They shouldn't be long now.

Barrett pictured the Chamberlain hurrying out of his evening robe and into his tunic, storming after Reymond with a mind to clout the back of his head. No doubt, he'd been enjoying a game of royals with the Captain of the Guard or reading the memoirs of some famous general when Reymond had appeared at his door.

"Your Baron ain't here. Is he?"

The image of the Chamberlain's ugly face shattered, replaced by the girl's muddy, mischievous grin. What she had to smile about was beyond him. The Chamberlain would soon be handing her over to the guard, where she'd receive a good beating before being sent on her way.

"What was that?" Barrett narrowed his eyes at her. "What did you say?"

She shrugged her skeletal shoulders. "He ain't here, your *Baron of Krämise*. I heard servants talking. He's away on some quest, ain't he? So, who does that leave in charge around here?"

"That" –and Barrett raised a finger to illustrate his point– "leaves the Baroness in charge of the barony and the Chamberlain to run matters of the estate." He shook his head, coming to his senses. "Not that it is any concern of yours. What is your name? Answer me."

His attempt at sternness sounded contrived to his own ears. He only prayed the Chamberlain interrupted this botched interrogation before the cracks revealed the true fool he was.

"Name's Vilka," she said, frowning. "For all it's worth."

"*Vilka?* What kind of a name is that?" The words spurted from his mouth.

She appeared unperturbed. "The kind I were given. You haven't given me your name yet. All you have is questions, questions, questions."

Vilka was fearless, in both word and mannerism. She stared at him, expressionless, unafraid and unwilling to look away.

Vilka. He chewed the name around the inside of his lips, nibbling on the walls of his cheeks. It wasn't a name he was familiar with, not even in the history books. He couldn't fathom a Gadian parent issuing such a strange moniker. She had to have originated somewhere westward. All the harsh words came from that way.

"This town... *Bale*-mead, did you say it were called?" Her wit faded as soon as it had arrived.

"*Balen*meade," he corrected her, as impatient as an old schoolteacher. "And Balenmeade is a city, not a town. It has a cathedral, and it is the capital of the Krämise and seat to..."

She spoke over him, turning away. "Bit small for a city, ain't it?"

Barrett opened his mouth to rebut, but only a whisper of air flowed from his lips. He followed her eyes as they explored the wine cellar.

"Where have you come from?" he demanded. She was *really* starting to try his patience.

"Some place far off." She spoke the words slow, like Barrett was simple and the answer was obvious. She sniffed at the air like a curious rat and grimaced. "No point in talking about it. Can't go back there. Wouldn't if I could."

"Which is *where*, exactly?"

Her expression was impossible to read. "Were on the road a good few days. Or were it weeks? A month? No, couldn't have been." She shrugged, sighing. "Either way, it ain't a direction I'll be taking again.

No time soon. Your man can do what he wants with me, but if he kicks me out of your *city*, as you call it, I'm going east."

Barrett laboured a deep sigh. "King Halmond's realm isn't something you can just pass through at leisure. There are procedures, laws..."

"What laws?" she interrupted him, folding her arms and sinking into the stool. "I'm cold. I need a blanket."

Barrett ground his teeth. The sheer cheek. She didn't seem to comprehend the trouble she was in. She had admitted to sneaking across the border without filling out the appropriate paperwork.

"Listen to me," Barrett said, steadying his temper. "When the Chamberlain arrives, you have to be careful with your words."

"I'm cold," she repeated, folding her arms tighter to her chest. "Why should I be careful? Is your Chamber-Man really so scary?"

For a second time, Barrett was at a loss for words.

"Your coat looks warm."

"My coat is covered in horse..." He held back from swearing. "Manure."

"Don't care," she said, frowning.

Barrett chewed his cheeks. This girl was relentless, and the Chamberlain was taking his sweet time. He only prayed the old bastard hadn't been sleeping when Reymond arrived with the news, else there would be even greater hell to pay.

"Fine."

He stood and released the toggles of his coat. The stench of the stables bit at his nose as he folded it and passed it over to Vilka. But he surmised the garment didn't stink half as bad as she did.

"Thanks."

Vilka might as well have dressed in a tent. She had asked for a blanket and a blanket she'd received. The coat's arms were almost twice as long as the human stumps slotted into them. The coattails flapped against her ankles as if she was wearing an ill-fitted dress. At least it shut her up.

But the silence didn't last for long.

"Where's your Chamber-Man? What's taking him so long?"

She'd read his mind.

"Chamber-*lain*," he corrected her. The syllables echoed in the chasm of his skull. He swallowed a heavy ball that took forever to pass through his throat.

Then, as if they had both summoned the beast by speaking its name, the cellar door creaked open.

Warm brazier light pulsed from the doorway, trickling down the staircase. Vilka covered her eyes with her hands, though her crusty hair seemed to serve as its own shield.

Barrett's heart was in his mouth. As he struggled onto his feet, the shabbiness of his appearance was all too apparent: his exposed shirt was untucked and open at the collar, sweat and stable stains soiled his trousers. He turned to find the Chamberlain's pig-like form descending the stairs, each step sighing under his weight.

"What is the meaning of this interruption?" the Chamberlain boomed, his snout's aim alternating between steward and stranger.

Barrett fingered the arm of the chair behind his back. "My apologies, sir, but Reymond and I..."

The Chamberlain waved him away as he reached the final step. He panted, holding the banister for support. "I don't require your apology, boy. And your partner-in-crime has more than filled me in on your current disposition."

Disposition? What exactly had Reymond said?

Barrett glanced up at the open door, expecting... *hoping* he'd see Reymond, but the Chamberlain had come alone.

"And this is the morsel in question, I suppose?" The Chamberlain motioned past Barrett, craning his neck around him for a better view. "Why does she wear your uniform, boy? Has she come to enlist in the Baron's service?"

Barrett searched in vain for the right words. *Think... think...* The moment had gone.

"Actually, yeah," Vilka said, as confident as she'd been with Barrett.

Barrett shot her a look of suppression. "Vilka, keep your mouth shut," he hissed, a volume designed for her ears only.

"What's this?" the Chamberlain remarked, his thin lip curled in amusement. "The girl has bigger balls than you, boy. Tell me, girl, what is your name?"

"It sure ain't *girl*," she snapped, her arms still folded. "Tell me *your* name first. Barrett here said you were some sort of *chamber-man*. I'm guessing that ain't your real name."

The Chamberlain laughed. "So, my evening has been rudely interrupted for what, a peasant's comedy? You should have listened to the boy's advice and shut your mouth."

"Suppose I won't work for your Baron then." She shrugged. "See if I care."

The Chamberlain's eyes were thin as slits, his mouth curling into itself.

Barrett mouthed toward Vilka, rotating his head so the Chamberlain couldn't read his lips. "Be quiet. Allow me to speak." He turned back to the Chamberlain, wearing the smile he knew worked wonders for the man's ego. "Sir, please allow me to explain. I'm not sure how much Reymond has told you, but the situation is simply this: we discovered Vilka in the corner of the stables, toward the end of our shift."

"*Vilka?*" The Chamberlain chewed the name around in his mouth, expressing it with a prominent *ahh*. *Villkahh*, like some mysterious, ancient city whose inhabitants uttered the strangest of dialects.

Barrett was unsure what his next sentence would be. Indeed, it wasn't like the Chamberlain to allow him the time to explain or elaborate. He was accustomed to being cut off, not having to worry about how he might have to end a conversation.

"You make me sound so unworldly," Vilka said, though Barrett was unsure who she was addressing. And *unworldly* was an unusual word to hear uttered by a peasant girl.

The three of them existed in disharmonious silence for a time, during which the Chamberlain reviewed the situation, and Barrett cursed his inability to articulate himself.

"So, we gonna stand here all night?" Vilka broke the silence. A blunt arrow into the invisible wall between both men.

"You will do as you are told," the Chamberlain snapped. "Still, it is not wholly my place to determine such a matter as this. I shall have to raise this conundrum with the Baroness, but it shall have to wait till the morrow." He bit down on his bottom lip, still thinking. "I would speak with you on the morrow also, Barrett Barrett, after your morning duties have been fulfilled."

Barrett paused in shock, aware that his mouth was gaping open. The Chamberlain didn't refer to servants by their full name, especially when that someone was Barrett.

This is it. My time as a steward is over. I'll be out of work, forced to sell my home.

"In the meantime," the Chamberlain said, "house and feed the girl. And for the love of the Goddess, fetch some water for a bath. Mister Vinerman won't be in the least bit pleased when he denotes the new odours gracing his cellar."

Barrett bowed his head. "Yes, sir, of course. At once."

The Chamberlain grunted as he began to ascend the stairs. The door slammed shut behind him, eclipsing Barrett and Vilka into blackness once more.

"You hear that?" Vilka said, wearing something of a smile. "Housed and fed, he says. You know what, I think the Chamber-Man likes me."

"He called me Barrett Barrett," Barrett thought aloud. *That could mean I am in his favour... it could mean my discovery of Vilka is reason enough to dismiss me.* He searched frantically for some minor breach in procedure. *Should I have kicked her out onto the street without question? Handed her over to the dungeon-keeper? Have I, by taking pity on the girl, written my own dismissal?*

Vilka was staring at him. "*And?* Ain't that your name? Goddess above, the people round here ain't half strange."

A New Arrival

U nease lingered in the air like a putrid stench. Mavrian seemed to be alone in detecting the foulness, the uncertainty weaved into the wind.

As her fingers caressed the smooth edge of the balustrade, the cool metal forced a chill up her wrist, tickling her forearm. A welcome change. With her nails, she tapped curiously, the sound a dull ping racing from one side of the banister to the other.

The view from the balcony was astounding, no matter how many times she saw it. The northern edge of Kleäm was all cliff and stone-beach, but the residents had carved grandeur from the rock: upon the cliffs overlooking the sand that wrapped around the island stood the castle of Meelian. Mavrian beheld the spiralling towers, gaunt murder-holes, and sharp, triangular roofs. In this moment, she was a virgin to its beauty.

The idea of beauty turned to dust as her gaze rested on the tallest tower. *Eplin's tower.* Lorr Garr had been gone from Kleäm for over a week, but still, his words invaded her mind: *When next we meet, my dear, you will be carrying our child.*

Mavrian discerned sick in the depths of her throat. Her stomach lurched. She fought the urge to vomit over the balustrade.

Her attention turned to the marketplace at the bottom of the hill as she inhaled the brisk salt air. In the shadow of Meelian, the courtyard was a booming centre of trader stalls, peddler wagons, and the eager patrons that scurried between them.

Do they not know what day this is?

She strained to listen and could hear their busy voices in the wind. They had no form, but she imagined they were saying, "Come one, come all, browse my exotic wares. Potions to cure, poisons to kill. Delicious fruits, wines to sate."

Mavrian hadn't left her quarters in days. The Dräege was due to take place in a few hours, and then she'd have no choice but to venture outside. She'd been dreading the ceremony as soon as Eplin had sailed from Kleäm. Though in many ways, the lord's absence spelled her liberation, it had also resulted in her exile from court. *Which is no bad thing.* But the ceremony would mean her facing the Loress Meels once more, this time without the Lorr Garr's protection.

A sudden commotion in the marketplace drew her attention. A crowd of people huddled around a single stall, listening to a tradesman. She was too far to discern their words or expressions, but the crowd appeared rapt, still with intrigue.

Whatever can be so interesting? The question lingered as Mavrian left her chambers and descended the steps of Vicker's Tower like a hound in search of fresh meat.

Outside, at last, the fresh air filled her lungs like a rich, soothing beverage. The sky burned orange, muted with pale violet clouds. She realised the storm hadn't finished with them just yet, as the horizon to her left revealed inky splotches of grey. The past few nights had been ghastly, spent listening to waves crashing into Hobe Rock, the fierce downpour singing its chorus. And all the while, she'd dreamed of Eplin's ship sinking to the bottom of the sea, praying that if such an event occurred, the Twins would be unable to save him.

A flock of birds cawed overhead. Twenty-or-so journeyed

southward in search of a better autumn. Mavrian had a mind to take flight and join them.

Vässa take me from this place, from the cursed shadow of this castle. Lend me wings. Let me fly with these beasts. Then, as though they sensed her folly, the birds let loose a volley of white excrement in their wake, missing Mavrian only by a fraction. *The Twins have a sense of humour today.*

As she followed the street southwards, she realised the birds' bombardment had spattered the statue of Drente that guarded the entrance to the market. Sticky, slow-dripping shit covered the shoddy interpretation of the once-great emperor.

"Fucking rats with wings," muttered a man, shaking his fist at the retreating birds. He'd been leaning against the statue's plinth when the rain of white fire fell.

Mavrian stifled a laugh as the man locked eyes with her. His flesh was unusually pink, his eyes a cool shade of blue.

"Vermin o' the *fucking* skies," he said through gritted teeth.

"Well, you won't have to worry about them until next spring," Mavrian said, spotting the wet faeces dripping down his jacket as she passed by.

"Mayhap, *you* won't. I won't be here day after the morrow," he called after her. "And good riddance to this bloody isle, I says! When spring comes, you can keep your shitty winged rats. Keep 'em for good."

Mavrian winced at the stranger's peculiar accent. She didn't dare turn back to confirm her fears, but she was certain he was Kinsmeer. She shuddered at the thought. Kinsmeer weren't an uncommon sight on Kleäm, but they remained an unwelcome one. To think she might've conversed with one left her queasy.

Mavrian shook the idea as she passed under the rusty gates, atop which bore the symbol of a trident – a thing that had baffled her since the day she'd landed. There was no correlation between tridents and Kleäm. Though, perhaps the square had once been a fishers' market.

She wandered the stalls in particular direction, except to avoid her usual route. The tradesmen of Kleäm knew her weaknesses, what she couldn't avoid spending her coin on. She hadn't visited the marketplace in weeks, but the same traders perched behind their tables laden with goods, ready to sell her anything and everything. And they weren't in the habit of forgetting their favourite patron.

She searched for the stall that the crowd had gathered around, avoiding the tradesmen's widening eyes and emerging grins.

Madam Vanet's eyes lit up as Mavrian passed her dressmaking stand. "Oh, good morning! Come here. Come here, child. I've a fine new range of silken gowns that would complement the unmatched beauty of your crimson eyes. Come, come."

Mavrian pretended not to hear the eager woman. Dresses and trinkets seemed unimportant for the moment. There was only one thing interesting her. She would discover the cause of the crowd's fascination if it was the last thing she did. Whatever it was, she wanted a part of it.

She took a right, then a left, then another left, then a right, then kept straight for a time, then turned left once more. As she stopped to catch her breath, she realised she was in an area she'd never visited before. Here stood the temporary traders, the stalls that were here today and gone tomorrow. Mainlanders from Ryne, and the occasional Kinsmeer visiting from across the sea. Her usual inclination was to avoid this place, as rumours encircled of illegal, pirated goods and shoddy replicas of finery being sold here. But the mesmerising salesman *had* to be around here. No permanent merchant would have generated such intrigue.

"Morning, lass." An old man's toothless grin blocked her path. "Can I interest ye in a humble man's collection of rare and precious oddments?"

The trader's proposition was far too vague. And he reeked of fish. Without a glance or reply, she dodged his sparse teeth and took a sharp left, passing several bookstands.

Before she had a chance to review her bearings, a display of fresh fruit stole her attention. The rich multi-coloured collection included fruit she'd never seen before and several that appeared almost fake, handcrafted from wax. As she glanced over everything on offer, a red apple caught her eye, bundled among varied shades of green, much smaller fruit.

She searched for a box that contained more of the red variety, to no avail. *It must have been stuck here by mistake. Much like myself.*

"You gon' buy summit or just stand there gawking?" The grocer's crude voice brought her eyes toward him. He had several chins and brown dots for eyes. She couldn't help but notice his belly hanging over his belt, threatening to burst out of his shirt. "Mayhap you seek to alter the apple's shade by staring at it?"

The ethnic origin of the man wasn't debatable. Everything, from his coarse voice to his piggy skin, screamed Kinsmeer. Though he carried the scent of crushed flowers popular in the Meelian court, and his ill-fitted frilly shirt was quite fashionable in Kleäm. Even his quaint mannerisms were blood skin in nature.

Mavrian almost choked. She'd been holding her breath without realising it. "I'd like the red apple... if you please." She gestured at the fruit in question, feigning disinterest. Doubtless, a Kinsmeer would charge her double if he thought she was willing to pay it.

"So I see." The man's smile revealed brown teeth to match his muddy eyes. "The young lady seeks a taste of the exotic. Handpicked from the vineyards of the Jade Isles were me apples. And polished to please the eye, no less. Only the finest will do for this fine young lady." He smacked his hand against the table. "And so, a piece of the exotic this young lady shall have. And promptly, as she likes." He withdrew a roll of brown paper, cut it to size, and placed a green apple on top, ready to roll.

"No, n-not that one," Mavrian protested. "The *red* one."

The man raised his eyebrows and tossed the green fruit back into the pile. He wiped his mouth with the used brown paper, threw it aside, then retrieved a fresh strip.

"Well, well." His voice suggested mirth, despite his deadpan expression. "So you *do* have the exotic taste, lady." He wrapped the red apple up carefully. "Though I must point out, this here's the rarest variety, no less. Costs but a smidgeon more than the rest of me fine apples. 'Tis quite the delicacy, so I hear. From the Ruby Isles, no less. Last of its batch."

The Ruby Isles? This pig takes me for a fool! Mavrian knew the Jade Isles produced such delicacies, but the Ruby Isles she'd never heard of. And she had heard of everywhere. This *Ruby Isles* did not exist.

The trader's arm reached across the stall, holding out the packaged fruit. "That'd be three silver pieces if the lady don't so mind." His brown grin hung on her every breath.

Three silvers? Three silvers would have purchased her a necklace from the tinkerer – albeit a counterfeit – or an ivory comb from the poacher's stand – albeit not actually made of ivory. Even one silver would have been an insult for a single piece of fruit.

The man's smile faded as she withdrew three silver coins from her purse and dropped them into his sweaty hand. Muttering under his breath, he stuffed the pieces into his breast pocket, eyes thin as murder-holes. It seemed he hadn't planned for the Bloodkin to meet such an extortionate fee. Unbeknownst to him, Mavrian's coins were not her own.

He shooed her away with a sharp wave of the hand. A gentleman browsing melons had caught his attention, and before Mavrian could blink, the grocer was creeping towards him.

Mavrian laughed under her breath, unwrapped the apple, and tossed the worthless paper onto the grocer's desk.

The marketplace was busy for a morning. She guessed half the gentry of Kleäm were out and meandering amongst the stalls. *Perhaps they too seek to distract themselves from the upcoming Dräege.* Though she dreaded any of them despised the event as much as she did. The Dräege was lauded as a great spiritual occurrence, filled with jubilation and triumph. It was a time when the Twins basked amongst their people, bridging the gap between the mortal and immortal planes.

Most greeted the Dräege with undiluted delight. But most hadn't experienced the Dräeges Mavrian had.

Her first bite of the apple was sour, the aftertaste bitter. She avoided eye contact with the doublets and tunics that passed her, as her face contorted due to the potent flavour. After her fourth bite, the sourness subsided, and what remained was sweet as sugar.

As she turned a corner, Mavrian spotted Cäda and Reesa standing by a meat stand, watching in disgust and awe as butchers hacked without mercy at indiscernible carcasses. One butcher, twice as wide as the rest, barked orders and spittle in every direction. A plump woman was sitting behind the butcher's desk out front, poring over a massive book. She didn't seem to notice the two young ladies staring over her shoulder as the butchers chopped away.

Mavrian bit into her apple as she approached. "What are you doing here?"

Both ladies jumped in surprise.

"*Mavrian!*" Cäda shrieked, recovering from the shock. "Where have you been and... and... what have you got there? When I heard you'd left Vicker's Tower, I didn't imagine that..." Her words trailed off. She scratched at her thin eyebrows. "You left your quarters to find... an *apple?*"

Mavrian shrugged. "I was hungry." She flashed her eyes toward the butchers. The burly men sliced through the immense carcasses with practised ease. "*You* left Vicker's Tower to ogle at butchers? Or is it the butchery itself that has you mesmerised?"

Cäda giggled at that. Reesa shook her head.

"Mock away, Mavrian," Reesa said, plain faced. "Cäda and I were discussing their barbaric technique. The way they slice and dice without regard for what they're doing. It's... it's... simply barbaric."

Mavrian hid her smile. "What difference does it make? The things are already dead."

Reesa studied Mavrian for a moment. "Really, Mavrian. Believe it not, the meat belonged to a living creature once. Would you care so little if these men were to chop *you* up so carelessly?"

Cäda itched at her temples, confused. "And why would they do that?"

Mavrian couldn't shield herself from laughter this time. "Reesa, you didn't seem to mind when you were dining on pork last night."

The maids of Vicker's Tower had served them enough chicken and sausages to sate an entire ship's crew, and Reesa had eaten more than Mavrian and Cäda combined.

"Ah, but you see..." Reesa faltered. "It's all so different when you *see* the slaughter for yourself. It's just so... ghastly."

Cäda had, Mavrian noticed, turned pink in the face, her eyes darting around in a nervous frenzy.

Mavrian realised the woman behind the desk had looked up from her book. "Can I help you, dears?" she asked, her voice falling somewhere between a kind mother and an unkind brute.

Reesa ran a hand through her hair. "We're fine, er... thank you." She cocked her head back over her shoulder. "Come on, let us take our leave," she hissed at Mavrian, knowing Cäda would follow.

"Well," the woman behind the desk said, unsmiling. "If you dears ever have need for a hog or steak, you know where we'll be."

"Come," Reesa snapped, grabbing both Mavrian and Cäda by the arm. "We should be making our way back to Vicker's Tower. Won't be long before the summons will be heard sounding from Meelian." She slipped Mavrian a smile. "*Then* we'll know the Dräege is about to begin."

Reesa led them away from the market stalls, where the shit-painted statue of Drente stood proudly.

"Why did you really come here?" Reesa asked Mavrian. "And don't tell me it's because of that apple."

"I heard a commotion from my balcony," Mavrian admitted. "Saw a crowd gathered around one of the stalls, and I *had* to see for myself what the fuss was all about."

Reesa and Cäda shared a look. Mavrian knew that look.

"I didn't find what I was looking for," Mavrian added, grimacing down at her apple. The inside of the fruit was a shade of golden. *But*

I did find the world's most expensive apple. She couldn't wait to see Meels's face after learning her coin was squandered on fruit.

"A commotion, eh?" Reesa narrowed her eyes at Mavrian.

"The crowd wasn't gathered around a market stall," Cäda said.

A chill prickled Mavrian's spine.

A flock of blackbirds swooped overhead, declaring their presence with a series of squawks.

Reesa sighed. "What Cäda *means* to say is that what you saw from Vicker's Tower *may* have been the same gathering that we ourselves joined. You see, when we entered the market, a boy was running up and down, yapping at all who'd listen that tremendous news had just landed in Kleäm."

"We followed the boy to a newsman," Cäda continued the story. "*Rejoice,* said the man, *for a vessel's docked in Kleäm baring the esteemed flag of the Bloody Hand.*"

"The Bloody Hand?" Mavrian thought aloud. "*The* Bloody Hand of the Veerkasn?"

Reesa and Cäda nodded in unison.

"The Veerkasn ship bares none other than Scarmane Trokluss," Reesa said. "And yes, *the* Scarmane Trokluss. The Warlock of Blanders. He's come to pay his respects to the Loress Meels, and, so they say, comes bearing some news of his own."

Scarmane Trokluss? What's he *doing here?* The Warlock of Blanders was one of the most prominent members of the Veerkasn. A hero of the war. *What does he want with that old bat Meels?* Mavrian doubted it was to *pay his respects.* Nobody respected the Loress, not even Eplin.

"Come," Reesa said, grabbing Mavrian by the wrist. "Madam Corr will be none too pleased when she learns of the three of us venturing outside without permission."

"Since when do *I* ask for permission?" Mavrian muttered, but the others – thank the Twins – didn't seem to hear her.

"Zamrian won't be pleased either," Cäda added. "In fact, she'll be very unpleased."

"Speaking of which, where *is* your sister at present?" Reesa asked Cäda. "I don't suppose she remains cooped up with the madam. I certainly wouldn't choose such a fate."

"Perhaps we should check the gardens?" Mavrian suggested, tossing what remained of her apple onto the ground.

Reesa frowned at that. "And risk stumbling over that oaf Gäne? No. No, I don't think so."

"Come now, ladies," Cäda said. "Today is special. We can't forget that."

Mavrian's skin prickled at the very word. *Special*. She would use many words to describe the Dräege, but special wasn't among them. The ceremony meant brushing shoulders with the Loress Meels and her wretched daughters, swallowing bile as the men of court undressed her with their eyes. They knew she belonged to Eplin Garr, but that didn't stop them staring, fantasising.

And, to make matters worse, the men of Meelian were the least desirable creatures in the world.

Scarmane Trokluss, on the other hand, was the most handsome man in all of Ryne, according to some. He was also said to be a fiend, an honourless bastard who tortured the innocent and murdered the Overlord's enemies. But then, every Veer carried that reputation.

Perhaps Scarmane Trokluss will attend our Dräege, she considered. The idea was a welcome distraction from the thought of those vassmirs that led the ceremony. Their soulless, listless eyes had haunted Mavrian ever since she was a child. The way they glided across the marble floor like formless, ethereal beings stayed with her for days after every ceremony. She supposed that was due to their auras. Their spirits were tied to Väss, their souls tethered to the Twins. Others claimed to feel safe around vassmirs, that standing near them brought them closer to Vässa and Vällas. Mavrian felt nothing but unease around them.

Perhaps I don't bleed myself enough.

Bloodkin were compelled to bleed themselves at least once per day, according to the vassmirs, but thrice was preferable. Most days,

Mavrian forgot to bleed, but nothing dreadful seemed to befall her, as the vassmirs claimed would happen.

Unless my lack of bloodletting is what anchors me to this forsaken island. Then, in that case, the Twins had indeed cursed her.

They walked back to Vicker's Tower in silence, save for the wailing of the wind and the whispers of those they passed. It was an uphill climb from the market to the line of towers that peppered the eastern edge of Kleäm. Here lived the Bloodkin with plentiful coin but not enough renown to quarter in the castle.

Mavrian was just glad her chambers were far enough that she didn't experience the scents and sounds of the docks.

"Do you suppose that sailors practice the Dräege?" Mavrian asked no one in particular.

Madam Corr was inspecting the planters in the yard as they approached Vicker's Tower.

"Some do," Reesa stated. "Most commoners in Kleäm have black blood. Most are filthy scavengers from Gammôr and Myrakäss, where the Dräege is not practised. And there are far too many Kinsmeers among the crews of these trade captains. The piggies pray to a moon goddess, I hear. Bloody wretches."

"There you girls are!" Madam Corr boomed when she noticed the three ladies, her layers of stomach jiggling as she bounced over to them.

"I wonder what Scarmane Trokluss would think of these heathen captains and their love of Kinsmeer labour," Reesa said under her breath. "I wonder what he'd do about it."

Madam Corr reeked of sweat and tobacco. "Twins above! I feared you ladies wouldn't make it back in time for luncheon. Don't you know what day it is? What *time* it is? There's a Dräege to prepare for! And how do you propose to prepare yourselves with empty stomachs? Think, ladies. Think!"

The keeper of Vicker's Tower snatched Cäda's sleeve. "Your sister worries after you. Come. Come, the lot of you! I'll have you something rustled up. Need to maintain fortitude if you mean to honour the Twins with all vitality."

Reesa held her hand out in front of Mavrian to hold her back and allow the plump keeper to wander off, gaining some distance as she led Cäda inside the tower.

"Mavrian. Scarmane Trokluss's appearance means something."

"I know." Mavrian swatted Reesa's arm away. "I'm no fool. Of course it means something."

"But what does it mean?" Reesa folded her arms tight to her chest. "We all know Trokluss was present at the peace negotiations in Carthane. I'd warrant a guess that the news he carries pertains to the talks. Things turned sour, I'd guess."

"But why would he land in Kleäm of all places? That bitch Meels commands no respect in the Capital. Eplin wouldn't lie, not about that."

"Perhaps there is someone else in Kleäm he seeks an audience with."

"Lorr Garr isn't here. There's no one else in Kleäm of any importance."

Reesa shook her head, eyes narrowing. Mavrian knew that look, knew it far too well.

"I hope you're not insinuating..."

"You are the daughter of Havarian Morr," Reesa spoke over her. "Your father may be long dead, but that name means something in Plargross. Even now."

Mavrian opened her mouth to retort.

Madam Corr's massive face emerged from the door of Vicker's Tower. "Ladies! Come quickly, now. I'll see that your stomachs are plump if it's the last thing I do."

"He will seek you out," Reesa muttered as she grinned and waved over at Corr. "But in the meantime, we've the simple matter of a Dräege to prepare for."

Words, Bloody Words

The Baron Without Sorrow. That's what the commoners called him, through stew-stained teeth and ale-infused spittle. The words whispered over tavern tables, breathed into ears over dinner. None would day utter the words in his presence.

Barrett's first encounter with his liege and employer had been underwhelming. Disappointing, even. For Hanzus of the House of Irvaye appeared, on the face of it, no more foreboding than any other man in Balenmeade. In fact, Barrett considered Merrian, the Honest Mule's lazy-eyed bard, to be much more frightening.

To Barrett, the moniker *Baron Without Sorrow* evoked the image of an impassive brute, a warrior whose mercy had abandoned him long ago. A malicious, conniving monster.

In truth, Hanzus Irvaye hid his sorrow well.

"Barrett! Barrett!" somebody barked into Barrett's ear.

A huge blob, somewhat resembling a face, loomed over Barrett. Huge, bulbous eyes studied him. The face was hideous: pocked with acne scars, skin dry and flaking at the scalp. It was Ache, he realised. Or, to be precise, the man they *called* Ache. The soldier's real name remained a mystery, but one thing was certain: Ache was as unpleasant a man as his moniker suggested.

"Morning," Barrett said, avoiding the giant's stony gaze.

When Barrett was a child, Ache had made a habit of chasing the youths of Balenmeade, bellowing abuse after them. Barrett had always been quick on his feet, and so escaped the pursuing giant with ease. As to what fate befell the children Ache caught up to, however, he'd rather not imagine.

"I suppose you've some sort o' audience with the Baroness," Ache stated, scratching a raw pink lump on his forehead.

Barrett nodded, gazing at the door over the man's shoulder. And an ornate door it was: a rich shade of emerald, a flowery gold leaf border around the frame, its polished bronze handle shaped like a twisted branch.

Ache narrowed his eyes at Barrett. "Suppose you been summoned."

Barrett inhaled a sharp pocket of air. "Yes, Ache, the Baroness is expecting me." As Ache loomed over him, his throat dried up, tightening, an invisible hand choking him.

Ache scratched his stubbly chin with one hand, leaning on the blunt middle of his two-bladed axe with the other. According to Ache, artisans forged the immense weapon in the infamous pits of Dulenmeake, and it had once belonged to Vestar the Thirsty. Whatever the truth, one fact remained undeniable: Ache was the only man in the Balenmanor strong enough to lift it off the ground.

"Why've you been summoned?" The guard's breath reeked of breakfast, a blend of eggs, bacon, and stale bread. Barrett was sure, if he dared look, he'd find evidence of the meal slotted between Ache's goofy teeth. Fortunately, the giant's gullet remained shut, his puffy lips curling into a snarl.

Barrett searched for the right words to move this oaf aside. Ache was stupid, but he could detect sarcasm like a hound sniffing out a rabbit. "It would be impertinent of me to say." *Will he understand impertinent?* Barrett might as well have spoken in Nerblyss, judging by the giant's dumbstruck face. "I'm here on business," he added. "*Confidential* business."

Ache itched his dry cheek. "Much as I'd like to believe you, Mister Barrett, I can't just take your word for it." And he turned and pounded one troll-sized fist on the door. A disgruntled cry came from the other side, and Ache pushed the door inward a crack, squeezing his fat face through the gap. "Barrett Barrett's here to see you, milady. Says he's 'ere on business, though he won't say the sort."

"Send him in, Ache," the Baroness commanded in a shrill voice. Hers was a stark contrast to Ache's harsh accent. Every word sounded preened and polished.

"Very well, milord... uh... milady." Ache turned back to Barrett, holding the door open with his fist. "Now, no funny business. We've already had a steward causing 'avoc this morn. Don't want no more trouble, you 'ear?" Barrett thought better than to question the man's statement. Ache leaned in close, the stench of egg assaulting Barrett's nostrils. "If I hear a whisper o' trouble, I'll be rolling in after you. You understand me, boy?"

Barrett faked a smile as he took the weight of the door from Ache. "I understand." He could feel the giant's pervasive eyes tearing into the back of his neck until the door closed behind him.

Funny business? If Barrett wasn't so gripped by fear, he'd have laughed at that. Did Ache *seriously* believe he posed more of a threat to Heatha Irvaye than she did to him?

As he staggered into the dark room, Barrett inhaled dust. The study was filthy. Piles of dusty books and rolls of parchment covered the tables and were stacked irregularly on the bookshelves. The curtains were closed. Penetrating sunlight revealed clouds of dust around the window frame.

The Baroness, eyes red and droopy, could have been chair-bound for a century. Small journals and hefty tomes sat piled high on her desk, alongside tea-stained rolls of parchment and several dried-up inkwells. She would have hidden behind the stack of leather and parchment if she were only a few inches shorter.

"My lady," Barrett said, inclining his head as he reached the foot of the desk. He noticed that thick layers of ghost-grey dust coated everything.

Heatha Irvaye attempted a smile as she raised her stubby chin to greet him. "Mister Barrett," she rasped. "Thank you for arriving with such haste. News has reached my ears of a... shall we say, distressing nature."

Barrett's heart sank. *Vilka...* This had to have something to do with the girl.

"Please sit, Mister Barrett," the Baroness said, flashing her eyes at the empty chair beside him.

As he slumped down, Barrett could not peel his eyes off Heatha's hollow, impassive void of a face. It was the first time he'd seen her in weeks, and in his absence, she could have aged a few years. Or decades. The Baroness was only forty, but her hair was a shock of white, her skin taut in places and saggy in others.

She rapped her skeletal fingers against the desk. "This morning, Chamberlain Jupe paid me a visit. It was a most disturbing visitation, I might add." Her eyes widened. "The news he carried was most perturbing."

We're talking about Vilka, aren't we? There was surely no other reason the Baroness would take a break from locking herself away in this decrepit library.

Heatha straightened in her chair. "Jupe tells me you discovered a wayward child lurking in my husband's stables." She rubbed her hands together slowly. "An insipid creature, from what I hear. Possesses as much merit as an infested rodent. And to top it all off, she's foreign." Her lip curled in disgust.

Barrett found that ironic, as Heatha was a foreigner herself. Still, he kept his mouth shut.

"Jupe informs me that you spoke to the girl for some time. That you went as far as to lend her your coat."

Barrett picked at the fabric arm of his chair. Were those good or negative actions to her eyes? *Am I about to be lambasted? Is that what* this was about? He knew he should have kicked Vilka out onto the street the moment he laid eyes on her.

Heatha's eyes were assaulting him, appraising his every movement, penetrating his soul. Sweat trickled down Barrett's back. His cheeks burned.

It was meetings like this that could end a man's career.

"She... was cold, my lady." It was all he could muster. When she did not respond, he added, "We were holding her in the cellar. She... was frightened." That was a lie. Vilka was fearless. She hadn't shown the faintest hint of anxiety. Not a drip. But whatever he said now might very well seal her fate. "I believe the girl was lost and happened upon the warmth of the stables. Like a fly drawn to the light." He cringed at the weak metaphor. Could he really compare Vilka to a fly? A mouse, perhaps. "I believe her to be of no threat... to anyone." He was digging himself into an even deeper hole. *She didn't ask if Vilka posed a threat, you bloody fool.*

Heatha considered his words. She rested her elbows on the edge of the desk. "Please continue."

Barrett considered his position. Was Vilka on trial, or was he answering for his own crimes? Condemning Vilka would see her banished or imprisoned. On the other hand, if he outright lied and Heatha caught him out, he could be mucking out stables every day for the rest of his life. *I suppose I should just tell the truth.*

"Her name is Vilka, my lady. She didn't say much, but she did tell me she travelled east to get here." He stopped to catch his breath. Heatha's stare was impossible to read. *Am I talking my way out of a corner, or am I writing my last will?* He had no choice but to continue. "She was blunt and rude. Obnoxious. But... but I believe she was acting that way out of fear, as a sort of defence mechanism. From what I could garner, she has no place to go. Nowhere to call home. Nowhere to return to. She's fleeing something, perhaps. Or someone. She's... she's... desperate."

That last word lingered in the air like a bad smell. Barrett was now desperate himself, desperate to leave the room with his head still resting on his shoulders.

If he wasn't mistaken, Heatha was smiling. She pointed at one of the books lying flat on the desk. A dark illustration sketched onto the open page. Barrett squinted at it, trying to make sense of the image. He could make out a humanoid shape whose skin seemed to be glowing, their hair black as night, their eyes as red as the setting sun.

"Bloodkin," Heatha answered the unvoiced question. "Accursed vermin. Their ilk has not been seen or smelt in this barony for many, many years. Emperor Hovane sent as many as he could across the Northern Sea, banishing them to Ryne for all eternity. They are a forsaken, Goddessless people." She faltered then, appearing disgusted by her own words. "I shouldn't say *people*. They are no more *people* than we ourselves are insects, making homes out of shit and mud. And now they believe that the land of Ryne is their own." She cackled into her hand, a laugh that graduated into a cough.

Barrett was familiar with the Bloodkin of Ryne and their ongoing war with the Sylvian Empire. The war had been the newspapers' favourite topic for months, and it was with an eye to end that very war that Hanzus had vacated his seat in Balenmeade and sailed across the Northern Sea. King Halmond believed the Baron's presence at the peace negotiations would convince the Bloodkin to sign an armistice. An impossible task, in Barrett's opinion. The Bloodkin had been warring in their supposed homeland for centuries.

But what has this got to do with Vilka?

"My husband will soon return," Heatha said. "I have no doubt that he will arrive in time for the Harvest celebrations."

Barrett inclined his head, wondering where all of this was leading.

"The Bloodkin will be our downfall." She exaggerated a sigh. "I don't know *how* or *when* it will come to pass, but I have this terrible feeling in my heart. It will one day be so."

Barrett was speechless. He searched and searched, raiding the library of his mind for some idle platitude to dish out. "The Bloodkin are far from our realm, my lady. Far across the Northern Sea."

Heatha's eyes widened. "Only, it is there you are wrong. Your girl, Vilka, told Chamberlain Jupe quite the tale when he paid her a visit this morning. And her claim may surprise you." Her eyes narrowed, the bags under them darkening. "Bloodkin, Mister Barrett. Bloodkin here in the Krämise." She sighed, straightening her shoulders, which produced a sharp *click*.

"Bloodkin?"

"In the Krämise," Heatha repeated. "Vilka marched for days and days to reach Balenmeade, under rain cloud and thunder, her only shelter in the trees and knolls of the Krämisen wilderness. She encountered all manner of monsters and men but was able to sneak past them all. That was until she encountered *them*."

Barrett realised he'd stopped breathing. For a moment, life itself seemed to inhale his surroundings and hold them in its lungs. His throat filled with sick, and he choked.

By all accounts, Bloodkin were wicked men with black hearts and black minds. Stories circulated of blood sacrifice, worship of multiple gods, debauchery of the most fiendish nature. They couldn't be in the Krämise, or anywhere near here for that matter. A few hundred Bloodkin worked in Vinerheim, but they were as good as slaves. Had some escaped and headed south?

Barrett had never met a Bloodkin in the flesh, but if the stark illustration in Heatha's book was accurate, they were monstrous. *What if they're here in Balenmeade? Mother... Lerry... We aren't safe.*

The Baroness seemed unperturbed. "Vilka has been bathed and clothed. You'll be pleased to know. And your coat was cleansed scrupulously. The child had near enough soiled it." Barrett's cheeks flashed red. "But she was cleaned up, and this morning she was presented with a breakfast fit for a lady. That did enough to loosen her lips." She chuckled. "Really, when you consider, jailers often spend days trying to loosen the tongues of their prisoners. And

Chamberlain Jupe managed it in less than an hour with no more than a few sausages and strips of bacon."

Barrett cringed at the thought of the fat Old Chamberpot interrogating Vilka over breakfast. Sauce dripping down his many chins as his chubby fingers reached for her young flesh.

He vomited a bit in his mouth.

"You have questions," Heatha said, straightening her back. "Well, let's hear them then."

Sweat caked Barrett's chest. If only he could unbutton his shirt without revealing the evidence of his anxiety. "Is she in good health?" The question slipped off his tongue and lingered in the air for more than one agonising moment.

"So, so," Heatha said, pursing her lips. "I believe she returned to her bed after Brendal left her side. She's a precious little thing, he tells me. Though she is somewhat lacking in decorum and charm." She sighed. "Come, Barrett. You can do much better than that. What is your next question?"

Barrett paused. Was there such a thing as a good question when evil lurked on their doorstep? He wanted to probe more on the subject of Bloodkin, but for some reason, Vilka was central to his thoughts. "What's to become of her?"

"Really?" Heatha looked disappointed. "I tell you a child sighted Bloodkin, and all you care to know is how the *child* is doing? Bugger *her* fate. What about our fate? *My* fate! *Bloodkin*, Mister Barrett! Bloodkin here in the Krämise!" Her anger simmered down. "You must forgive me, Mister Barrett. I... have not slept in some time." She blinked around the bleak room. "If true, do you understand what Vilka's sighting could mean?"

Of course, he understood. The thought of Bloodkin crawling through Lerry's bedroom window was frightening indeed, but so was the thought of Vilka's captivity. Old Chamberpot's hands raping her... Heatha torturing her for more information.

"As to whether the girl is telling the truth, I am undecided." Heatha sighed, staring at the Bloodkin illustration before her. "By rights, the matter should be settled by my husband, for I know his arrival is only days away. Should I await my husband's will so that he can decide the veracity of her claims? Even there I am undecided." She pursed her lips and scrunched up her eyes. "Perhaps your words can sway me, Barrett Barrett. Tell me, why *were* you named Barrett Barrett? Seems rather odd to me."

The diversion threw Barrett's thoughts into disarray. Would the truth suffice, or should he devise a diversion of his own? "My father named me Barrett, after his father."

"A humorous family tradition then," Heatha mused. "You know, I think I'm starting to understand what my Hans sees in you."

It took him a moment to realise that *Hans* referred to the Baron.

"The girl is in no immediate danger," she continued, sighing through her nostrils. She chewed over her thoughts in silence, tapping the desk with one long fingernail. "I suppose that leads me to the reason I summoned you. I am aware that Brendal tasked you with preparing the stables. A job I have no doubt you excel in." She offered him a smirk. "I do, however, require your services elsewhere."

"Does this new service have something to do with the girl, my lady?"

Heatha smiled. "Vilka has been offered temporary residence here in the Balenmanor. It would please me greatly if you could make her feel at home. To see to her every requirement."

Barrett felt an initial pang of relief. Spying on someone was without doubt better than shovelling manure. "Of course, my lady. May I ask, though... what will become of Reymond?"

"Hm?" Heatha's brows furrowed deep into her skull. "Who is... ah, you are referring to Mister Morgen? The young steward will continue his good work in the stables. It *was* you that discovered Vilka, was it not?"

"Yes, but..."

She waved him away. "Then it is settled. I was certain there had been a mistake when the two of you had been allocated the same task. A sleight of hand, perhaps. For though the preparation of the stables is, I do not doubt, an arduous one, it is also quite clearly a one-man job."

Bile trickled down Barrett's throat as he nodded along. He had a feeling Reymond wouldn't see Barrett's escape from stable duties in quite the same way. It was true that Barrett discovered Vilka, but Reymond had helped him escort her inside the Balenmanor and had risked his neck by going to fetch the Chamberlain.

"I'm sure you understand, Mister Barrett. Vilka's claims cannot be blindly accepted. I have, I will admit, espoused my own untruths from time to time when the situation demanded it." She gasped, eyes wide and panicked. "A man's mind can be a confusing place, let alone that of a little girl. One might utter all manner of things. Perhaps, when spoken enough, one might even begin to believe their own lies." She folded her arms, working the words around her mouth. "Vilka is a vagrant, Mister Barrett. No more, no less. And a vagrant would say anything... *anything* to steal a few sympathetic platefuls of meat." She leaned over the table. Sweet perfume masked the aroma of sweat wafting over the books. "I will be frank with you, Mister Barrett. I see something in you. Intellect. Guile." She leaned back in her seat and pouted. "I want you to get to the bottom of Vilka's tale. I want you to learn the facts about these Bloodkin. The *real* facts. By any means necessary."

Barrett nodded. What else could he do? "I understand, my lady."

By any means necessary. The words echoed in his mind.

Heatha had asked him to turn informer. And not the Baron's informer, not even the Chamberlain's. *Her* informer. Her spy. A snitch, a snake – the role Jupe had made a career of. But why wasn't she getting the Old Chamberpot to do her dirty work now? *Why was I chosen for this sordid task?*

Heatha's frown deepened as silence reigned.

"Believe me," she groaned, shattering the silence. "I would have no problem sending you back to the shit-infested stables. And perhaps you would stay there, serving as the master's lackey, feeding his pigs and sifting through haystack after haystack. I hear that he rather likes sweaty, stinking young men. Perhaps you would serve as his mistress, also."

The bile was rising now, infusing his tongue, staining his teeth. His stomach leapt and jumped and swished side to side. He was on the verge of puking, spewing his guts up all over the Baron's collection of books.

Barrett didn't have a choice. He could not afford the rent on his house on the wage of a stable hand. His family would be forced to live on the street. Lerry would never have an education. They would all be begging for scraps, selling their bodies for coppers.

What choice did he have?

Heatha was glaring at him, breathing heavily, chewing on her thin lips.

"I will do as you ask, my lady." As the words reached his lips, shame coursed through his body. *You're sworn to the Baron... You're bloody well sworn to the Baron.*

In any other barony, it would have been quite possible, even expected, to serve the lord and lady equally. In Balenmeade, Heatha was her own entity. It was no secret that the Old Chamberpot sailed in her direction – a wind that Barrett had always tried to steer away from.

"Good," Heatha said, shutting the book with the Bloodkin illustration with a *thud*. "I will leave the task with you. On the day after Harvest, I expect you to return to me with a full report."

Full report? Barrett's hands were trembling. *By the Goddess, what have I done?* He belonged to Heatha now, and in so doing, was betraying the very man he owed his life.

"Leave me now," Heatha grumbled, shooing him away as she turned her attention to a book. "When next we speak, I expect you will know the truth of these Bloodkin. The *real* truth."

The Dräege

The Dräege arrived like the claws of death, clutching her throat, tightening, tightening as the afternoon faded. The Holy Hour was upon them.

Madam Corr had helped Mavrian into a dress of black velvet. An ensemble that, according to the mistress, directed attention to Mavrian's *beautiful face*. The material caressing her skin made her think of Eplin, and that was the last thing she wanted on her mind. Especially now, seated in the temple pews.

Mavrian had been placed in the middle of Mudgar Vane's stale breath and Lucian Grögg's sweat. She hoped that her placement between the two least desirable members of the Meelian court was no more than a stroke of bad luck. But it wouldn't surprise her to learn she'd been dumped at the back of the hall out of spite. She recalled Meels's words to her at their last meeting: *Your father was a treacherous, worthless blot on the legacy of our kin. I suppose it's no surprise that his offspring is following in his footsteps.*

Cäda and Zamrian sat in the middle of the hall, next to their uncle, Kölle Kamarn, who was whispering with the man to his right.

Mavrian couldn't pick Reesa out of the crowd, but when they'd entered the temple together, Reesa had veered off towards the front pews.

The Loress despises me more than she does the others, Mavrian mused, watching Mudgar Vane pick at his nose. She wondered whether to rejoice at that thought or sob. It was no secret that the Loress despised the name Morr, but Mavrian's placement at the back of the hall was a terrible insult, even by Meels's standards. *Perhaps she heard about my trip to the market. Perhaps she's realised how I squander the puny allowance she sends me.*

Mudgar Vane kept grinning at Mavrian. She was certain he'd whispered something in her direction at one point, but neither understood nor wanted to understand its meaning.

In the courtyard outside, the clock chimed the hour.

Mavrian's heart pounded with each *twang* of the bell.

When the clock tower fell silent, the audience stood.

Mavrian sucked her stomach in, angling her hips to ensure she didn't rub up against Lucian Grögg. Mudgar Vane was staring at the side of her face, as gormless as ever. *Vässa have mercy on me.*

The doors at the rear of the hall burst open. Musicians blew trumpets from the mezzanine level above. Awe gripped every dumb face that was stuffed into the pews.

As the doors shut, every head turned toward the white-robed man that was gliding through the corridor in the centre of the pews. He crept toward the altar. The vassmir, Käl, carried an air of feminine grace. His movements were soft and slick, his chin aimed at the ceiling. Two small boys were scurrying after him, clutching the ends of his trailing robe. He was some macabre form of bride; only, instead of inspiring delight and joy, he radiated dread and sorrow.

When Käl stepped up onto the platform and took his place behind the lectern, the boys dispersed into the crowd. The vassmir's eyes scanned across the pews – blank, emotionless, expressionless orbs. As his eyes fell on Mavrian, he appeared to be looking *through* her, penetrating flesh and bone, peeking into her mind, evaluating her soul.

She dismissed the idea. The vassmirs of Väss maintained a close relationship with the Twins, but they couldn't read minds. But Käl's eyes lingered on Mavrian, studying her features.

Käl's attention graduated from Mavrian to the book that lay open on the lectern. He shut his eyes, his crooked nose pointing at the audience like an accusing finger. Then he outstretched his arms, signalling for the audience to be seated.

As Mavrian lowered herself into the seat, she ensured she was an equal distance away from the two oafs on either side of her. Much to her horror, she realised her dress had got caught under the great weight of Lucian Grögg. As she yanked the fabric free of his immense buttocks, her shoulder barged Mudgar Vane, who shot her an accusing glare.

Käl glanced over through the book before him. Then he stood back from the lectern, moving around to stand at the front of the platform, tucking his hands behind his back. He inhaled a sharp breath, closing his eyes once more. Mavrian could see his eyelids twitching from across the room.

His words started as a low rumble, inaudible at first, before raising just loud enough to hear.

"Children of Blood. Children of Väss..." His eyes snapped open, searching the pews for answers. "We remember the fallen. Gods below, we remember the fallen. Those blessed kin that gave their blood to ensure our liberation." He pointed at his own chest, jabbing one bony thumb into his heart. "It is true that we have lost good men and good women, without whose sacrifice we would have remained slaves to the whims of foreign forces until the end of time. But even so, it is with the *Gods* that we place our gratitude, without whom our cause would have crumbled into nothing. Without whom we are, but empty shells. Gods below, hear our sacred vow!"

The audience echoed, "Gods below, hear our sacred vow!"

The words left a bitter taste in Mavrian's mouth, as they reminded her of Mother. And Father. And Dravan. She pushed the thought out of her mind. *You are in the presence of the Twins. They're watching you. They can hear your thoughts.*

Käl closed his eyes, his breathing laboured, exaggerated in through the nose and out of his mouth. A sick smile crossed his face.

"And yes, gracious Gods of Our Blood, Vällas and Vässa, we honour the exalted one's breathing still!" The crowd repeated his words. "We look to our past endeavours, for we are reminded of the momentous task set out before us. Young and old. Rich and poor. Ours is a people united by common blood!" He opened his eyes and surveyed the Bloodkin on the front column. "Yes, gracious Gods of Our Blood, a day shall come for each and every one of your children. Your sacred presence is yet to reveal itself. Yet to be bestowed. Yet to *penetrate.*" He lowered his voice to an intimate, almost reassuring tone. "Yes, let it be prophesied before each one of your children gathered here today. The sacred presence *shall* reveal itself. For it is the will of the gracious Gods of Our Blood and the want of their children that shall make it so." His voice grew in volume, his words clear and crisp as they echoed throughout the hall. "Yes! Let it be known before the children gathered here, when such a day arrives, every soul shall be scrutinised! For every breath... every *drop* of blood must be given in servitude to Vällas and Vässa! We live in an age, my children, where a single drop spilled for any purpose other than the furthering of their cause breathes life into the enemies of salvation!"

Mavrian studied the reactions of those around her, careful not to draw any attention to herself. Every pair of eyes presented the same basic theme: ecstatic desire, fierce flames burning bright. Zamrian's smile widened with every breath, which was flustered and high in her chest. Even Cäda appeared to be gripped by the vassmir's message.

Lucian Grögg grinned at Mavrian as their eyes met for a second. The imbecile's dog-like features were gut wrenching at the best of times, but his sick smile and the way his eyes hovered over her bust made her want to climb over the pews and escape.

Focus, Mavrian, focus. She turned her attention back to Käl, who was pacing up and down the platform, his hands gripped tight behind his back. *What is wrong with you? You are in the presence of gods. How can you allow yourself to be distracted?*

The more she thought about it, the less she felt connected to the Twins. There was something curious, something not quite right about the vassmir's affirmations... then she realised: *They're the same words he spewed at last year's Dräege. The same exact words.* Though he dispersed passion through every fibre of his being, the words were hollow, something false in the way he weaved them.

"Behold!" Käl boomed, his eyes nearly popping from their sockets, his trembling hand pointing down the aisle toward the doors.

The audience twisted their necks toward the entrance. Like obedient children, they waited.

Then the doors swung open, and a procession of crimson-robed vassmirs strode into the hall. They were carrying a black coffin-shaped box on their shoulders, painted with floral patterns interwoven with an illegible script. The contents weighed down its carriers – and they were large men, as far as vassmirs went.

As the procession passed Mavrian, she realised the men were no vassmirs at all but men of the Loress's court. Six of Meels's favourites, her eldest son, Revarian, among them.

The Dräege had been predictable so far, but Mavrian didn't remember this part of the ceremony.

The men placed the black box at Käl's feet. The lid heaved off and taken aside. As the red-robed men took their places in the audience, the vassmir bent down, placing his hands inside the box.

Mavrian craned her neck to get a better view, but it was hopeless. All she could see were the flaps of Käl's robes draping across the box's opening.

When Käl arose, he was clutching a bronze object – a small blade, it seemed, sharpened on one side, glimmering with a beautiful menace. He walked to the edge of the platform, eyeing the front row with such glee. A knot tightened in Mavrian's gut.

"A time of words has obscured our vision. A vision seen through the drapery of blood." Something of a smile creased his leathery features. "The Gods teach us that *we*, the children of that very blood, glorify this world by our very presence. But such essential loyalty cannot remain untested... unresolved!" His smile crumbled with bitterness, disgust. He muttered, just loud enough for Mavrian to hear, "And tested it shall be." Clearing his throat, he thrust his arms into the air, embracing an invisible figure. "Bring forth the willing!"

The doors opened a third time, their painful groan as they swung shut, serving as an announcement. A lone figure entered the hall, gliding towards the vassmir. A woman wrapped in coarse linen, barefooted and bruised at the ankles, her wild frizzy blonde hair tied up in a bun. As she passed Mavrian, her face revealed a patchwork of pink blemishes, black moles, and untamed warts.

Kinsmeer, she realised, as she denoted the creature's stone-grey eyes and warm complexion. A servant, perhaps, or one of the dockside workers.

The woman stopped before the vassmir and curtseyed.

Käl spat at her with his eyes, pointed an accusing finger in her face. "Stand before the Children of Blood and accept their scrutiny. Quiver before the eyes of the Gods and accept the shame of yours, a race untrue. For the Gods created you, not in their image, but in the image of the forsworn. Black beings of the Nether. Vällas! Key furgtao blessa!" Like a mummer in a play, he recoiled away from the Kinsmeer, wearing a face of disdain and piteous disgust. "Almighty Vällas, bathe us in your blessing. Rid us of this spiritual plague!"

Tears thrashed against his cheeks.

The Kinsmeer lowered their head in submission, resigned to their fate.

Käl lunged forward off the platform, snatched her by the scruff of the robe, and spun her to face the audience. He grabbed the back of her hair, squeezing the bun and yanking her head upwards, forcing her eyes level with their faces. He held it there in suspense.

Not an utterance or a single breath broke the rapt silence. Though Käl's prey was Kinsmeer, some part of Mavrian pitied the creature. She searched for the sympathy in others. Friends she had known for years and acquaintances introduced to her in the past months, united in their thirst for blood. Even Cäda's eyes gleamed with anticipation.

The puppeteer Käl still held up the Kinsmeer, his emotionless face looming over her, an extension of her body. The woman was docile in his firm embrace, her ugly features expressionless. She was a hollow vessel without mind or soul.

"Behold!" the vassmir shattered the silence. "Behold the past!" His free arm wrapped around the woman's body, tight to her chest, his fingers clasping her wart-ridden face, pushing her cheeks together. Still, she did not flinch. "The past is primitive. Cold and fearful. As is Kinsmeerkind, in all its decadent, flawed form." He stepped back suddenly, his release of pressure causing the woman to lose her balance, but she stood her ground. He wrapped his hands behind his back and began to pace up and down behind her. "Now, the Bloodkin are a race perfected. The inferior race will learn this. By Vässa's grace, they will learn this." He fell into a smile once more. "And so, rejoice, for the vassal shall bathe in the inferior's weakness and ignite the superior soul!"

Käl launched himself forward once more, like an assassin from the dark, yanking her back by the hair so that her face aimed at the ceiling. He rested her neck on his clenched fist. "And now, through the power of the Twins of Blood, the children are charged in their rebirth! Behold the power of Vässa! Behold the power of Vällas!"

In one swift motion, his clenched hand retreated behind his back, then reappeared clutching the bronze blade. In one fluid motion, he slashed it across the front of her neck. Dark blood sprayed in an arc. Once relieved of his grip, the Kinsmeer's body fell to the ground in a heap, her robe blackening with blood.

The Kinsmeer writhed in silent agony, her legs twitching. Death hissed from her lips, just loud enough for Mavrian's ears. Then the body stopped its dance.

Mavrian was numb. Her buttocks ached against the hard seat, the sensation shuddering up her spine. She couldn't look away from the vassmir's dripping red hands.

She supposed she ought to feel something. Jubilation. Disgust. She felt nothing, no shred of emotion, no spiritual tether binding her to the Twins. Nothing.

Only souls that carried blood worthy of the Twins were supposed to be sacrificed. That basic principle was preached by every vassmir Mavrian had ever heard speak. The books of Aegal taught them such.

This sacrifice was nothing. It was butchery.

Käl lifted his red hands. The blade slipped from his grip, hitting the ground with two metallic thuds.

"In death, we rest. In death, we pass on to the next life. Oh yes. But there is no time for rest. Not now." Käl fell to his knees before the corpse, inspecting its gushing wound with his fingers. He closed his eyes and began chanting a low hum, rising in volume and intensity as the river of blood painted his arm with its rich stain.

A tear came to Mavrian's eye, though numbness prevented her from feeling anything.

"Don't let the others see you," Lucian Grögg whispered in her ear. "They will misunderstand."

Before she could think to reply to him, the vassmir ambled onto his feet, almost slipping on the pool of blood around him. His indiscernible chanting formed something of a melody. Abruptly, he broke off and opened his eyes. "Child of dirt, Vässa forbids your passing! Vällas forbids your passing!" He waved a finger in the corpse's face. "I forbid your passing! Arise now before the Children of Blood. Awaken in honour of our Gods! Awaken now and banish the shadow that is your wretched soul!"

The pews filled with gasps of abject horror. Mudgar Vane reached for Mavrian's trembling hand, which she slapped away.

A chorus of wails echoed throughout the hall, emanating from the front row. They jumped out of their seats, recoiling from the platform.

It was seconds later that Mavrian, through a gap in the flailing arms and frantic faces, glimpsed the cause of their hysteria.

The dead woman had arisen from the pool of blood and stood nude beside the vassmir, her robes a bloody heap by her feet. The blood had dried over her neck, shoulder, and breasts. A thick layer of black clotting sealed the gash.

"Alas, my children!" Käl shrieked with an orgasmic glee. "The Gods have sought to bestow us a sign!" He gestured frantically between the woman and the crowd.

The living corpse raised its hands, silencing them all. Her eyes had faded into nothingness, leaving only white orbs to gaze in no particular direction, and yet everywhere at once. She spoke words that became masked by the audible confusion of the crowd, but as she did so, they fell into awed silence.

"I have been resurrected in the Blood of the Gods," she said, her booming voice reaching every corner of the hall. "And now that the power of Vässa has been witnessed, the Children might journey forth and rejoice in the victory that she has promised. Now that the power of Vällas has been witnessed, the Children might bathe in the blood that he has promised. And so, the future is paved for their coming."

The hall erupted, all at once, into a sea of madness. Every manner of emotion came pouring from their faces: floods of tears, frenzied applause, manic laughter, lamentations of despair. A swarm of people approached the stage, falling to their knees and audibly praying. Hands reached for the woman's pink flesh, feeling her all over. She was a living relic. They clambered for a touch of her bloodstains and the pool permeating the stone surface.

"She is Kinsmeer no longer!" someone proclaimed. "She is born from the ashes of her own blood!"

Mavrian froze. She watched as Vassmir Käl backed away from his army of frantic admirers as they asked him for blessings and praised his work. Before he turned to leave, he whispered something in the resurrected woman's ear.

The Baron's Return

The afternoon was dying. Black clouds wept, rain pattered against the slanted outbuilding roofs, trickling down the stone wall that surrounded the Balenmanor. The ditch skirting the wall was overflowing, and Barrett saw the stable master's son, Olex, playing with a paper boat in the new makeshift river.

A spider raced across the cobbles, deftly avoiding the droplets of watery hell. When it reached the ditch, it stopped. Too late. The spider's hesitation spelled its demise as a volley of raindrops forced the creature into the ditch, washing it away.

Barrett swallowed. The sky was grey everywhere.

"Straighten your shoulders," the Chamberlain snapped at one servant further down the steps.

Barrett straightened his spine, eager not to attract Jupe's attention. He wondered if the old snake was privy to Barrett's new position.

They'd all been standing there for what felt like several hours.

The balcony overlooking the Balenmanor's main doors sheltered Barrett and his fellow stewards from the torrential downpour, but the lower-ranking servants were not so fortunate. The groomsmen were stood in a line in the centre of the yard, their clothes already soaking. The maids occupied the opposite side and appeared wetter still, their long hair plastered over their faces.

The entire household was present, arranged like some puny army awaiting its general's return. And in a way, Barrett mused, they were.

Suddenly, the band started up. Drum and symbol crashed in unison, trumpet and trombone buzzing their practised tune. The Ballad of Balenmeade, so named – it was the farthest thing from a ballad Barrett had ever heard.

Everyone lifted their heads, squinting through the onslaught of rain. A dull humming echoed from the streets beyond the wall. It was cheering, muffled by the rain, if he wasn't mistaken.

The metal gatehouse doors creaked inward, and three horses trotted into the courtyard. Lion, the Baron's personal stallion, was much taller and muscular than the other two horses. Barrett was certain the immense steed had grown in the months it had been absent.

And the lord it carries has shrunk. Barrett remembered the broad, almost plump lord that had departed for Carthane all those months ago. Were he not astride Lion, the Baron Without Sorrow could have been mistaken for an unconvincing imposter.

The Baron dismounted in the centre of the yard, his mud-encrusted boots thudding against the cobbles. His beard was thick, matted, grey in places. His oily hair almost touched his shoulders. If there was one thing that revealed his true status, and one thing only, it was his walk: confident, purposeful. His sky-blue eyes surveyed the commoners gathered around him.

The two other arrivals dismounted their horses and hobbled after the Baron. Their poor postures betrayed them as uncouth commoners. Cay's inability to grow a beard meant that only dirt covered his pink face – or was it blood? Stains peppered his long coat, the blue fabric obscured by purple splotches.

Lew had aged a decade in a few months. With his grey-and-white beard and spoiled rags, he looked like a wandering wizard.

"Jupe," Hanzus said, slipping out of a pair of leather gloves as he approached the manor steps. He placed a firm hand on the Chamberlain's shoulder, spun him round to face the door. "Tell me, where is my wife?"

"Ah..." Brendal's eyes shifted between his lord and the door, then to the nearest servant, then back to Hanzus. "She is at prayer, my lord."

A lie. A lazy lie. The Baroness hadn't attended a single chapel in months, not even the Balenmanor's shrine to the Goddess. It was common knowledge.

Hanzus's eyes narrowed, his thick moustache twitched. "Fetch my wife, Jupe. She will see me at once."

The two men passed Barrett, one reeking of perfume, the other worse than the stables. Had the Baron bathed in cow dung? The stench lingered in his nostrils even when Hanzus and Jupe reached the doorway.

The Chamberlain wore a brittle smile. "My lord, might I suggest I have a bath prepared for..."

"I *said* at once," Hanzus spoke over him, his voice dry as stone.

Brendal held the doors open for his master. "Certainly, my lord. Certainly, yes. At once. Yes, yes."

The voices faded as the doors shut behind them. The battalion of servants broke ranks at once, gliding this way and that, chattering as they sought shelter from the rain. But before Barrett could follow them, Lew and Cay's crooked faces appeared in front of him.

"Barrett Barrett," Cay said, wearing a tired smile. "Can't tell you how pleased I am to see your face again. Well, anything's better than *his* ugly mug..." He nodded in Lew's direction.

Cay and Lew didn't smell quite as foul as Hanzus, but whiffs of horse and sweat encircled them like a pestilence. Barrett glanced around and was relieved to discover the three of them were now alone in the yard.

Lew winked at Barrett. "How the hell are you, lad? Goddess, it's good to be back. Trust our lady's been 'olding the old fort good and proper?"

Barrett nodded, unsure what to say. Surely Lew knew he couldn't speak about such things. Not here, at least.

"Pissy weather," Cay groaned, grimacing as the rain trickled off the balcony. "Can't say it was much better out in the sticks. But what a greeting..." His voice trailed off as he glanced around. "It never rained up north."

"Don't mind the lad," Lew said, running a hand through his greasy hair. "We've had quite the fucking journey. How's about I tell you all about it over a pint? Shit, I'd kill for an ale about now." He sucked in the air, puffing out his otherwise gaunt cheeks as he peered around the yard. "Course, we was expecting the Lady Heatha to be here. Handkerchief drawn. Sobbing and all that."

Was that Lew's crude idea of a joke? *Or have the summer months burned all memory of Heatha Irvaye from his charred brain?* When Heatha had watched Hanzus depart Balenmeade, her eyes possessed more joy than tears.

"Well, I didn't entertain the thought for a second," Cay said. "Hanzus was rather adamant his wife would greet him, though. Fool's hope, I suppose."

Hanzus? Hanzus? They're calling him by his Goddess-given name now? It was a small wonder Cay still possessed his tongue. *Did things really become so informal out there on the road?* Though, Barrett couldn't pretend to relate to their experiences out there in the wilderness. *The open road changes a man.* He'd seen it written in many a memoir. But did it strip a man of his professionalism?

"Well, these ancient bones o' mine won't help me stand much longer," Lew said. He placed a dripping hand on Barrett's shoulder before ambling over to the door. "This old chap needs me a nice hot bath."

"As does this young one," Cay said, hobbling after him.

Barrett watched in horror as both men dragged their boots over the steps, leaving trails of brown sludge in their wake. The thought of that mud and filth decorating the hallway carpet brought a lump to his throat. He had no choice but to follow them. No one else would shield them from the Chamberlain's wrath.

The men's stench was much worse when they stepped inside the manor. Barrett denoted traces of piss and sweat, and there were other foul elements he couldn't quite put his finger on. The only certainty was that Lew and Cay had been in a fight. Old blood spattered across their clothes, and a purple bruise imprinted on the side of Lew's neck.

"Did you encounter highwaymen?" Barrett asked as they turned into the hallway that connected the front rooms to the rear of the manor.

Cay shrugged. "I guess. Highwaymen of a sort."

"Dogmen," Lew elaborated. "Cursed shits. The darned beasts tried to scavenge our camp while we slept. But they weren't expecting no fight. Not the one we brought to 'em. We bruised them up proper, ain't no two ways about it."

Dogmen? Several adventurers' books referred to those wretched dog-headed men. But he'd scarcely believed such tales were true. "Goddess above. Where did you encounter them?"

"Not twenty miles from here," Lew grumbled. "Where the Kingswood meets the Krämise."

Barrett's heart sank. *Now there are* Dogmen *in the Krämise? What would he learn next? Giants ripping Krämisen trees up from their roots? But what does it all mean? Bloodkin lurking in the Krämise... Dogmen on our border... What is happening?*

"Baron tore them to pieces," Cay said, grinning. "Had the dogs weeping blood down to their bastard breeches. Mark my words, no dogs'll be troubling us any time soon."

"Truly," Lew sighed. "Mind, a few did escape with our food. And speaking o' which, I'm bloody starving."

"Here we are," Barrett said, rushing forward to open the doors at the end of the hallway, so their grubby hands didn't get there first. "You must be famished."

"My arse hurts, mainly," Cay groaned as he passed through the door.

"Cheers, lad," Lew said, taking the weight of the door from Barrett, pressing his dirty fingers into the handle.

Barrett cringed as he stomped after Cay.

The servant hall they'd entered was a hive of activity. Maids scurried from door to door, carrying piles of folded towels and buckets overflowing with water. Porters sprinted up and down, caked in sweat, carrying crates of Goddess-knows-what.

When they reached the bathing rooms, Old Nuttel sprang up from her chair. The knitting she'd been working on clattered to the floor.

"The 'ell are *you* doing here?" she barked, her grey eyes darting between the three men. She poked one bony finger into Barrett's chest, her gloomy gaze settling on him. "*You* don't bunk in these quarters, boy. Get out. Now. Afore the Chamberlain 'ears of this."

"Cay and Lew need to use the facilities," Barrett explained, swallowing fear. "It's not for me. It's... for them."

"Ain't for *you* to decide," she growled, her half-blind eyes studying the filthy men before her. She muttered under her breath as she squinted at Cay. "Young'un can enter. Old'un will 'ave to bathe elsewhere."

Without a second thought, Cay pushed past them both and disappeared through one of the bathing room doors. Lew didn't seem shocked in the slightest.

Some fellowship you two share. "Lew needs a bath also," Barrett sighed, ignoring the voice in his head, begging him to be silent.

Old Nuttel growled like a dog. "Cay bunks in these 'ere quarters. Old'un don't." She sank back into her chair, considered reaching for the knitting needles at her feet, but decided against it. "*I* don't make the rules around 'ere, boy. Take it up with the Chamberlain."

A surge of adrenaline coursed through Barrett. He knew that arguing with Old Nuttel was akin to debating an old nut, but Lew looked exhausted. Surely she could make an exception. "Please. Lew has just returned from a long, long march. He's... he's fought in a battle!"

His words were in vain. Of course, they were in vain. Old Nuttel had been following Brendal Jupe's orders down to a tee since the beginning of time. He doubted she would deviate from that strategy now.

"Don't matter," she hissed, staring at the ground. "Now, leave me. Don't you know not to bother poor old ladies?" Her gaze attached to the knitting needles by her feet.

Barrett could have picked them up and passed them to her, but help was the last thing she deserved. Nuttel was a vicious old bat, consumed with disdain for every man that wasn't Brendal Jupe.

"Hush now, lad." Barrett felt Lew's hand grasp his shoulder. "Come, let's drink at my place."

Lew's home was a decrepit shack on the edge of town. The eastern quarter housed the poorer citizens of Balenmeade: lumberjacks, farmhands, muckers, and the like. The buildings were narrow, averaging three or four storeys. The area reeked of mould and stale piss, and the interior of Lew's home was no exception.

From Lew's front window, Barrett could see the dark stone wall that surrounded Balenmeade, designed to keep vagrants like Vilka out. He wondered whether living in the shadow of the wall was reassuring or made one feel imprisoned. If an army ever besieged the city, Lew's shack would be one of the first buildings to burn.

Barrett had visited Lew's house only once before, after the old man insisted he and Reymond sample his wife's cooking. As he recalled, the soup on that day was the same grey sludge that was placed before him now. Barrett's stomach professed its hunger, but the slop was scolding hot, even after blowing on his spoon.

Lew had no such problem as he wolfed the stuff down, pausing only to stuff bread in his mouth and cool his throat with ale. Barrett supposed this was his first proper meal in days.

Freda glared at her husband over the brim of her cup, breaking every so often to direct a smile Barrett's way. She'd refused to embrace Lew when he'd entered and made him scrub himself down with a damp rag before sitting him at the table. She was a warm lady, but fierce. Barrett had witnessed her drink the men of the Dancing Buck under the table and hold her own in the regular arm-wrestling competitions Drodger would instigate.

"It were so good o' you to escort my Lew home," Freda aimed at Barrett, swallowing a mouthful of ale. Her rosy cheeks wobbled as she spoke. "And so nice to 'ave you with us. Ain't so often Lew brings a guest to my table."

Lew paused from slurping and stared at his wife. He held his spoon close to his narrowing eyes, the contents dripping back into his bowl. Then he went back to his food, shovelling it in as if his wife hadn't spoken.

Barrett offered Freda a smile. "It's a pleasure. Really."

He'd just stepped between a marital feud. *Perhaps Lew's invited me here just to prevent an argument between them.* He took a spoonful of soup and blew on it. Brown chunks poked out of the grey goo. He hadn't a clue what he was looking at, but he knew better than to ask.

"You're always welcome at my table," Freda said. "Though I 'ear lunch up at the Balenmanor is plentiful and hearty. What with all those fine ingredients the Baroness gets delivered, you lot must be spoiled."

"Only if you're Old Chamberpot," Barrett remarked, kicking himself for speaking so freely.

Lew paused once more, his dark eyes studying them both.

"Don't suppose *your* meals were so hearty," Freda snapped at her husband.

Lew chuckled at that. "It were me what cooked, dear. So o' course, the serves were dire. Master Cay couldn't boil a stew to save his life, and the Baron couldn't be expected to hunt for himself, could he?"

Barrett realised he'd been blowing on his spoon for some time. The mouthful he swallowed was cold and tasted of chicken, leek, and salt. There was a bitter aftertaste, some herb that didn't mix well with the rest. But he voiced polite groans to indicate his satisfaction.

"You must've 'ad your work cut out," Freda remarked, glaring at her husband.

Lew set down his spoon and wiped his moustache clean of soup. "Oh, my work were cut out for me, all right." He reached for his ale and downed it in one.

"You must be exhausted," Freda said, her tone softening somewhat. "How's about you go and lie down?"

"I *was* exhausted," Lew grumbled. "Now I'm just tired. Won't be lying my head down no time soon, mind. Got too much to do. Many folks to visit."

"Do you have work back at the manor?" Barrett asked.

Lew shook his shaggy head. "Baron's give Cay and me three days to rest up. We rode hard, and we sailed hard and true, the lad and me. Then we sat, and we waited while finely dressed cunts and forsworn heathens argued over land and politics." He took a deep breath as he stared out the window. "I'm tired. There'll be no work for this old bugger for the next few days. These old bones need resting."

Barrett had a thousand questions swirling around his head. *How fared the negotiations in Carthane? Is the war between Bloodkin and Men over at last? What was it like to sail on a ship? How did you fight off a band of wild Dogmen?*

Barrett held his tongue. By Lew's dishevelled appearance, he was in no mood to tell stories.

"I'll pop to the merchant's," Freda said, shifting from her stool and pacing over to the door. "Nimforthe will be pleased to 'ear o' your return. Besides, we need milk."

"Tell that greedy Nocryn that his pleasure's none o' my concern," Lew muttered, too quiet for his wife to hear.

The moment Freda had left the room, Lew sighed in relief and relaxed on his stool. "More ale?" he asked, refilling Barrett's cup before receiving an answer. "Freda ain't happy, as I'm sure you can tell. When I left her, I promised to return within the month. Fool words. And fool lady to believe it."

Barrett accepted the ale with both hands.

Lew downed his own new serving in one and quickly refilled his cup. "She should be counting her blessings. Coin don't make itself, now, does it?" He sighed again, grimacing into his cup. "Bah. I shouldn't 'ave spoken so cold. She ain't deserving o' it. The long road does queer things to a man. Hardens him. Squeezes his soul. I know it better than any man in this Goddess-forsaken town."

Lew seemed inconsolable, full of fatigue and bitterness. Barrett supposed this was a bad time to bring up Carthane and Dogmen.

Barrett searched his own recent memories for something that would take Lew's mind off things. "Weather's been foul here in Balenmeade. Nothing unusual there. You haven't missed much at all here, really." He thought on the events of the last few days, hoping for a cheery subject to make itself known. Indeed, he realised there'd been nothing joyous about the past few months. The nights he'd spent drinking his life away in the Dancing Buck were a scant consolation for the Chamberlain's tyrannical rule of the Balenmanor and the Baroness's gross mismanagement of funds.

Then there was Vilka. On that subject, Barrett didn't know where to begin.

"Folly," Lew said, meeting Barrett's eyes. "Damnable folly were those negotiations. We're just boys acting as men, and failing even at that."

Barrett's back prickled. "So, the diplomacy between Sylvia and Ryne failed?"

Lew laughed, but his face was devoid of humour. "*Failed?* You could say something like that, yeah. The talks were a bloody mess. No more than a diversion. When we arrived in Carthane, Hanzus were treated like the fucking King of Gadensland. Shown to a royal suite in the Tower of Frame, treated to the fattest banquets the lad and me had ever seen." He finished his ale and immediately refilled the cup. "It were a ruse. All o' it. A con. The negotiations were nothing, led nowhere. And then, after we'd boarded the ship back home, guess who tries to slit our good baron's throat? None other than His Majesty's royal captain, Edgar Morske."

Barrett sank onto his stool. The ale had turned to bile in his throat. *Edgar Morske, famous captain, turned cutthroat?* "Surely not," he thought aloud.

Lew raised an eyebrow. "You think I'd lie? Think I'm in the habit o' queer jests? I saw the captain's body with my own eyes. Hanzus managed to kill the bastard before his evil order could be carried out. He wanted Hanzus dead, you 'ear? Nearly had him and all."

Barrett's hand was trembling as he reached for his ale. "Order? But who..."

Lew waved him away. "I've said enough. Too much. Leave an old man alone to rest." And with that, he sprang from his stool and rushed to the door to hold it open. "Be gone now, lad. Quick as you like."

Barrett wiped his lips clean of ale before scampering over. "Look Lew, I'm sorry if I said anything to upset you."

"I said be gone!" Lew hissed, then he slammed the door shut behind Barrett.

Barrett's heart was pounding. What kind of dark force could have willed an esteemed hero of the high seas to do its foul bidding? How could Morske stoop so low? *Is Lew telling the truth? Is his mind muddled?* Barrett could see no reason for the old man to lie, and his mind was as sharp as his tongue.

Barrett almost tripped. As he came to rest his hand on the wooden wall beside him, he became lightheaded, his vision blurry.

Somebody wants the Baron dead... The negotiations between the Sylvian Empire and Ryne have failed... Bloodkin have been spotted in our barony, and I am now under oath to the Baroness...

Barrett had a feeling that when the Harvest commenced, he wouldn't be among those celebrating.

The Baron's Sorrow

Balenmeade was Hanzus's first love. Years before he knew the ladies of the Vinerheim court, long before the sweet numbing of wine became his favourite pleasure, he'd fallen for the smells and sounds of the Krämise's capital. The narrow, cobbled streets weaved in and out of four-storey townhouses and taverns that never closed.

To the educated mind, Balenmeade was a den of louts and imbeciles, a rat's nest of poorly constructed and seldom-maintained shacks that would better serve the kingdom on fire. The Balenmeaders were, according to the experts, a boulder-fisted, pebble-brained people who preferred slobbering down their own chins to a hard day's work. The published works seemed to forget that the Krämise produced enough hops and barley to fill the kingdom's alehouses. They also forgot that without Hanzus, the Battle That Never Was would have gone ahead, and the people of Gadensland would now be hailing Jesmond as their king.

To anyone with eyes, Balenmeade was a wholly unremarkable place. But the city was the last bastion of civilisation. The gateway to the Middle Kingdoms. Without the Krämisens to guard the southern-most borders, the plagued Rooksfolk and heathen Gunnic tribesmen would ravish the land, burning and raping as they marched to Vinerheim.

Gadensland needs the Krämise far more than the Krämise needs Gadensland. The barony had not always belonged to the Kingdom of Diamonds. Before the emerging kings and emperors annexed the lands of men, the Krämise was a free realm. A pure realm, free of foreign influences.

Hanzus had witnessed the Capital's influence spread across his barony like a fetid plague. Jurgen had attempted to save the dying language of Krämisen during his reign, but his efforts were all in vain. As merchants and labourers moved in from all corners of the kingdom, the true essence of Balenmeade had diminished and died.

Balenmeade was Hanzus's first love, but it wasn't the city he'd grown up in. It wasn't the even city handed over to him after Jurgen's abdication.

Hanzus had been in Balenmeade for almost a week. And with his return, the Harvest festival had been constructed around him. Flags were draped out of every window down every street. The banner of Gadensland flew paramount – a golden lion wearing a crown of diamonds, standing on its hind legs across a sea of deepest blue. The banner of the Krämise flew outside the home of every true Balenmeader – a brown boar walking across a field of emerald-green. He spotted a few anomalies thrown into the mix: the tower banner of Vinerheim, the bleeding heart of the Artenshold, and the hooting owl of the Tyldar.

Musicians skipped up and down the roads, layering the ambient merrymaking with their flutes and lutes and fiddles. Mummers stood on street corners, dramatising the failed peace negotiations in Carthane – and the common misconception seemed to be that Hanzus's presence at the talks had somehow prevented the whole world from taking part in the Empire's foolish war. Jugglers and jesters kept the rabble entertained as carriages and cabs came rolling in through the city gates, smuggling in gentry from across the barony.

Hanzus had avoided his family in the days following his return.

He'd ordered his meals delivered to his chamber and spent much of his time reading by the window. When he did venture outside, he accepted only a single guardsman so as not to draw attention. For all the good it did. As he wandered the streets, commoners bowed before him and sang him platitudes and invited him into their homes for an ale and a bite to eat. He declined them all with a smile, promising to raise a mug with them after the Harvest feast was over.

They were lies, of course. The last thing he wanted to do was to dine with his noxious courtiers, to be forced to tolerate his wife in the company of stewards and aldermen. And he had no intention of prolonging his suffering by breaking bread with commoners afterwards.

He already wanted to escape the Balenmanor, to escape Balenmeade, to ride back out into the wilderness. *And perhaps I will when this is all over.* Perhaps he would visit the inns along the Old Road, then spend the winter in Dulenmeake.

Hanzus inhaled a sharp breath as he left his chamber. He hadn't visited his study yet. He had to ensure his collections remained in order.

He approached the ornate study door and halted. It was ajar. A knot formed in his throat. His study was off-limits, even to Heatha. He had been sure to lock the oak door before departing Balenmeade and made a point to draw the curtains so nobody could peek in from the outside.

He pushed the door inward, swallowing fear and bubbling anger.

The study was a ruin.

Somebody had violated the collection. Spoiled it. Devastated it. As his fingers brushed the leather volumes, he noticed several books were placed on the wrong section of shelf. Books of contrasting size and bindings of various colours had been jumbled together. Geography and history books were mixed with works of poetry and prose. Books he'd never seen before – that must have come from the library or Balenmeade bookshops – had found their way into *his* space. Discarded books littered the floor, some worth ten times the average servant's salary.

Any commoner could have found their way in here, spotted the most lavish cover and sold it to a festival peddler.

Heatha's behind this. Only the Baroness possessed a skeleton key. Only the Baroness possessed the malice and guile to spoil what he held dear.

And it was Heatha he'd promised to meet this afternoon, to share a drink before supper. The wretched woman had been harassing him for days, inviting him to dine or to go for strolls. Realising he'd have to see her at some point, he'd chosen a few goblets of wine over enduring an entire meal in her company.

Now he'd rather strangle her than drink, but the Baroness had been cunning. When Hanzus agreed to meet her for goblets, he learned she'd also invited his cousin, Denzus Irvaye the Younger. *So I don't berate her.*

Reluctantly, he inspected the room further. He stepped over pages that had been ripped out of books, scrunched up and tossed onto the floor. The desk by the window was a graveyard of disorganised piles of torn volumes.

This study had once been his retreat, his fortress. Now that his one prized possession was ripped from his heart, there was nothing tethering him to Balenmeade. Heatha had delivered the final blow to all he held dear in the city.

Hanzus sighed in exasperation as he sank into his chair. With his head in his hands, he camped there a while, picturing all the ways he could murder her.

So long as she remains, he realised, *my days are numbered.*

Heatha wanted to break him, to render him useless. Meanwhile, the Despot wanted to see him writhing in blood on a dank cabin floor. *Enemies want me dead at every turn.*

And it was not just Hanzus's life endangered. If the Despot wanted him gone, then he wished Arwel Nate dead as well. He remembered the note Arwel had sent to his cabin aboard Captain

Morske's ship. *Something's brewing. And what started with Morske's fumbled attempt at assassination can only mark the beginning.*

Something caught his eye.

Amidst the destruction upon the desk, an open book beheld a bold illustration. The picture of a man, he realised as he blinked through the darkness. Then, upon closer inspection, he reasoned it was no man at all. Under the drawing's mop of black hair, a set of blood-red eyes stared back at him. For a split second, he thought he saw the illustration blink.

Bloodkin.

Text accompanied the grim image on the opposite leaf, a sordid description of their milk-white skin seeming to glow with the moon and their bloody eyes pulsating with inner fire.

Fantasy.

He closed the book and ran his fingers over the embossed title: *Beings of the World.*

The thought of Heatha studying Bloodkin brought a chuckle to his lips. *You concern yourself with Bloodkin when you are as wretched a being yourself.* When his eyes lifted from the leather and set on the lamplight oozing through the door, his thoughts sobered. *You will be my downfall, dear wife. As sure as Man must triumph over Bloodkin, I must triumph over you. But, like Man and Bloodkin, I fear evil will victor. I fear those black of heart will soon have their day.*

Heatha Irvaye was a shadow. A mockery of her former self. The beauty Hanzus had met in Vinerheim all those years ago had long since withered and perished. The memory of that pale goddess dressed in Thelian finery had all but faded from his mind. That her poisonous lips had once screamed his name in pleasure was the only thing that kept her memory alive. The memory of the *real* Heatha. The uncorrupted Heatha. *My love.*

"My love," she declared. "I'd almost forgotten the sound of your voice. For months you have haunted my dreams, bearing the face of your former self." Her narrow nose seemed to scrunch up, to shield itself from an unpleasant pong. "If you were without voice, I might be inclined to believe that the old face before me belonged to a stranger."

Would that it did. Hanzus hid his reaction behind his silver goblet. He inspected its intricate etchings and dull rubies up close. Even its vile imperfections were a more welcoming sight than Heatha.

In the time he'd been gone, age had murdered the final echoes of her charm. And no amount of makeup could mask her vile features. She'd been beautiful once, inside and out. But time had gnawed away at that beauty, boiling it alive and burning the remnants. What remained of the daughter of Lord Wurtz-Worley of the Artenshold was a shell filled with nought but bitterness.

Hanzus supposed fools said the same about him. The commoners called him the Baron Without Sorrow. The most treacherous thing of all was that the moniker was incredibly false, for Hanzus knew sorrow all too well. Heatha was his sorrow, a curse that threatened to haunt him forever.

"Perhaps I was wrong," Heatha said suddenly, startling him. "Perhaps the old face before me does not belong to my husband. I have no way of knowing, for the stranger does not speak."

Turning from the window, he appeased her with his gaze – a gaze that frightened most but did nothing to diminish her mask of calm. "I'm here, Heatha. I'm here where you want me. What is it you want me to hear?" *You wouldn't be insistent we meet if you didn't want to gloat or complain about something.*

She considered him, sipping wine in calculated doses. "Perhaps I simply wish to speak for the sake of speaking." She tensed, her prominent cheekbones protruding from stretched skin. "Come, let us speak plain. You have avoided my company for seven long days, during which time I have continued to rule your barony. The least you could do is look me in the eyes."

Hanzus narrowed at her. "The Krämise is mine. It has always

been mine and mine alone. You have no more ruled my realm than a chamberlain rules his master's house." He stopped himself from unraveling further. He wouldn't be able to upset her, couldn't break her if he tried. What would have offended another lady only fuelled this creature's malice.

"You misunderstand me, my love." A thin smile cracked her rouged lips. "I have no desire to rule anything, least of all things a slice of marshland gifted to a once-honourable family."

She was, of course, referring to the Irvaye dynasty that once ruled Gadensland over one hundred years ago. The Irvaye kings were not unkind monarchs by any means, but the people disliked them, and the courtiers of Vinerheim saw to their downfall one plot at a time.

"Where is Denzus?" Hanzus asked, eager to change the subject. If there was one person in the Balenmanor that knew the knight's movements, it was its baroness.

"Holed up in his chamber. His cock plugged into some harlot."

"A servant must be sent to summon him," Hanzus groaned. "Shall I call for it or will you?"

Heatha was unmoved. Her gaze betrayed the thoughts festering behind her skull. *I never truly intended for your cousin to join us,* she was saying. *I sent word that Denzus would join us in order to coax you here. And now that you're with me, you're mine to devour. But I'm going to savour this. I'm going to take my time as I peel at you slowly.*

"How are the children?" Hanzus asked. "Where did you get this wine?"

She raised a quill-thin eyebrow at him. "Which do you wish for me to answer?"

Hanzus set his goblet down on the tablecloth. "The Chamberlain tells me Francessa has taken to her bed. He assures me it's nothing more than a dry cough that will have run its course by the time the feast takes place."

Heatha's features offered him nothing.

The news of Francessa's illness had come as no surprise. Their daughter had been feigning sickness from the moment she'd learned how.

Heatha was inspecting her nails. "Her life is under no threat." She flashed her narrow eyes at him, a sick smile creeping across her pale face. "The girl's condition is not of the body but the mind. She hides in her chamber for days at a time. Plates are sent to up to her, and they seldom return empty." She paused for a time, then added, "You should speak with her if you've a care. She's your daughter."

"Have *you* not spoken with her?" No answer. "Not even attempted to?"

Heatha grimaced. "You imply she would listen to me? Don't play the fool with me, Hans. Your daughter loves you, and you alone. If I had to guess, her ailment is nothing more than a longing for affection. From you."

Hanzus sighed. Heatha was wrong, and she knew she was wrong. Francessa wanted nothing more to do with her father. She'd been hiding away from him for weeks before he departed for Carthane.

"And what of Hessan? What of my son?"

"I'm quite aware whose son he is. Fortunately, there are more pressing matters to waste our time with." She fingered her goblet's intricate handle, her many rings clinking against the metal. "Your absence has proved costly to us. Your folly in Carthane might well have resulted in the collapse of your barony had I not been here to steer this ship into calmer waters. Not to mention your children have been pining for you like sick little puppies. The festival arrangements are almost complete, and they've proved costly. Brendal assures me your coffers have suffered fiercer blows in the past, but the current climate remains volatile." She lifted her goblet and took a swig. "*Extremely* volatile."

So, it's Brendal *now, is it?* He sipped his wine, welcoming the numbness it offered his troubled mind. Jupe's desire to bed Heatha had always been apparent, but he'd never have guessed the attraction was mutual. *Has my chamberlain grown brazen with the power I bestowed upon him? Has my harlot of a wife stooped to bedding servants common as copper?*

"I pray *Brendal* has spent my gold wisely," Hanzus said. He was certain this was the first time he'd ever spoken the chamberlain's Goddess-given name aloud. He hoped it would be the last. "Harvest is a time to celebrate, but we mustn't lose our heads. One can be *too* festive."

Heatha studied him as she poured herself yet another cup. "My lord, you should tell that to the hundreds of souls flocking to your gates. Can you imagine the scandal if your celebrations were as uneventful as the northern barons' meek affairs?" She laughed aloud. "I never thought I'd see the day the great Baron Irvaye spoke warily of Harvest, when a man must fall to his knees and thank the Goddess she allowed the sun to smile upon his crops. One might consider such notions as blasphemous." She lifted her goblet to toast him, then took one long sip, smiling over the rim. "Imagine such a scandal reaching the Capital. Imagine such word reaching my father."

"I'm sure your father finds himself all too occupied with his own scandals," Hanzus said through gritted teeth. He fought the urge to yelp as his front tooth nipped the end of his tongue.

Heatha was unmoved. "Doubtless. Only one more scandal might just nudge him over the edge." And she refilled her goblet, perhaps only to illustrate her point. "As much as I'd love to linger on the thought of home, the matter of Harvest owns my thoughts." She shrugged. "Brendal assures me we're in for the finest spectacle witnessed in decades. Around these parts, at any rate. He tells me every one of our invitations were returned."

"*All* were returned?"

He had every reason to doubt it. He could recite every name on that list of invitees, and one of those men never returned his letters *except when I'm aboard the HMS Temper.*

"Well, yes." She hid her smugness, but not very well. "Though, I'm afraid to say, not all of the responses were welcome ones."

"Who declined?" he asked, already knowing the answer.

"Arwel Nate." The name oozed from her lips like poison. "The Baron of the Tyldar is grieved to declare he cannot attend your feast. He has his own to host, you see. His own dignitaries to impress."

Arwel Nate, the one man he would have wanted at his feast. But of course, he'd declined. He had for the past five or so years, and every year Hanzus proved himself a fool for getting his hopes up. When they were younger, Hanzus and Arwel would take it in turns to attend each other's Harvest, to celebrate the Goddess's grace together, merrymaking into the early hours, singing songs of hope and gaiety.

Long had Arwel's priorities steered from frivolity. The man had changed. Something was brewing deep within him. Fear of the Despot's reach had exiled him from the world of Vinerheim politics.

Not that I can blame him. Hanzus had also distanced himself from the Capital for a number of years. Of course, he attended council whenever the King commanded him to do so, but so long as court remained optional and the Council of Barons did not require his presence, he chose to stay in Balenmeade.

Though, staring into Heatha's lifeless eyes, he wondered whether such a plan needed revision.

"No matter," he said, feigning disinterest.

"Indeed." Humour had left her voice. "Alderman Marman and Alderman Karston will be your guests of honour this year. The seating arrangements, therefore, will be thus: we will ourselves be seated at either end of the table. Marman and Karston on either side of you. In the middle we have Francessa. Bishop Clarayne..."

It was around then that Hanzus stopped listening. From the sound of it, their placements at the table were identical to last year and the one before that.

The courtiers of Balenmeade and Dulenmeake were a sorry bunch. Overdressed vagrants drunk off cheap wine and mead, basking in the one night they rubbed shoulders with true nobility. They were shadows of real men, carrying near-useless titles thanks to some distant link to the houses of Irvaye or Marman or Karston.

None displayed the Bravery of the Boar. They were worse than the rabble.

"Hanzus? *Hanzus*! Do you hear me?"

Hanzus almost knocked his goblet to the floor.

"I *said* that the Abbot of Eldersley has accepted your invitation. Now, let me see, that would make the abbot and myself the only guests in attendance not born of the Krämise." She was grinning again. "Quite the diverse bunch we'll have. And they say Baron Marret's feast will boast a guest from every barony."

Hanzus scratched at his head. "Then who is his guest from the Krämise?"

She shrugged. "Well, *almost* every barony," she said, but she meant to say *well, every barony of importance*.

"Well," he said, rising to his feet and patting down his clean shirt. "I'd best take my leave. After all, the preparations you've made require my seal of approval. They are, you understand, worthless without my signature."

"Leaving me so soon?" She pouted with derision. "I've yet to pleasure you with the most pressing news of all."

Hanzus considered her smile as he sank back into his chair. *What do you torment me with now? Will you ever let me rest?*

Heatha basked in the rapt silence, sipping from her goblet like a baby savouring milk. She sighed, sucking in the tension. "Something has occurred. Something that, even in my maddest dreams, would not have seemed possible." She fell silent once more, drinking wine with lips etched with pleasure. "I'll start from the beginning, shall I? Where all things are pure and unspoiled." Her eyes rolled over to the door. "*Boy*! Come here, boy!"

A plump little thing dressed in servant's finery came strutting into the room, his face flushed pink. "Milady?"

"Have we food to feast upon?"

The frightened creature stared at her, aghast. "M-milady, supper shan't be prepared for many, many hours."

Heatha waved him away. "No, you stupid boy. Appetisers,

delectable appetisers. If I am to judge you by your girth, you are no stranger to such pleasures. Fetch your lord and lady a plate of something. Berries and seeds will do." She looked at Hanzus. "Or would you prefer something a little more substantial?"

Hanzus shot her a cold glance. "I'll wait for my supper." His stomach cried out to accept the woman's proposal, but he'd rather dine on ash than spend another moment in her company. "Can we return to your pressing news?"

"Berries and seeds," she snapped at the servant, who fumbled a bow before skittering out of the room. "Now, where was I? Ah, yes." She gazed out of the window. "After I realised our festival resources were stretched thin, Brendal came to me with a plan to allocate the household servants with additional tasks to aid with the preparations." She smiled at the window. "The house and grounds servants went about their additional duties, as you'd expect. However, the stewards of your house appeared to be simply... outraged."

Hanzus studied her profile, her cold skin aglow with the sun's warmth. *What madness does the creature espouse now?* Was she trying to goad him into battle?

She continued, "Still, they got to work eventually. The taxers were tasked with overseeing the scrubbers. The scribes oversaw the cleaning of moss and mould that plagues the exterior. The bookkeepers... and this is where our pressing news begins to unfold... oversaw the cleaning of your stables."

Hanzus ground his teeth. He wanted to reach across the ugly tablecloth and strangle her with it. Not till she was dead. No, that would be too quick, too kind, just enough to steal her breath and bruise her neck for good measure. If he could only forget who her father was for just one moment...

Was she suggesting the Chamberlain had reassigned his stewards with menial labour tasks? Relegated them to the status of a common servant?

Heatha's attention remained outside the window. "Reymond

Morgen and... Garrett, was the other one?" She waved a dismissive hand. "This Garrett stumbled across something in the stables. Something *most* curious."

Hanzus's agitation faded away. His thoughts were silenced. "Pardon?"

She turned back to him then, her eyes wide with menace. "He discovered a vagrant, Hans. A wretched gutter-child hiding herself away in the hay, stealing shelter in your stables." She paused for a reviving swig of wine. "She is a wholly unremarkable creature, I'm told. So far as appearances go."

Hanzus tried to make sense of her story. "Someone was *living* in the Balenmanor stables?"

Heatha folded her arms as she considered him, the goblet still wedged between her fingers. "Did you lose your wits somewhere across the ocean? The vagrant slipped into the stables after sneaking past a dozen of your finest guardsmen. After, I'm told, she begged her way across the outskirts of Balenmeade. Probably whored herself out as well, I've no doubt." She creased into a scowl. "She was feasting on the pig's food, would you believe? Do you know what goes into their feed? Disgusting. Pitiless wretch of the gutter. A stain on this world."

Her hollow protest came to an abrupt halt. She stared at Hanzus, awaiting his reaction, basking in the scent of wine under her nostrils.

Why was she troubling him with a crime so trivial? It was no great surprise a street urchin preferred the warmth of the stables to the bitter night's air.

Before Hanzus could even formulate a response, the door opened, and the plump serving boy came jogging over to the table.

"What berries did you find?" Heatha shot at him, slamming her goblet against the table. Hanzus could already see several wine stains on her portion of the tablecloth.

"Raspberries and blackberries, milady." The peasant wiped his forehead clean of sweat. "And an assortment of seeds that..."

"Good, good, very good." She waved him away as he laid the

platter down beside her. "Now begone. We require nothing more, so ask the Chamberlain for further orders. Make haste."

Hanzus scoffed at the woman's parody of assertiveness. After the door closed behind the servant, Heatha went about picking at her food.

Hanzus finished what little remained in his goblet and wiped his lips clean. "Well, is that all? You trouble me with the fact that petty criminals exist? Well, I do hope the appropriate punishment was delivered before the girl was tossed into the dungeons. Let me see... stealing of one pig feed, trespassing on noble property... that would cost the girl's hand and one year of imprisonment. The urchin should learn her lesson from that."

"Actually..." Heatha stuffed a handful of berries into her mouth, her face dripping with bloody juices. "I chose a different course of action." She flashed him a smile, her lips dyed crimson from berries and grapes. "The girl has been given quarters here in the manor."

A silence followed – a silence so palpable Hanzus could have reached out and strangled it. Heatha's sweat wafted across the table, mixed with aromatic perfume. Outside the window, labourers barked at each other.

"You did what?" *What crude form of jest is this?*

"The girl told Brendal quite the tale," Heatha stated. She was being serious. *The mad cunt's lost her mind.* "I thought it only proper I await your verdict on the matter. Initially, I believed the servant that discovered her... *Garrow*, was it?"

"What *tale*?" Hanzus spoke over her. "First, you tell me a vagrant has made a home of my stables, then you tell me you offered the fiend quarters in my manor?"

Heatha didn't flinch. "The vagrant's name is Vilka. And I'm told she possesses quite the tongue for one so young and lowly. Her accent places her origins somewhere west. From Rookland, by Brendal's estimation. He tells me she claims to have slipped past your border guard with some ease."

Beggar, trespasser, and now border sneak? This madness defied belief. He wondered if Heatha was fabricating this story just to torment his brittle mind, to play on his weariness and send him reeling over the edge. It wouldn't have taken much.

"This vagrant is a Rooklander?" It went without saying, but he reminded Heatha of the law: "The Rooksland border is closed. Famine and plague ravish that forsaken realm." *Goddess knows I'd visit my father if it were otherwise.*

Heatha's smile was thinning. "I will say no more. You must speak with her, Hans. Speak with her yourself. Only then will you learn the reason I saved her from the dungeon." She chewed on some seeds. "As for her tale, I will say only this." And she flashed him a smile, revealing several seeds stuck between her teeth. "Vilka is not the only sordid soul that has invaded your borders."

Raw, relentless anger poured through Hanzus. *Riddles and mistruths and treachery... This woman will see me dead. Or at least a blubbering mess rolling around at her feet.* Her intrigued eyes and lingering smile betrayed her lust for his displeasure. She knew she was taunting him well, weaving his woes around her bony finger.

He couldn't take it anymore.

Without thinking, he lifted his goblet and chucked it across the table. It flew well over Heatha's head, but she ducked for good measure. With a deafening clink, the silver chalice crashed into a wooden panel next to the window and rolled around the floor.

"You will tell me this little slut's tale, and you will do so now!"

Heatha's cheeks were reddening, her grey eyes gaped in panic. "How *dare* you raise your voice at me!" She struggled onto her feet, her trembling finger pointing at him. "How dare you... how *dare* you..."

She repeated the words over and over, her breathing rapid, her fingernails clawing at the tablecloth.

As Hanzus rose from his chair, the anger drained from his body. Heatha fell silent as the floorboards creaked beneath her husband's weight. He padded around the table. Heatha recoiled as he neared her, but he didn't stop at her chair, passing her to stop instead at the window.

The sight that met his eyes calmed him further, sobering him in an instant. A dozen or so tents and gazebos lined the field beyond the yard. Immense fabric halls that would soon play host as the epicentre of Harvest. In a few days, that central tent – which rose almost to the height of the Balenmanor – would hold every guest of worth, lining long tables filled with pheasant and boar, honeyed vegetables and berry pies. It would see the sharing of fine wines and fabricated tales. Minstrels plucking away at miserable instruments.

"Forgive me." Heatha was sobbing somewhere behind him, in the back of his mind, whimpering like a beaten hound. "I've longed for your return all these months... for what seemed several lifetimes. All I want... all I've ever wanted is for you to look at me the way you used to."

"Tell me this vagrant's tale." Hanzus kept his gaze outside the window. His body was numb, tingling all over. He'd been bled of emotion. He was empty, hollowed out. He couldn't face her. Invisible hands rooted him to the spot. "Tell me everything."

Spilling Drinks and Secrets

It didn't make sense.

Vilka was now, in all but name, a prisoner of the Chamberlain. She'd been stowed away in the manor's attic, to be dealt with after Harvest. Barrett had tried to visit Vilka on several occasions, but none other than Pamen Ostarne, who had been ordered to allow none to enter, guarded her room.

None but Brendal Jupe.

Barrett could only imagine what the Chamberlain planned to do with Vilka. He pictured the wretched fossil's hands probing her virgin skin. His rotten breath enveloped her.

Or perhaps Jupe would torture her, rip off her fingernails one by one, peel off her skin, or boil her alive. Perhaps he'd strangle her, or slit her throat ear-to-ear, or order a servant to drag her into the woods and hang her from the nearest tree.

And what would happen to Barrett then? Would the Chamberlain have his steward murdered, his tongue cut out, his house burned down?

Fuck. I need a drink.

Barrett had witnessed the girl, spoken with her. If the

Chamberlain wanted to hush all memory of her existence, he'd have to rid himself of Barrett, as well.

Logic told him that the Chamberlain would do no more than question the girl further before kicking her out onto the street. But something gnawed at him. He had a terrible feeling something bad was going to happen. Something bad always happened.

I need to get to Vilka before Jupe. But how? With Pamen guarding her, he didn't stand a chance. There was no way to sneak past him, no obvious means by which to trick him.

Heatha will have me strangled in my sleep if Jupe doesn't get to me first. She'd handed him an impossible task. How was he supposed to *get to the bottom of her tale* if he couldn't even speak with her?

My only real hope, he realised as he passed Oddison's bookshop, *is that the Baron's return will be enough to distract her from Vilka. And me.*

"Any spare coppers, sir?" a ragged voice came from a nearby alley.

Barrett halted. A beggar was dragging himself toward Barrett, emerging from the shadows.

Barrett could see the Dancing Buck's green-and-blue sign swaying in the breeze at the other end of the street. *I'm so close.*

"Spare change, lad?" The beggar was holding out his grubby hands, his eyes full of eagerness.

As Barrett turned to the vagrant, he realised that there were no *eyes* at all but a single pale-blue orb, and in place of the other, there existed a void of scar tissue.

"Uh... here." Barrett tossed him a coin. He didn't want to be rude, but the man was too repulsive to look at.

"A thousand blessings, kindly sir," the vagrant blubbered. "If I might be so bold, sir, I wish ye a fine eve. I do."

Barrett made to escape the man's stale aroma, then a thought crossed his mind. "Say..." He turned back to the man, facing his toothless grin, bent jaw, and the black hole where an eye once lay. "Have you been loitering around this area for long?"

The vagrant blinked at Barrett, scratching at dry skin. "Believe so, sir. Then, tis an 'ard thing to say. Time means nought to an old codger as me. The days melt to one, ye see, the hours pass in a blink and..."

"Yes, yes," Barrett spoke over him. *I've got my own problems to deal with. I don't need to hear yours.*

The wretch jumped in surprise, his one eye wide with panic.

"Listen," Barrett said, softening his tone. "You see that alehouse over there? Have you been watching who's been coming and going?"

The vagrant picked at his nose, his listless eye darting between the steward and the Dancing Buck. "Ah, yes. That place. Stepped into its warmth not too long ago. Managed to snatch a few coppers afore the inn's heavies kicked me out. Managed to snatch a keen look at those buxom lasses."

Barrett's heart skipped a beat at that. *Please say she's not working tonight.* "Tell me more about the... lasses."

The beggar curled into a grin. A solitary tooth slotted over his bottom lip. "Devoted to fine crumpet, are ye? Well, they was buxom lasses all. Don't take much to please this old eye nor make this shrivelled pecker stand. And these lasses was fine as the Goddess herself. Hektor as me witness."

Barrett bit down on his tongue. *Blasphemous arse.* "Just tell me, was there a woman with red hair? She's young, no older than me."

The beggar's eye lit up. "Locks like fire? Sure, I seen her. Seen her good and proper."

The lump rose in Barrett's throat, infusing his tongue with bile. *For Hektor's sake, can this day get any worse?*

"Finest of the lot," the man continued, slobbering over his gums. "Hell, if I was a young'un such as ye, nothing could stop me sticking it to her sweet little arse. Goddess as me witness I..."

Barrett walked away, leaving the old coot talking to himself. His boots grew heavy as he approached the Dancing Buck.

As he stepped outside the door, he froze. Fear and embarrassment had him gripped.

Should I just find another inn? Then he reasoned with himself.

It's possible she won't remember me. And even if she does, I bet she's propositioned by punters all the time. Perhaps my drunken advances were nothing out of the ordinary. The Dancing Buck wasn't the most civilised place in Balenmeade.

He strained to recall what he'd even said to her, but he remembered her shaking her head at him.

The building wafted the sweet scent of bread pudding and well-seasoned pie. The stale aroma of ale and dry puke came next, stinging his nostrils. A chorus of conversation poured from the door, low, gruff voices exchanging crude words.

"Buy me another round, pup!"

"Joke's on you, Kenner!"

"Bet you five coppers he barfs! No, make it five silver!"

A bard's song carried over the voices: a female soprano accompanied by a lute.

Barrett sucked in the bitter air. All he needed now was a plan. A plan to get drunk in peace, without fear of humiliating himself further.

He'd seek out Old Drodger as soon as he got inside. There was no way he could embarrass himself any more than Drodger did on a daily basis. And he had no doubt the legendary drunk would be inside. The Buck was as good as his home.

Barrett took a deep breath and grabbed the door handle. The act of turning it was like dragging a knife through his own stomach. As he opened the door, the collective odour of wine, vodka, ale, mead, hints of fresh bread and mystery spice assaulted his senses.

The Buck was a hive of activity. A thousand voices met him at once. The bard's sweet song soothed his ears, welcoming him, reassuring that all would be well.

The musician was a young woman dressed in blue-and-red faux-finery and a leather flat cap bearing a single yellow feather. She had powdered her cheeks pink and framed her eyes with bold crimson makeup. Her appearance struck him as more jester than a bard, but her features were charming, the perfect complement to her voice. She sat on a booze crate at the back of the room, surrounded by a dozen gormless faces engrossed in her performance.

Loud conversation bubbled up from the ten-or-so tables between Barrett and the bard. Wild laughter, brazen boasting, drunks spitting at each other with reddened smiles. Sweaty faces, protruding stomachs, and drooling mouths filled every inch of the narrow room.

Barrett searched everywhere for Drodger's signature smile. His eye fell on a bush of ginger hair, and his heart sank.

It's her.

Much to his relief, when the person turned around, they revealed a set of bulging cheeks and a thick moustache.

Barrett scanned the dim room, picking out a few recognisable faces, but none he knew too well.

"Barrett, me lad!" a voice assaulted him, booming above the rest. Old Drodger's bulbous head emerged from the milling crowd. He sat at the table closest to the bar, slotted between two men.

Barrett wore a smile as he approached the man. "Drodger. I've come to take you up on your offer after all."

The drunk's leathery features creased, his eyes glowing with blue fire. "Course you are! Come, make a home of me table." He nudged the man to his left in the side, who relinquished his chair with a reluctant groan and wandered over to the bar. "I've an ale for you here someplace." He rummaged around the assortment of wooden mugs and metal tankards on the table. "Ah, here it be. Only taken a couple sips, so she's good as new."

Barrett squeezed past the sweating bodies seated around the neighbouring tables and slotted himself into the chair beside Drodger. The ale tasted like a mixture of drinks, but it was booze, and that was all that mattered.

Barrett would forget about Vilka and the schemes of Brendal Jupe and Heatha Irvaye if it was the last thing he did. He would numb his mind. He would revel in the crooked company of Balenmeade's rabble. He would lose himself in the beautiful bard's music. He would stop thinking.

At last.

Drodger seemed to read something in the steward's face as he paused from his drinking and met him with hard eyes. "Come, what ails you, lad? Tisn't the hour to fret. Come, I'll lend you an ear a while, but then we'll drink, and we'll forget, and we'll drink some more. The Harvest will soon be upon us, me lad. Tis a time for celebrating, not for troubling."

"Huh?" Barrett had already forgotten the man's question.

"There must be something the matter," Drodger said, spitting brown saliva everywhere. "Come, Old Drodger ain't no fool. When were the last time you accepted me offer to drink? Your brain's clogged with all the goings on in that manor house. Tis always so. Sometimes, lad, I think you bog down with those matters and forget what's important."

Barrett raised an eyebrow as he sipped his mystery brew. What did Drodger know about matters of import? He wasted every copper and hour of his life on his long love affair with ale.

"This old sod smells something quarrelsome afoot. Tomfoolery, no less. Harvest preparations turned sour, have they? Bah. Best decision I ever made was to walk out of that place."

Sure, excellent decision, you old fool. Drodger had quit his job in the manor long before Barrett had started as an accountant. Rumours suggested Drodger departed due to an argument with the Chamberlain that he refused to carry out orders, while others speculated that Drodger's ale habit had forced him out.

Barrett didn't much care for the hearsay passed around Balenmeade taverns.

Drodger seemed harmless enough. Honest and predictable. He was nothing like that monster, Nipp Brewman. *Now there is a dangerous drunk.* Drodger was an ear when one wanted to talk, a trove of tales when one wanted to listen.

"So, what is it?" Drodger's eyes widened, and his crow's feet thickened. "I can't lie, lad. I'm a friend to gossip this day."

Barrett opened his mouth to speak but reasoned not to mention his ordeal. "Well, work at the manor is increasingly difficult. There are several payments to finalise, countless loans that have been taken out and will need..." He stopped, realising Drodger wasn't listening.

"Oi, Bracker!" Drodger waved his fist at a group of bearded men in the centre of the room. "Don't be forgetting that pint you owe me from last night!"

The man in question grunted, shook his head, and turned away from Drodger. Clearly, Drodger wasn't the most popular man in the Buck. Barrett noticed folk grimacing at him and turning away when he met their eyes.

What on earth am I doing here? Barrett glanced down at the watery-brown substance in his hand, then looked up at his woeful company.

Drodger's table consisted of a slender man, a wrinkled woman, and two portly men who were, judging by their eyes, no older than Barrett, though their balding heads and enormous cheeks gave them the appearance of two old pigs.

The butcher Frode was standing close by, conversing with a group of unshaven men. He'd settled his pint mug on Drodger's table and glared at the old drunk every time he reached over to grab it.

"'Ere," the old woman said, her eyes lighting up as they met Barrett. "Who's this 'andsome hunk o' meat what's dressed so fine? 'Ave we a nobleman for company?"

Barrett blinked down at his torso. Ale marks stained his shirt and jacket. *You call* this *finely dressed?*

Frode had overheard the woman and craned his enormous neck towards Barrett. "Who's noble? *Him?*" He chuckled a low bark. "That ain't no lord, you stupid slut. That there's one of Brendal Jupe's men. He's no nobler than you or me."

Barrett's cheeks flushed warm as the butcher turned back to his friends.

It was no secret that Frode disliked Barrett. The stone-faced man was the direct rival of Fester Gace, who remained adamant that Barrett should marry his ugly child-daughter. And Gace's interest in

Barrett had not gone unnoticed by Frode, as the latter often shot Barrett daggers whenever he passed his shop.

"Goodness gracious," Drodger said, clutching his chest dramatically. "Have me manners deserted me entirely? Friends, this here's Mister Barrett Barrett, son of Rena Barrett."

"You work at the Balenmanor, eh?" the old woman asked Barrett before taking a swig of her brew. "Suppose that means you'll feast with the lord and lady during 'Arvest? Tis quite the honour."

Barrett's voice was stuck in his throat. The woman was correct in a way: as a steward, Barrett would be in attendance for the Baron's banquet, but they wouldn't seat him near anyone important.

"This here's Margaret Barrow," Drodger introduced the old woman, then he went around the table. "Lyle Cornickle." The thin man bowed his head. "Dans Hanson." One of the portly men nodded. "And his brother, Willy Hanson." The other grunted, then buried his face in his tankard.

"A pleasure," Barrett said, raising his mug. He finished the remnants in one, and Drodger pushed another cup toward him.

"Have another... ale... I *think* this one's ale."

Barrett brought the mystery substance to his lips, smelt hops before tasting the dark, bitter liquid. He took several more sips before slamming the mug onto the table.

The surrounding faces grinned their approval.

"There's me, lad!" Drodger cried, smacking Barrett across the back. "Drink up, lad, and I'll buy us another round."

The room was already spinning around Barrett. Whatever the drinks had been, they were potent.

Lyle Cornickle's sharp features seemed to be pulsating, his long nose and flappy ears breathing in and out. The Hanson brothers poured ale down themselves as they drank, stuffing what appeared to be chicken drumsticks into their mouths between sips. Margaret Barrow watched Barrett with intent, and at one point, if he wasn't mistaken, she licked her lips and winked at him.

"You know," Drodger said after a time, whispering in Barrett's ear. "Earlier, I overheard an interesting thing. Piqued me interest, it did."

Barrett spun to face Drodger. "What?"

Drodger's gappy smile widened. His breath was horrendous. "You know that girl everyone's talking about?"

Barrett's heart sank. *"Girl?* What girl?"

He wasn't referring to Vilka? *He can't be.*

"The one they found sleeping in hay. The one they found lurking in the Baron's stables. She's a crafty little shit, you ask me. To be good at hiding away, to be good at hiding anything. From anyone."

Barrett repeated Drodger's words over and over in his mind, trying to make sense of them. *Drodger knows about Vilka?* This was the first time he'd heard anyone mention her existence, save for the Baroness. *If Drodger knows about Vilka, then Balenmeade knows about Vilka.* That meant the Chamberlain wasn't keeping her locked away, to keep her a secret. *So why then has he imprisoned her?* A shiver ran down his spine. *Is there more to Vilka's story than meets the eye?*

"What *about* the girl, Drodger?"

"Well." Drodger stretched out his arms, resting his hands on his head. "I can only tell of rumour, lad. These lips can only tell what their ears've heard. If folk speak true, the girl in question escaped the Balenmanor this afternoon. She were being kept there, but I'm sure you knew that already." He nibbled on his lip, digesting the steward's reaction. "This girl were involved in a pilfering a few hours past, in good Frellar's shop no less."

"Frellar? The sweetshop owner?"

The drunk nodded. "Little bitch stole treats enough to indulge a whole bloody orphanage."

A dozen thoughts crossed Barrett's mind at once.

How had Vilka sneaked past Pamen? Unless she'd found an alternative means to escape. But why, if she was on the run, would she draw attention to herself by thieving so close to the manor? Why not flee Balenmeade before anyone noticed she was gone?

"'Tis but a rumour," Drodger said, shrugging. "Though you could learn the truth of it, I guess, if you've a mind. Why don't you go ask Frellar yourself? He's around here someplace. Saw him not long ago."

Barrett didn't wait to finish his drink. He excused himself from the table with a promise to return, then he began his search. The sweet shop owner wore a quill-thin moustache. That was all Barrett remembered. He'd frequented Frellar's shop as a child, and back then, the man towered over him like a finely dressed giant.

Ugly, sweat-soaked faces stared at him as he pushed his way to the back of the room. For a split second, he met eyes with Fester Gace, but he was able to disappear back into the crowd before the fat butcher could speak of marrying off his daughter.

"Watch where you're going, little shit," a gruff-faced man barked at him.

Barrett didn't pay him any mind, nor did he acknowledge the sneers aimed his way as he patrolled the room. His search centred on a moustache, and all he could see were beards or shaven faces. Indeed, moustaches were a symbol of the wealthy, and rich folk seldom visited the Dancing Buck. There were tea rooms and wine saloons for people of such ilk. But Drodger was certain he'd seen the sweet seller here, and if the famous drunk was good at one thing and one thing only, it was his memory, especially if the thing he remembered pertained to gossip.

Barrett scanned the line of men queuing at the bar. It was then that his eye lingered on a familiar set of features: a carrot-shaped nose drooping over a thin moustache. It had to be Frellar.

Barrett pushed his way to the front of the bar, ignoring the insults and accusations levelled his way.

"Frellar?"

The man's misshapen nose turned to greet him. "Yes? Who are you?"

There was no time for pleasantries. "I heard that a theft took place in your shop today. Is that so?"

Frellar narrowed his grey eyes at him. "Thefts happen from time to time, stranger. Tis an unavoidable occurrence. What of it?"

"This incident is of interest to me," Barrett said. He stopped there, not wanting to give too much away. The thief in question could, after all, have been another young vagrant that someone had mistaken for Vilka. He imagined a sweetshop attracted all manner of ill-begotten children who would slip in and stuff their pockets with free chocolate.

Frellar turned to face Barrett head-on, leaning back against the bar. "Today's incident is nothing new. Hundreds of whippets come to my shop to gaze at my wares. How many of those do you suppose possess the coin to acquire their desires?" He folded his arms, frowning. "But what of it? You haven't given me your name, young sir, so why should I give you my time?"

Barrett sighed. "Sorry. My name is Barrett Barrett."

Frellar's brows rose with interest. "You're Rena's boy? Why, your mother paid my shop a visit a couple days ago. It may be improper of me to say, Barrett, but that brother of yours is spoiled." He turned back to face the barmaid. "Two pints of Krämisen, if you please." He accepted two mugs of beer, then passed one to Barrett. "Here. Tis the least I can do to return your mother's custom."

Barrett cringed at the thought of all that coin being squandered on chocolate and boiled sweets for Lerry. *My coin.* Not to mention the havoc those sweets would cause Lerry's teeth. *I'll be damned if I have to pay for any more extractions.*

"Drink with me, and I'll indulge your curiosity of this theft."

Barrett couldn't tell if Frellar was mocking him, but he drank all the same. The ale tasted like proper brew, the sort he'd been craving.

"My name's Sanders Frellar," the sweet seller said, guiding Barrett to a vacant spot to stand by the door. "But you knew that already, didn't you? Tell me, why does this theft interest you? Do you know something about it? That little bitch ran away with more sweets than I often sell in a day."

Barrett sipped his ale. "I'm afraid I'm no wiser in the matter. But I do believe the girl that stole from you today is also the one I seek."

"You missing a sister or something?"

"Something like that."

"Tell you what," Frellar said, sighing over his mug. "You buy my next round, and I'll tell you all you want to know."

It was more than a fair exchange.

Barrett returned to the bar and was about to place his order when he realised the barmaid blinking over the counter at him was the same red-haired woman he had tried to bed a few nights ago.

Shit.

"Can I help you?" she hissed. Her sternness told him she remembered his feeble attempt at seduction. She was far from the beauty of memory: her features were flat, uninspiring, her makeup looked like a child had applied it. But she had a twinkle in her eye, a flash of assuredness, determination.

"I... uh..." He couldn't look away from her emerald irises.

"Two pints of Krämisen if you please!" Frellar shouted over.

"What he says," Barrett said, wearing a thin smile. When the barmaid folded her arms, he added, "Look, I'm... I'm sorry for all I might have said the other night."

The woman raised an eyebrow at him, and for one horrible second, he thought she was about to reach across the counter and slap him. Then she laughed, loud enough to silence a few men in close proximity.

"Ain't no need to apologise, mister. Was you what came out of that moment worse? You know, I ain't never seen a lad as brazen as you was that eve. You must be, what, sixteen years old?"

Barrett ignored the chuckles that chittered around him. He wouldn't dignify that jibe with an answer.

"Two pints of Krämisen, were it?" she said coldly, realising he wasn't going to answer. "Very well. Coming up."

No sooner had Barrett placed a fresh mug of ale in Frellar's hands did the sweet seller's lips waggle.

The theft had taken place around the same time that Barrett had spoken with Pamen. The thief pilfered enough butter bars, sugar sticks, and lemon biscuits to fill a large sack. *They're stockpiling for a few days on the road.* The thief's choice to steal from a sweet seller wasn't hapless after all. Biscuits and hard sweets would last a lot longer than bread or meat.

Frellar described the pilferer as a skinny young girl, their hair a muddy blonde, their eyes bulbous and searching.

Vilka. It has to be Vilka. She had indeed escaped from Pamen, someway, somehow. And if Drodger knew, then it would only be a matter of time before word reached the Chamberlain. Then the whole city would be searching for her.

If Vilka's stocked herself with that much food, she's long gone from Balenmeade by now. It was just as well. Without Vilka, there was no reason for the Baroness to keep him as her informer. The Chamberlain would force him to muck out the stables again, but at least that meant Reymond would befriend him once more.

Barrett thanked Frellar for his time and, after buying another pint of Krämisen, made his way back to Drodger.

The old drunk sat at the same table, but his company had changed. *Probably scared the others away.* The four gormless strangers gawked at Barrett as he seated himself next to Drodger.

Drodger burped into his hand, then slapped Barrett across the back. "Barrett, milad, I'd like to introduce you to some fine lads." He grabbed Barrett by the arm, offering his hand for the strangers to shake. Their grips were firm but sticky. "Where'd you say you was from?"

"Dulenmeake," one stranger said, the youngest of the four. He had a patchy beard of stubble and one very lazy eye. "Took us three and an 'alf days to get 'ere. Long march." One of the man's eyes landed on Barrett. "Name's Brice. These are me brothers... Sarren, Egan... oh and this 'ere's Arren."

"Name's Barrett," Barrett said, offering a weak smile, then he leaned close to Drodger and whispered, "What more can you tell me about the girl that fled the Balenmanor?"

If there was one man who'd heard anything else, it would be Drodger.

The drunk looked through him, not hearing or not interested in what he'd heard. "They say the best swords in the land are forged in Dulenmeake, don't they?"

"And they are," Brice replied. "Never bought outside Dulenmeake, 'ave we, lads?"

The three brothers grunted in approval, more interested in ale than conversation.

"You wanna know what we do best here in Balenmeade?" Drodger said, grinning over his mug. Then he pointed down at his pint, jabbing one meaty finger into the liquid. "Won't find no finer ale than Krämisen, trust. And it's all brewed here in Balenmeade. To boot, our meaderies give those northern county folk a run for their coin, that's for sure."

"Interesting," said Brice. "Ain't never had no Balenmeade mead, that's for sure. But I'd surely like to."

Drodger raised his mug. "'Tis where our fine city gets its name, kindly sir."

Barrett sighed into his cup. *Bloody fool.* Everyone with a brain knew the city was named after the defunct House of Balen-Meade.

The next drink Drodger slipped his way, reeked of something foul. He glanced over at the redhead barmaid and hoped she hadn't mixed his drink with piss or spittle. A sip confirmed the ale was pristine. The cup was not clean.

He pushed the thought to the back of his mind and carried on drinking, half-listening to Drodger and Brice's conversation about the various meads and ales one could find up and down the kingdom.

Barrett considered returning home, but the thought of listening to Mother rattle on about coin and Lerry's education pushed the idea out of his mind.

He returned to the bar, had his mug refilled, and found a spot in the corner of the room where the conversation was quieter.

The bard had stopped playing and was now engaged in a game of cards with a pack of bearded brutes. Frellar was locked in a debate with Nipp Brewman about Harvest, with the former in favour of the frivolities and the latter arguing against the whole affair. Deana Carrow was flirting with everyone she laid eyes on. Whether a regular or an outsider, no one was safe from this spinster's unwelcome gaze.

Barrett moved away from his corner when he spotted Deana heading his way. He searched for Drodger's face in the milling crowd, but his sight was blurry. As he looked around, his head was spinning. He tried to count the number of ales he'd had. Six? Seven?

The bard had started playing her lute again.

The streets outside the window were dark now. The lamps were being lit, and the regulars were filing into the Buck after a hard day's work.

The bard's tune had become a melody now. *The Lord of Every Realm*, if Barrett wasn't mistaken – a comical song that questioned the relationship between a lord and his subjects. The bard was brave for playing such a controversial tune in the Dancing Buck, of all places. *Or stupid.*

Still, a good portion of the revellers hummed along, punching the air during the chorus. Barrett even found himself mouthing along with the lyrics:

A man, a man from Ecclestand, went rambling on the moors,
Dressed in false finery, a vagrant of the hills,
Went dancing into Herrinbridge, a' laughing as he came,
Said, "I am lord of every realm, and every realm's the same."

Davey Cobb

Look there, oh there, that hero from the hills,
He's no king or noble thing. He's the luckless lord of nil.

This man, this man from Ecclestand did keep his lips a' sealed,
As folk from up and down his realm refused to come to kneel,
And standing proud before the crowd, a common lad proclaimed,
"That there's a lord, now turn to see, for his cloak is maintained."

Look there, oh there, that lad he speaks the truth,
For here's the king of every realm, bow or face the noose.

This king, this king of Ecclestand and Herrinbridge to boot,
Dressed in all the finery his tailors made to suit,
And as he died, grinningly, our lord did tell them all,
"You crowned a peasant, you fools and men, and now my sons shall
rule."

Look there, oh there, our king has passed away,
And now his sons shall rule his halls as folk piss on his grave.

When the music stopped, the room erupted in applause, a hundred whoops of praise and whistles of admiration.

The bard grinned around the room. "And what now should I sing, you fine lot of bell-ends?"

122

A dozen voices responded with various requests, but by far, the most audible response was, "The Diamond of the Day!"

"Ah! Now there is a song!" the bard said and began singing the song that many considered the anthem of Gadensland.

Barrett pushed his way back to the bar. The room was becoming hot and stuffy. So much sweat in one small space. But he would have one more pint before he made his way home.

For a moment, everything seemed to stop. The music washed into the background, the raucous crowd faded to silence. Barrett had to blink several times to ensure he didn't imagine things. For there at the bar with a tankard in her hand stood Vilka.

Goddess, do not play tricks on me. Not now.

Vilka was laughing at the man beside her, a tall, broad-shouldered figure with long brown hair. The man looked out of place in his fine clothing. He had to be a merchant or perhaps some minor noble.

Barrett approached them clumsily, knocking into a passing patron and almost spilling their drink all over himself.

"Vilka? What are you doing here?"

The girl turned to face him, her smile diminishing in an instant. "*You.*" She was expressionless, sipping her ale like a veteran drinker.

"Is there some sort of problem?" the noble said, sneering down his nose at Barrett. "Deana, do you know this man?"

"*Deana?*" Barrett thought aloud, spitting out the name like a badly worded joke. Last he checked, Vilka bore scant resemblance to the middle-aged spinster that frequented every tavern in Balenmeade.

"I know *of* him," Vilka said, glaring at Barrett. "What do you want?" she asked him under her breath.

Barrett didn't know where to begin. "I... Well, I want to know what you're doing here, for a start."

How have you the gall to slip free of the Chamberlain's clutches and then parade yourself in front of the people of Balenmeade?

"Don't see how that's none of your business." She shrugged. "I'm with Sir Denzus now, can't you see? Now be gone."

Sir Denzus? Barrett knew that name. *Sir Denzus Irvaye.* He was one of Hanzus's cousins, but... this man was far too young to be Denzus Irvaye. Perhaps he was one of Denzus's sons, given the same name. What little he knew about the Dulenmeake branch of the House of Irvaye was nothing good. Denzus the Elder was an infamous layabout who whored his way across the kingdom, spending every drop of coin on wine and women.

"You heard the lady," Denzus said, his voice shaky. "I'm warning you now, peasant, vacate yourself promptly from my presence."

"Vilka," Barrett said through his teeth, trying to ignore the man. Denzus might have been a knight, but the threat Barrett faced if he neglected to return Vilka to the Balenmanor was far greater than the wrath of one man. "You need to come with me."

"*Need* to?" Vilka slipped her empty tankard back onto the bar counter, then folded her arms. "I don't need your opinion on what I *need* do, Mister Barrett. I've already had enough of your chamberman telling me how I'm supposed to act. Perhaps I don't wanna sleep in your mansion no more. Perhaps I've found another place to stay."

"What are you talking about, Deana?" Denzus said, dumbstruck.

"Nothing, milord," Vilka said, placating him. "Barrett, here's an old associate of mine."

Sir Denzus was nodding along. "Ah, I see. When you used to work in the manor."

Barrett was incredulous. "You what?"

He stared at Vilka in amazement, words failing him. He couldn't leave her with this man, but he feared what Denzus might do to her if he learned the truth. He could guess the lies Vilka had fed him with. The knight's wish to bed her was obvious, but *her* motives were unclear.

"Was nice seeing you again," Vilka said to Barrett. She was smiling with her lips, but her eyes told another story: they were begging him to be silent, pleading with him to leave.

"Yes," was all that Barrett could manage. "Nice seeing you again."

He walked away, confused. Numb.

He couldn't leave her with Denzus. He couldn't allow this man to steal what remained of her purity. *If anything indeed remains.* The noble would use her flesh, then kick her to the gutter. He'd seen it happen before after Alderman Caine visited the Buck and forced himself on Lucindra Cockles – the common folk hadn't dared intercede, as the noble dragged the young girl outside and thrust himself inside her. And after the sordid act was over, Caine pulled up his trousers and walked away, grinning. Soon after, Lucindra's parents sent her away to the convent outside Blueharrow, forced to repent till the end of her days. Lucindra's name became a dirty word in Balenmeade thereafter, used to chide daughters and shame spinsters.

I can't let Denzus bed her. I can't let her become another Lucindra.

But then, how could he return her to the Balenmanor against her will? She appeared content with Denzus. She was swindling him somehow.

He couldn't risk exposing Vilka. If Denzus learned that this *Deana* was a foreign vagrant who'd escaped the Baroness's clutches, he'd have her stabbed with the tip of his sword before anything else.

Vilka was playing a dangerous game.

But there was nothing he could do, no clear action.

He needed air to rouse his senses, to help him think. He was tired. His temples throbbed.

He stepped outside onto Hacker's Row. The pale moon peeped over the thatched roofs and wonky chimneys, illuminating the buildings with its blue hue. A few blinking streetlamps offered the cobbles its warmth. Black shadows hugged the street's edges, casting darkness over the ground floors.

As Barrett stumbled into the road and his eyes adjusted to the gloom, he made out a dozen bodies leaning against the four-storey building opposite. A young lad was making his way down this line of men, lighting their smoking pipes with metal strikers in exchange for a few coppers.

A few drunks were leaning against the Buck's low wall, sipping from their mugs, nattering quietly. They eyed Barrett with suspicion as he passed.

The bard's music seeped from the alehouse, humming over the night's silence. Most in Balenmeade were sleeping.

He staggered over to a vacant space along the Buck's wooden wall and dropped to the cobbles with a thud. His arse was numb, but he knew it would ache come morn.

He ran his hands through his greasy hair and over his stubbly chin. The smokers across the street were watching him behind their grey cloud. He pondered his next course of action.

Then, as though the Goddess herself was answering him, the door of the Dancing Buck opened, and the short figure of Vilka scurried into the lamplight. Even in the darkness, he made out her shadowy scowl. She picked his face out in an instance, drawn toward it.

Barrett struggled onto his feet as she edged toward her. Much to his relief, neither Denzus Irvaye nor any other crook had followed her outside.

"Barrett Barrett," she said, halting in front of him. "I'm sorry... Sorry you found me this eve. Weren't my intention to stumble on you like this."

Barrett didn't speak. He didn't know what to say. The smokers were watching the pair with heightened intrigue. One even waved the lighting boy away to pay them further attention.

"You should go on home," Vilka said, her words as firm as Mother's. "You shouldn't be here... that is... we shouldn't be... together."

Anger was bubbling inside Barrett. "What is going on here? What are you talking about?"

He wanted to grab her by the arm and drag her back to the Balenmanor. He had half a mind to inform the Chamberlain of her escape. Jupe would have her whipped, then cast into the Balenmeade dungeons.

No.

Something stopped him. Reason calmed his mind, drew him back to reality. He didn't want to harm her. There and then, looking at her placid features, her sorrowful eyes, he realised he *wanted* her to escape. He didn't want her to return to the Balenmanor, no matter what that spelt for his own fate.

Barrett sucked in the rancid air. "Look, Vilka, I only want to see you safe. Today and yesterday and the day before, I tried to visit you in the manor, but I wasn't allowed to see you."

Her frown deepened. She didn't believe a word he was saying.

"Then," Barrett continued, "I spoke with Drodger, and he told me you'd escaped the manor. Then I spoke with Frellar and learned you'd pilfered a sweet shop. I surmised you were fleeing Balenmeade, that you were stocking up for a long journey." He stopped to breathe, but she didn't interrupt him. "Now I find you flirting with one of the Baron's relatives, in full view of every man and woman of Balenmeade."

Vilka laughed, but the sorrow didn't leave her eyes. "*Flirting?* How little you know, Mister Barrett. Besides, none know my face." Her eyes fell to the cobbles, unable to meet his gaze. "I know you've likely been given some charge to question me further, to continue our talk in that wine cellar." She lifted her head then, her amber eyes meeting him. "You needn't fret. I ain't left your beloved manor for good. Just needed to stretch my legs out, is all. A girl needs to breathe. I ain't some sort of animal. You wanna know how rotten it is, being cooped up in that dusty attic?"

"Would you rather be sleeping in the stables?"

She considered with cool eyes. "I ain't returning to the manor tonight, Mister Barrett. But I'll be there come the morn, you wait and see. I give you my word for all it's worth. Not a one of them will know where I've been, nor *that* I've been gone. That's if *you* keep your mouth shut." She laughed at him. "That gormless guard that were outside my prison today don't even know I'm missing."

The anger was mounting inside Barrett, threatening to animate his fingers and wrap them around her throat. Vilka was no guest of the Baron and Baroness. She couldn't come and go from the manor as she pleased and enjoy the city like a travelling merchant.

"That *gormless guard* is none other than Pamen Ostarne, the most skilled warrior in all the Krämise," he spat through his teeth. "You may not respect me, but Hektor as my witness, you will respect my kin, you will respect our land, you will..."

As his words trailed off, so too did his animosity.

She flashed him a smile. "Most skilled in the land, is he? That certainly says something."

Anger flashed back into his body, but his mind had mellowed. He was able to control his body to prevent himself from lashing out.

Vilka was a menace, a fiend. She had manipulated him into thinking she was some poor fragile creature, and in truth, she was no more than a brigand. A vagrant who cared not where she lay her head. A brigand who was willing and able to sneak out of her prison. A pilferer, and now, it would seem, a pickpocket who would use her charm and persuasion to get a man drunk and steal him of his riches.

And her prey was no ordinary man. Denzus Irvaye was the Baron's family, a noble with direct ties to the Seat of the Krämise. If he discovered he was being manipulated, he would have Vilka thrown into a cell and tortured to death.

"Come back with me," Barrett said, admitting defeat. "I can smuggle you back inside the manor. Please. We can forget any of this ever happened."

Vilka laughed, a hollow snort. "I can find my own way back." She looked him up and down, then raised an eyebrow. "Think it's you what should be leaving round about now. How much you drank?"

"Not that much." It was a lie, of course, but lying didn't seem so immoral in the company of this wretch. "Still, it's none of your concern. I am not a prisoner."

His smile waned as he realised the inaccuracy of his statement.

He'd been a fool to worry after her safety. The girl *was* a vagrant, an immoral cur. *Perhaps it's true what they say of foreigners.* He ought to leave her, to allow Denzus to have his wicked way, to let her get caught by the Baron's guards.

"I'm going back in now," she said. "Perhaps we'll meet again someday."

He couldn't do it.

"Wait." Barrett grabbed hold of her arm. She was cold to the touch. All life had abandoned her. "I *can't* let you go."

"You don't have... any choice."

"It's my duty to... watch over you."

"I don't need watching over."

She struggled to escape his grasp but couldn't so much as peel a single finger from her arm.

"Come with me. Now."

"I said I don't need you!"

Everyone was watching them now. A few windows had unlatched, and dark faces filled the frames, intrigued or angered by the noise in the street below. The smokers and outdoor drinkers had paused from their whispering to stare at Barrett.

"I haven't been told to watch over you for *your* benefit," Barrett hissed at her. "The Baroness won't let you escape, you know. No matter where you run, she'll send searchers after you. And it's your own damn fault for mentioning these Bloodkin inside our borders. If you hadn't brought it up in the first place, the Chamberlain would've cast you out on your arse."

Her eyes widened with fear. She stopped struggling. "Then tell them I lied."

"That won't wash. Not with them. And don't lie to me, Vilka. You're coming back to the Balenmanor, and I'm telling the Baron all about your little escape."

All of a sudden, tears were rolling down her cheeks. Her face was pink with exasperation. "You can't tell me where to go. You ain't my pa."

Barrett spoke through his teeth. "Perhaps if you'd stayed with your parents, you wouldn't be in this mess."

"They're dead," Vilka shrieked. "They're dead. They're dead. They're dead! Why'd you think I left home in the first place? I told you, I ain't got nothing to return to. *Nothing*, Mister Barrett."

There was something about the sadness in her eyes that immobilised him. All strength faded from his hands. His anger subsided as soon as it had arrived.

"I'm sorry, Vilka, I..."

She snatched her arms free of his grasp. "I watched my pa murdered before my eyes, while my ma screamed in my ears, begging he be spared, puking her guts up at my feet. There was nothing we could do. None of us."

Barrett just stood there as she backed away from him, rooted to the stone and dirt. "I don't know what to do."

He closed his eyes, and when he opened them again, she was gone.

She'd returned to Denzus.

A handful of men voiced their contempt at what they'd just witnessed, then most of them filtered back inside the alehouse. The windows that were opened slammed shut.

Vilka had broken Barrett. His body cried out for the warmth of his bed. His mind wanted to leave this place and find solace outside the city walls.

He fought the urge to wander off into the woods and made his way back home.

Vilka's parents were dead. *Of course.* It made sense now. She'd left her home because she no longer had one. She retained no sense of home, of family. She was an orphan, a refugee.

As Barrett started down the street in the general direction of home, he puked down his shirt.

The Veer

Mavrian watched as her blood flowed, mesmerised by its perfection. As her life force dribbled from the gash, warm droplets rained on her thigh, trickling down to her knee like holy rivers of crimson.

"Vässa, I beseech you," she said, ignoring the pain. "Take this blood as your own, for I am a vessel bound to your name." She strained to remember the rest of the prayer, recalling Father's words. "Vässa, yours is the name whose grandeur I do feed. Yours is the name whose desire I do sate. Yours is the name for which I do offer my servitude."

The Twins had consumed the blood's true essence, the magic that coursed through every one of her veins.

Vällas drew power from men, but there were elements of a woman's blood that satisfied his base desires. Conversely, Vässa consumed woman's blood to feed her being, to breathe life into her undying lungs, to pump her eternal heart.

Mavrian sensed that most, if not all, of her offering had nourished Vällas's lust as opposed to feeding Vässa. Though that was not her intention, she was relieved to learn the blood wasn't wasted.

The tingle below her stomach was a sign of Vällas's presence that her offering had satisfied him a great deal. Despite the dull throbbing in her clitoris, she felt no real gratification. She supposed that was a good thing, though. The offering was not intended to pleasure *her*.

Mavrian dripped vinegar into her wound, biting down against the sting. She'd have liked to think herself familiar to the pain, but the searing discomfort was never pleasant. *Though, I supposed that's the point of sacrifice.*

Reesa and Zamrian often spoke of the bliss they experienced when cutting themselves, how they felt Vällas coursing through their bodies, how they pleasured themselves as they watched their blood dry.

She wished she could say the same. Her sessions were painful, awkward. Though she had to admit, the way her blood glimmered in the sunlight was a thing of beauty.

She gazed at her nude reflection, wondering if she was desirable enough for Vällas. *Perhaps that's why I don't feel him inside me, pleasuring himself in my anus like Eplin used to.*

A few ugly courtiers had pursued Mavrian, but did that make her good enough for a god? Probably not. Reesa was far more beautiful than she was, and although Zamrian's face wasn't the prettiest in Vicker's Tower, many in Meelian enjoyed the plump curves of her body.

Mavrian was a skeleton in comparison.

When she'd first arrived in Kleäm, her appetite matched her enthusiasm for life. Kleäm had eroded her spirit piece by piece, sucking the plumpness from her body. But there was still beauty in her face, and as she smiled at herself now, she saw the face that had first entranced Eplin Garr.

Her smile died as she remembered Eplin's words the day he departed. *When next we meet, you will be carrying my child.*

She looked down at her flat belly, thankful nothing had grown. The last thing in the world she wanted was to be tied to the name of

Garr. Eplin's words had either been wishful, or his ability to predict was not as it used to be. Either way, her decision to drown herself in wine the day after he'd left had turned out to be no more than a precaution.

Your seed is not as potent as you think, Lorr of the Garren.

She pushed his awful image out of her mind, robed herself in black cloth, then approached the balcony. As soon as her eyes greeted the auburn sky, she heard something over her shoulder.

Turning back to the room, she scanned the vanity table, four-poster bed, and shelves lined with leather tomes. She spotted nothing awry, but she had a dreadful feeling someone was watching her.

A chill raced down her spine. Had somebody been hiding there all along, observing her nude ritual?

There was no one there, she realised, after scrutinising every corner of the chamber. She was about to turn back to the balcony when something caught the corner of her eye.

She turned to find a small square of parchment on the floor by the door. Someone had slid a letter under the crack.

A wave of relief rushed over her as she went to retrieve the envelope. As she bent down to pick it up, she heard a sound on the other side of the door. A low humming. At first, she thought it was the wailing wind, a draft sweeping under the doors in the corridor, but the sound was methodical, as if it belonged to a pair of lungs.

Mavrian snatched up the envelope and hastened over to the balcony. As her fingernails ripped at the envelope, the letter's red seal caught her attention: the image of a hand, the bottom turning to droplets, melting away, the diagonal Cross of Drente etched into its palm.

The Bloody Hand.

The letter was from Scarmane Trokluss. It had to be. He was the only member of the Veerkasn to have arrived in Kleäm. He'd been in residence for about a week now. The Loress had given him the grandest quarters in Meelian.

But what would he want with me?

Reesa had insisted Trokluss was in Kleäm to speak with Mavrian, but if that was the case, why had it taken him a week to establish contact?

She realised her hands were trembling as she unfolded the letter. At first glance, the parchment appeared empty, and she wondered if the letter was some trick, but then she noticed a line of writing scribbled in green ink:

Meet me in the library. As soon as you can.

Mavrian swallowed bile. Dread clawed at her flesh, whipping her into action as she replaced her chamber robe with a dress of heavy cotton.

She made eye contact with her ghostly reflection. Self-pity painted her beautiful features. She knew what Veer summons usually entailed for a lady of high standing: a test of loyalty to gauge one's devotion to the Overlord.

Whatever the case, she couldn't delay.

She studied the letter's script as she descended Vicker's Tower. The words were sloppy, and she couldn't help but linger on the misspelling of *library*. She supposed that was the result of rushing. Or perhaps Trokluss was a man of scant education.

All she knew about Scarmane Trokluss came from insidious rumours: knives in the dark, dragging Kinsmeers out of their hiding holes and impaling them alive, the slow poisoning of his former master.

The gossip had intensified in the last few days. Zamrian, who was the only lady of Vicker's Tower the Loress allowed inside Meelian, had dined twice in Trokluss's company. She described the Veer as a happy, outgoing gentleman. Trokluss's kindness and charisma had Zamrian speculating that the rumour he'd killed his master had to be bogus, but Mavrian wasn't so sure.

Father was always sceptical of the Veerkasn, often referring to them as the *Underhanded Bloody Hand*.

But even if Scarmane's intentions were crooked, she had no choice but to obey his will. Father was dead now, and her uncle would do nothing to protect her from the Veerkasn.

The Meelian library would be busy on a day like today, at least. If Trokluss wished her harm, he wouldn't act in the presence of others.

At least, she assumed he meant for her to meet him in Meelian. The only library in Kleäm was the one inside Meelian's west wing. Getting inside the castle, however, would be easier said than done.

As she approached the gigantic wooden doors of Meelian, two halberds appeared in front of her, blocking her way. The guards holding them stared at Mavrian, impassive behind their black masks.

"Stop right there, lady," one of them mumbled. "What business have you inside the stronghold of the Loress Meels?"

"I need to get inside," Mavrian admitted.

The guards exchanged looks, then burst out laughing and relaxed their stance. She would have loved to know what was so funny.

"Lady Morr," one said, pausing from laughter. "I'm sure you haven't forgotten the words of the Loress."

"You're not welcome here," the other spat, all humour fading. "Look at this fine structure. Meelian was built by the first Lorr of Kleäm in order to promote purity on this isle." He hunched sideways, leaning his weight on his halberd. "Your name isn't lost on me. *Morr.* Our Loress Meels banished you from Meelian with good reason." He leaned close to her, his rotten breath detectable through his mask. "Your family's been a stain on this nation ever since the revolution was won."

"Scurry back to your tower, Lady Morr," the first guard added, "and we shan't inform the Loress of your appearance."

Mavrian considered her next move. She could argue over her family name till the moon was up, but they still wouldn't allow entry. Still, the audacity of these common louts was astounding. A just and fair loress would have these two flogged for their insolence. But as it was with all things on this forsaken island, injustice reigned.

"My uncle is the Lorr of the Morren," she reminded them. "There is no fiercer advocate of the Overlord than Vanan Morr." She glanced up at the Sigil of Meels displayed above the immense doorframe: a beautiful siren holding a shield that depicted the Cross of Drente. "That's more than can be said for your wretched lady."

The guard on the left stiffened. "Speak ill of our Loress Meels and face her fair judgement."

Mavrian laughed. "Oh, so *that's* what I must do to gain an audience? So much for not being allowed inside."

The other guard shook his head at her. "You waste your words on us."

"Look," Mavrian spat, grinding her teeth. "I have neither the time nor patience to stand here exchanging words with some watered-down blood offering. I *need* to enter Meelian."

"And *I* said you waste your time. Any dispute to our lady's rulings must be submitted to her in writing."

Writing? *Of course.*

Mavrian unfolded Scarmane Trokluss's letter and held it up in front of them.

"Here. See this. If you don't let me inside, you'll have to explain your actions to the Veer."

The guards glowered at the parchment.

They can't read, she surmised from their silence. She rummaged around in her pouch, withdrew the envelope, and flashed the seal at them.

The guards did not deliberate for a second. Without question, they stepped aside, angling their halberds away from her path.

A wave of relief rushed over her. *I guess the fear of the Bloody Hand will always be greater than that of Meels.*

"Thank you, kinsmen," she said, bowing her head at them as she opened the door. "Now, if the Veer asks me why I was late to his summons, I'll be sure to tell him the two reasons."

"Only following orders," she heard one of them say as the door closed behind her.

Mavrian chuckled as she imagined the frightened faces behind their masks, but her mirth turned to ash as she stepped into the vestibule and beheld the black marble staircase that led to the Loress's quarters.

And Eplin's old chamber. How could she forget the dozens of times Lorr Garr led her by the hand up those dreadful stairs?

She escaped the gaze of the vestibule's servants and took the corridor leading to the west wing. The intricate library door came into view at the end of the hall, the knotted wood painted ocean-blue and marked *Meelian Library* in gold lettering.

The door creaked as she yanked it open, its hinges crying out for oil, proclaiming the room's neglect. And indeed, the first thing she was aware of as the door groaned shut behind her was that she was alone in the immense room.

The library was a long hall of long-forgotten tomes, the final resting place of many hundreds of centuries-old books and weathered scrolls. The Meels collection was worth more than the castle itself, a fact the Loress boasted about whenever the situation allowed it. And yet, neither the Loress nor her late-husband had purchased any of the books here. They had inherited the collection from the great Västian Meels, who'd stolen most of the tomes from Sylvian trade ships and Carthanian pirates.

A foul taste lingered on her lips as she scanned the books lining the shelves and noted several more titles written in Sylvian than in the Bloodkin tongue of Nerblyss. She was literate in Sylvian, owing to her upbringing in the Kinsmeer-infested south of Ryne. She made a point to avoid Kinsmeeric literature, as the race's inherent wickedness seemed to infuse their writings. But it seemed Västian Meels had possessed a penchant for decadence.

As she stepped into the middle of the immense hall, she couldn't shake the feeling she was being watched, probed from every angle. Darkness pressing her flesh, sucking the sweat out of her pores.

Shadow blanketed the hall. The only light source slivered out of a single window at the end of the room.

She strained to see through the darkness, searching for a recognisable form, for any kind of movement.

She was alone. Alone in a tomb of worthless books and scrolls.

Where is he?

The library took form as she adjusted to the dim. The hall was an impressive sight, its high ceiling a wooden masterpiece of intricate, carved crosses and swirls weaving in and out of each other. Wood panelled the floor, but years of neglect had loosened the cuts, and they creaked and groaned as Mavrian stepped on them.

A formation of tables lined the centre of the hall, the dark slabs of oak arranged like guardsmen presenting to a lorr. Shelves filled with every shade of dyed leather lined the walls. The books were thick with dust. It appeared their existence eluded the servants. Above the ground level, a mezzanine floor spanned the length and width of the hall, accessible only by a single spiral staircase at the end of the room.

She gazed up at the mezzanine but made nothing out of the shadows.

Is this some sort of trick? Had the Veer summoned her here without intending to meet her? Was she being tested? Was the promptness of her appearance the part of some study?

She wanted to escape, to pretend she'd never seen the letter. But she'd rather face a thousand haunted libraries than refuse the summons of a Veer.

"Hello there."

The voice tickled her eardrums, puncturing flesh and bone and echoing in her skull. At first, she thought she'd imagined the words, that her grave surroundings were playing with her mind. But then the voice spoke again, precise, crisp.

"Your name is Mavrian Morr, is it not?"

She spotted a black figure descending the spiral staircase, its form roughly resembling a Bloodkin, silhouetted by the window.

Anxiety washed over her, glueing her boots to the floorboards. The realisation that she was about to face an agent of the Bloody

Hand seeped doubt into her flesh. She was unable to look away from him, from the dreadful eyes that would soon be upon her.

The figure emerged from the staircase, slithering around the formation of tables as it approached her.

The first thing she noticed was the intensity in his eyes, the fire seething from his scarlet irises as he probed her through the gloom.

Scarmane Trokluss was handsome... he *would* have been handsome if it wasn't for the thick pink scar that ran from his right eyebrow to his gaunt cheek.

That explains the name. She'd always wondered the reason for his unusual moniker. *His scar explains the first syllable.* Though his short slicked-back hair didn't strike her as befitting the title of *mane*. Regardless, the most curious thing was that the name comprised of two Sylvian words.

"Mavrian Morr," he said, reaching for her hand. His words were soft, sweet as a bird's morning song. "Word of your beauty precedes you."

He brought her fingers to his lips and kissed them. His aroma was godly, a treat for her nostrils. She couldn't put her finger on the scent, but it reminded her of Father – hints of chopped wood, of fresh dew weeping from the trees.

Mavrian couldn't move. She was entranced by his perfection.

His eyes were like magic penetrating her flesh, prickling her skin. Her sacrificial wound throbbed as he let go of her hand. The pain was delightful. His smile possessed a charm that reminded her of Eplin, though, unlike the Lorr of the Garren, Scarmane's was a promise of mischief. He gazed at her, evaluating her temperament, seeking to recognise her ills and rectify them with his tender tongue.

As his supple lips parted, the pulse between her legs told her she was wet for him. He spoke beauty into this dusty coffin of ancient books, his voice a beautiful flower spraying seeds into a garden of rotting corpses.

"Mavrian," she heard him saying, watching the subtle movement of his moist lips. "I have been looking forward to this moment."

Mavrian curtsied. As she looked away from him, she was set free from his alluring spell, and the terrible truth of his station shot panic into her chest. But as she regained her posture, his welcoming smile quelled her fears.

"Veer Trokluss," she managed. "The pleasure is mine."

Scarmane's smile seemed to wane at that. "I'm afraid I must apologise to you, my lady. I wished to speak with you several days ago, but several unforeseen happenings occurred in the wake of my arrival."

He couldn't have been much older than Mavrian. His skin was free of wrinkles, but there was wisdom behind his warm gaze, a sharpened perceptiveness.

She was grinning at him, exposing her misaligned teeth, contorting her face in an unappealing fashion. And yet, his eyes told her she was the most desirable Bloodkin in existence.

"There is nothing to forgive," she returned. Her body yearned for the return of his touch, for his hands to explore her in any way they deemed fit.

"Oh, but there is." He grimaced at his surroundings. "I would not have chosen such a vulgar place to meet had I the time to prepare." He frowned at a discarded book on one of the tables. "To learn that Jessa Meels keeps such literary filth in her stronghold wounds me greatly. You know, some scholars claim that to keep decadent items is akin to keeping a decadent mind. I pray to Vällas that sentiment is not true. For *her* sake."

The sweetness had waned from his voice. Agitation had seeped in, infusing his words with disgust and loathing.

Mavrian held back from commenting. It was strange to hear the Loress's forename spoken aloud, especially from one of common stock. Though, she supposed Veers were exempt from such a paradigm and were, in many ways, superior to nobles.

"Veer Trokluss," she said, eager to soothe him. "It is an honour to meet with you. When I first heard that a member of the Veerkasn was among us..." She stopped herself, thinking the sentiment improper.

She'd never met with a Veer before. Thinking on it, she was unsure how to conduct herself in front of one. The rules of conversing with a lorr and with a commoner were quite simple, but the members of the Veerkasn stood apart from that world. They were neither above nor below nobility, a law unto themselves.

"*Yes?*"

"Please... forgive me, Veer Trokluss. I've... I've... I speak out of turn."

He met her with a smile once more, seeming somewhat amused by her crumbling resolve. "Please, my lady, you misunderstand my station." He bowed his head. "I am but a humble servant of the Overlord. One sliver of thread in a great tapestry. You, my lady, symbolise all that is untainted in our realm. You are the daughter of a great family. A pure family. Tell of the greatness of your blood truly precedes you." As he rose to greet her, his beautiful eyes touched her with kindness, an offering of peace. "So no, my lady, you cannot speak to me out of turn, for I am but a humble servant of this realm."

Mavrian offered him a smile. "In that case, shall we sit?" She dragged one of the chairs out from under the table and seated herself.

As he seated himself opposite her, he fought to maintain his smile. "I'm afraid I must be brief here with what I am about to say my lady, for my impending departure, draws nearer by the day. Firstly, I ask that you join me this evening." His eyes darted around the room, searching for the right words. "To dine here in Meelian, that is to say."

She could feel her cheeks flushing. "Veer Trokluss, I..."

"Please," he spoke over her. "Call me Scarmane."

She swallowed her nerves. "*Scarmane*, I would love nothing more than to accept your offer, but I'm afraid the Loress Meels has banned me from dining inside the castle."

"I'm aware," he said, unmoved by her statement. "But alas, my lady, I am the Loress's honoured guest. It is for me to choose who accompanies me to the banquet."

Mavrian swallowed bile. He wasn't simply asking her to dine

within his quarters. He meant for her to feast with the whole court of Meelian. Keeping Mavrian away from her banquets was the Loress's main reason for dismissing her in the first place.

Scarmane's smile was comforting enough to push the dreadful image of Jessa Meels out of her mind.

"It will be okay, my lady. You have my protection, for now until the end of time." Everything about his demeanour told her his words were genuine, that, for whatever reason, he would risk his entire livelihood to keep her from harm.

"I would be honoured to accompany you," she found herself saying. Her legs were trembling under the table.

He folded his arms and narrowed his eyes at her. "And now I must relay my foul news, my lady. The primary reason for my summons."

He watched her in silence, eager to discover something from her eyes. There was sorrow in him, a terrible regret.

Mavrian wasn't breathing. She couldn't feel her stomach expanding, her nostrils flaring, her lips parting. She looked down at her robe and noted the movement of cloth around her sternum – she *was* breathing, but she'd lost all feeling.

Terror peeled at her skin. Dread seeped into her soul. As Scarmane studied her, biding his time to strike, she had a horrible feeling that what he was about to tell her would alter her very existence.

"I must inform you, with regret, that your uncle had taken ill. Gravely ill."

Relief brushed over her. *That explains the rareness of his letters.*

"And that brings me to my news, my lady."

You mean that wasn't the foul news?

Scarmane straightened in his seat. "The Overlord has called for every lorr and loress to attend council in the Capital. With the Lorr of the Morren suffering ill health, someone must present themselves in Sela'Fundor on his behalf."

Mavrian's mind raced with thoughts and fears. "And he has chosen *me*?"

It couldn't be. Vanan would sooner see her perish than assume his position.

Scarmane turned his attention to the ceiling, unable to meet her gaze. "I am afraid your uncle has not the awareness to make such a decision. He is sleeping, my lady, and the healers predict he will never again awake. My master has tasked me with electing an ambassador to represent the Morren, and I see none better suited than yourself. I sail for the Capital in three days, weather permitting, and yourself and the Loress Meels will accompany me."

"Veer Trokluss, I..."

Before she could utter another word, he rose from his seat, bowed his head, and walked away from her. "I regret I must leave," he said as he strode towards the exit. "For time is a failing commodity. I will see you in the eve, my lady. The merriment commences at seven o'clock, I'm told."

As the door creaked shut behind him, Mavrian found herself frozen to her seat.

Uncle is dying? The thought didn't seem as foul as she imagined it ought to. She ran her fingers down her robe, lifting the fabric up past her knees, probing between her legs. She was soaking wet, her chamber throbbing from the whole ordeal.

Uncle is dying. The thought was pleasant. *Vanan did not deserve the title of Lorr of the Morren. He stole it from me.* The result of his death would only mean one thing. *Now I'll be recognised for what I really am, what I always should have been... the Loress of the Morren.*

As she slid her fingertips over her clitoris, jubilation coursed through her body. She pictured Jessa Meels's face when she heard the news, her clever words turning to ashes in her throat as she realised she could belittle Mavrian no longer.

Meelian no longer felt like a place she shouldn't enter. Kleäm no longer seemed a place she didn't belong to. Jessa Meels was her superior no more.

The evening's banquet would be one to remember. As she teased her lower lips, biting down on her tongue, she found Scarmane's dazzling smile entering her thoughts.

The Eyes of the Future

Something was brewing in Balenmeade, something more than the mere coming of Harvest.

Word of the mysterious girl found hiding in the Baron's stables had spread. Rumours as to her origins abounded: she was an exiled Sylvian peasant one minute and a Nocryn fleeing the Lerthian purges the next. Barrett even heard the suggestion that Vilka was a Bloodkin who'd used black magic to disguise herself as a young girl.

Barrett amused himself as he imagined Vilka with glowing red eyes, blood dripping from her lips, her milky-white skin almost translucent.

He stiffened as the image of Vilka flashed before his mind's eye, judging him with her fiery-brown beads. Her face followed him everywhere he went. He couldn't drink with Drodger or even take a shit without her childish visage appearing before him.

Barrett still rued his decision to walk away that fateful night outside the Dancing Buck, allowing her to make an awful decision with Sir Denzus. Whatever she'd done that night, it can't have been good. Whether Vilka had stolen from him or slept with him or both, she had set herself up for a world of trouble.

He visited the Dancing Buck almost nightly, hoping to spot her there again, but she never made an appearance. Indeed, Drodger seemed to have forgotten he'd ever mentioned her, which was undoubtedly a good thing.

No matter how many drunkards insisted that the girl must be an Imperial spy, the one thing that clawed at the back of Barrett's mind was: what if she was innocent? What if the child really had sought refuge in the stables because she had no other place to go? What if she really had fled the scene of her parent's murder? What if she was telling the truth all along? What if she posed no threat to anyone?

The thing that put him at unease the most was that he didn't know what was happening to her, whether she was being bathed and fed or whipped and beaten and locked away to starve.

Every morning, after an hour or so of filtering through the logbooks, he visited the fourth floor to see if Pamen still guarded the way to the attic. And he still did, most days at least. When it wasn't Pamen, Ache patrolled the area.

Barrett knew he had a better chance of discovering diamonds in his boots than convincing Ache to let him visit Vilka. Still, so long as someone was guarding the attic, he knew Vilka was still up there. *The clever little shit did manage to slip back up there after staying with* Sir *Denzus.* There was *some* relief in that. At least she wasn't sleeping out on the streets.

The only thing that distracted Barrett from Vilka was Reymond. After the Chamberlain's announcement that the stewards were relieved of their additional duties, Reymond's mood had lightened. He hadn't quite forgiven Barrett – after all, he'd mucked out the stables on his own for the past two weeks – but Reymond was far too excited about the festival feast and commoners' dance to dwell on that sordid subject.

Reymond claimed he would bed half a dozen ladies by the end of the second night of Harvest and invited Barrett to match his number. Most curiously, Reymond showed no real interest in the subject of

Vilka. Whenever Barrett mentioned her, Reymond would shrug, then continue to drone on about ale or breasts.

As was Harvest custom, the stewards of the Balenmanor were relieved of their duties for three days – a time Barrett traditionally used to drown himself in ale and kiss every girl that was willing. But this was no ordinary harvest, and no matter how many pints and monotonous words he consumed, he couldn't shake the feeling that something dreadful was going to happen.

"What do you think about Hetsy Docker?" Reymond asked, pulling Barrett's thoughts back to reality. He had seated himself on the stone wall next to the fountain.

Morske Square was Barrett's favourite spot in Balenmeade: a small square of peach-coloured stone pavement, ornamental flowerbeds, and a series of stone statues. It was situated away from the shops and marketplace of central Balenmeade. Still, it was close enough to hear the excited chatter of revellers carrying over the tall stone structures surrounding it. They had named the square after the great naval hero Edgar Morske, who had sadly passed away a few weeks before Hanzus's arrival in Balenmeade.

As Barrett came up alongside Reymond and peered into the pool of water by the fountain, he spotted several crowns at the bottom. Blasphemous strangers must have dropped them in to muster good luck. As he inspected the big-bosomed statue, whose upturned jug was the origin of a steady stream of spurting water, he reasoned he could do with some fortune of his own.

He searched his purse for a worthless coin, then tossed a copper into the water behind Reymond's back.

"Actually, no. Not Hetsy. What's her sister's name, again?" He met Barrett with half-closed eyes as the morning sun beamed on his face.

"Letza," Barrett supplied. The Docker sisters had moved to Balenmeade with their father only a few years ago. Like many of the city's artisans, they had emigrated from Vinerheim. Apparently, the Capital had an oversupply of clockmakers.

"Letza. Ah yes." Reymond grimaced, tugging his jacket tight to his neck. Though the skies were clear and sunny, the autumnal breeze carried a chill. "Which would you choose?"

"What?" Barrett groaned, exasperated. The steward had been poking him with hypotheticals involving women ever since they'd met up. Reymond shared Barrett's enthusiasm for wanting to escape his family on a day of no work, but they didn't share a favourite topic of conversation. Though he supposed the thought of Letza and Hetsy Docker flashing their bosoms was better than Vilka's torture.

"Which one would you choose?" Reymond repeated in the same tone. "If both were stood before us now and I gave you the option, which sister would you bed?"

Barrett could picture the occurrence now: arriving at his home with Letza Docker under his arm, then Mother chasing her away with her broom.

"Letza, I guess."

Reymond considered him with narrow eyes. He sprang to his feet and wrapped his arm around Barrett's shoulders, guiding his feet into action. "What's on your mind? And don't lie to me now. I've seen that face before, and it rarely speaks of good tidings."

They walked out of the square, turning onto Candle Street, which the Harvest planners had transformed into an impromptu marketplace. Wooden stalls lined the exterior walls of the permanent shops, each with its own collection of crates and barrels filled to the brim with fresh produce.

They passed fishmongers and toy makers and fruit peddlers, even an old crone who was selling tatty old books. The street reeked of several aromas, some sweet and others foul. The aroma of fresh bread and cakes wafted over from the bakery, mixing with old wool from the clothes peddler, and piss and shit from the privy house stationed halfway down the street.

"It's nothing," Barrett lied, amused as he watched women queue for the makeshift privy, while drunk men bypassed the line and pissed against the nearby wall.

"Well, you best not be wearing that face tomorrow," Reymond said, patting him on the back before removing his arm entirely. "I'm going to ask Maisie Taverner to the commoner's dance."

Barrett sighed. *Not this again.* "Reymond, Maisie Taverner has already accepted an invitation to the dance. *You* told me so."

"That may be so, but I don't care if Maisie's partner was Hektor himself. I'll change her mind. Just wait and see. I'll have my dance before the night is through."

Barrett scanned all that was on offer along the lines of the market stalls. A tall, slender man was selling small objects that were stuffed into glass bottles. They were boiled sweets, he realised upon closer inspection, but they smelled something foul.

A jester dressed in mock-finery was juggling leather balls before a crowd of young children, making them laugh as he pulled funny faces. Barrett was sure he recognised the man. For a split second, he thought it was Nipp Brewman in costume, before he remembered the guards had thrown the old drunk into the dungeons many days ago for brawling outside the Buck.

"Come," Reymond said, gesturing down the street. "I'm too sober for all this cheeriness. Fancy a pint in the Red Sparrow? I'm buying."

Barrett couldn't say no to that. He found himself smiling for the first time in a while. "Lead the way."

The Red Sparrow was not Barrett's favourite alehouse, by any means. Unlike the Dancing Buck and the Irvaye Arms, which offered open drinking halls where folk traded songs and stories, the Red Sparrow consisted of one small room split into six booths. There was no entertainment, no space for a bard to stamp their feet as they plucked away at their lute. The relative quiet of the Sparrow made Barrett feel uneasy. Every nearby patron was a potential eavesdropper.

After Reymond had instructed Barrett to sit at one of the tables, he came over carrying a tray of drinks. Each of the four beverages appeared different. Reymond had instructed the barmaid to fill the tankards with anything that would get them drunk fast. Goddness only knew what the maid had picked.

"Here," Reymond said, handing Barrett the darkest of the drinks. "Think I can safely say this one is Krämisen." He scratched his head as he inspected the other beverages. "As for this one... I'm going to say Rooksbrew?"

Barrett creased at that, remembering Vilka telling him she'd come from the west. "Why would they be serving Rooksbrew here? Place is plagued."

"The cellars here are filled to the rafters with the stuff," Reymond explained. "Barmaid told me they can't *give* the stuff away. Don't see why. Doctors say plague is carried in the air, not in liquids. Besides, I've read that the numbers are thinning over there. Will only be a matter of time before the border's open again."

Barrett mused on that as he gazed out the window. Many revellers had taken to drinking in the street outside, carrying tankards and bottles as they browsed the wares of the recently arrived peddlers. He noticed a man leaning against a shop window being caught in the line of fire as a woman emptied her chamber pot from the apartment window above. As the woman began to apologise, the man picked up an apple from a nearby fruit stand and chucked it at her. Then a nearby guard ran over and tackled the man to the ground.

"Balenmeade," Reymond mused, sipping on his mystery ale. "Don't you just love it?"

Barrett sighed. His Krämisen tasted like an unclean tankard. "Don't you ever wonder what's out there, beyond our walls?"

Reymond considered him for a moment, wondering if he was jesting. "Outside Balenmeade, there are moors and wilds and swampland. And beyond that, there are more towns like Balenmeade that are just as bland and rotten as ours."

Barrett shrugged. He supposed Reymond was right. He wondered what Vilka's town or village was like, whether it was anything like Balenmeade. He'd always wanted to venture out into the wilds of the Krämise, but reason stopped him every time. There were monstrous creatures out there. And heathens that prayed to false spirits and would sacrifice any wayfarer they encountered.

"Your mind should be here. Right here and right now." Reymond tugged on Barrett's sleeve, shocking him. "Tell me your troubles, Barrett. Let them be spoken so they can then be forgotten."

"You sound like Drodger," Barrett said, sighing. The man who'd thrown the apple was being dragged away by the guardsman now, no doubt, toward the dungeons.

"Ah, yes. I've heard you've been spending a lot of time merrymaking with that old coot. Listen to me, Barrett, if you linger on your troubles, you'll grow to be as old and bitter as the Baron." Reymond had his full attention now. The steward was foolish indeed to make such a statement out in public. "We've known each other since we were nippers. I know you. Know you better than any other. And I *know* you don't enjoy the company of Drodger. Save for the last few weeks, you've spent most of your life avoiding him, for Hektor's sake." He wrapped his fingers around Barrett's wrist, squeezing hard. "You're not yourself. You haven't been ever since we discovered that girl."

"Says you," Barrett retorted, snatching his arm free. He returned his attention to the street outside. They had taken the piss-stained man away now, and a few people who had witnessed the scene were gossiping and laughing. "You could barely look me in the eye for two weeks just because you had to clean the stables on your own."

Reymond scoffed at that. "That *wasn't* the reason I didn't want to speak with you, Barrett. You were acting strange. Obsessing over that girl. And you're still doing it. You have the same look in your eye. But you have to forget about it. She's none of your concern now."

"You don't know what you're talking about," Barrett muttered. "You only know half the story." He'd piqued Reymond's interest as the steward then held his tongue.

"I don't want to bicker anymore," Reymond said when it became clear Barrett would tell him no more. "The girl... *Vilka*, was it? Her fate lies with Hanzus and Heatha now. There's nothing you or I can do to make it otherwise. Besides, the girl's lucky she hasn't been thrown in the dungeons already."

Lucky? I'm sure she won't be lucky when Hanzus learns of her manipulation of Denzus.

Barrett had decided not to tell Reymond about his encounter with Vilka outside the Dancing Buck. He'd decided not to tell anyone, for that matter. The fewer ears heard of her gambit, the better, for her sake. He wasn't sure why, but he didn't want to see Vilka harmed. She might have been insolent and impulsive, but the pain he'd seen in her eyes the last time he saw her... Her parents were dead. She needed to be comforted, to be soothed with kind words, not locked away in some attic prison.

"Push her out of your mind," Reymond said, intercepting his thoughts. "Balenmeade has plenty of lasses to go around. Not to mention the amount of fresh meat that's arrived from across the barony."

Barrett faced him, incredulous. "I'm not... *attracted* to her."

Reymond cracked a smile. "Come, now. She's all you ever speak of."

Barrett shook his head, drowning his discomfort in ale. "You don't know what you're talking about."

"Oh, really? Again, Barrett Barrett, I know you better than anyone else." He reached for another drink – a yellowish beverage with a pungent odour. "In fact, I'd wager I know you better than you know yourself." Then something changed in his face. At first, Barrett thought he was grimacing at the taste of the yellow beer, but a thought struck him. "I know something that'll clear your mind."

"What?" Barrett folded his arms, not at all confident in the nature of Reymond's proposal.

"Look outside. The festival is upon us. Tonight will be a night of celebration. We'll drink more ale than we've ever done before. But there's more to Harvest than ale and women."

"Why do I have the dreadful feeling you're about to propose something ridiculous?"

Reymond was grinning, yellow foam dripping from his chin. "We'll put your mind at ease by visiting someone who can tell you more about yourself than even *you* know. We'll visit an oracle."

Barrett laughed. "You can't be serious?"

"Come, Barrett, it's only a bit of merriment. And, you never know, the oracle might tell you something about Vilka."

"Fortune-telling is blasphemous," Barrett reminded him. "An oracle's words are no more than lies and trickery. They're charlatans. Most are Nocryn heathens."

"If you know their words are false, then speaking with one won't do you any harm. And don't give me that blasphemy crap. I know you and your family don't attend Mass anymore."

"Quiet down," Barrett hissed, glancing around at the other booths within sight. Fortunately, the other punters seemed too interested in their friends to pay the stewards any mind. "Watch your tongue."

"I'm not speaking ill of you," Reymond said before glugging down his beer. "I haven't prayed in Goddess knows how long." He gazed up at the ceiling and winked at nothing. "Forgive me, Sacred Lady, for you're not the only lass in my life." He looked back at Barrett, grinning. "Besides, I don't believe the Goddess gives a damn whose nonsense we listen to. Don't the priests say a son of the Goddess will remain so until his last breath?"

"You're uncouth," Barrett groaned, downing his Krämisen. He reached for the fourth and final tankard filled with an welcoming gold liquid. *Vickan's Goldblend from the Tyldar,* he reasoned, though its light flavour was difficult to place.

"And you're a bore," Reymond quipped. "Now, finish your beer. There's an oracle hut on the corner of Halmond Square. We'll visit the oracle, then we'll get some luncheon. I'll pay for both, and I *won't* take no for an answer."

As they walked down Accles Road, they passed a pileup of carriages and cabs stationed outside the Four Blades Inn. The drivers and their finely dressed clients exchanged foul language. The inn was fully booked and so had turned them away. The frantic sons of aldermen and wealthy merchants sat in the carriages shook their fists and lamented at the sky as if it was the Goddess's fault they had arrived in Balenmeade late and were not important enough to be given quarters in the Balenmanor.

A commotion caught Barrett's eye further down the street. What appeared to be an elderly vagrant, dressed in ragged robes and mud-encrusted boots, was flapping his arms about, shouting at any stranger that met his gaze.

"I sense lunacy ahead," Reymond whispered in Barrett's ear. "Keep your head down. Don't say a word."

As they neared the man, a small crowd had gathered around him, a few young men of low station pointing at him mockingly.

"I must speak with him!" the vagrant declared to the closest lad. "I must speak with him at once! Before it's too late!"

"Eat shit, old man!" the lad shot back, then, when the vagrant approached him, he recoiled and spat, "Get away from me, you plagued coot!"

The vagrant lunged toward the young man, but the lad stepped out of the way. The vagrant tripped over something and fell, crashing into the cobbles. The lads burst out laughing.

"We should do something," Barrett said, quickening his pace toward the scene.

"No, wait." Reymond pulled him back by his jacket. "Look." He gestured at a couple of guardsmen who were walking by and who, upon noticing the vagrant, stormed over to him.

"What's going on here?" the taller of the two boomed at the group of lads before the heap of an old man on the ground caught his eye. "What's this then?"

"Thank the Goddess, good sir," the vagrant croaked, extending his arm in the hope that the guard would help him to his feet. "You bear the Boar of Irvaye! Tis a welcome sight indeed."

The guardsman grimaced at the vagrant. "You've a questionable accent, mister. What's your business in Balenmeade?"

"Please... help me."

"I asked you a question, you old wretch!"

As the vagrant offered his hand a second time, the guard unsheathed his sword and smacked the man's hand with the hilt. The group of lads applauded with glee, egging the guard on.

"Leave this place!" the guard bellowed at the lads, causing them to flee in fear. Then he turned on the vagrant. "And you... we don't want your kind here. Least of all during this holy festival. Leave Balenmeade before the gates are shut for the night, or you'll spend the rest of Harvest in a cell."

After the guard sheathed his sword and re-joined his fellow soldier, the two muttered together and walked away.

Before Barrett could even consider approaching the vagrant, the old man struggled onto his feet and staggered away down the street.

"What on earth was all that all about?" Reymond asked, scratching his head.

"I... I don't know," Barrett admitted. The guard's reaction told him the man was some kind of foreigner. Perhaps a Nocryn, or a Rooklander who'd sneaked across the border. *Surely there's not another one?*

What Reymond had described as an oracle hut turned out to be a tent of patchwork cloth stitched crudely together. The wooden sign hanging over the entrance read *Travelling Oracle*, above the symbol of an iris-less eye.

The fact the festival planning committee had allowed a blasphemous crone to do business within the city walls surprised

Barrett. There was a time when they would hang such heathens from the nearest tree. Though, it was no great surprise to Barrett that the wig-wearers in Balen Hall cared more for coin than the purity of their souls.

Not that Barrett could talk. Reymond was right – he couldn't remember the last time he'd attended Mass or even knelt down to pray. And now he was visiting an oracle, a crone of black magic or an immoral, shrewd charlatan. If there was one person who'd turned their back on the Holy Mother, it was Barrett.

Reymond paused at the tent's entrance. "You'll have to enter alone."

"Scared of an old lady, are you?"

Reymond gestured at the smaller writing at the bottom of the sign. "One soul permitted at a time," he read aloud. "And with that being the case, I'll wait for you..." He scanned Halmond Square before his eyes rested on a tent stitched with the words *Cheap Ale Imports*. "Over there."

"Fine," Barrett sighed. He had a feeling he was making a stupid mistake for even listening to Reymond's suggestion to visit an old sorceress... but what if Reymond's hunch was right? What if she could tell him something about Vilka?

"Oh, and here." Reymond handed him a few copper and silver coins. "That should more than cover it." He patted Barrett's back with encouragement, then marched over to the booze tent and disappeared inside.

Barrett glanced down at the handful of coins Reymond had left him with, pressing his fingers into their warmth. Barrett didn't know the true value of an oracle reading, but he was sure it would cost more than two silvers and four coppers.

Steeling himself, Barrett peeled back the flap of the oracle's lair and stepped inside.

The interior was almost black, illuminated by a single candle pulsating on the other side of the room. The whiff of damp cloth and a mixture of herbs swam in his nostrils, stinging his eyes as they adjusted to the gloom.

He made out the rough shape of a body lingering by the candlelight, which emanated from a small table littered with books and papers. The crone sat on the far side of the wooden surface, her wrinkled features bold from the shadows. The face looked up from the papers and studied him for a few seconds before returning its attention to the table.

"Are you an... oracle?" Barrett asked. The words sounded ridiculous.

The crone chuckled. Her voice was deep and coarse. She might have smoked a pipe for several hours. "I am *the* Oracle." She lifted her chin to study him once more, her eyes penetrating the dark and etching into his skin.

Barrett's cheeks flushed warmly. Cool sweat relieved his face. "I've come for a reading." He shook off the fear peppering his mind. *Get a grip on yourself. It's just an old woman.*

"Ten silver," the Oracle hissed, her lisp telling him she had little to no teeth. The thing that disturbed him most was that her accent sounded distinctly Krämisen.

"*Ten silver?*" Barrett echoed, incredulous. "You jest, surely? Ten silver could buy me a carriage ride to Dulenmeake. It could rent me a horse for several days."

"Could also purchase your reading," the Oracle quipped. "Ten silver. No more, nor less. There ain't no other that does what I do in Balenmeade."

"How do you know that you're the authentic one?"

The crone's ancient features creased into a smile. "Be seated, Mister Barrett. We've much to discuss."

Barrett edged closer to the table and noted the low stool next to the table. He seated himself there, and found himself uncomfortably close to the witch's face, on the other side of her heaps of parchment and leather-bound books. She was perhaps the oldest person he'd ever seen. Her skin reminded him of the result of scrunching up brown paper, then flattening it out again. Her eyes were bulbous black beads, the pupils swallowing the irises entirely.

"You know my name," Barrett stated, aware it was a possible trick. Had she overheard Reymond speak his name outside? Perhaps she'd spoken with Drodger during a merry night in the Buck.

"The spirits tell me many things, young Barrett. An open eye is not always an open mind, nor does a closed eye always mean a closed mind."

Riddles. The crone wouldn't earn her silver with clever words alone. He scanned the papers littering her desk. The first thing that caught his eye was a list of words or names, not a dissimilar sight to the pages that haunted his logbooks. The page of an open book caught his eye, wherein the illustration of a fiery red eye stood out from the page, threatening to take form and float away from the parchment.

"Ten silver, you say?" Barrett said, unable to take his eyes from the illustration. "And what would I receive for ten silver?"

The woman closed the book with the red eye, and with it, something changed in Barrett. He felt relief, the crone's action saving him from a great evil.

He blinked up at her and realised sweat was trickling down his face.

"The spirits do whisper in my ear, Mister Barrett. Your coming is of no surprise to these wizened eyes, for your coming was foretold. My ability is shared by none other in Balenmeade, and so, the spirits of this city pay me great mind. Hand me ten silvers and I will do more than inform you of *their* wisdom. There are higher powers we can contact, powers whose knowledge reaches beyond the past, and whose influence extends beyond the future."

A chill shivered up his spine. Though all reason told him this crone's words were false. She'd weave any lie she could to bleed him of his coin. Something touched him deep down within himself, pressing its ethereal fingers into his ribcage, caressing his heart and playing with his other organs.

But his gut told him this crone was genuine, that she held some innate power that could communicate with other planes of existence.

Ten silver might be extortionate, but if his gut was right, the Oracle could tell him things he'd have no other way of learning.

She could tell me about Vilka. Help me learn the truth of her appearance in Balenmeade.

Reymond was right. Speaking with this witch would enable him to find closure, to know the truth about Vilka so his brain could stop guessing. *Though I wish you were right about this crone's fee.* Barrett withdrew his purse and explored its contents. He'd allocated himself five crowns and thirty silvers to enjoy Harvest, and a few spare coppers made up the rest. He reached in and handed the crone ten polished silver coins.

"Very good," she said, stuffing the coins into some invisible pocket of her dark robe. "Before we begin, I must warn you. That which we are about to do cannot be done lightly, nor can it be undone. Do you understand?" When Barrett nodded, she continued, "When I tell you to do something, you must do so without question. Our reading will consist of three stages. For the first, you must give me your hand."

Before Barrett could react, the crone reached across and snatched his right hand, holding it above the table. She held him tight with one leathery hand as the bony fingers of the other stroked his palm. Her eyes shut tight, revealing tiny identical marks on both of her eyelids. Tattoos, he reasoned, but before he could make them out, the woman's eyes snapped open again.

"There exists a great sorrow in you," she said, frowning. "A part of you is broken. It prevents you from being whole, from being the man you ought to be. No... no, they're wrong. It's like some part of you never grew to be in the first place. Like something or someone prevented it from growing."

Barrett blinked at her, unsure how to feel. Her words were so abstract, he wondered whether she was indeed a charlatan and thought him easy enough to appease with vague claims.

Then she said something that grabbed at his throat, strangling him with its invisible fingers, forcing the air out of his lungs. "Your father is not with you." Her eyes narrowed at him. "And yet, in so many ways, he has never left you."

Barrett fought against tears. *How can she know?* "My father is... gone. Most probably... dead."

The crone shook her head dismissively. "The spirits that guide you also surround another. The two of you are bound together in spirit. Your fates are intertwined. But... but..." She creased her brows at him. "There is another... A third spirit. Another living soul whose fate is bound to your own."

"Does she have a name?"

The crone's thick brow creased at him. "You speak as if you know the name already. And know it you do."

Vilka.

"But all is not as it seems." She snatched her hands away from him, rummaged around in one of her pockets, and withdrew a tiny glass vial filled with some kind of powder. "I invite you now to gaze into the flame."

"I want you to tell me more about this girl," Barrett demanded. "Her name is Vilka, isn't it? Tell me. That's what I paid you ten coins for."

The crone seemed unmoved. "The flame is our second reading. Wherein the whispers of spirits will take form." She nodded toward the candle. "I invite you to gaze into its flame, removing your gaze for nought. I invite you to clear your mind and to allow the flame to show you. To teach you what you ought to be taught."

"Teach me?" He'd heard stories of witches conjuring spirits into the flames, but he was no witch. Just when he thought he was paying this crone to blaspheme on his behalf, she was suggesting he cast spells of his own.

"Your soul's purity remains intact, Mister Barrett," the crone said. "That *is* what you fear, is it not? That you will not one day reach the Gardens of the Goddess and cleanse your immortal soul? The flames will do nothing to compromise your spirit. They will do nothing to alter you. The flames simply allow us a glimpse of ourselves. Our *true* selves."

Barrett took a deep inhalation and let it exhale slowly from his lips. He decided to ignore his better judgement, allowing his eyes to focus on the flickering flame. For the first few seconds, the light was blinding, and he wasn't sure how long he could gaze at it before being forced to look away. But his eyes adjusted, or the light adjusted, and his body seemed calm.

"What am I supposed to do?" he asked.

"You need not *do* anything. Allow your mind to wander as you keep your gaze true. Watch as the orange blends with the yellow hues of the sun. The flecks of crimson and white that want you to believe they're there. The suggestions of grey and charcoal as our flame becomes smoke."

The woman's voice had changed. It was soothing to his ears, soft where once it was harsh. The more she spoke, the less her voice seemed to belong to the ancient body sat close to him. The voice sounded a year younger with every syllable until the voice instructing him was that of a girl not much older than Vilka. In fact, had the crone's shadowy suggestion not been visible behind the flame, he might have believed Vilka sat across from him.

"Bring your mind back to me," the girl said, her sound pleasing, melodious. "Your mind is open to me now. And as I speak to it, it whispers back to me, unguarded. It whispers back to me without thought or reason. It simply answers when spoken to."

"Yes, it does," Barrett found himself agreeing with her. Still, he didn't see anything inside the flames, only the dancing flecks of warmth.

"Your name is Barrett Barrett, is it not?"

"It is."

"And what is your profession, Barrett Barrett?"

"I am an accountant. A steward in the home of Hanzus Irvaye, the Baron of the Krämise. But I do not do my job well. I spend most of my coin on booze, for I seek to numb my brain, to stupefy myself."

"Very good," the beautiful voice told him. "Your mind is open to me. Now allow your mind to open to itself. I want you to picture a door. It is at the end of a long corridor and is the only thing of interest. The only thing of interest in all the world. You're walking toward it, approaching it slowly."

As sure as the beautiful words suggested, Barrett could see the door inside the flames. He drew closer to it, or it to him, the ornateness of its boar's head handle making itself known with his approach. As his fingers went to touch it, he realised the boar's head was alive, its black eyes blinking at him, evaluating him with scorn.

"When you open the door, I want you to tell me what greets you on the other side. Tell me *everything*. Do not forgo a single detail."

The boar, satisfied with its appraisal, melted away, transforming into an ordinary door handle. As Barrett pulled the door open, a wall of blackness greeted him. Then, as he passed through the doorway and entered the gloom, the blackness swirled into shapes around him. The form of a girl appeared in front of him, its form the same height and girth as Vilka, but its face was blurry, indistinct.

"*Vilka?*" he queried, but the form offered no answer.

"What is it? What do you see?"

"A girl," he admitted. "She is... taking shape, presenting herself before me. She wears a dress of fine silk, peach in colour and detailed with purple lace. Her cheeks are pink and glowing. Life itself pulsates from her. Her eyes are... they are green. And beautiful. Alluring. She is not Vilka. She is... someone else."

"*Who?*" Cracks had appeared in the beautiful voice, revealing the crone's true crooked tongue. "Who is she?"

The image of the girl was changing, the form that was her face shifting into something else. But her eyes did not alter. Their emerald glow retained their hold over him. If the stranger had somewhat resembled Vilka before, it strayed further from that likeness now. Wrinkles appeared above the woman's brow, bags appeared under her magnificent eyes. The glow of her cheeks faded to greyness. At first, he thought she was ageing before his eyes, but then black splotches formed on her skin. He realised she was naked, her small supple breasts presented to him like a votive offering. But blackness was corrupting her flesh, turning pale skin to charred grey. She was burning, being cooked alive. Those beautiful eyes, trapped inside the flame, begged him to be set free.

"Who is the woman? Who do you see? Tell me her name!" The crone's raspy voice had resurfaced, sundering the illusion entirely.

Barrett's eyes snapped away from the flame drawn out by the wretch's words. "I... I don't know who she was."

"Lies! You know her!" The Oracle's bark snapped him out of his confusion. "Those green eyes are your future. Those green eyes are your purpose."

The crone reached across the table, her skeletal fingers clawing at the space between them. But he recoiled his hands away from her reach.

"What are you talking about?" Barrett retorted, managing to get himself onto his feet. His vision was blurry as he tried to focus on the flame once more. The image had disappeared from the slit of fire. The candle had returned to being a simple light.

"Be seated, boy. Our reading isn't concluded."

"I don't want to see any more," he admitted, staggering back toward the entrance. "You... you have your coin. I made a mistake in coming here."

He couldn't remove the image of those emerald eyes from his mind. They were indelible, etched into his brain, a solid memory. As they lingered in the fore of his mind's eye, they appeared to smile at him, happy to see him acknowledge them. A voice told him they had always been there, and they were thankful he could see them at last.

"The woman you see is your future," the crone reminded him. "You will not escape her. You *cannot*. Some folk live their lives never knowing their purpose. Most do not have one. But your purpose is undeniable, Barrett Barrett, whose father's spirit walks beside him. Your path is set out before you. And it *cannot* be rejected."

"Enough," Barrett snapped at her, turning back to face the

entrance flap. He couldn't tolerate another moment in the presence of her leathery features and raspy voice.

He made his escape before the Oracle could say more. Daylight hit him like the first glimpse of morning. He staggered toward the booze tent, shielding his eyes from the sun.

Reymond would never believe him if he told him what he'd just witnessed. He struggled to trust it himself.

Was the image in the flame some sort of trick conjured up by the crone? He remembered her withdrawing a vial of mystery contents before he'd gazed into the light, but he couldn't remember her doing anything with it.

His gut wrenched with the terrible idea that the emerald-eyed woman had been real. That this stranger was somehow bound to him. But he didn't recall ever meeting a woman with green eyes.

And what does the crone mean by my father's spirit walks beside me? He gripped a nearby sign to steady himself. *I should never have visited a Goddessless crone. I should never have listened to Reymond.*

The Turn of the Tide

"Splendid. Most splendid."

Zamrian was chewing on her lip as she inspected Mavrian. Her cheeks flushed with excitement. Her eyes glowed with... was it pride? If her smile stretched any wider, her skin would surely split.

Zamrian had appeared at Mavrian's door as soon as she returned from her meeting with Scarmane Trokluss. Mavrian had told her everything about the incident, after which Zamrian insisted on helping her prepare for the evening's banquet.

"You really think so?"

Mavrian gazed at her flat, lifeless reflection. A dark allocation of silk draped over her like a smooth sack covering a signpost. The dress was loose at the shoulders and tight everywhere else. She looked a clown. If she took a long enough stride, the whole dress might slide up past her waist.

That would be quite something, exposing myself before the Meelian courtiers. Perhaps it would distract the Loress and her gaggle of arse-lickers from the real threat that Mavrian posed.

She could picture Jessa Meels's venomous snarl now. As soon as the Loress learned of Mavrian's invitation to the banquet, her hatred would reach boiling point. Vässa only knew whether she would act on that anger. The old bat had slighted Mavrian during the Dräege by placing her at the back of the hall. She had then insulted her further by refusing to acknowledge her as they exited the temple. Indeed, Jessa had despised Mavrian long before she landed on Kleäm. The Meelses had been spitting on the name of Morr ever since the Overlord named them rulers of what became the Morren.

Uncle Vanan had to have known Jessa would detest Mavrian's presence. His justification for shipping her to Kleäm was that it would help her learn the ways of court, but the real reason was to be rid of her. Likely, he'd hoped Jessa would have his niece stabbed in the night.

At least I'll never have to worry about that. Meels is too great a coward to declare open war on my bloodline. But now that Vanan was sick and Mavrian was the effective the head of her house, the Loress's perspective might have changed.

Then she remembered Scarmane's promise to sail with her to attend the Overlord's council. No matter how much Meels despised Mavrian, she would never defy a Veer.

Mavrian sighed. The silk pressed on her belly, preventing her stomach from expanding. As much as she wanted to rip the dress into pieces and pick something else to wear, the azure gown was the most expensive thing she possessed. *And if there's one thing that'll silence the courtiers, it's the one thing they'll never attain...* True wealth.

"What's got you looking so thoughtful?" Zamrian asked.

Mavrian faced the archway that led to the balcony. The day was dying, the sun bleeding into her chamber. The balcony's balustrade cast bold shadows under the arch, the blackness creeping closer and closer to her bare feet. The Twins' watch over the world was ending. The tether between their realm and the mortal plane would soon snap, at least until the sun rose again.

"Nothing." Mavrian shrugged her shoulders, the loose silk flapping.

Zamrian sucked in air. "Well, if negative thoughts brew in that little head of yours, cast them out." She lifted herself out of the chair and padded over to the balcony, pausing at the archway. "They say he's a bachelor, you know."

Mavrian stared into her mirror, meeting her reflection's grimace. "Pardon?"

"Scarmane Trokluss," Zamrian confirmed, folding her arms as she gazed at the sunset. "He's a bachelor."

Mavrian felt a tingle between her legs. The thought of the Veer prickled her skin. She stepped away from the mirror and sank into the chair, hiding her shame. "What of it?"

"The Gättengor ladies tell me they visited the Veer's chamber a few nights ago. They asked if he'd care to enjoy their flesh, but he declined."

Mavrian scoffed. "So? Häta and Henreesa would fuck Lucian Grögg if he asked to. Am I supposed to be surprised they'd lust after a Veer?"

Zamrian turned back to Mavrian, her face obscured by shadow. "I've spoken with him myself, Mavrian. Several times. The man offers me no advances. He pays no attention to my cleavage. His eyes do not wander down my shift."

Mavrian considered her friend, trying to gauge an expression on her darkened face. "What are you insinuating?"

Zamrian shook her head slowly, her long locks glimmering purple in the sun. "Members of the Veerkasn abstain from pleasures of the flesh. I'd seen it written before, but I always believed it was an old myth perpetuated to discredit them."

Mavrian lounged back in her chair, gazing up at the stone ceiling. Her tables and bookshelves projected bold shadows onto the grey surface to create magnificent wild art.

She'd heard the rumours that the Veerkasn practised celibacy, but that idea had melted away as soon as she'd met Scarmane Trokluss. A man *that* handsome had to have enjoyed his fair share of ladies. Perhaps gentlemen, as well. If he so chose, he could bed every courtier in Meelian. How could he deprive himself of such pleasure? How could he deny others of his inviting flesh?

"If that's the case, how would that make him a bachelor?"

"Come again?"

"You said he was a bachelor, suggesting marriage is a possibility. If Scarmane abstains from mortal pleasures, how can he be a bachelor?"

"*Scarmane?*" Zamrian whispered in shock.

Mavrian shrugged. "That's what he told me to call him."

"Is that so?" Zamrian's dark eyes narrowed. "Do you know *why* he carries such a peculiar name? Do you know *why* it's made up of Sylvian words?"

Mavrian did find it odd that the Veer's name consisted of the Sylvian terms for an old gash and a shaggy head of hair. "No. But I suppose you're about to tell me."

"His true name is Valgoth. Alongside his brother Darlgoth, he grew up on the streets of Tyrägatt, during the years of Sylvian occupation. The Trokluss brothers possessed an innate power, a holy blessing from the Twins. And discovering their magic, the Kinsmeer captured them. Forced them to serve their degenerate will."

"Vässa have mercy," Mavrian whispered. She couldn't imagine succumbing to such a wretched fate. "I thought Kinsmeer deplored the use of magic?"

Zamrian turned to face the horizon, her plump frame filling the archway. "When it suits them. But the Trokluss brothers possessed abilities never before seen by Sylvians. They tortured the brothers for years, draining their souls of their gods-given power. Until one night, as a storm brewed over the Gatten, the brothers managed to escape and ran for the hills in search of the border. But Valgoth was recaptured, and Darlgoth had a chance to save his brother, but he chose the path of cowardice and fled to save himself. Valgoth was presented before the people of Tyrägatt and tortured slowly. They scarred his body from scalp to toenail. They cut his long hair and fashioned it into a whip for his body. And then, after days of public torment, the time came to execute Valgoth once and for all. But as the executioner lifted his axe, Valgoth called out to Vällas, and our god spoke back. The executioner burst into flames, and Valgoth escaped."

As Zamrian paused, Scarmane's beautiful eyes flashed before Mavrian, but instead of inspiring lust, a deep sorrow cut into her heart. Those eyes had seen terror. That perfect flesh had known torture.

"Despite evading the axe, Valgoth died that day. The tortured soul that escaped Tyrägatt and joined the Bloody Hand named itself Scarmane Trokluss, a shadow of the boy he'd been before."

"How do you know this?" Mavrian asked. Zamrian liked to believe she knew everything there was to know about everyone. But learning secrets about a Veer not only seemed difficult, but dangerous. She was sure Scarmane didn't want the world to hear about his ordeal and might well silence those that spoke of it.

Zamrian turned back to Mavrian, her shadowy face twisting into a smile. "He told me so. Why do you think he named himself using Sylvian words? He wants his tormentors to be known."

Zamrian padded back over to Mavrian, pausing to admire herself in the mirror. She was the only other lady of Vicker's Tower to be invited to the Loress's banquet. She enjoyed a permanent place at the Meels table, owing to her impressive ability to talk her way into the hearts and beds of every cock-wielder at court,. A bittersweet luxury that did not extend to her sister, Cäda, who much preferred to hide away in Vicker's chamber.

Zamrian inspected herself in the mirror, folding her arms tight to her chest, pushing her breasts up to her neck. Her cleavage was the envy of Kleäm, stealing every lustful eye in every room. Mavrian wished her own weren't so flat that she could share in just a smidgeon of Zamrian's plumpness.

There came a knock at the door, and the serving girl, Mäga, shuffled into the chamber, carrying a pile of fresh linens.

"Set them down over there," Mavrian instructed her.

Mäga folded the sheets and organised them in a neat pile on top of the dresser. "The call for dinner will be soon, my lady."

"Thank you." Mäga reminded Mavrian of herself at thirteen: sheepish and submissive. "Now get yourself to the kitchens and ask Madam Corr for soup and scraps."

"Thank you, my lady. I... I will." The plump-faced little girl scuttled out, patting the door shut behind her.

"You spoil that girl," Zamrian groaned, meeting Mavrian's eyes through the mirror. "Treat your servant as your peer, and your peer they'll become."

Mavrian strained to remember who Zamrian was quoting. She'd heard the phrase spoken by a vassmir, or perhaps she'd read it in a work of philosophy.

"Who said that?" she asked, succumbing to curiosity.

"Your father." Zamrian stated, inspecting her nails. "I remember it vividly."

Meelian castle was a stone monolith that rose from the cliffs, warning all who beheld it to steer clear of the island. To the blind observer, the inhabitants had to be bloodthirsty marauders or omnipotent warlocks, but in truth, the courtiers of Meelian were a group of noxious carousers, preferring feeding and fucking than bothering about the world outside their walls.

Mavrian wasn't sure how long had passed since she'd last stepped into the great hall, but she knew she'd been holding Eplin's hand as he led her to his chamber. The memory was awful, but things had been a lot simpler back then.

"Announcing Zamrian Kamarn!" the fat herald boomed as Mavrian and Zamrian stepped through the open doorway, arm-in-arm. "She is the daughter of the esteemed Lennanite Kamarn, an honourable magistrate of Sela'Fundor!" He peered down his spectacles at Mavrian, noting her as an afterthought, sniffing the air around her as if he detected a stench. "And announcing Lady Mavrian Morr," he muttered, almost inaudible to the cackling courtiers that filled the hall.

"Think nothing of it," Zamrian whispered in Mavrian's ear. "They might spit on the name of Morr here, but you won't be around to hear it for much longer. Listen, when you get to Sela'Fundor, I want you to stay with my father. His manor is in the Spyre District, and he'd be more than happy to host you."

"I'll bear that in mind," Mavrian said as they entered the fray of pale faces amassed before them. For a brief moment, everyone stared at Mavrian, before returning to their conversations.

The court of Meelian was made up of the relatives of the Meels bloodline and the intermarried families of Grögg and Garr, and a few titleless sons of lorrs who had decided the indolence of Kleäm was the ideal lifestyle. There wasn't a pleasant face among them. Reesa was not worthy of attending court, and Cäda's reputation as a prude had seen the Kamarns' place at the table relegated to one seat.

The great oak doors shut behind them, sealing Mavrian's fate. She'd been locked in a prison of finely dressed monsters, a den of muzzled wolves.

She spotted Vassmir Käl, the man who had sacrificed a Kinsmeer and resurrected them into a Bloodkin. She'd imagined a man of such high standing with the gods would remain isolated in his temple, cutting all day and praying all night, but here he was drinking wine and conversing with dandies. The man he was talking to had his face obscured with a blood mask, signifying him as a participant in the fortnight of sacrifices that followed the Dräege. Such a commitment required a great deal of reflection, as the mask-wearer was repenting for the sins he'd forgotten to bleed for. Such a holy image seemed perverse in the midst of these sinners.

As they melded into the crowd, Mavrian tightened her grip on Zamrian's silk dress.

The men dressed in fitted robes draped to their ankles, their leather boots buckled with ornate silver finery. As was customary on the mainland, they'd slicked their hair back with oils and fat and outlined their eyes with black makeup. The women wore velvet gowns of azure and canary and crimson and a few donned imported cotton. They pinned their hair high above their heads, decorating their curls with shells and flowers. As she looked around, Mavrian noticed she was the only lady wearing her locks loose on her shoulders.

"I'll fetch us some goblets," Zamrian whispered in her ear, disappearing before Mavrian could suggest otherwise.

As Mavrian entered the maelstrom of warm bodies, wine-breath filled the air like a suffocating incense. She searched the maze of grinning faces for Scarmane Trokluss, but before she could register a single handsome feature, the drooling dog-face of Mudgar Vane filled her vision. His makeup gave him the appearance of a canine disguising itself as a Bloodkin.

"Lady Morr," he said to her, his snout twisting into a parody of a smile. His sweet aroma was overwhelming. He must've doused himself with a pint of perfume. "Been a long time since I seen *you* in these parts. Haven't seen you since... since..."

"The Dräege," Mavrian supplied, wishing she had a goblet to hide behind. *You better be quick, Zamrian.* She'd always abhorred the standing around that preluded the Loress's banquets. The courtiers took the opportunity to drown themselves in cheap Kinsmeeric wine and bark utter nonsense, and most were drunk by the time the food was served.

"Ah, yes," Mudgar said. "Spectacular sight, was it not? Vassmir Käl is truly blessed by Vällas's grace." He glanced around furtively, likely to ensure Käl wasn't within earshot. "Imagine wielding that power. The power to breathe life into the dead."

Mavrian groaned. Now she remembered why she detested conversing with this basic creature. Though he didn't loathe her like the others did, his inaptitude was painful to endure.

"Vassmirs do not *wield* power." *I can't believe I have to explain this to a grown man.* "The Twins work through them, as they do us all. The only difference is that people like you and I possess minds." *Poor choice of words.* "Wills of our own. Vassmirs open themselves up to serve as empty vessels. To allow the Twins to act through them."

Mudgar gaped at her, as if she'd spoken every sentence in some obscure Kinsmeeric language.

She glanced over at Käl and wondered if her words were any more valid than the dark utterings of the Kinsmeer. The vassmir was guffawing with a couple of smiling ladies. Back home in the Morren, the saying *vassmirs own no will, but that of our gods* rang true, as the clerics she'd witnessed were the embodiment of their faith. Vassmirs were supposed to keep themselves away from the rabble. And yet, though Käl had integrated himself into the infidel court of Meels and played her petty game of politics, the Twins blessed him with their gift.

Zamrian returned with two goblets of red wine. She handed one to Mavrian, then noted Mudgar's presence with a raised brow. "Lord Vane. I'm surprised to see you without a blood mask."

"What makes you say that?" he barked, spilling wine down his chin.

Zamrian glowered at him. "Last I recall, you were bemoaning how long it had been since your little pecker last slipped itself between a woman's legs. A *grown* woman, that is."

Mudgar blushed pink. "How did..."

"I learn of your indiscretions?" Zamrian finished his sentence. "You should pick your friends more carefully, Lord Vane." She flashed her eyes in the direction of Masser Bome and Lucian Grögg, who were engaged in deep conversation.

Mudgar followed her line of sight, then stormed over to the two young men and began jabbing his fingers into Masser's chest.

Mavrian dug her shoulder into Zamrian's side, stifling laughter. "That was cruel."

"Mudgar Vane is cruel," Zamrian corrected her. "Last night, he enjoyed a young serving girl against her will." Mudgar Vane screamed at his two friends, waving his arms about as he raved at them. "When you do leave this place, Mavrian, do the sensible thing and never look back."

———————

The reception lasted for what seemed like hours. Mavrian devoured three helpings of wine as she partook in idle chatter with Zamrian and the only tolerable Meels in existence. Mäs Meels was two years older than Mavrian, but her unintelligent statements and slow responses betrayed her as an inferior. Still, the way she raved about Mavrian's return to court made her feel somewhat welcome, even if she was the only courtier to harbour such an outrageous view.

As she scanned the drunk and almost-drunk faces around her, Mavrian noted two important absentees. It was customary for the Loress to make a grand entrance as the food was about to be served, and she'd evidently instructed Scarmane Trokluss to join in her tradition.

As the bells chimed high from the tower above the great hall, Mavrian's heart rose high in her chest. The servants reclaimed the goblets from the courtiers after many lords and ladies had downed what remained in their cups.

In a dance of sideways glances and fine shoes scuffing stone, the guests made their way to the long table at the end of the hall and found their places among the high-backed oak seats. The white linen tablecloth depicted scenes of shelly beaches lined with Crabfolk in silver thread, and Bloodkin and mermen engaged in a war of spears. The crockery was the same silver collection as always, but they'd been polished into mirrors.

Mavrian sat between Zamrian and an empty space that had to belong to Scarmane. As they sat and waited, whispers punctured the silence, and as the minutes passed, the chattering spread. Lucian Grögg flicked his brows at Mavrian from across the table, and Häta Gättengor scowled at her with plain disgust. Mavrian struggled to hold their gazes. *Pull yourself together. It's only a banquet, just like all the rest.*

"Are you ready for this?" she heard Zamrian whisper in her ear. "Remember, the fact you'll soon replace your uncle as loress means nothing to these people. The only thing stopping them from tearing you open is that you are the honoured guest of Scarmane Trokluss."

"Is that supposed to be reassuring?" Mavrian returned, shielding her lips from the watchful gaze of Vassmir Käl. "I'm surprised these infidels even respect the Veerkasn."

"The influence of the Bloody Hand is not lost on these people, Mavrian. Most owe their very existence to the Veerkasn in one way or another. Without the Hand, the Overlord could not have re-founded Plargross." She paused, considering her words, then dropped her voice even lower. "But it's not mere respect that holds their insults at bay. Look around you. These fragrant fools don't just eye you with contempt. They fear you."

Mavrian scanned the Bloodkin seated around her. Those that weren't engaged in their own conversations were staring at her, searing their eyes into her flesh.

"Why would they fear *me*?"

Zamrian half-smiled, and then frowned. She stared Mavrian dead in the eyes, but before her lips could part, the creaking of the great oak doors stole her attention. Every neck along the table twisted toward the sound. Two figures had entered the hall and were striding toward the table.

Everyone arose from their chairs and began clapping to welcome the arrivals.

"Announcing Jessa Meels, the Loress of Kleäm!" the herald announced. "And announcing Scarmane Trokluss, venerable Veer of the Veerkasn."

"Why would anyone fear me?" Mavrian repeated in Zamrian's ear, but her friend's focus did not waver from the approaching couple. "Is it because of Scarmane?"

Zamrian remained speechless as Jessa and Scarmane reached the table. As the couple took their respective seats, everyone seated themselves and began to don their napkins. Their eyes darted between Meels and Trokluss, awaiting permission to speak.

"Lords and ladies, I thank you for that warm welcome," the Loress said, addressing each one of them – except for Mavrian, who she skipped over. "And indeed, for your patience. I see before me a mass of hungry faces."

The courtiers buzzed with well-mannered amusement.

The Loress clapped her hands together, and the servants that had been hanging on the periphery approached the table bearing jugs of wine and water and started filling the silver goblets. Mavrian noticed, much to her astonishment, that when a plump serving girl leaned over Scarmane and filled his cup, the Veer smiled and thanked her. Still, he did not turn to acknowledge Mavrian, directing his placid smile in the Loress's direction instead.

"This feast marks a special occasion," Jessa continued. "I've gathered you all here, not only to share the finest wines this side of Ryne." The courtiers hummed with an appreciation of her humour. "I dine with you tonight in order to bid you all a fond farewell. You see, I have cause to leave this cherished place, for there are matters of highest importance for which I must attend to." Shocked whispers and irritated groans bubbled up along the table. "But fear not, friends... blood of my blood... it shan't be for long. There is no place for sadness or sorrow. Tonight we celebrate the pact of our friendship. Tonight we bask in the sanctity of this place." She raised her filled goblet, and in turn, the rest of the table followed suit. "Wine will flow like the richness of our blood. Purest of Bloodkin, untainted kin of my kin, tonight we sup in luxury. Tonight we dine among friends."

As Mavrian followed the rest of them in bringing her goblet to her lips, Jessa flashed her loathsome eyes upon her. There was something brewing within her, something conniving. Her umber orbs were assessing Mavrian as if for the very first time.

"To friends!" Scarmane happily agreed. Then, as the table returned to its ambient chatter, he turned to Mavrian and said, "You look spectacular, my lady. Truly. I see your mother in you, as fiercely as I detect your father's guile."

Mavrian offered a smile before retreating into her goblet and turning her gaze to the tablecloth. *How could he know about Mother?* Morella Morr died when Mavrian was a child and, according to Uncle Vanan, was a witless woman with no friends. And could he really have known her father? *Or does he seek to butter me up with false compliments?*

Before she could think to answer him, Scarmane rose from his chair, goblet in hand, and the table fell silent once more.

"To the Loress of Kleäm!" he proclaimed, lifting his goblet. The courtiers echoed his sentiment and sipped their wine. "I want to thank you, my lady, for your fine... no, *excellent* hospitality. I had heard of the kindness and compassion of Jessa Meels, of course. Your reputation truly precedes you. But never did I expect to be welcomed into your home so heartily. So readily. Like I were one of your own. My lady, truly, you have humbled me." He raised his goblet once more. "To the bonds that bind us, old and new!"

The courtiers echoed his words before drowning their encouragement in the sweetness of wine.

"You shall forever be welcome in my halls, my Veer," the Loress returned as Scarmane lowered himself into his seat. Then her eyes landed on a nearby servant. "Now, where is our feast, boy?"

The servant bowed low and scurried off toward the doors.

The table erupted in cheers as the doors opened once more, and two orderly lines of servants came streaming into the hall carrying silver dishes. As they reached the table, they laid fragrant servings of slod and mulefish and sea-sausages out for all to enjoy. The aroma was both appetising and revolting. Mavrian wasn't sure whether to eat or excuse herself to vomit. A serving girl leaned over Mavrian and slopped a fat grey slice of indiscernible fish onto her plate and drizzled white herb sauce all over it.

"Let the feast commence!" Jessa boomed over the cheerful prattle as a servant placed slodfish on her plate.

Mavrian stared at her plate, poking the soggy substance with her fork. Covered in greenish cream sauce, it looked and smelled like the least appetising thing in the world. Still, she couldn't recall the last time she'd eaten seafood. Most of the stews Madam Corr made consisted of shrooms and root vegetables.

"Not hungry, Lady Morr?" Scarmane spoke under his breath, not looking at her. "You know, the journey to Sela'Fundor can take weeks. I suggest you enjoy this while you can."

His tone was gruff, irritable. She had no idea how or if she should respond. Mavrian followed his suggestion – or instruction – and nibbled at her food. It was slod, and sweeter than any slod she'd sampled before. The Loress's feasts were always indulgent, but this fish was special.

The table existed in polite chatter for several minutes. Most spoke of the calm weather they'd enjoyed the last few days.

Häta Gättengor had turned pink from the wine. She was swaying in her seat, irritating those around her with inappropriate comments, digging her elbows into the ladies on either side of her. As she brought her goblet to her lips for the hundredth time, her sister, Henreesa, said something that made her slam her palm on the table.

A rapt silence rippled across the table. Häta's indistinct expression made it impossible to tell if she'd smacked the table in anger or good humour.

"You know," she barked, pointing her goblet at Scarmane. "When I first heard that an honourable Veer courted among us... Do you want to know the first thing that crossed my mind?" Her heavy eyelids blinked directionless at the bewildered faces around her. As she fell into a pause, the courtiers turned their attention to Scarmane, their eyes wide with fear.

"Nothing at all, because your mind is empty?" Lucian Grögg suggested, gaining a few chuckles, though Häta and Scarmane didn't seem to hear him.

Mavrian could feel the unease radiating from Scarmane. He

wiped his lips clean of wine and sauce with a handkerchief and set his goblet down gently.

"No, Lady Gättengor," he crooned. "What *did* cross your mind?"

Häta stared at him, dumbfounded. "Come, Veer Trokluss. I'm sure you're aware of the rumours that surround your order."

Scarmane's mask of calm was peeling away with her words and the silence that followed. Mavrian cursed herself for not taking the opportunity to escape to the privy when she had the chance. She had known that Häta Gättengor wasn't the smartest of ladies, but now the Loress's niece was proving herself to be no wiser than the slaughtered fish adorning the table.

"Stop this," Jessa Meels hissed over the whispers, raising her hand to silence them.

"The girl knows not of what she speaks," Vassmir Käl said to Scarmane, his widening eyes betraying his fear. "Some cannot handle the wine's alterations to the blood. And the moon's gaze solicits mistruths."

"Enough," Scarmane said to silence the vassmir, narrowing his eyes at Häta. "So, my lady, what *did* cross your mind when first you saw me? I'm dying to hear it."

Häta grinned at him, pouring wine down herself as she attempted to drink it. "You see, it's strange. When first I heard of your coming, I'd pictured a fearsome fellow. A cruel, conspiring bastard whose magic could be used to maim and torture." She shrugged her shoulders. "And yet you're quite the opposite. Kindly... virtuous. No different than the rest of us."

Mavrian realised she was digging her nails into the armrest of her chair. She remembered Zamrian telling her how the Gättengor sisters had attempted to lure the Veer into their bed. This wasn't the first slight Häta had enacted upon Scarmane.

"No different than the rest of us." Scarmane chewed on the words, trying to understand them. He paused for an agonising moment, staring at Häta. Then he lifted his goblet to his lips and slurped.

Mavrian noticed the terror etched into the Loress's face: her mouth gaped wide, her fat cheeks flapping like the wings of a fleeing bird. But she wasn't worried about Häta's hide. On the contrary, the look she gave her niece was one of undiluted abhorrence. Mavrian was quite certain the Loress would have slain her niece right there and then if it meant she could save herself from harm.

For as long as Mavrian had known her, Jessa had ruled Kleäm uncontested. But the Veer held supremacy in her court now.

As Scarmane continued to gaze at her, Häta Gättengor's drunken grin faded as she realised she'd just slighted one of the most powerful men in Plargross.

"My... my Veer," she stammered, her lips trembling. "Please... forgive me. The wine loosens my tongue. I know not of what I speak."

Scarmane rose to his feet, his goblet gripped tight in his hand. He inclined his head at Häta, then drew a long sip of wine as he basked in the silence. "Among such fine and admirable Bloodkin, I take your words to be a great honour."

The collective relief around the table was palpable. Jessa hid her reaction behind her goblet. As she moved the cup from her lips, Mavrian was sure she muttered something.

"Thank you, Lady Gättengor," the Veer continued. "These past days in your company... in the company of you all will be a memory I will not soon forget." He lowered his goblet then, his lips descending into a frown. "But I regret I must now deliver news to you that is far, far from welcome. I wish I could exchange pleasantries with you all through the night, but my time on Kleäm nears its end, and our companies will soon be parted. But before that comes to pass, there are things that must be said. Tidings that must be relayed."

The only thing Mavrian could hear was the sound of her own breathing – ragged, irregular. Scarmane scanned over them all, appearing indifferent to their fright.

"The Overlord has asked me to inform you all that the ceasefire between Plargross and the Sylvian Empire has come to an end."

A chill teased her spine. The news didn't surprise her. After all, it was only a matter of time before the war would again continue – but it was no less daunting a prospect. The war with the Kinsmeer had claimed the lives of her parents and brothers, Zamrian's mother and Reesa's entire family.

Rushed whispers echoed throughout the hall. Even the servants were in on the act.

"I attended the negotiations with Sylvia in Carthane myself. The Overlord's offer was gracious and just and far exceeded what the vermin deserved. But the Kinsmeeric swine rejected our peace, declaring that our war will only end when the Bloodkin race has been wiped off the face of this world."

The courtiers raged with disgust, waving their fists above their heads, knocking their goblets over, and spilling wine everywhere. They muttered and groaned and spat and insulted the very existence of Kinsmeer.

"Now," Scarmane spoke over them, raising his hands to quiet the crowd. "The Overlord has called for every lorr and loress in Plargross to attend his council in Sela'Fundor." He turned to Jessa and bowed his head, then flashed his eyes at Mavrian. "If it is war the Kinsmeer want, then I say it is a war they shall have!"

The courtiers confirmed their assent with loud cheers. Scarmane raised his goblet to toast, and the rest of the table followed suit.

"My lords and ladies... Loress Meels... our kin will triumph. By the grace of the Twins, they will triumph. By all that is pure in this world, our kin will triumph!"

"Our kin will triumph!" the courtiers echoed, guzzling their wine with a newfound fervour, joy returning to their faces.

As Scarmane dropped into his seat, he glanced at Mavrian, impassive. "And now you know why the Morren must be represented in Sela'Fundor. The standing army of your uncle's realm exceeds five thousand. Five-thousand souls that must bolster the Overlord's army."

Before Mavrian could respond, Lucian Grögg barked for all to hear, "You know, my Veer, there are Kinsmeer on Kleäm! I saw a few this morn. With my own eyes, no less."

"We should have them impaled!" a woman close to Jessa hissed. "No less than they deserve."

"Yes!" Lucian proclaimed, pointing at the woman who'd spoken out. "Loress Meels... Veer Trokluss... with both your leave, I shall lead this charge myself."

Mavrian remembered the Kinsmeer she'd encountered in the marketplace, the wretched people that had tried to sell her stock they'd likely stolen in order to trick foolish Bloodkin. She could picture their faces, their pig-pink skin, their eyes as blue as the ocean. Though she harboured no love for the creatures, the thought of Lucian Grögg butchering them in their sleep left a foul taste in her mouth. Though she supposed it was no less than their impure souls deserved.

Jessa exchanged a look with Scarmane before nodding at Lucian. Lucian and Mudgar Vane rose together, staggered back from their seats, and almost fell on their arses.

"My lady," they each said, bowing before the Loress before turning to Scarmane. "My Veer."

After the two men excused themselves, Scarmane returned to his meal and said to Jessa, "Have the defence preparations been met, my lady?"

"Yes, my Veer," the Loress replied, returning to her own plate, though she didn't appear to be enjoying it. "Our outer defences are impenetrable. Meelian has supplies enough to hold out for several months. But it would never come to that. There are twenty-four watchtowers overlooking the shores of this isle, each as fortified as a citadel."

"I know well the defences of Kleäm, my lady, having spent the last week studying them in some detail." Scarmane offered her a wry smile. "I do not fear an attack on your isle. Far from it. Though I must ask, who have you elected to rule in your stead after we set sail for Sela'Fundor?"

"My eldest, Bënar," Meels said, offering her son a weak smile.

Bënar Meels was a fat blob of existence, much like his mother. His hobbies included placing bets on slave duels and terrorising the courtiers with expulsion if they did not satisfy his whims. He was the foulest player in the game of the Meelian court. But he smiled at the Veer with grace, moved his chubby arms and bulbous face with exaggerated poise.

"Very good," Scarmane said to Bënar. "You shan't be without the aid of your Overlord. Nor that of my order. For it cannot be forgotten that, in years past, the towers of Meels were some of the first to fly the red flag of Plargross."

"They were *the* first, my Veer," Bënar said, bearing his crooked teeth. "And we shall be once more." He raised his goblet to make a toast. "There will always be a Plargross!"

The table raised their cups and echoed his sentiment. As she sipped her wine, Mavrian found Bënar's words humorous, as the Loress's son hadn't even visited the mainland. Though Kleäm belonged to the realm of Plargross, the island existed miles off the coast of Ryne.

"The faith of this isle is strong, my Veer," Vassmir Käl said as the cups were lowered. He'd remained unusually quiet during the meal, his iris-less eyes studying the table, awaiting the perfect time to strike. "No invader could break the spirit of these peoples."

"Ah, yes. *Faith.*" Scarmane chewed that last word over. "That is in no small part thanks to *your* good work." He offered the vassmir a smile, but Mavrian detected contempt twinkling in his eyes.

"I cannot credit myself alone," Käl said, wearing a proud smirk. "The faith of this isle has always been strong. Long before my coming. As Bënar says, the people of Kleäm were the first to rally behind our Overlord. Upon these shores, the purest of blood dwells."

Scarmane's eyes narrowed at him. "Only, I *do* credit you, Käl." He let the statement linger like a bad smell, invading the nose of every Bloodkin. "You have spread to these kinsmen the teachings of Aegal. You have performed miracles in front of their very eyes.

Wonders of godly intervention. In fact…" He paused, taking a drawn-out sip of wine. "I had the pleasure of witnessing one of these feats myself. And it was quite the spectacle, wasn't it, Käl? In fact, I'd hazard to say, your actions were enough to quell any descent here for years to come. With your good work, the people of Kleäm will be cutting themselves for centuries."

Käl's grin had disappeared. Like Mavrian, he'd surely realised the miracle Scarmane referred to was the one performed at the Dräege, when he sacrificed a Kinsmeer and saw her reborn as a Bloodkin.

"I do not understand your meaning," Käl said, twisting his fork around his fingers with one hand and tapping his goblet-handle with the other.

"Are you sure about that?" Scarmane downed his wine and slammed his goblet onto the table. The whispers that were being exchanged up and down the table ceased with a collective gasp. Every eye fixed on the Veer and vassmir.

"My Veer," Käl began. "I…"

"You're a fraud," Scarmane spoke over him. "You're a deceiver. Your miracles are no more genuine than your words of appeasement."

A lump formed in Mavrian's throat, as though an invisible hand had wrapped its fingers around her. Her body tingled with dreadful anticipation.

A warmth emanated from Scarmane. His anger radiated heat. He locked his snarl on Käl, who seemed more confused than insulted. The Loress blinked her bulbous eyes between the two men like a fearful frog.

Zamrian tugged on Mavrian's sleeve, leaning into her ear. "We should leave."

Fear rooted Mavrian to the spot, her gaze glued to Scarmane. She parted her lips to whisper back, but the indistinct gurgling of her tongue offered no words.

Käl was the first to speak. "My Veer. Perhaps there has been a misunderstanding."

Scarmane straightened in his seat. "I was there, Käl. I was there in the fourth row. I've witnessed seventeen Dräege miracles during my lifetime. And only the seventeenth was staged."

Käl's face creased – at first, Mavrian thought he was about to burst into tears, but his brows furrowed deep into the bridge of his nose, his lip curling in disgust. "You should watch your tongue, boy. Holding the title of Veer does not give you the right to address me like some common brigand. I know not what you accuse me of. I say you should keep your forked tongue firmly behind your teeth and *think* before you spit venom, you tortured son of a pauper!" He twisted into a goading smile. "Oh, yes. That's just it, isn't it? The Sylvians tortured and scarred your flesh from top to bottom. Pray tell me, when they carved into your face, did the blade touch your brain?"

Scarmane jumped to his feet, his flailing arm knocking Mavrian's goblet over, splashing wine all over her dress. Still, she remained rooted to her chair.

Käl ambled to a standing position, his complexion pink.

Jessa's face was a mask of terror. "My Veer... *please.*"

"The Dräege was a lie!" Scarmane spat before turning to Jessa. "Your vassmir is a peddler of lies. You see, when I came to board my master's ship in Sela'Fundor not three weeks ago, I happened to pass a slavers' auction. A merchant offloading captured Kinsmeer and Hei, and traitor Bloodkin. Now, I never forget faces, my lady. And when I saw the Dräege offering in your temple, I saw the same wretched face that had belonged to a Bloodkin slave. The *Kinsmeer* Käl transformed had *never* been Kinsmeer! Käl here used trickery to make these people believe the Twins work through him. To suggest Vällas and Vässa would deign to make Bloodkin of Kinsmeer is to spit on the Twins' very existence." His ire returned to the vassmir. "The Twins do not speak to you, do they? They don't so much as whisper in your ear, *do they?*"

Käl slammed his fist into the table. Much to Mavrian's horror, she noticed that a sliver of red had appeared in the man's eyes, a narrow ring surrounding his iris. Vassmirs lost the colour in their irises after consuming their potions during initiation. But Käl had not.

He was no vassmir.

Käl seemed unaware of the exposure of his lie. "I have *never* in all my long years been insulted by such callous... belligerent nonsense. You speak ill... You speak out of turn, Scarmane Trokluss." He lowered his voice, the grin returning to his face. "Or should I say... *Valgoth.*"

The Veer's true name was the last thing Käl ever spoke. A blinding light flashed in front of him. As Mavrian closed her eyes, piercing screams stabbed in her ears.

As she reopened her eyes, she saw the vassmir still standing there, but where there had once been a head, there was only a void. Blood oozed from the stump that had once been his neck, squirting dark liquid all over the tablecloth. As to where the head had vanished to, that was a mystery. As the headless corpse fell backwards and collapsed in a heap, the hall filled with terror.

Zamrian fell out of her chair, dragging Mavrian with her as she staggered back from the table. The courtiers ran in every direction, smashing into each other, yelling indiscernible nonsense as they fled the table.

"What have you done?" the Loress was screaming. "How... how *could* you?"

Zamrian pulled at Mavrian's dress. "Come with me... *now!*"

"No," Mavrian snapped, swatting her hand away. "If you want to leave, then leave." Her friend didn't need any convincing. She retreated as fast as she could.

Mavrian couldn't leave the Veer now.

In a matter of moments, Mavrian and Scarmane and Jessa were standing alone at the table.

"The man was a pretender," Scarmane said, turning to Mavrian. "One cannot take the names of Vällas and Vässa in vain. One cannot claim to speak with them and work against Aegal's teachings. You understand that. Don't you?"

"I do," Mavrian answered, her body vibrating with energy. At first, she thought fear gripped her, but as a smile crossed her lips, she realised it was something else.

"How *could* you?" Jessa was saying. "I welcomed you into my home! My courtiers treated you as one of their own. And you repay us by *murdering* our *vassmir*? You cannot act this way. I will not allow it. Käl served my father before me. He was an honourable man."

Scarmane spun on his heel to face her. "Käl was a traitor. You see, as I explored your archives, I came to inspect the temple records, and I learned that your *honourable man* was funnelling temple donations into his personal estate in Versalan. And do not presume to tell me what I can or cannot do, my lady. My master sent me here to ensure the defences of your shitty island can withstand Sylvian assault. Not out of love or respect for you, but because this fucking *speck* of land holds strategic significance to the Overlord."

"You're a pig!" Jessa spat, her cheeks wobbling with rage. "You're a monster! And I will not sail with you! Not anywhere!"

Scarmane narrowed his eyes at her. "Unfortunately for you, my lady, you have no choice. The Overlord *demands* your presence in Sela'Fundor. Both of you." He turned to Mavrian. "And it is not only the Overlord that sends *your* summons, my lady. I have been asked to relay the message that Lorr Eplin Garr awaits you in Sela'Fundor."

Feast of Sorrows

They say that when summer fades and the brown autumn is upon the world. The Goddess turns away from us. Away from the kingdom, away from the king. And from now until the winter ends and the colours of the world return, the Goddess has deserted us.

Jurgen Irvaye had uttered that verse the day he left Balenmeade. After casting his finery into the fire, he'd donned a simple habit and abandoned the Krämise forever, leaving Hanzus alone to rule his Goddess-forsaken realm.

Despite the signet ring strangling his finger and the cloak of nobility around his neck, Hanzus did not feel like a baron. Not a legitimate one, at any rate. So long as Jurgen was alive – albeit in exile – the Balenmanor would never be his home. The very walls reeked of Jurgen. The tapestries, paintings and ornaments were all his. Jurgen consigned everything that came before him to the fire. None had escaped his wrath, not even the artwork. And his wrath still haunted this place.

"My *lord?*"

The voice tickled the insides of Hanzus's ears, stirring him from the world of thought. The image that was Jurgen's twisted features cracked and darkened like a damaged painting, and in its place, the chubby face of Myles Erman appeared before him.

"My lord, your people await you," the voice came again, confirming it belonged to Sheriff Erman. As his bovine features took form, his droopy eyes revealed nervousness, darting between Hanzus and somewhere off to his right.

"What are you talking about?" Following the sheriff's eyes, Hanzus realised he stood before a crowd of a hundred eager faces.

"Your people await your speech, my lord. Without your word, the festival cannot commence."

Of course... It all came back to him. He was about to deliver a speech that would usher in the beginning of Harvest. The sheriff had been addressing the crowd before him, and it was then that Jurgen had crept inside his head like a pregnant spider, laying its eggs of dread and doubt and despair, drawing him away from his people. His purpose.

Hanzus stiffened, addressing the attentive, excited crowd. Their eyes lingered on his every move, respect and fear sealing their lips. All they required was their lord's permission to flock to the ale-and-dance tents now plaguing the Balenmanor's grounds to make merry into the early hours.

Hanzus approached the edge of the low stage, stepping into the light of the staked torches surrounding the platform. He unfurled the parchment that was tucked into his coat and read the speech aloud:

"Folk of the Krämise. Fellow kinsmen. We are gathered here this eve to celebrate all of our achievements. To acknowledge the dedication and hard work that has allowed us to reap such a remarkable harvest. And we thank Our Lady, who shines her grace upon us nightly, without whom our crops would not grow, and our hearts would not beat." He paused, reading the last few lines of the speech over and over. They were the same old words he repeated every year, the same tired platitudes and recurring promises. Gazing out at the crowd, he tucked the parchment inside his pocket and, against his better judgement, echoed Jurgen's favourite verse: "They say that when the summer fades, and the brown autumn is upon the world, the Goddess turns away from us. Away from the kingdom, away from the king. And from now until the winter ends and the colours of the world return, the Goddess has deserted us." The crowd blinked up at him, radiating confusion. He let it simmer a while before continuing. "Those words were told to me once, many, many years ago. But I've come to realise that the Goddess does not turn away from us. The love of Our Lady, our Eternal Mother, is unconditional. The Goddess will never turn her back on her people, so long as her people do not turn their backs on her. Tonight, we make plain our love and devotion. Tonight we rejoice in the evidence of her love and care. For we have plentiful food and drink, and it is all of her making. Tonight, my people... my *friends*... we devour it all!"

The crowd erupted in hysterical applause. Cries of joy and whoops of assent filled Hanzus's ears as he descended the stage. Young ladies handed him flowers of affection, and gentlemen bowed and shook his hand.

Heatha's scowl greeted him as he emerged from the crowd, murdering the momentary joy. Their children scurried after her.

"My lady," he said through gritted teeth, before turning to his children.

Francessa was a woman now and never had it been so evident than in this moment. Her sequined gown of honey-yellow complimented her regal stance and eloquent figure. The fire in her eyes told him the spirit of his blood flowed through her veins.

"Father," she said, flashing a pretty smile. Despite inheriting Heatha's flat jaw and long neck, she possessed brilliant-blue eyes and a chiselled nose befitting of the name Irvaye. "Your speech was... different."

"Your speech was incorrect," Heatha snapped. "We do hire scribes for a reason, you know."

Hanzus ignored her and ruffled Hessan's curls. "My son and heir." The boy had dressed well for the occasion. Though only ten, he was clearly a lord in the making. His smile possessed charm. His

Irvaye-eyes would one day pleasure ladies with no more than a look. He would command aldermen and lead armies in the field. He would rule.

"What was that about the Goddess turning her back on us?" Heatha hissed, linking with his reluctant arm. They walked ahead of the procession, leading the courtiers towards the feasting tent at the end of the field.

"You wouldn't understand," Hanzus returned. After all, she had loved Jurgen once.

The entertainment began with Krämisen dancers, which was followed by a short rendition of *A Mourner's Good Morning* by the Mummer's Guild, the actors delivering their lines over a musician's playful lute.

Hanzus's table was situated back behind the stage, encircled by his noxious, most esteemed guests. Heatha and Francessa sat on either side of him. Hessan sat beside Denzus the Younger, whose face was red from the day's flow of wine.

The mummers and musicians alternated their attention between Hanzus and the four long tables situated on the other side of the stage. There the other guests sat – lesser-aldermen and knights, merchants and magistrates, and the stewards of the Balenmanor.

As the play came to an end, the tent filled with polite applause. After the mummers filtered off the stage, a group of bards equipped with various instruments joined the lutist. Their song was lamentably light and cheery.

Hanzus sighed as he scanned the faces seated at his table. Fritt Karston, the chief administrator of central-Krämise, was dressed more like an emperor than an alderman, though he slurped his wine like a Gunnic savage. His enormous stomach rested on the edge of the table.

Denzel Marman, the ward of the west, was a skeleton in

comparison. The elderly alderman wore a simple mustard tunic with indigo buttons, his black wig only partially hiding the evidence of his baldness. He was joined by his son, Sir Mavery, who, as far as appearances go, was a younger version of the same man.

The only other notable guest was the ancient Bishop Clarayne, who'd presided over the Balenmanor's masses since Hanzus was born.

Hanzus would have traded them all for a gang of thieves if it meant avoiding the same jokes and pleasantries that he heard every single year. They all wanted something from him, even now, as they stared into their reflective silverware, waiting to be fed.

A line of servants stood along the length of the canvas wall, like soldiers awaiting their call to battle. And it came. Within moments, invisible hands pinned back the various entrance flaps, and floods of servants entered, holding trays and dishes. The turkeys and chickens were sweating with a glistening glaze. The honeyed vegetables oozed with oil and chopped herbs. They laid the symbolic crown of the feast, a boar holding a red apple between its jaws, in front of Hanzus. It appeared to be grinning at him, full of mocking and contempt. Still, the large beast served as a means to shield himself from the foul faces gathered around.

A serving boy took a knife to the boar and presented Hanzus with a generous slice. Hessan was salivating like a dogman as a buxom serving girl carved away at the boar and slapped a thick slice on his plate. The boar's grin remained intact even as the servants ripped and pulled and sliced away at its body.

The servants replaced the pre-banquet wine with the feasting variety.

"Gelemonian," Denzel Marman remarked, holding his goblet to his nostrils. "Imperial era. From Theanes, if I'm not mistaken."

"You know your wines, my lord," Heatha said, sipping her own with practised poise. She wasn't fooling Hanzus. He'd seen her drink it from the bottle before. "The Baron and I have amassed quite the collection here in Balenmeade. Isn't that right, my lord? Wines purchased from as far as the cliffs of Stemgrosa to the bays of Nanderra. I must, though, confess that my personal favourite is the Bervanoux of nine-hundred-and-forty-four." She waved a servant over, who then filled the alderman's goblet with a different wine.

"Nine-hundred-and-forty-four," Marman said, sipping the beverage. "Terrible year for the Empire. Excellent year for wine."

The guests chuckled politely, applauding the alderman for his knowledgeable wit.

"Terrible time for the Krämise," Hanzus added, stripping the man of his accomplished smile. "If I'm not mistaken, the Middle Kingdom Blight started around that time."

Heatha's lip was quivering. "And yet, my lord, was it not your ancestor Wendel that survived said blight and filled your cellars with much of the wine we have today?"

Hanzus considered her impassive face as he chewed on the boar. "A couple, perhaps, but the majority appeared much later. That Bervanoux is no older than you and I. But still, fine wine it remains." He raised his goblet to call for a toast. "To the existence of wine. May it fill our cups and bellies till the end of our days."

"To wine," the guests echoed, seeming bemused but drinking all the same.

As the table returned to polite, cautious chatter, Hanzus turned his attention to the bards upon the stage. He found himself entranced by their bright finery and the exaggerated expressions they pulled as they strummed away on their lutes and blew on their pipes.

He gazed past them, scanning the four tables spanning the length of the tent. The guests tore at their meat like savages. Flakes of carrot, broccoli and apple sprayed the air. Ale and wine splashed the grass-floor, spilling onto the tablecloths and trickling down their chins. Some seemed unsure whether they should eat or drink, and several attempted both at the same time.

He saw the chamberlain, Brendal Jupe, conversing with Myles Erman. He spotted Reymond and Barrett laughing with Cay and Lew. As Hanzus watched, it became clear that Barrett felt uncomfortable in his surroundings. He didn't once move to speak, and when he did laugh along with the others, he did so nervously, glancing at the canvas walls, perhaps expecting a monster to slice through them at any moment.

Then Barrett turned his head in Hanzus's direction. Their eyes met for a moment – baron and steward united by disillusionment – before the boy shied away and stared into his cup.

Hanzus remembered Heatha telling him Barrett was the one that found Vilka hiding in the stables. He wondered if the girl had revealed anything to the young steward. Though he supposed it mattered not. After all, the girl would soon be gone.

A clattering of cutlery stole his attention back to the table.

"The sweet potato's a fine complement to the duck, my lord," Fritt Karston said with his mouth full, gesturing for a servant to fill his plate with more vegetables. "A most delectable grouping."

"The plum sauce is Goddess-sent," Bishop Clarayne said, bowing his silver head. "'Tis a fine tribute to Our Lady. A fitting ode to a successful harvest."

Hanzus inclined his head to the bishop.

"May I have a cup of wine, father?" Francessa spoke in his ear. "Just one. I'll have no more, I swear it."

"Now, Francessa," Heatha intercepted. "We spoke about this." She looked at Hanzus, searching for his support, and, receiving none, glowered at her daughter. "The answer is no."

But Francessa's eyes stayed fixed on Hanzus. "Father?"

The whole table was anticipating his answer now. All had paused from their gluttony, fat, and wine dripping from their lips.

"I don't see the harm in a cup or two," he said, prompting a few to raise their eyebrows.

"Oh... thank you, father. Thank you so much."

Hanzus clicked his fingers, and a portly servant poured some Thelian red into Francessa's goblet. Heatha's eyes ground into her husband. She stabbed her slice of boar, no doubt wishing it was his flesh.

"Have you sampled the Krämisemead this evening, my lord?" Fritt Karston asked, delighting everyone with his diversion. "The meaderies have achieved a new standard of perfection." He flashed the baron a wide, almost painful grin that revealed a large gap between his two front teeth. He looked like a giant rat. "Yes, quite excellent."

"I haven't tried it, no, Lord Karston."

"*You*, boy!" Karston snapped at a nearby servant. "Fetch your lord and lady some Krämisemead. With haste!"

Two servants made to leave at the same time.

"Surely one of you is enough. We require mead, not another bloody boar," Heatha joked, winning her a chorus of exaggerated laughter.

"You will be able to taste the improvements from last year's brew, I'm sure of it," Karston said, as one of the servants disappeared behind the flap that led to the kitchens. "I sampled a batch only this morning. Exquisite. Absolutely exquisite."

Hanzus wondered how it had come to pass that an alderman had sampled the mead stock before his liege lord, but he couldn't bother to question it.

"Will you be partaking, my lord?" Heatha directed at Marman.

"I would be delighted to, my lady," Marman replied. "I hear you had some input in this year's flavour. Is that so?"

"*Is* that so?" Hanzus echoed. This was the first he'd heard of it.

"I confess," Heatha said, unsmiling, "I may have given a few passing suggestions. Though I cannot say, I contributed much. Krämisemead is, after all, a staple of this great barony. There is little room for improvement."

Well, you would have to say that in case the brew tastes like shit.

"My lady, you are as humble as you are talented," Marman said. "I'm sure your suggestions proved invaluable."

When the servant returned with a bottle of honey-brown liquid and a tray of empty cups, the table fell silent with anticipation. They poured the baron's first. A nutty aroma emanated from the bronze cup, and as the metal reached his lips, the thick taste of honey and spices filled his mouth. It was, without doubt, the sweetest mead he'd ever tasted. That seemed a welcome alteration at first, but then, as the aftertaste kicked in and his throat burned, the sweetness turned bitter.

"Delicious," he lied, licking the substance now stuck to his lips. "Most... delicious." Krämisemead was a staple export. If news circulated that the Baron of the Krämise disliked his own brew, the gossipers would riot.

"I'm glad you think so," Heatha said, but she was wincing as she lowered her own goblet.

Karston groaned with satisfaction as he lowered his cup. "A tremendous sampling. Truly." Then he turned to Hanzus, his grin unwavering. "My lord, if I may be so bold, might I make a speech to your people?"

The request came as a surprise to everyone.

Hanzus stifled a laugh. Karston had his head in the clouds if he believed the gathering wanted to hear another speech. They all wanted to stuff their faces with chicken and boar and to drown their sorrows in ale and wine before the grasp of winter had them.

Past the stage, he saw smiling, laughing faces seated at the four long tables. Many were moving their heads in time with the bards' instrumental arrangement. They wanted to forget their miserable lives for the evening. They wanted to drink so much their hangovers would last them days.

Hanzus had no doubt that Karston's speech would bore them all to death. He would drone and ramble, stumbling over the clunky words his scribes had provided him with. It would be entertaining.

"Very well, Lord Karston."

Fritt's face turned red as he lifted himself from his seat, panting. When a serving girl hurried over to aid him, he swatted her away with his fat fingers. He straightened his frilly collar, took a deep breath, then marched over to the stage and whispered to one of the bards.

The music ceased, and the entire tent fell silent. Knives and forks and goblets clinked as they rested on the tables. Every neck craned toward the stage. They blinked dumbly up at Karston, many clearly drunk, but none dared protest the interruption.

Though a minor nobleman in every possible way, the people of Balenmeade were well aware of Fritt's longstanding friendship with Heatha Irvaye. He didn't have their respect, but they feared Heatha enough to humour him.

"My Lord and Lady Irvaye! Ladies and gents of the feast!" Karston waved his tree-trunk arms about, his grin alternating between Hanzus and the common tables. "It is my pleasure to address..."

The alderman dropped his arms, pausing indefinitely as he gazed out at the mass of petty lords and commoners. Hanzus was about to question why the fool had stopped, then he heard a guttural cry.

Hanzus rose from his seat, surprise willing him into action, a chill grasping his spine. The sound came again as a rasping shout, a low gurgle filling the canvas hall. Most of the guests had risen and were glancing around in search of the noise's owner.

Another cry sliced through the air.

Hanzus noticed the lines of bodies seated between the two central tables were stirring. The guests were jumping out of their chairs, pushing themselves up against the tables, creating a pathway carving through the centre of the tent. A dark figure was passing through the gap, pushing past the few bodies that remained in its way.

A skinny wretch of a man, dressed neck-to-toe in rags, waddled over to the edge of the stage. His skull of a face glanced up at Fritt Karston. "Hail, my lord. Are you the Baron of the Krämise?"

"Who let this beggar inside?" Karston barked over the man's shoulder. "Guards! Guards! *Where* are the guards? Remove this brigand from our sight at once!"

Protesters roared at the intruder, pointing at him accusingly. The beggar's eyes passed over Karston and explored Hanzus's table.

Hanzus craned his neck around Heatha for a better look at the man. He was quite elderly, perhaps as old as Bishop Clarayne. He looked to be on the verge of death. His eyes sank deep into his skull. Bruises mottled his wrinkly skin. His robe was torn in several places. Matted grey hair obscured much of his face.

The vagrant had some nerve interrupting the feast of a baron. Perhaps he had consumed too much Rooksbrew or had swallowed the wrong sort of mushroom.

"What are you all standing around for?" Karston croaked in disbelief. "Arrest this fiend at once!"

The guardsman, Ache, stood and unsheathed his sword. Pamen jumped in front of the beggar, shielding him from the stage.

"Have him cast out!" Karston shrieked, waving his hands. "And see to it, this does not happen again! Take him *away!*"

"Hanzus... Irvaye," the beggar groaned, clutching at his chest. "I must speak with him. Where is the... Baron of the... Krämise?"

Hanzus pushed Heatha out of his way. As he approached the stage, Pamen and Ache grabbed the old vagrant by the shoulders.

"Who is this man?" Hanzus called out, his voice silencing the room.

"Simply an old scoundrel, milord," Ache replied. "Pamen and I'll cast him out. But not before we show him what it means to interrupt the feast of Baron Irvaye."

"Wait," Hanzus instructed them, stopping beside Karston on the edge of the stage. "Tell me your name, beggar."

"My lord!" the man cried, close to tears. He struggled against the guards' grip, but his slender frame was no match for their thick arms. His eyes were brown pits of despair, betraying him as a foreigner. He stared at Hanzus, his body trembling. "Lord Irvaye, it's... it's really you. I come to you as a messenger. My lord, I've been sent."

"*Messenger?*" Karston scoffed, almost choking. "Do you take us for fools, man? Where are your colours then, *sir messenger?*" He turned to Hanzus. "My lord, wretches will say anything to win them a warm meal."

Hanzus waved him away. "Message? What message? Who has sent you?"

"I... I... beg your gracious pardon, my... lord..."

"Spit it out, cur!" Karston roared at him. "The Baron of the Krämise asked you a question!"

The messenger didn't seem to hear him. He kept his tearful eyes locked on Hanzus, begging him for forgiveness with a look. "It's your father, my lord. Your father is... your father is..." He faltered, lowering his head to the ground.

Hanzus could feel his heart pounding in his chest. The face of Jurgen flashed before his mind's eye, beholding him with a frown. *Look at what you've become,* it was saying, shaking its head in disappointment. *See how little you've achieved.*

"My father?" he found himself saying. Jurgen's face merged into that of the old messenger.

The messenger blinked up at Hanzus. "He's sick, my lord. As a matter of fact, he's... he's soon to die."

The old man squirmed and was quick enough to wriggle free from the guards' grip. He staggered forward, but before he could take another step, he collapsed in a heap on the ground.

One of the aldermen's daughters rushed forward and inspected the body. "He's alive, my lord. He's still alive!"

"Jurgen is sick?" Hanzus asked himself, retreating to the table and sinking into his chair. "Jurgen is... going to die?"

Heatha was beside him, squeezing his arm, her fingers cold to the touch. She was talking to him, hoping to placate him with words of encouragement, but he didn't hear a thing she said. The tables tweeted with chatter, melding into a single sound of fury and distress.

The face of Jurgen appeared in front of him once more, floating somewhere between thought and reality. This time the head was nodding at him, its leathery flesh creased in a smile. *Even now, on the other side of the kingdom, you mock me.*

"Hans... *Hans?*" Heatha was saying, tugging on his sleeve.

Four years had passed since Jurgen's last letter. The former baron's silence had come as a reprieve, as welcome as the end of a bone-gnawing dirge. And now, his memory was flooding back into Hanzus's mind, filling him with its poison.

"You don't think it could be plague. Do you?" Heatha hissed in his ear.

"Have this *messenger* escorted to the dungeons!" Fritt Karston boomed over everyone.

Ache lifted the man's limp body with ease.

The mocking face of Jurgen had faded. Denzus the Younger was staring at Hanzus, swallowing his drink with measured sips. Francessa and Hessan were sobbing as Bishop Clarayne failed to comfort them.

Hanzus turned to Heatha and offered her a weak smile, swallowing bile. "I think I shall retire for the evening, my dear."

"But Hans... what about the dance?" She blinked at him, incredulous. "A baron cannot forgo his own dance. The courtiers will ask questions. Imagine the scandal. And... and... the feast is not yet over."

"Jurgen is dying, you heartless bitch. You alone have spent all my coin on this fucking festival. Now you alone can enjoy it." And with that, he stood and stomped out of the tent.

Vodka and Mead

His name was Hanzus of the House of Irvaye, but the people called him the Baron Without Sorrow. A man of iron will and unyielding resolve. A man who'd overseen torture and ordered hundreds of executions. A man who could fight a pack of wild Dogmen without breaking a sweat. A warrior. A diplomat. One of the most powerful and feared men in the whole of Gadensland.

And yet, the man had unravelled in front of his entire court, his thick armour penetrated for all to see, revealing weakness, brittleness.

The Baron of the Krämise had refused to take any further part in his own festival, his own celebration of the Goddess. The courtiers would celebrate Harvest without their liege lord. And they were already whispering.

"Baron don't care about Harvest," the Baroness's lawyer, Marc Kest declared to all the stewards. "Baron don't care about his people."

"The night is ruined," Edvard Linn groaned. "What will folk be murmuring on the morrow? Imagine what the papers will say."

"You speak out of turn," Edgar Vassel grumbled at them. "Do not forget what house you serve, gentlemen."

Barrett and Reymond escaped from the squabbling stewards as

they all left the feast, slipping into a commoner's ale tent situated close to the Balenmanor. The other stewards chose to follow the Baroness and her courtiers to the dance pavilion, where they would watch knights and aldermen dance as they sipped their wine and politely discussed the downfall of the kingdom. Barrett decided sharing ale with peasants was a far more interesting prospect than watching Alderman Karston's belly bouncing as he danced with the Baroness, and Reymond needed no convincing.

"Does the Baron realise how much coin has been thrown at this night?" Reymond sighed, accepting the ale Barrett had purchased from the bar. "How much *effort*? Goddess, have mercy. I slaved in those stables for nothing."

"You did what now?" Lew asked, scratching at his scalp. Lew and Cay already sat at a table when Barrett and Reymond entered the commoner's tent. Seemingly, they too preferred cheap ale to fine wine.

"Never mind," Reymond muttered into his cup.

Considering how rowdy the taverns and alehouses became during Harvest, this tent was perhaps the calmest drinking establishment in all of Balenmeade. The punters sipped their Kramisen and whispered amongst themselves. They were all much older than Barrett and perhaps found the intense merrymaking found in the rest of town too much to bear.

"'Tis an omen," Lew said, staring into Barrett's eyes. "Baron's cursed us all for the winter. To hold Harvest celebrations without the one's baron... Lads, it don't bode well for none of us. Soon as the Baron took his leave for the eve, the feast and dance should've been called off."

"Never thought I'd see the day," Cay concurred, wiping his lips clean. "Fancy fleeing your own feast."

"Shouldn't you have taken your leave also?" Reymond muttered at the valets. "You're his attendants."

Lew shrugged. "Far as I'm concerned, Baron retiring for the night means the lad and I are off the hook. We can do as we please, for now."

"And speak as we please," Cay added, grimacing at Barrett. "We're well and truly fucked, aren't we? Soon as the papers print that our baron abandoned his feast, every literate man in the kingdom will come to distrust the Krämise. Even more than's customary. What bodes ill for the baron bodes ill for the barony."

Cay had spoken those last words loud enough for all to hear. The old faces gathered around them broke from their conversations and glared at the four servants.

"*Quiet*," Barrett hissed at the valet. "We don't want this night to get any worse."

Reymond didn't seem to hear him. "Can you imagine the King's face when he reads of all that transpired here? When he hears that Jurgen Irvaye is dying."

"I don't think King Halmond will pay much mind to the ramblings of an old vagrant," Barrett said under his breath. "You speak like you believe the old man."

"It doesn't matter what the scandal *is*," Reymond said. "*Any* scandal is bad when it comes to the attention of the King. My father says Halmond already watches Balenmeade with a cautious eye. He awaits any hint of a whisper of rebellion. Some believe he *wants* a rebellion in order to supplant the House of Irvaye. To be rid of them once and for all."

Barrett scoffed much louder than he'd intended. A few scowls shot toward him. "*Rebellion?*" He tried to whisper. "Why on earth would anyone suspect the Krämise of rebellion?"

Reymond bit on his lip. "Kings have feared rebellion from the south ever since the formation of the Krämise. Come, you know that. You know the House of Irvaye once ruled the kingdom, and it would do so again if it had the opportunity. At least if Heatha had her way."

Barrett sighed in disbelief. Reymond Morgen, ever the peddler of conspiracies. This deep talk was too much for his weary mind. He needed another drink, and fast. "What does that have to do with an old man blabbering about Jurgen dying?"

Reymond narrowed his eyes at Barrett. "You see that man over there? One with the black hair, drinking on his own, needing a cane to stand up." He pulled Barrett close and grabbed his chin with one sticky hand, forcing his head to peer left. Barrett squinted through the sea of commoners. Sure enough, seated close to the bar, a dark-haired man was sipping ale with one hand and clutching his cane with the other.

"I see him. Who is he?"

"Be damned if I know," Reymond whispered. "But he joined us for the feast, and he wasn't on the list. And I read the list of attendees over and over."

"So what?" Cay and Lew were staring at the two of them with raised eyebrows.

"My guess?" Reymond said. "He's a Verstecian spy, sent by the King to keep an eye on proceedings. If he hasn't already, he'll soon be reporting that Jurgen is dying."

Barrett scoffed. "You seriously believe the old man's words? He was clearly just some street vagrant. Alderman Karston was right. He was in search of a free meal."

Reymond swallowed. "Didn't you see the mark stitched into his robes? It was... unmistakable. The moment I laid eyes on the old fool, I realised what he was." He glared at Cay and Lew, lowering his voice further to ensure they couldn't hear him. "A monk of the Order of Mutlen. And seeing as how the Baron scarpered, I'd wager he recognised the monk for what he was too."

"A monk of... *Mutlen?*" Barrett was about to ask what the word meant, but then he remembered. The place of Jurgen's exile, Freestone Monastery, belonged to the Order of Mutlen, a holy Hektorian order. But then, that could mean... "The old man was telling the truth?"

Cay heard that last bit. "Come on, Barrett. You could tell by his stench he was no more than an unfortunate rover."

Barrett wasn't sure what to believe. He had no cause to doubt Reymond, but he hoped he was somehow mistaken. If the messenger was indeed a Mutlen monk, then he'd travelled hundreds of miles to deliver his message. If word reached the King of a monk being thrown into Hanzus's dungeons, then Jurgen's impending death would be the least of their concerns.

"If you knew who he was, why didn't you say anything?" Barrett whispered in Reymond's ear. "Why didn't you stop the guards from dragging him away?"

Reymond sighed. "And risk my hide in front of the Baroness? I know it's easy for you to worm your way out of hopeless situations, but not me. I don't fancy mucking out the stables for the rest of the year, thank you very much." Then, before Barrett could respond, he said to Cay and Lew, "Baron or no baron, this night is ours for the taking, lads. The commoner's dance will be under way in no time, and you'll never guess who's agreed to partner me."

Cay's eyes widened with anticipation. "Surely not?"

"That's right." Reymond turned to Barrett with an accomplished grin. "I told you Maisie would accept my invitation, did I not?"

Barrett groaned. He wasn't anywhere near drunk enough to endure such talk. "I thought she was partnering Jasper Granite?" Perhaps if he downed enough Krämisen, he'd be able to forget the evening's events.

Reymond knitted his brows, his smile unwavering. "I told you I could be persuasive. Now, I believe you have something that belongs to me."

Barrett reached into his pocket and placed ten silvers in the steward's hand. "I'm taking your word for it. You best not be lying."

Reymond's grin widened. "Have I ever lied to you? Don't be glum, now. With this silver, I'm buying the next two rounds. More ale, lads?"

Lew and Cay raised their cups and cheered. Downing the last of his ale, Reymond gathered their empty cups and pushed his way toward the bar.

"You stewards and your secrets," Cay groaned at Barrett. "Tonight's a night to celebrate. I hope you'll remember that. What were you whispering about, anyway?"

Barrett held his tongue as something caught his attention. A man with a reddened face stepped up onto the stage, holding a lute. He could hardly walk.

The bard gazed out at the crowd and chortled, turning every head in his direction. "This here's the sorriest lot o' drinkers I ever did see!" The punters fell silent, gaping at the man, bewildered. "There's an 'arvest happening outside, you know." He strummed his out-of-tune instrument and thrust his head back in laughter. "Come now, is there a singer out there brazen enough to 'elp me rouse this cheerless lot?"

"Go on, lad." Lew dug his elbow into Cay's side. "We all know you can sing."

Cay seemed unsure of that. Barrett knew the valet enjoyed singing, but never in front of a large gathering.

"You don't want to 'ear my awful squawking over this 'ere lute," the bard jested. "You'd sooner flee like our lord than sing along with me!"

There were a few cries of complaint and disgust at the man's poorly timed joke, but most of them chuckled.

"Over 'ere!" Lew barked at the stage, holding Cay's arm up for all to see.

Cay slapped his hand away, then, realising every head had turned toward him, cursed under his breath, and stomped over to the stage.

The crowd applauded as the bard helped Cay up onto the stage.

"What shall we play?" the lutist asked the crowd.

"The Night Before Us!" an old crone called out.

"I don't know the words to that," Cay admitted, shrugging.

"The Diamond of the Day!" another voice suggested.

Cay exchanged whispers with the bard, then the lutist began strumming. Cay wasn't the best singer, but Barrett found himself smiling as the valet grew in confidence. The commoners hummed and sang along with the lyrics. A man in the crowd passed Cay a drink, which he glugged down before performing a jig. As Cay returned to the singing and passed the first few verses, he belted out the most iconic lines of the song:

From fields of Nare to the Honeydew Downs,
And the shores of Marlin Bay,
True Gadians protect their realm,
And still, I hear them say,
Hurray! Hurray! The lions sing hurray!
Here stands the finest man, the Diamond of the Day.

This diamond lord, he gathered strong,
On Tyldar fields before,
The silver fiends sounded their retreat,
And now the lions roar,
Hurray! Hurray! The lions sing hurray!
Here stands the finest man, the Diamond of the Day.
Hurray! Hurray! Good Hektor sings hurray!
Here stands the finest man, the Diamond of the Day.

As the music reached its climactic conclusion, the punters cheered and smashed their cups together.

Cay and the lutist linked arms and bowed low before the applauding revellers. Smiles and laughter had replaced the dour faces. With only one song, Cay and the bard had transformed the tent into a den of excitement.

After Cay jumped off the stage and made his way back to his friends, grinning drunks patted him on the back and shouted praise in his ear.

"Let's get out of here," Cay said to Barrett as he emerged from the sea of admirers. He wrapped his arms around Barrett and Reymond. "What say we head to the dance pavilion?"

The world was shifting around Barrett. Reymond had his arm around him, leading him through the muddy field. Men huddled together in groups to fight off the chill breeze, exchanging stories and songs as they clashed their tankards together.

Blurry faces flashed past Barrett, red wine and brown ale dripping down their chins. The aroma of hops and piss invaded his nostrils. A woman belched in his face before turning to laugh with her friends. A stilt walker loomed over them, juggling leather balls before a crowd of happy air-punchers. Fireworks crackled and boomed overhead, lighting the black sky with dazzling shapes and colours.

Suddenly, the sky became a canvas ceiling.

Barrett blinked around at the commoner's dance pavilion. Peasants packed the tent to the brim. Most dressed far above their station, adorned in faux-finery and the tunics of stewards and merchants, rubbing shoulders with paupers in rags. The commoners joined together in one unholy mass, laughing and singing, without a care in the world. Music screeched over them from somewhere, drums and lutes scarcely forming a tune. Then the band came into view, tucked away on the far side of the tent – a crude, primitive version of the band that had played during the feast.

Something wet splashed Barrett's hands and neck, and a skinny man staggered away from the sea of bodies, bumping into Cay. The man patted Cay on the chest and shouted something in his ear before continuing on his way.

To Barrett's surprise, Cay turned back to his three companions and grinned. "Now, *this* is a party."

A sped-up version of the Diamond of the Day was playing. The revellers jigged along to the inconsistent beat, spraying spittle at one another as they sang along.

"Ooray, ooray... the Diamond of the Day!" a pig-faced peasant boomed in Barrett's ear, punching the surrounding air.

Someone slotted a wooden mug into Barrett's hand, overflowing with brown froth.

"Afraid they's out of mead," Lew screamed in Barrett's face. "Barman said this were Rooksbrew."

It tasted like the water left behind after cleaning spoiled clothes. And Barrett should know, Reymond had once dunked his head in the bowl Mother had been using to wash the linens. Barrett wasn't sure he could drink anymore, and the others looked equally appalled at the taste of their brews.

Cay's bottom lip was wobbling. "Why the fuck are we drinking Rooksbrew in the Krämise?"

"All the good ale must be gone," Reymond suggested.

"Well, this brew should stay in the Rooksland where it belongs," Cay grumbled.

"Beer's beer," Lew said, shrugging. "Might as well make do, lads."

The thought of the Rooksland reminded Barrett of Vilka. He wondered how the girl was tolerating all this noise bleeding through her attic window. That was if she hadn't fled again.

"Reymond Morgen!" a shrill voice carried over the music. A portly woman caked in sweat pushed through the crowd and thrust her wobbly arms around Reymond's neck. "I'd recognise that dashing face anywhere I would."

Reymond was blushing. "Kerlina." He staggered back, smiling gingerly at his friends. "How... uh... lovely it is to see you."

"It is?" She narrowed her eyes at him. "Well now, I've been waiting for a man with balls big enough to ask me to dance all eve." She wore an unbearable smile now. "And I accept your invitation."

"But I..."

The plump maid latched onto Reymond's hand and yanked him away. The crowd swallowed them both whole. Barrett blinked several times, half expecting he'd imagined the whole thing, but Reymond was gone.

"So much for dancing with Maisie Taverner," he groaned. "What a waste of ten silver."

"Well, better him than me," Cay said, cringing as he sucked the froth of his brew. "But the crazy mare's right about one thing. What are we doing just standing around? Let's join the dance."

The night had turned to madness. A couple of hours ago, he'd been feasting with aldermen, playing a civilised member of court, and now he was rubbing shoulders with ploughmen, miners, and lumberjacks.

Faces swam by, dribbling with sweat and Rooksbrew, men and women acting as equals in this frenzied show of decadence. They slapped their knees and waved their hands and twisted on their heels. Drinks sprayed everywhere, drooling from mouths and spilling from cups. He was witnessing a blasphemous ritual, a ritual he was now a part of.

"They carved into the mountains, a sign from the Goddess. Here lies the land they call the Kingdom of Diamonds..." Barrett sang along, slurring the words, forgetting which order the verses went in, humming the general tune. There was no judgement in this hall of brew and sweat.

When the instruments screeched to a halt, the commoners hooted and raised their cups to the canvas sky. A fat man embraced Barrett. His breath reeked of rotten eggs.

Barrett glanced around and realised he was among strangers. He craned his neck around the gaunt grins and fat faces in his way, searching for his friends without success. The crowd had dragged them all in different directions.

Barrett fought his way to the edge of the tent and leaned back against the taut fabric. He imagined the safety and warmth his bedsheets would offer if he somehow escaped.

Rooksbrew clung to the walls of his mouth. The dirty liquid was like granite on his tongue, rendering him thirstier with each sip. *I'll leave after this drink. Just this one.*

He took another sip, which triggered a searing pain in his throat. Revulsion and discomfort swelled as one. He almost dropped the cup in surprise. *Could slip outside, and nobody would notice... disappear into the night with all the other wayward drunks.* The others wouldn't learn of his departure until it was too late.

The last sip of Rooksbrew. It didn't seem so bad. The lingering froth was tasteless. He dropped the container onto the balding grass and wiped the bitter residue from his lips.

A wave of dizziness overcame him. He had to close his eyes, grabbing a handful of canvas to steady himself. His eyes throbbed as if alcohol infused them. As he opened them, he realised the crowd had become blurry. He had consumed his fair share of foreign beers, but nothing had affected him quite like this.

He rubbed at his sockets, trying in vain to restore his vision. He could tell no one was looking at him. They were far too occupied to pay him any mind. Then, as fast as it had arrived, the blurriness faded. Clarity returned at last.

And there she was.

No... you're mistaken. Look again.

As he looked closer, he was certain he'd made a mistake. Ever since Vilka's appearance in the Dancing Buck, he'd expected her to pop up at any turn, and now his drunken mind was sketching her into the faces of others. He was looking at a chambermaid. Yes, that was it. Only the maid didn't seem right. She seemed awkward in the sea of her peers, like she didn't belong. No, this was no manor-maid.

The girl was alone, seated in the centre of a line of stools. A group of dishevelled men sat nearby, watching her every move.

He had to get a better look at the girl's features. It wasn't Vilka, surely. But his gut told him it was. He strode right, trying to peer around the dancers without arousing their attention, but the blur of bodies seemed to move with him, blocking his view.

The band's volume and rhythm increased, and so too did the

crowd's fervour. A primal rendition of *Sir Darter's Red Rose*. The drums were indifferent to the melody, a law unto themselves. It seemed the band was as drunk as the revellers.

Barrett edged further to the side, manoeuvring around a guardsman and chambermaid who were slobbering over each other's faces. He skirted the perimeter of the tent until he reached the far side of the crowd.

As he approached the chairs, the girl turned toward him, looking through him. It was beyond any doubt this time. It *was* Vilka. She had escaped the Balenmanor again.

She glanced around at the dancers, transfixed by the marvellous freak show, a metal tankard clutched to her lap. The group of men seated nearby seemed sober as they stared at her, and only one held a drink.

Vilka's eyes grew wide with fear as they fell on Barrett. She gripped her tankard for dear life.

"Vilka." Barrett reached for her shoulder, but she recoiled so quickly she almost fell off the stool. He staggered back.

She blinked up at him, squinting and straining to make sense of his face. "Mister Barrett?"

Barrett struggled to look at her without crossing his eyes. "Vilka, what are you... doing here?"

Her attention trailed off to the dance floor. As she stared at no one in particular, her mouth gaped open. "I heard laughter." She sounded uninterested, her mind elsewhere. "Laughter from my window. I heard happy voices. People sounded so..." She closed her eyes, smiling to herself. "So happy. Fortunate."

She's drunk... or worse. The very thought was sobering him up. This time she'd crossed a line, drinking in plain sight of the servants of the Balenmanor. *If the Chamberlain hears of this... If the Baroness hears of this...*

"Vilka, you... you shouldn't be here. It's not safe for you to be here alone." He dropped his voice as low as he could. "The whole of Balenmeade is in celebration and..."

"And that's a *bad* thing?" She was smiling still, but she couldn't keep her eyes on him for more than a second. "People celebrating... *together?*"

The girl was in a trance, hypnotised by the ensuing madness. Barrett wanted to escape from it all, but Vilka prevented him from leaving.

"You know," she said, stretching out her arms, about to yawn. "That baron of yours, he's no good. Mark my words."

"What?"

She frowned at him. "I saw you, but you couldn't see me. I followed you from the mansion, but you went into that food tent with all those dress-wearers, and it didn't look much fun." She gestured at the surrounding crowd. "So I found this place. These folk know how to celebrate."

"You followed me?" Barrett wasn't sure what to say.

The men seated nearby were narrowing their eyes at Vilka and glaring at Barrett.

"Don't flatter yourself," Vilka quipped. She took a swig of whatever was in her cup. Barrett peered into the container. It was a clear, hazy liquid. Water? He surely hoped so, though he somehow doubted it.

"Look, Vilka, I'm going to head home. If you want, you could..."

"Then go." She sipped some more of her drink, curling her lip in an exaggerated frown. "You know, you don't look too well."

"Don't change the subject. I think you should come with me."

"Think I'll stay here, thanks."

Barrett reached for her cup. "What have you got in there?"

"None of your business." She snatched it back.

She was trying his patience now. Perhaps the others had been right all along. Perhaps the girl was a vagrant and nothing more. A runaway. A castaway. A whore affordable to the lowest bidder, the bidder being Sir Denzus Irvaye. The man's crooked features floated around his mind. He could only imagine the unspeakable acts a man like that would inflict upon Vilka.

"What are you drinking?" he demanded.

Concern ate into her face. She glanced around, searching for aid, turning all the more anxious when she noticed the group of watchful thugs beside her.

Barrett couldn't hide his frustration. The image of Sir Denzus's invasive hands made him sick to his stomach. "I asked you a question!"

A few dark looks shot Barrett's way as onlookers paused from dancing, but they soon returned to their merrymaking.

Barrett turned back to Vilka. "What's in the bloody cup? Please, tell me."

"I dunno," Vilka hissed at him, growing teary. "I asked for water, and the man said all the water were putrid. He handed me this instead."

"Give it to me." Barrett reached for the tankard, but her grip was strong. Cool liquid sprayed Barrett's hand as he wriggled it from her grasp. He held it to his nostrils, but all he could smell was the surrounding sweat. He took a sip. A bitter sting surged down his throat, like poison pouring into an open wound. He felt it plummet into his belly. The urge to gag was irresistible.

"Girl... this 'ere fella troubling ye?"

Barrett lowered the tankard, his hands trembling. A square, unshaven face was looming over Vilka. He belonged to the shifty cohort who'd been watching them, and the rest of his friends were still leering at Vilka, poised to intervene at any moment.

A drop of adrenaline coursed through Barrett. The man was immense in both height and girth. He was sweating profusely, and although he could have crushed Barrett with ease, there was uncertainty in his dark stare.

Vilka said something that Barrett couldn't make out. Square-face looked from Vilka to Barrett, his lips pursed in brutish thought. Then, without warning, one sausage-sized finger shoved against Barrett's chest.

"Lass don't want you round her no more." Square-face's voice carried over the music. "Says ye be poking yer nose where it don't belong." He shook his head, his greasy hair flapping about his shoulders as one side of his mouth curled in a grin. "I see ye for what ye are, cunt. Seen you snatching this 'elpless lass's booze, and now yer confronted by a real man, yer running scared." He threw his head back and laughed, revealing a host of missing teeth. "Ye 'ave the look of a Krämisen and the gut of a Rook."

Barrett could feel his lip trembling. He bit down until a rush of pain seeped down his chin. He wasn't sure whether he'd gone delirious, but he was sure he heard Vilka say, "What's your problem with Rooklanders?"

The brute's head snapped in her direction, confirming Barrett's fears. "Yer fucking what?"

Vilka looked as nervous as Barrett now. She was fidgeting in her seat, leaning into an invisible back.

"Your quarrel is with me," Barrett heard himself saying. As the thug's snarl angled back toward him, he had the overwhelming urge to flee.

Square-face was close to frothing at the mouth. His crew balanced on the edge of their seats, eyes darting between the three players.

"Ye has to be slow." Spit sprayed against Barrett's cheek. "Slow or mighty stupid."

Barrett leaned toward the latter. If it came to running away from this brute, slow was the last thing he'd be.

"I'm sure there's been a misunderstanding," Barrett said. "This girl is my sister, and I was simply giving her what any Goddess-loving brother would after finding vodka in their cup, and that's a good scolding."

"Sister, is it?" Square-face narrowed his eyes in Vilka's direction. "That right, lass?"

Vilka was looking at Barrett, wobbling with fear. Barrett nodded back at her, willing her to play along. The brute shot a raised eyebrow toward the steward, and there it lingered for a few long moments before he returned his frown to Vilka. "*Well?*"

Vilka swallowed. "Yes. That's right."

"As I say," Barrett said, eager to drag the man's attention from Vilka. "Found her with vodka. Isn't something a girl her age should be drinking. As a smart man, I'm sure you understand that."

"Vodka?" The man peered into the tankard Barrett was holding. "Ain't it fucking obvious? What ye got in yer hand's the finest soot-vodka ever known to man." He grinned back towards his friends, and they laughed, even though they couldn't have heard him.

Barrett stared at the man's flat chin and dirty stubble. "Soot-vodka?"

"None other." The man tapped his nose as though relaying some great secret. "And I should know. I fucking live off the stuff." He slapped his chest, laughing like a madman, then plodded back over to his friends.

Barrett looked down at the clear liquid, the cup rattling in his shaky hand. It certainly tasted like vodka, but *soot*-vodka? He'd never heard of such a thing.

"Listen, Vilka..." When he looked up, Vilka's eyes were closing. "*Vilka?*" She was slipping out of the chair now, her limbs weak and floppy. Before she fell, Barrett grasped her by the arm, dragging her onto her feet. "We need to get you home."

Home? Where's home? He couldn't very well return her to the Balenmanor now. Even if he was somehow able to sneak her back into her attic room, how would she explain her hangover the next day? He was sobering up with every couple of strides as he led Vilka through the hordes of bodies and out into the fresh air.

The field was empty, save for a few stragglers and the odd servant picking up discarded cups. The music inside the tent was droning on like a storm in spring, its tuneless melody all the more evident from afar.

"Vilka?"

Barrett felt her weight shift from under him. She would have crashed into the grass had he not reached an arm underneath her and swept her over his shoulder. She was even lighter than she looked, or perhaps it was some drunken illusion of strength.

Her breath was warm against his neck as she leaned into his ear and whispered, "Mister Barrett... that messenger man... he'll lead the Baron to his death."

The Messenger

It was a cold, bitter morning. The kind he would rather spend neck-high in blankets, dreaming of anything, *anything* but a Krämisen winter. And yet it was in that exact barony, at the beginning of that very treacherous season, that Hanzus now found himself inhaling the howling wind.

"He's late," Hanzus said, searching around.

The crowd had gathered for almost half an hour, barely a word or second glance traded between any of them.

Arwel's eyes had not left the stage. Even now, his sight lingered on the macabre display arranged before them. "He's waiting."

Hanzus would have laughed if he'd had any laughter left in him. "*We're* the one that are waiting. Don't you see that?"

Arwel was breathing heavily, laboured exhalations. "He's waiting for the moment in which we've been waiting long enough. Then the waiting will be over for all of us."

There was movement behind the stage. The curtain rustled – wind or man? – then the fabric swept aside, and a procession made its way out onto the stage. Jurgen was leading the parade, an axe slumped over his shoulder. Expressionless, he shepherded his line of guards out onto the stage, one by one, then he ordered them into a formation, facing the crowd. Last onto the stage was a hooded figure, who was being led, seemingly backwards, by the helping hand of Pamen.

"There he is," Arwel said, though Hanzus wasn't sure which one he was referring to. "This is it, Hans."

Pamen marched the hooded figure over to Jurgen, and it was then that Hanzus realised that the man hadn't been walking backwards at all. The hood was actually a sack covering his entire head.

"Fair people!" Jurgen exclaimed, waving his hands about dramatically, eyes to the heavens, nose aimed at the top row of seats. "As promised, we are gathered here for your viewing pleasure. To carry out the noble task of execution!"

A patter of applause and a few positive groans rippled across the stand.

"Mister Granite has been found guilty of crimes against honest folk," Jurgen continued, his voice a low rumble. "He pleaded innocence before a court chaired by myself, but after conclusive evidence came to the fore, a decision was made!"

"Traitor!" someone bellowed from the crowd.

"Fucking pig!" yelled another.

"People, people!" Jurgen held up his hands, silencing them all. "Mister Granite has met the justice of the Krämise. Now he goes to meet *Her* justice!"

The crowd yelled their frenzied support. It was hard to believe the sun had not long since risen.

"Bring him forth!"

Hanzus nudged Arwel's arm. "Remind me, what's he guilty of again?"

Arwel flashed him with his devilish grin. "Really? You mean you don't know? Or are you playing me like an old lute?"

He couldn't remember the nature of the man's crimes. Furthermore, he wasn't exactly sure what he was doing here. He hated executions.

The accused was facing the crowd now. Jurgen peeled the sack off his head. As the fabric drifted to the ground, shock and confusion echoed around the enclosure.

Hanzus squinted. At first, he wasn't sure what he was looking at, then...

Holy Mother...

There, staring back at him, equally bemused was... himself. The prisoner had the face of Hanzus, but with greasy hair and a week's worth of stubble.

"What... what is happening?"

"Really, Hans," Arwel chuckled in his ear. "You do like to play the fool from time to time."

The Hanzus on the stage was being led to the block. Pamen knocked him down onto his knees as Jurgen ran his hand along the smooth axe handle.

"This can't be real. This isn't happening."

Before he proceeded to the block, Jurgen turned his attention to the audience. He stared directly at the Hanzus in the stand, picking him out in an instant. He mouthed what looked like, *Goodbye, my son*, and before he took another breath, the axe fell.

Hanzus jolted upright, bursting from a veil of thin fabric. Everything was dark. He was panting, short hoarse breaths forced through his teeth. Sweat trickled down his face. He reached out, clawing at nothing, then he found a bunch of fabric grasped in his hand and pulled it back.

Light exploded, forcing his eyes shut. He opened them slowly, testing, adjusting to the brightness. He was blinking out into his bedchamber, warm light shining through the lace curtains.

It had been a dream, and yet it felt so real. He looked down at his hands: they were watery, sticky with sweat. The other side of the bed was empty, and it was just as well, as goodness knows what had soaked the sheets. Had he truly pissed himself? His body ached all over. His bones were stiff, as if unused for days.

He rolled over, patting the sheets in search of the opposite curtain. He grabbed a fistful of coarse rags, turning his head to discover a ginger cat curled up next to Heatha's pillow.

Franzus.

Hessan's pet was a bloody nuisance, always appearing when it wasn't wanted. It looked up at him now, a vacant smile etched into its brown eyes.

"What are you doing in here?" Hanzus had managed to stop it from entering the chamber for days, despite its frequent clawing sessions with the door outside.

The creature closed its eyes to him, purring.

The dream flashed back through Hanzus's mind. Arwel's smile, the way Jurgen had carried the axe as if it was a toy. *Jurgen... Jurgen...* Then the thought he truly feared crept back into his consciousness: *The messenger!*

Hanzus leapt from the bed. Franzus jumped after him, darting across the floor and out through the door. *The door!* Somebody had left the door ajar, and the cat's fat body must have smacked it fully open.

Hanzus saw the shape of a body flash past in the corridor.

"Stop, you!" he cried.

Seconds later, a dishevelled servant popped their head through the doorway. "Yes, milord?"

"Dell, prepare my clothes for the day." Hanzus looked down at himself. His nightgown was damp with fresh piss stains. "And a cold bath." *No time for heat. No time to delay.*

The oil lamp provided scarce illumination, but Hanzus could have recognised Olken in the pitch-black. The jailer was leaning over a low table, his crooked nose pointing up toward Hanzus like a threatening crossbow bolt.

Olken flipped through a thick, cracked leather book, his thin eye slits jumping around the pages before they caught Hanzus's shadow flickering over the parchment.

"What'cha want?" Olken croaked, not looking up. He wet a finger and turned the page. "Your break dragged well over an hour, you swine."

Hanzus slotted one hand into his armpit, holding the lamp close to his own face with the other. "Oh? Sounds like you're being lax with that apprentice of yours."

Olken's head jolted up, his eyes gaping wide with horror. "Milord, I hadn't imagined that..."

"No, I don't suppose you did." The air was tight down here. Hanzus fought for breath, his lungs constricted. "I have to tell you, Olken, that some most distressing news reached my ears this morning."

The jailer chewed every word, nodding like a sycophant. When it was obvious Hanzus had finished speaking, he said, "What can I assist you with, milord? Name anything."

"Better still, I'll name you a *man*." Hanzus placed the lamp down on the table, peering at the leather book Olken had been reading. A ledger of some sort. A list of prisoners? "A man was brought to you yesterday evening, I believe."

Olken's eyes widened further. He nibbled at his lip, his hooknose scrunched up to shield himself from an unpleasant pong.

"I scarcely believed the news," Hanzus continued, wiping sweat clean off his brow. The hundred or so steps that led down into the dungeons took it out of him every time. He was dreading the climb back up to daylight. "Had the words reached me from an unreliable source, I would've laughed them away." He leered down upon Olken, his lip curling its contempt for the vile cretin. "Or seen them punished."

Olken shifted against the back of his seat, pulling himself up to stand, his nervous smile not moving from the baron. "You speak of the monk, milord? He's right this way if you'd care to follow me."

He should never have been brought here. Hanzus could remember

Alderman Karston ordering the guards to transport the messenger to the dungeons. He'd been unable to intervene. The ringing realisation that Jurgen was dying had immobilised Hanzus, rendering him as useless as a peasant.

Pathetic. Undone in front of your own courtiers. He only prayed the monk was unharmed. The Balenmeade dungeons were no place to store a messenger, welcome or not. Folk came down here to become food for rats.

"The monk was not brought here on my orders," Hanzus admitted. Not that it made him feel any less guilty.

Olken alternated between a frown and a smile, undecided about the appropriate expression. "I only receive the prisoners, milord. Where they come from ain't for me to comment or dwell on. When I saw the monk being carried down here, I wondered, I admit, what on earth could have happened."

Hanzus waved him into silence. "Enough. Just hand me the key to his cell." *This folly has gone on long enough.*

Olken's face settled on a scowl. He pursed his lips, dark eyes squinting through the dim. "With respect, milord, the dungeons are a dangerous place. I could lead you to the cell in question in no time at all."

Hanzus thought about it. It was true, during his tenure as the Baron of the Krämise, he'd scarcely ventured into the depths below the city. Jurgen had taken a rather hands-on approach when it came to ensuring his jailers and torturers were providing an adequate service – and criminals packed the Balenmeade dungeons to the brim in those days – but Hanzus preferred to leave the dungeon dwellers to their own devices. Myles Erman was more than happy to supervise these sun-starved leeches himself.

Hanzus swallowed dust. "Lead the way."

The passageways were barely wide enough for one man. It was a challenge to tuck in one's shoulders and keep from brushing the damp stone. Hanzus had pissed himself during the night, and now he'd ruined his clothes a second time. Tiny box-lanterns hung wherever there were gaps. Their feeble glow, and the pulsating lamp Olken carried, were their only protection from the swallowing darkness.

It had been years since Hanzus had last slipped through these passageways. All he could remember were the wails that echoed throughout the labyrinth, cries for help that had stayed with him for days afterwards, entering his dreams and poisoning his thoughts. The perpetrators surely deserved their suffering, but where was the line drawn between punishment and torture for the sake of torture?

The dungeons were now an eerie contrast to the home of shrieks and groans they had once been. Rapt silence hugged the stone walls, interrupted by the occasional drip and Olken's heavy footsteps.

"If I were you, milord," Olken's voice drifted back over his shoulder, "I'd cover me mouth. Foul lot down here. Wouldn't want you catching nothing untreatable."

It almost sounded like a threat. Regardless, Hanzus pulled out a handkerchief and held it over his mouth and nose. "*You* seem healthy enough."

Hanzus meant it as sarcasm, but the jailer replied, "I've learnt to wash myself of these people, milord. Thing is..." They made a sharp turn, and Olken's words seemed to evaporate.

"What's that you say?" When the jailer didn't respond, Hanzus patted him on the shoulder.

"We're close now, milord. I've taken you the safe way."

Safe way? Hanzus dreaded to think what the *unsafe* way might be. He was already dreaming of the surface and the certainty it brought. Down here, anything could happen. Down here, he didn't feel like a baron. A ceiling could give way, stone crumbling into a thousand tiny pieces, crushing anything and anyone unfortunate enough to have been lurking below. A man could scream and bellow and yell, and the people up on the surface would never hear him.

"Folk get lost down here," Olken explained. "Since I been working here, we've had two fresh recruits just disappear. One turned up days later, head smashed in by a large chunk of rock. The other lad still ain't appeared to this day. You see these lamps dotted about the place? Each one's lit by me. Ain't no other guard skilled or man enough to take the long walk. Perhaps, milord, you could ask about sometime... see if there's some man in Balenmeade strong enough of gut to serve down here. Best I've got is Old Skuller and that weedy lad Dellon."

Hanzus amused himself with the thought of Ache and Pamen stumbling around in the dungeons, watching their backs, and jumping at their own shadows – that would knock them down a peg or two, although come to think of it, knocking those men down was the last thing he wanted. What use would they be then?

"I'll see what I can do." The truth was, he had no intention of maintaining this place. The dungeons were a long tradition of the House of Irvaye, and Jurgen's legacy, but they wouldn't be his. While he understood the necessity of locking up crooks, torture for the sake of torture was an evil he'd ignored and abetted for too long. Thievery was an abhorrent crime, but this was no place to house the human race.

I should seal these tunnels for good and build a prison above land.

Olken halted. Hanzus almost stepped onto his back. "And here we are, milord."

They stepped into a room, or at least, it was a room in comparison. As his eyes adjusted to the light, he realised it was just another passage, only wider and lined with wooden doors. There was a slit carved in the ceiling, allowing a sliver of blue light to beam down onto the floor. The lamps were just as dim here, the air just as close.

The place was unnervingly silent. Hanzus didn't move an inch, slowing his breath in order to hear some verbal clue behind one of the doors. Nothing. He was expecting moans and groans, some sign of life.

"Which door is it?"

Olken blinked at the formation of doors. He scratched his scabby forehead, shining his light towards the closest door. There was a crude *one* etched into the wood, red ink oozing out of the carved grooves. "Uh, let me see now..." Olken shuffled over to the second door, gripping his chin in thought. He started talking to himself, his words barely audible.

Hanzus coughed into his hand. "We haven't all morning, Master Olken."

The jailer didn't seem to hear his baron. "Just need to remember, was it a two or a six... not *twenty*-six. No, no."

Hanzus ground his teeth. "For the Goddess's sake, man. The prisoner was brought in here *last night*. Surely you remember the bloody number?"

Olken moved over to the third door, displaying no more confidence than he did with the previous two.

Hanzus cleared his throat. "Messenger of Jurgen Irvaye, I'm here to speak with you!" Nothing more than Olken's surprise filled the silence. "Answer me now!" The words echoed around the chamber, shooting down the passageway.

Olken was pulling at his collar. "Milord, if I may, some of our inhabitants are a rather nervous bunch. That's to say..."

"*Yes?*" Hanzus interrupted. "That is to say what?"

Olken's gaze shifted sideways, landing on something that made his face light up. "But of course! Number eleven." He rummaged around in his pocket and withdrew a chain of keys.

A rush of adrenaline surged through Hanzus as the key slipped into the lock.

Click.

Cool sweat beaded his brow. *The truth lies behind this door.*

The door creaked inward, like a feeble elder being forced from their bed.

"And here he is, milord. As requested."

The cell was like another passageway, long and unbearably narrow, not wide enough for a man to stretch out his arms. A window-slit beamed light onto the slab floor from high above. Despite its scarcity, Hanzus was relieved to glimpse at sunlight.

Just beyond the light's reach, a dark figure stood with his back to the far wall. The person shuffled forward, exposing one mud-encrusted shoe.

"You're certain this is the man?" Hanzus whispered to Olken.

"Certain as can be, milord."

"Then you may leave us."

Olken bit at his lip. "Uhm... you sure, milord? Never know. Could be a dangerous one, this."

Hanzus wore a smile. "Then wait outside the door, Master Olken."

Olken blinked at the baron, then nodded, saliva dribbling down his lip. "Certainly."

The door creaked in protest as Olken slotted it back into its frame. Hanzus could hear the jailer's breath on the other side of the damp wood. No doubt he would be listening to their every word.

Hanzus sucked at his gums. The sunlight was illuminating his face to the prisoner.

"Truly, you've come," the stranger spoke, their words carrying across the cell like a subtle stench. His voice was strained, coarse, thick with the Rooksland accent.

Hanzus squinted at the man's vague shape. He could make out the roundness of a head, but none of its features. "Who are you? And why do you not address me by my title?"

The figure's arm made some kind of gesture. "That will not be necessary. We are, after all, equals under the Goddess."

Hanzus had to disagree there, but he hadn't the time nor patience to play such petty games. "I believe I asked for your name."

"Actually, you asked me who I was. Not my name. And to answer your first, I am nothing more or less than a brother. A brother to your father, and by extension, a brother to you."

Hanzus was uncertain of the man's quality of education, but he surely understood that families didn't work that way.

"Edennel is my name," the man continued.

Of course. How fitting that he's named after a Sage.

Edennel swayed forward some more, a section of dark trouser emerging from the shadows. "And you are Hanzus of the House of Irvaye. Brother Jurgen speaks kindly of you."

Hanzus couldn't hold back the laughter. Bitter, tooth-grinding laughter. "*Kindly?* Perhaps you've mistaken me for some foolish chambermaid who might readily lap up the ramblings of a monk. That is, providing you are who you say you are." He swallowed the knot forming in his throat. "Step into the light."

Edennel hesitated, wiggling his visible foot as though testing a pool of water, then he stepped forward. The same famished face that had ruined the previous evening's banquet presented itself before Hanzus. The tattered fabric of his robe frayed at the wrists and neck. His wild, matted hair reminded Hanzus of a stray dog.

"Brother Hanzus." The monk straightened his back; at least, he attempted to, before his body made a creaking sound not dissimilar to the door, and he stumbled forward, his back hunched like a beast. "Brother Jurgen clings to life like the bird upon the breaking branch. The branch strains and eventually snaps as the elements work against it." His eyes pulsated like an irregular heartbeat. "It's only a matter of time before the branch snaps, and the bird is undone."

Pain gathered in Hanzus's chest. "Speak sense. What did Jurgen say to you?"

Edennel was swaying on the balls of his feet, his pupils dancing around the floor. "He says little. Looks to the ceiling in prayer, making peace with the Goddess. I have, as have my brothers, been attending to Brother Jurgen ever since he became bound to his quarters. It's only a matter of time, Brother Hanzus. Only a matter of time."

"Why should I believe you?"

The monk's eyes snapped suddenly into focus. "All I possess, Brother Hanzus, is the skin on my back and the message I have been entrusted to deliver. Brother Hanzus, last night I slipped my way past every post, every fence, every gate." He lifted a point-making finger.

"And every man that came to see my face had not a doubt in their heart. They knew well that I am a Brother of the Order of Mutlen."

Hanzus wasn't sure what to say. He was certain the old monk told the truth, but accepting it meant accepting Jurgen was dying.

"A girl has come into your care," Brother Edennel said, his eyes glazed over. His mind was elsewhere. "Beware of her, Brother Hanzus. Mark my words on that. She means nothing more nor less than despair."

Hanzus was incredulous now. Was the mad monk referring to Vilka? How could he have known about her appearance in the Balenmanor? Did he know something about her origins? Did he know something as to the reason why she was here?

Hanzus opened his mouth to pose the question, but the monk spoke over him. "Take note of my words, dear brother, for I am Brother Edennel of the Order of Mutlen and I..." The words caught in his throat like a mouthful of rotten food. He looked up at the window, then he turned back and gaped toward the door. "I *am* Brother Edennel of the Order of Mutlen."

Hanzus had met some shrewd charlatans in his time. He'd met some truly blessed holy men, but this dishevelled monk was something else entirely. There was something not quite right about his presence in Balenmeade. Despite his apparent authenticity, his appearance raised more questions than it provided answers. Surely, if Jurgen's impending death was true, the Order of Mutlen would have equipped Edennel with some sort of letter or sent a message by pigeon ahead of his arrival.

Suddenly, the monk's pupils seemed to disappear, consumed by the whites of his eyes. His shoulders convulsed. His knees shook violently. Before Hanzus could react, Edennel had crashed to the floor.

Hanzus rushed to his side, flipped the brittle body onto its back, and lifted his neck off the cold stone. The monk's eyes were still open, blinking at him.

"Baron Hanzus of the House of Irvaye," Edennel croaked, a faint smile stretching across his sick face. "I see it now. Brother Jurgen spoke highly of your character. Your resolve. The embers burn slow in him now. Not long before they are extinguished."

Hanzus shook Edennel, hoping to snap him out of the confusion. His eyes were closing, tiny flames about to be snuffed. "Brother Edennel, wake up. I order you." The eyes weren't blinking anymore. Hanzus patted him on the cheek. "Brother Edennel? Brother Edennel? For Hektor's sake, what illness has taken my father? Was he poisoned? *Brother Edennel?*"

It was no use. The body was limp, the skin already cold.

The door creaked open. Olken's twisted nose was soon looming over him. "Milord, what... what happened?"

"He's dead." Hanzus wiped the saliva from his lips, letting the monk's head drop to the floor. He reached out a hand, and Olken helped him onto his feet. "Jurgen is dying. My father is dying."

The jailer stared at him, dumbfounded. "Baron Jurgen? Uhm... that's to say the *former* baron..."

"Olken," Hanzus spoke over him. "You need to listen to me very carefully." His hand was trembling, the hand that had laid Brother Edennel down to rest forever. "Tell me, did anyone else question the monk before I arrived?"

Men didn't just die because they had spent a night in the dungeons.

Olken wore a nervous smile. "Well, it is our custom to question the prisoners ourselves. But come to think of it, another man did visit the monk in the early hours. Said he had questions. Said he'd give the monk his broth on my behalf."

Goddess above. Why didn't he tell me this earlier? Someone must have poisoned the monk. *Heatha is behind this. She has to be.*

He would punish Olken for his negligence, but first, he had to get to the bottom of all that had transpired. "Lead me back to the surface, Master Olken. And while we walk, you to tell me about this visitor."

Hanzus pushed the door with such force he was certain it would burst from its hinges. But the battered old thing was sturdier than it looked. It creaked and groaned in retaliation, a piece of ancient tree awoken from slumber.

Heatha was sitting by the fire, a shawl over her lap and a small book in her hands. She looked up from her half-moon spectacles, her face aglow from the hue of the flames.

"My lord," she crooned, closing the book and setting it down on the table. She looked him dead in the eye, challenging him to proceed, goading him to attack.

"You killed him," Hanzus stated, kicking the door shut behind him. "The monk is dead because of *you*."

She feigned surprise, taking off her glasses and folding them on top of the book. "The monk is dead?"

Hanzus skirted across the room until he was close enough to feel the fire's warmth. "Do *not* play the fool with me. I heard it from Olken's very own lips."

"That is unfortunate news indeed." She picked up the book and glasses again, bored with their discussion.

Hanzus grabbed her by the arm, knocking the book and spectacles onto the floor. "You treacherous fucking bitch! Do you realise what you've done? He was a holy brother of..."

"The esteemed Order of Mutlen," she supplied, looking up at him with undiluted scorn. "Yes, I was informed." She snatched her arm free of his grip, leaving him hovering over her, clutching at the air. "Though, if you'd even the slightest idea what you were talking about, you'd know I ordered the monk to be detained for later questioning. Why then would I have the man killed?"

Hanzus didn't believe her, not for a second. Though her impassive face offered scant suggestion of emotion, the subtle crease in her thin lips told him she was holding back a smile. A *knowing* smile. Perhaps she'd poisoned the monk just to spite him, to add to his torment. Or maybe, just maybe, there was more to this rueful mess than at first he'd thought.

First, I endure the negotiations in Carthane, then Edgar Morske tries to kill me and lets me know it was all the doing of the Despot... then I return to Balenmeade, and my wretch of a wife is harbouring some foreign vagrant. He remembered the monk's words before he finally succumbed to poison: *A girl has come into your care... Beware of her... She means nothing more nor less than despair.*

Heatha had to be behind it. She was the common theme in all of this. She had taken this Vilka in. She had poisoned the messenger, who had, in turn, warned Hanzus about the child. Perhaps he had been wrong from the very beginning: perhaps the Despot was not the Crown Prince after all. As he lived and breathed, Heatha was grinning at him after he'd declared that a monk of Mutlen lay dead in their dungeons. She was happy.

She was behind it all. Heatha *was* the Despot.

Her lip curled downward. "Hans, listen to me. Your father *is* dying. He now lays on his deathbed." She picked the book up from the floor and rested it on the table. "I'm not exactly sure what you're accusing me of, but you are distracting yourself from the bigger picture." She forced herself to smile. "You were right, Hans. You *were* right. Honestly, when you excused yourself from the Harvest feast, I wanted to kill you. To maim you for abandoning me. Do you have any idea how ridiculous you made me appear? I had to host the rest of the evening on my own, entertaining *your* wretched bootlickers."

"And what about now?" he intervened. "Do you still want to kill me? Come, I'm sure you've a knife tucked into that dress." He raised his hands in mock submission. "Strike me down now while you have the chance." Her smile turned to ashes as he lowered his arms. "Ah, that's right. You'd sooner have someone else do the deed, just as you had Brother Edennel poisoned by another."

She scanned the room, searching for a hidden eavesdropper. "These walls have ears, my lord. Do you understand the weight of your accusations? The implications if you're found to be correct. Do you believe the King would take kindly to hearing that a monk of Mutlen was murdered during the Harvest of Balenmeade? And do you seriously think he'd care whether the order to poison had come from the baron or his baroness?" She straightened in her seat, looking him up and down without fear or conscience. "We are one and the same, my lord. *We* are the Krämise. And as such, our fates are entwined." She sighed, exasperated. "I know you believe I wronged you, that I took action simply to harm you. But I do all that I do for the sake of this family."

Hanzus couldn't take this anymore. "Just... just... explain yourself to me."

He would never reveal the monk's dying words to her, of course. Brother Edennel had confirmed what he feared from the very beginning: that Vilka's appearance in the Balenmanor was no random twist of fate, that she'd been placed here for a reason. And Heatha's insistence that the girl had to be imprisoned here in the manor betrayed her involvement.

Hanzus was a fool for acting against his better judgement. When he'd arrived in Balenmeade and Heatha had informed him of Vilka's presence, he'd resolved to leave the girl alone until the Harvest had passed. *I'll have to question her at once, as I should have done days ago.*

"You wouldn't understand, even if I explained it to you." She folded her arms tight to her bosom. "But I will tell you this. Your father *is* dying. My man questioned him this morn, and the monk speaks the truth. Jurgen has been poisoned, by whom even the monk seemed unsure. But the poison is one designed to act slowly, to cause as much pain as humanly possible before allowing its victim the sweet release of death. He breathes, for now, but there is no antidote to save him. He *will* perish before the month is out."

Hanzus swallowed bile. Jurgen was a cruel man, but even he didn't deserve a death as slow as this. There were several potions he knew of that could take weeks to stop a heart, the work of vindictive alchemists who found pleasure in the torture of their victims.

If Heatha was behind any of this, he'd have her experience a fate worse than that.

"You appear pained," she said. "We both know you harbour no love for your father."

Hanzus could have throttled her there and then and put them both out of their misery. It was no more than she deserved. But he couldn't prove she was behind the murders of Brother Edennel and Jurgen or his own botched assassination attempt aboard the HMS Temper. Not yet.

"It is curious that you do not appear pained," Hanzus returned through gritted teeth. "We both know that you loved him."

She scoffed, laughter and disgust in equal measure. "Please, Hans. You know as well as I, that the affair was only a bit of fun."

Hanzus couldn't look into her repulsive eyes a moment longer. Jurgen was dying. Perhaps he was already dead. Regardless of what Hanzus thought or felt, Freestone Monastery was no place for a former Baron of the Krämise to be buried.

"What are you going to do?" Heatha wanted to know.

"What I should have done years ago," he said. *But first, I'll pay this Vilka girl a visit.*

Schemes

Barrett awoke with a smile.

He'd been dreaming of a beautiful woman kissing his neck, playing with his hair. As she tossed her blonde locks to one side, she flashed her green eyes at him. *Green eyes.* Was she the woman the oracle had warned him of, the one that *belonged* to his future?

He rubbed his eyes, rousing his senses, and as he peeled his fingers from his face, he realised that a pair of eyes were glancing back at him. *Real* eyes, not a part of some dream. These irises were far from green – a woody shade of brown – and their round face belonged to Vilka.

Of course.

The previous night's events flooded back into his mind like an ocean wave of ale and vodka. He'd lost his friends during the commoner's dance, and it was then that he'd encountered Vilka inside the tent. She'd been sat near a band of leering drunkards, no doubt planning to ravage her. But Barrett had taken her away, saved her, given her a place to stay, just to keep her safe.

But safe for how long?

The Balenmanor servants would soon notice Vilka's absence, then they would notify Hanzus and Heatha. And if someone... *anyone* had witnessed Barrett carrying Vilka to his home... *What was I thinking?*

He'd endangered the livelihood of his whole family by smuggling this prisoner into his home. When the manor learned of his indiscretion, the Chamberlain would summon him and shred his contract of employment into a thousand pieces. Brendal Jupe would take great pleasure in that charge and in escorting Vilka back to her attic cell. Perhaps he would allocate Barrett a cell of his own in the deepest dungeons.

What have I done?

"What you staring at?" Vilka snapped. She lay on her side with one hand rested under her chin, her dark eyes narrowed at him.

"I should never have brought you here," he thought aloud. *Imagine if someone saw us now, sharing my small bed like pauper lovers.*

"And I shouldn't have let you take me. But here we are." She glanced over his shoulder, peering around his bedroom. "Whether *here* is. What the fuck's *that*?"

He followed her eyes over to the scribbled drawing pinned to his wall. Lerry had presented him with that charcoal sketch when the lad was barely two. "That... that's unimportant."

"All right, all right. Forget I said ought."

He tried to swallow, but the walls of his mouth dry as pebbles left out to bake in the sun. He looked up at the ceiling. His head turned light as a feather. Cool sweat trickled down the nape of his neck. *Holy Mother, what am I going to do?* He remembered Vilka murmuring in her sleep as he carried her through the manor grounds. She'd said something about the monk, made out she'd known a thing or two about that old messenger. He couldn't quite remember. His head pulsated with an aching flush.

Barrett closed his eyes, bit down on his tongue to thwart the pain. *Vilka tricked Denzus Irvaye into believing she was someone else, and now she appears to know something about that messenger.* He strained to remember what she'd said to him, but his head was thick with fog. One thing was for sure: Vilka was hiding something, probably a lot of things. Heatha had claimed that the girl had spotted Bloodkin roaming around the Krämise. *What else has she seen? What else does she know? Who is she?*

"Vilka," he said, opening his eyes a crack. "Why are you here?"

She furrowed her brows, appearing confused. "You gone soft, now? You brought me here."

Barrett nibbled on his tongue. "Why are you *really* here? Why are you in Balenmeade?"

She considered a moment, ruminating on his words, seeking to decipher their true meaning. "I already told you. I were escaping... escaping my ma's and pa's *murderers.*"

"But why *here?*" He asked, gesturing towards the closed window. "Why stop in Balenmeade? And why sneak into the Balenmanor stables of all places? You must understand that seems suspicious?" Everyone that had heard of her appearance in the stables speculated she was some sort of spy. "And the matter that confuses me most, Vilka, is why when you had the chance did you not flee the city? Why, after I encountered you with Sir Denzus inside the Buck, did you sneak back inside the Balenmanor?"

He regained his breath, the weight of his words sinking in as his panting gave birth to silence.

"Look," Vilka groaned, rolling her eyes. "I understand you must be under a lot of stress..."

"Don't condescend me," he snapped. The girl had some nerve if she thought she could treat him as an inferior when he was the elder. "You're a spy. Just admit it. You're some kind of informant. An assassin who's biding their time."

The idea sounded foolish as it came to be spoken. He sounded like one of the gossipy drunkards that loitered inside the Buck, speaking on matters he knew nothing about.

She spoke slowly. "You think I'm a spy?"

Barrett felt his cheeks reddening. *Yes, of course, the thought's ridiculous.* She was just a pauper trying to make her way by stealing what she could and accepting whatever bed offered to her. How silly he was. His mind had run away from him as per usual. Once a fool, always a fool. He was a laughingstock. A blundering imbecile.

Vilka scoffed, offended by his silence. "And who do you suppose I'm spying for? And for what?"

Her lips were uttering one thing, but her eyes told a different story, a story of meddling and untruths, of mischief and outright lies.

Words...

Barrett stiffened, remembering Vilka's words from the past evening, as she lay slumped over his shoulder. *That messenger man will lead the Baron to his death,* she'd said. She had spoken that sentence, and he'd dismissed it as drunken nonsense.

Fool.

Vilka knew something about the monk.

Barrett lifted himself out of bed and padded over to the wardrobe. He caught Vilka's eyes on his bare chest before he threw a shirt over his body. He stomped over to the window and opened the flaps to allow the sun in. The shadows baring down on the street outside told him they'd slept in past midday.

"Just tell me what you're doing here," Barrett said, gazing out the window. The cleaners were sweeping and scrubbing the mess the revellers had made of the cobbles. It was all spilt booze, discarded food scraps and dried puke. "That's all I want to know. What are you really doing in Balenmeade?"

The bed creaked as Vilka sat up. "I'm hungry."

Barrett turned back to face her. She was stretching out her arms and yawning. "Tell me about the Bloodkin you've claimed to see."

"Feed me first," she suggested. "My belly aches too much for this talk."

Before Barrett could open his mouth, an aggressive knock came on the front door. He heard Mother's heavy footsteps thumping down the corridor.

He craned his neck outside the window. A man stood in front of the doorway, wearing a fine black jerkin with a frilly collar. It was Marc Kest, he realised, the Baroness's lawyer.

Fuck.

Barrett ducked away from the window. He prayed the lawyer hadn't seen him.

"Can I help you?" Mother's muffled voice spoke on the other side of the wall. But the lawyer's response was too hushed to make out.

"So, you want to hear about the Red Eyes?" Vilka said, sliding deep under the covers, so only her head peeped out of the sheets.

Barrett held a finger to his lips to silence her. "*Later*," he mouthed.

Barrett exhaled slowly, careful not to make a sound. Then a knock came on his door.

"Cover yourself with the blankets," Barrett instructed Vilka.

She seemed nonchalant at first, but as the knock came a second time, her eyes filled with fear, and she hid her head under the sheets.

He opened his bedroom door and was greeted by Mother's glowering face. "There's a chap at the door. Says he needs to speak with you." She tutted, shaking her head at his appearance. "You should be ashamed of yourself. Thought you was supposed to be organising the festival, not partaking in it like some common lout."

"Perks of the job," he groaned, closing the door in her face. He shouted, "Tell him I'll be there in a minute!" His heart skipped a beat as he turned back to the shrouded Vilka. "Look, I'm going to have to leave and speak with that man. Listen to me carefully. *Nobody* can find out you're here... not a single, sodding soul... not even my mother or brother. Do you hear me?"

She swiped the bedclothes from her face. "Oh, so you're my protector now, are you? A hundred thanks, but you needn't bother."

"I'm being serious," he hissed before lowering his tone. "Stay here until I return, and I'll... I'll feed you as much as you want when I get back."

She narrowed her eyes at him. "What your ma stocking?"

"We'll have ham, sausages, gammon, and some fresh vegetables."

"Fine. But what am I supposed to do if that ma of yours comes knocking?"

"She won't." At least, he prayed she wouldn't. "Just stay in this room, will you? When I return, we'll talk."

She grumbled her assent and rolled over in the bed to face the wall. He wasn't sure he trusted her to stay put, but what choice did he have? If Marc Kest was here, then the Baroness knew Barrett had Vilka. He would have to persuade the lawyer otherwise.

Steeling himself, he squeezed into some trousers and went to the front door.

Marc Kest was wearing a thin smile, his face weary from the night before. "Good noon, Mister Barrett. I must apologise for intruding on you like this, especially after all the merrymaking of last night, but I've been sent to escort you to meet with the Baroness."

A chill prickled Barrett's spine. "The Baroness? Why would she call for a meeting today of all days? We stewards have been given the day off. It's tradition. I'm not due back at the manor till tomorrow morning. In fact, have you not been given the day off also?"

Marc's smile was waning. "Alas, a lawyer knows no reprieve. My lady shan't take up much of your time, and your day spent away from the Balenmanor shall still be so. My lady awaits you in a room above the Crooked Sparrow."

The Crooked Sparrow? Why would the Baroness hold a meeting above a tearoom? *Unless, of course, the meeting was a secret.*

"Very well," Barrett said. It wasn't like he had much choice. He slid into his boots and followed the lawyer down the garden path.

He gazed back at his bedroom window as he neared the gate, wondering how long Vilka would remain before plotting her next escape.

"Lovely arrangement you have here," Marc said, gesturing at the loweflowers beside the fence. "You have good taste."

"My mother does."

They walked the rest of the way in silence. And the streets were equally quiet, filled with more empty bottles and discarded chunks of meat and bone than people. The few folks that did wander the streets looked almost dead.

When they reached the Crooked Sparrow, Barrett looked out onto Halmond Square. The labourers had taken down most of the tents and stalls and packed them away. He looked at the space where the old oracle's tent had been. She had abandoned Balenmeade to tell the fortunes of more luckless sods in Dulenmeake, Vinerheim, or beyond.

"Why have you stopped?" Marc said, looking puzzled. "You know you've nothing to fear from the lady, don't you?"

Barrett offered the man a meek smile. *If only you knew what your lady was capable of.* He accepted the door that the lawyer held open for him, and they ascended the steps to the apartment above the tearoom.

Heatha stood by a window overlooking the square, dressed in a black velvet dress and the largest pearl necklace he'd ever seen. *Hardly inconspicuous.* As she turned to face Barrett, she nodded at the lawyer, and he took his leave.

"My lady," Barrett said, knowing the words might very well be his last. If this meeting wasn't about Vilka's appearance in his house, it was surely about his lack of success in delivering information on the girl to her.

"Mister Barrett. Your face is the first pleasing sight I've seen all morn." Her words took him by surprise. She almost sounded genuine, and there wasn't a hint of malice seeping from her eyes. "But as much as I'd like to converse with you all afternoon, I'm afraid I must be brief."

"My lady," he repeated, bowing his head. The Baroness was caked in makeup. She was either about to experience a second night of Harvest celebrations, or she was covering up the evidence of last night.

"As you know, a madman invaded our banquet last night and delivered news of my father-in-law's untimely demise. What you may not know is that the man's claims were quite genuine. The old fool was telling the truth."

Barrett knew better than to challenge her assertion, so he just listened.

"I'm afraid this news has not settled well with your master. The Baron of the Krämise is greatly grieved by these ill tidings, and he has made it clear to me that he means to travel to Freestone Monastery, to return Jurgen's corpse here, to where it belongs. I've tried to talk him out of this madness, but my attempts proved fruitless."

She fell into silence and returned her gaze to the window. Barrett wondered if this room was her usual haunt, whether she had been watching him from up here as he entered the oracle's tent and was privy to that folly.

He stepped closer to her, clasping his hands behind his back. "What would you have me do, my lady?"

She seemed to chuckle. "See, that's why my husband likes you. And it's why I want you in my service." She turned back to him, frowning. "These are unprecedented times, you understand. Ordinarily, I would never ask this of you. I'm aware you have no background in this sort of field, but I want you to go with my husband. I want you to accompany him to Freestone, no matter how imprudent his quest may be. You need not pack all that much. I'll provide you with coin enough to buy some provisions and a bed at every roadside inn. And you will be more than supplemented for your troubles upon your return. How does five-hundred crowns sound?"

Barrett staggered backwards, almost tripping over a loose floorboard. Five hundred crowns were more than a year's salary... but he couldn't just *leave* Balenmeade. The farthest he'd ventured outside the city gates was Balwick Mill when he was on an errand to pick up some flour. He was an accountant, a house steward who stared at logbooks and records of receipt for a living. His seat was an office chair, not the unforgiving saddle of a horse.

He opened his mouth, but no words came to pass his lips. He had to accept her offer, of course. It wasn't an offer, really. It was an order.

He lingered in the middle of the room, like driftwood floating on the river. Heatha was asking him to act as her informant, but this time she wasn't simply asking him to watch Vilka. She was ordering him to spy on her husband, the Baron of the Krämise, the Baron Without Sorrow, his master. Hanzus Irvaye was the reason Barrett had a job in the first place. He owed the man his life.

Heatha cleared her throat, still gazing out the window. "Without your keen, watchful eye, your unadulterated judgement, Mister Barrett, I fear I could not, in all good conscience, allow my husband to leave my side again. But with *you* at his side..." She turned back to Barrett, and to his surprise, to his horror, her makeup was running down her face. Her unwavering resolve had washed away, leaving her sobbing. "I ask you to do me this great service. I know well that this charge goes well above your station. I know well that this charge goes beyond anything outlined in your contract of employment. But aside from the fact that my house employs you, I am the wife of your liege lord. You owe your lord *and* lady your service. Your unquestioning, unwavering service." Her face creased into one of distaste. "You *will* do as I ask, Barrett Barrett. The arrangements have been made."

You want me to act as your spy? He wanted to speak it, to have her confirm the true nature of his charge, but in so asking, Heatha might call Marc Kest back into the room to have him sink a dagger into his chest.

His body was trembling as he inclined his head.

"Good." Her voice was emotionless. The black makeup lines streaked down her cheeks were the only clue that she'd been crying. "Kest will provide you with riding clothes and provisions enough for the ride to Freestone."

Goddess, preserve me. Freestone was at least a hundred miles away from Balenmeade. It lay across the border, deep in the

Rooksland. *And the border is closed, guarded by the standing army of the Krämise.* How would they react if their liege lord passed by their defences, entering the cursed realm they were shielding the kingdom from? The Baron had truly turned to madness. What would happen if they encountered Rooksfolk carrying the plague? What if highwaymen captured the Baron and held him for ransom?

The disastrous possibilities were endless, but it wasn't his place to question Hanzus's motives or to refuse Heatha's orders. He was going to accompany the Baron on his foolish quest, no matter the consequences. It was either that or he had to pack his things and flee Balenmeade with Mother and Lerry in tow, jobless and homeless, carving out a primitive existence in the hills like a Gunnic tribesman, forever banished from civilised society.

He had to do this for the good of his family, whatever that meant for his own fate.

"I'll do as you ask, my lady." He bowed his head low, scarcely able to meet her eyes. *Dear Goddess, what have I just agreed to?* "How long do I have before we leave?"

She raised an eyebrow at him. She wasn't expecting him to consent so readily. "You will present yourself at the Balenmanor on the morrow, just before dawn, where a steed will await you. Now, Mister Barrett, I want it made clear that you shan't tell a living soul where you are travelling to. Nor will you divulge to any living soul the details of our meeting here."

"What... what if my mother asks?"

"Tell her you've business out of town. It will go on record that you are accompanying my husband on a tour of the meaderies off to the west. Your fellow stewards will be informed that your accountancy services are required for you to audit the meadery books."

Most of the stewards would lap up that story, but Reymond would never believe Barrett had fled Balenmeade without informing him first. Nor would anyone find it convincing that Hanzus Irvaye had suddenly decided to audit the Krämisen meaderies two days after

Harvest. Both lord and lady were acting without thought, reacting on impulse.

First, Vilka had turned Barrett's world upside-down, and now a mad monk messenger threatened to set it aflame.

"Accompanying you will be Ache and Pamen and the Baron's valets, Cay and Lew," Heatha continued, folding her arms. "And Mister Barrett, I hope this goes without saying, but my husband cannot know the real reason you are accompanying him. I have pulled many strings in order to gain you a place at his side. He suspects that I seek representation amongst his party. After all, it was due to that very fear that he decided to attend the negotiations in Carthane without so much as a single guard. But grief clouds his judgement. He will make mistakes, oversights. Regardless, he will at some point suspect you of informing me of his movements, and for that reason, I shall not ask you to relay any messages to me here."

She awaited his response. Disappointed by his silence, she straightened her back and narrowed her eyes at him. "Upon returning to Balenmeade, Mister Barrett, you will tell me all that transpired on your journey. *Everything.* Down to the last monotonous detail. You will be my eyes on this venture, the voice that comforts my husband on my behalf. You carry with you my interests, my will, my..." She faltered, fighting for air, overcome with emotion. "You will do no more nor less than to serve as my *interest*. Am I understood?"

Barrett inclined his head.

There was much more to this charge than Heatha was letting on, but he had a feeling he'd never hear the truth of it from her. Or perhaps this was just one last desperate attempt to torment her husband by making it clear he could never escape her. Every servant in the Balenmanor knew of their mutual hatred. They'd all heard the arguments, the screaming sessions, the bouts of hurling insults. And now Barrett was a pawn in their game. He was Heatha's to command, without question, without hesitation.

"Now, begone from my sight," she said, waving him away before turning back to the window.

Barrett's boots were heavy as he took his leave and trudged back to the house. The streets were alive with revellers sharing stories about the night before, killing their hangovers by consuming more ale. The market stalls were open once more, their greedy merchants eager to bag more coin before the guests departed, and the locals returned to their miserable lives of labour.

The statue of Sage Eturnos that resided on the curve of Jasper's Row smiled down at Barrett with implied benevolence. He realised he might be viewing the statue for the very last time. The previous night's ale surged back into his throat. An elderly woman shot him daggers as he puked at the foot of the monument. As he wiped the sick from his lips, she waved her fist at him and muttered unintelligible abuse.

Barrett sprinted back home, holding his stomach to keep the sick at bay. His mouth filled with bile as he turned the key in the lock and pushed the door inwards. There, standing outside his bedroom door enjoying a pleasant conversation, were Mother and Vilka.

"What did you tell her?" Barrett spat through his teeth, pushing Vilka's shoulders up against the wardrobe door. She was as light as a feather. Her feeble stature offered scant resistance. "You seemed rather friendly with my mother just now, after I told you explicitly to *stay in my room.*"

"Get... your filthy... hands... off me." Vilka twisted her arms in a vain attempt to wriggle free. She kicked at his shins, but there was no force behind her blows. "You hold no sway over me. Besides, your ma came into the room without knocking. What were I to do?"

He loosened his grip, anger subsiding. "What did you say to her? What were you talking about?"

"Get *off* me." She kicked between his legs, and the blow hit the mark. He staggered backward, clutching at his aching crotch, his knees wobbly. "I didn't tell your ma ought. Matter of fact, I saved you from a good smack across the head. When your ma found me hiding in your bed, she thought I were some slice of harlotry. But I set her straight. I told her you were a kindly man that offered me his bed for the night." She glowered at him, raising her arm as a threat to strike again. "Though I'm starting to reconsider your intentions. Why'd you really drag me here, eh? What did you do to me in the night?"

"*What?*" Barrett straightened, fighting the urge to yelp in agony.

"Relax," she said, cooling her tone. "I'm only fucking with you. You still don't get it, do you? I ain't about to rat you out, not to no one about nothing."

Barrett retreated to his bed and seated himself on the edge, holding his head in his hands. He couldn't stop the tears from pouring down his face as the terrible reality of his situation seeped in. He was going to leave Balenmeade to accompany and spy on his liege lord. And though he didn't want to, he didn't have a choice.

"What... what you doing?" Vilka asked, bemused. He could hear the floorboards squeaking under her weight as she paced around the room. "Look, I'm grateful for all you've done. I know what you did for me last night. Those crooks would've dragged me away and had their way if you hadn't taken me away. I appreciate that. I do."

"You don't understand," Barrett said, lifting his head. He was aware of his lips wobbling, of the tears trickling down his cheeks, that the last remaining drops of his manliness were seeping through the floorboards. It didn't matter what she thought of him, not anymore. He would ride out of the city gates in only a few hours, taking the road north and then west toward the border.

"Then help me understand." She smiled, exposing a warmness he'd never witnessed. "Where did you go to, just now?"

Barrett swallowed his better judgement and told her all that had transpired during his meeting with the Baroness, how he would soon depart Balenmeade on a fool's errand to Freestone.

Vilka sat on the bed beside Barrett and pursed her lips in thought. "It's a lot to take in."

"Vilka, while I'm away, I want you to stay here in my home. In my room, well hidden. Or else leave the city for good. It's not safe for you here in Balenmeade. If anyone spots you wandering these streets, the Baroness will have you captured again."

Vilka chuckled, staring down at the floor. "You *still* don't get it, do you? After all this time." She sighed, her eyes darting around nervously. "I'm no prisoner of Heatha Irvaye." She turned to face him, seeming somewhat amused. "Your Baroness made me a deal, just like she did with you. I ain't *imprisoned* by her, Barrett. I'm working for her."

Barrett laughed along with her, spurred on by her grin. But he wasn't amused, not in the slightest. Could it be that all along, the Baroness had been keeping Vilka locked away in the attic to serve some strange purpose? Was that the reason she'd been gallivanting with Sir Denzus, to spy on the knight on Heatha's behalf?

He felt sick on the back of his tongue. "So, all along, you've been *working* for Heatha?"

Vilka frowned. "Don't be acting like you're some sort of sage. You said it yourself. You agreed to serve as Heatha's agent long before that messenger arrived at your feast."

It was at that moment that he realised he had no idea who she was. Once again, she was a complete stranger to him. The few facts he knew about her were most likely inventions, falsities designed to fool him. And he was a fool to fall for them. Vilka had never been a prisoner. She'd never been helpless nor at risk of losing her life. She was much more than a petty criminal or a lowly vagrant – or a lot less – she was a spy of one of the most powerful women in the whole of Gadensland.

Then a horrible thought crossed his mind. "Vilka, why were you really sleeping in the Balenmanor stables?"

She flashed him a smile. "I was there for you, Barrett. Just for you."

"I don't believe you. Why would the Baroness place you there just for me to find you? What purpose would that serve?"

"Heatha said your loyalty had to be tested to see which direction it swayed. You didn't even know me, and yet you protected my honour over the interests of your liege lord. You witnessed me flirting with your master's cousin, and yet you said nothing. Not to Denzus, nor to Hanzus."

Barrett would have puked if there was anything left inside him. All life was drained from his body, and Vilka was poisoning him with every noxious sentence.

If Vilka was telling the truth, the Baroness had done much more than use Barrett as her pawn. She had been testing him, goading him to act in service to her husband. By failing to inform Hanzus of Vilka's misdeeds, Barrett had established himself as a disloyal servant. And perhaps that was what Heatha had been searching for all along.

The only question that remained was what did Heatha have in store for her husband? She had spent so much time and effort working against him. What sinister act had she plotted?

"I was trying to shield you from harm," Barrett said, tears stinging his eyes. "I stayed silent after seeing you with Sir Denzus and finding you during the Harvest dance... not out of some twisted devotion to Heatha... I did it to protect *you*."

Vilka shrugged. "All I know is your lack of service to your lord pleased Heatha greatly."

Anger was bubbling within him, melting away the sadness and grief until there was nothing left but revulsion, loathing. "Was *anything* you said true? The story about your parents... the Bloodkin... Are you foreign, or is your accent just another pretence? Are you some local Gutterfolk the Baroness found scratching a living on the street?"

The lingering hints of humour faded from her face, leaving behind a scowl. "I didn't tell no lies. I altered the truth is all." Her frown deepened, her brows folding into the bridge of her nose. "Your lady picked me up off the streets after I were begging for days and days for scraps and the odd flash of copper." She grabbed him by the chin, her grip strong and resolute, forcing him to face her. "My ma and pa were murdered by Bloodkin. I hid from them for a time, and

249

when I escaped, they chased me for days and days. *Weeks*. And before I knew it, I were here in this dingy excuse for a town." She lowered her hand and turned away from him, repulsed by his face. "Your lady lifted me up again. Gave me a home. A purpose."

"An evil purpose," Barrett hissed. "Heatha Irvaye despises her husband. She lives and breathes to thwart him. I wouldn't put plotting his death past her." He waggled an accusing finger at her. "And *you* have been aiding and abetting her. And you... you lied to *me*."

Vilka shook her head in disbelief. "And I'd do it again if it meant I were able to see another day."

"Get out," Barrett spat, and when she didn't get to her feet, he sliced his hand through the air, threatening to strike her. "Get *out*! Leave me alone! I don't *ever* want to see your face again!"

Vilka scoffed as she pounced onto her feet. She padded over to the door and spun back on her heel to face him. "You might despise me, but I'm still thankful you saved me."

"*Get out!*" He reached for the first thing he could find – a hefty book – and threw it across the room.

Ducking, she opened the door and escaped before his ire could threaten her further.

Barrett collapsed on his bed, haunted by Vilka's revelations and the impending journey he was about to embark upon. Tears rolled down his face as he repeated Vilka's words in his mind, over and over, like an insidious prayer. He couldn't believe he'd been foolish enough to look out for her.

He supposed that no matter what he thought or felt, he remained Heatha's puppet, hers to do with as she pleased. On the face of it, Barrett served Hanzus Irvaye, his liege lord and employer, before any other. But in truth, he was the Baroness's now, serving her in secret.

He was a traitor, a turncoat, a conspirator, whether willing or not.

The bitter thoughts encircled his mind like a pack of wolves waiting to consume him. If he wasn't careful, Hanzus and Heatha would consume him together, feast on his flesh and shit him out into the river.

As he drifted off to sleep, he realised that this was the last time he'd ever rest in his own bed. When the sun rose next, Barrett would be gone.

Solace

Please, Holy Mother, please forgive my father, for he has walked a path of impurity, broken bread with tainted persons, infected minds, and desecrated hearts. And yet I implore you to embrace him, though I know it is not my place to do so.

Vilka was gone, and judging by the piles of dirty clothes and overturned boxes left in her attic room, she'd fled in a hurry. Heatha must have realised her husband would pay the girl a visit and had smuggled her out of the city or had her corpse dumped in the river.

Hanzus had spent the afternoon pacing around his study, hiding away from Heatha and her spies, and although he was alone at last, he knew he would never be at peace. Jurgen was dying. Jurgen's soul would never be accepted by the Goddess, no matter how many times he prayed for it. It would fall and sink and drown in the endless sea of Oblivion, dissipating into a million pieces and feeding the eternal blackness.

Jurgen deserved his fate, that was beyond any doubt, and yet Hanzus's heart throbbed with sorrow and pangs of remorse. There had been countless occasions in which he could have intervened, where he might have guided his father down a holier path, but he'd done nothing, watching as the dread insanity of his black soul worsened, festering.

If Hanzus had acted differently, none of this would have happened. There wasn't much he could do now, but there was *something*. The only chance Jurgen's soul had of reaching the Goddess was to bury his body under the oak of his name – the great tree planted on the day of his birth, destined to absorb his earthly vessel when it returned to the dirt. Oak burial was a Krämisen tradition, passed down to the Irvaye lords by the first Gunnic converts to Hektorism. Jurgen would be the last Irvaye buried under an oak. Jurgen had not planted a tree when Hanzus was born, nor had Hanzus seeded for the births of Francessa and Hessan. Thus, the only oak that stood awaiting its corpse was the one Jurgen's father had seeded for his son.

Holy Mother, please accept my father into your care. I know he has sinned... gravely, gravely sinned... but I will have him repent. As sure as I beseech you now, Jurgen will turn to you before he draws his last breath. Or else allow me to atone for his sins in his stead.

Hanzus stopped himself from condemning his soul any further. Many years ago, a brother of the Order of Mutlen told him that a man could atone for the sins of another, inviting their trespasses unto themselves and cleaning the former's spirit of guilt. It was possible that the monk had been talking out of his arse, or that Hanzus had consumed too much wine to comprehend his true meaning. But perhaps it was feasible.

There was only one man in Balenmeade who could clarify such a theory. *And he might just be my only hope.*

"My lord," the bishop said with a warming smile as Hanzus opened the doors of the Chapel of Sage Burnardus. "Yours is a welcome face. Welcome indeed. Come, unburden yourself before the Holy Mother." His ancient features creased with concern as he noted the baron's disposition. "What ails you, my child?" He handed Hanzus a white candle and ushered him along the lines of pews, halting by the altar of the Goddess.

"Father, I grow weary." Hanzus wasn't sure where to begin or if he could explain all that troubled his mind.

Bishop Clarayne was the only man in Balenmeade whose loyalties he did not question. The man had been his confidant since he was a small child, a father when Jurgen was off fighting his wars, a guiding light when all was dark.

Hanzus scanned the pews to ensure they were alone. "Father, I come seeking solace." *And answers.* He closed his eyes and felt a salty sting under his lids. "My time here grows thin, so I must be succinct. Is it possible to atone for the sins of another?"

Clarayne's eyes widened, studying the baron in astonishment. "You refer to the practice of trans-atonement?" He retrieved the candle from Hanzus's grasp, realising this was no ordinary visit. "Please, my lord, take a seat."

They sat in the front pew, bathing in the Goddess's benevolent gaze. Hanzus had spent a lifetime gazing up at the regal carving that floated above the altar. Her impassive stare had soothed him countless times, promising to protect and bless him with her grace. But his prayers and implorations had fallen on deaf ears. Despite the purity of his thoughts and the righteousness of his actions, the Goddess had overseen his marriage to a monster and indentured him to a king who displayed not a shred of gratitude after Hanzus's intervention at the Battle That Never Was.

"Where did you come to read about trans-atonement?" the bishop asked. "The Hektorian church does not teach nor condone such a practice. False prophets have claimed that one soul can absorb the sins of another, yes, but theirs is a black twisting of our holy faith. Such a dark act as absorption cannot be countenanced nor accepted. Our prophet, Hektor, warned us against such black rituals."

Hanzus inhaled the cool air. He wasn't here to listen to another one of Clarayne's monologues. The last midnight mass had taken place not long ago, and the bishop's dire protestations still rang in his ears.

"I'm leaving, father. On the morrow, I ride for the border." The announcement drained the chapel of its calm, carving concern into the image of the Goddess. She gazed down at the two of them, her wooden face offering no more than a declaration of her presence.

Clarayne stared at Hanzus, his mouth hanging open. "You mean to leave us so soon? But, my lord, you've only just retaken your rightful place amongst your people." He searched the baron's face for answers. "You must winter here, in the manor. You... you must, as you have always done."

"I *must*? Father, do you question the righteousness of my will?"

"No... no, of course not, my lord. But why, with such haste, do you leave us? The flock here look to you to inspire them, to guide them in every manner of their lives. Without you here, the Krämise is starved of its beating heart."

"You are here," Hanzus said, trying to smile. "The city's conscience will remain. Under your tutelage, the folk of Balenmeade will be placated. Besides, I shan't be gone for too long. My plans to winter here in the Balenmanor have not been interrupted. I will only be gone for a few weeks at most."

"A lot can happen in a few weeks." The bishop's frown deepened. "My lord, may I speak freely?"

You mean you haven't been thus far? Hanzus nodded.

"My lord, during your absence over the summer, the people of Balenmeade suffered. Suffered severely." Clarayne lowered his voice, realising the enormity of his words.

"Go on."

"It's your wife, my lord," Clarayne whispered, his wrinkled face gripped by fear. "In your absence, she commits unspeakable acts in your name. Threatening persons at the point of a dagger. I know not her intentions, but I have heard dozens of confessions, from magistrates to chambermaids. She blackmails and extorts, raising the taxes of those that disagree with her. I've even heard tell that she dabbles in witchcraft."

Hanzus was already aware of the awful tactics Heatha employed, but that last claim was ridiculous. "Until Hessan is of age, Heatha rules my realm in my stead whenever I ask it."

"Indeed. Though Hessan is not the only young male to own the name of Irvaye."

Hanzus considered the man. Was he seriously suggesting that Denzus the Younger should be named as his temporary successor?

"Forgive my insolence, my lord," Clarayne said, lowering his gaze to the stone floor. "So, it would seem you do not come seeking my counsel. It appears that a lot has changed since last we spoke this way. As sure as your wife grows in influence and gall, your own vitality does wane."

Hanzus mulled over that. If any other had spoken those words, their severed head would soon adorn the gates outside the Balenmanor, but Clarayne's cloth and his unwavering loyalty to Hanzus was his protection.

But Clarayne had gone a step too far, and he realised such as he lifted his chin and met his baron's eyes. "Forgive me, my lord, but I am pained by your departure."

"And I am pained by the damnation of my father's soul!"

The words hung there like a bad stink, wafting in and out of the pews, infesting this holy place with their pestilence.

The bishop blinked with surprise before creasing into a smile. "My lord, you do not have to absorb Jurgen's sins in order to guide him to the Goddess. With prayer and sincere imploration, his soul might be spared. For the Goddess may forgive those..."

"Who ask her for absolution," Hanzus finished the phrase. "But you know Jurgen. He does not repent because he does not believe he has sinned. Why do you think he joined the Order of Mutlen after he abdicated his title? The Gadian orders would have asked him to absolve himself of sin, but the Mutlen brothers have their own way of doing things."

"You are leaving us to ride for Freestone," Clarayne concluded, nodding along with his own words. "You seek to convince your father to repent before he passes." He closed his eyes, cringing as if hurt. "I feared as soon as I heard that messenger at the banquet speak that he belonged to the Order of Mutlen." He opened his eyes and studied the baron's face. "So, it is true. You know well what the Order is, my lord. You know they cannot be trusted."

"The monk did not lie," Hanzus explained. "I do not condone nor sympathise with the Order, but I have never disputed their devotion to my father."

Clarayne inclined his wise, old head. "And yet you accept they will placate him with nonsense, that his soul will be accepted by the Goddess with his baggage of sin."

"Which is why I must reach Freestone before his soul is consigned to Oblivion."

Clarayne nodded, a firm jolt. "Then you must go, my lord. You must choose your leanest stallion and make haste across the border. I will pray nightly for the Goddess to bless you for this journey." He rummaged around in the loose flaps of his heavy robe. "Here, take this with you and wear it around your neck for good fortune. There may be dark forces at play, working in the shadows against you. But the grace of the Goddess will be with you always."

Hanzus accepted the wooden cross and looped the string around his neck. "Thank you, father."

"You must guard yourself from the false monks that surround your father." He placed an ancient hand on Hanzus's arm. "Your heart is true, my lord. Uncorrupted but not incorruptible. Keep the Cross of Hektor close to your heart, and with it, your resolve shall never crumble."

Hanzus nodded, realising the bishop spoke the truth. He seldom believed anything Jurgen had told him, even after his abdication. The former baron had spent the first few years of his abdication residing in the east wing of the Balenmanor, but as soon as Hanzus had uncovered the affair with Heatha, Jurgen exiled himself across the border. And now, surrounded by Mutlen monks, Hanzus would have to shield himself from much more than his father's weasel words.

"You must choose your companions carefully," Clarayne continued. "Those whose hearts and minds are pure."

Hanzus stirred, realising his buttocks ached. He'd chosen Lew and Cay as his valets, and he would have limited the size of his party there had Sheriff Erman not insisted – in front of Heatha and a gaggle of aldermen – that the city provide him with a guard. Hanzus compromised by choosing Pamen and Ache for that service after Fritt Karston tried insisting on an escort of ten knights. Later, Chamberlain Jupe had informed Hanzus that the manor's accountant, Barrett Barrett, would accompany him also. Realising the steward was one of Heatha's spy, he'd gladly accepted. After all, if he declined the services of Barrett, Heatha would provide him with an effective alternative.

"My companions have been chosen," Hanzus admitted, mulling over the five that would be joining him on the road. *Though I don't believe there is a pure heart among them.*

Departure

E very stride was a step toward oblivion. The sea of blackness was calling Barrett, beckoning him with its harmonious dirge. His boots were heavy, as though filled to the ankle with putrid sludge, seeping into his flesh, slowing him down with every footstep. Each step fought against his will, feeding his dread as he betrayed his gut.

Marc Kest had awoken Barrett before sunrise, inviting himself into his home and inspecting the clothes and provisions he'd packed for the journey. He provided Barrett with leather riding clothes, which were constrictive and uncomfortable, but Barrett had no choice but to squeeze into them, as he possessed no alternative of his own. Kest also provided him with a purse full of crowns, reminding him that the Baroness would award him with five hundred more upon his return.

If I return. Doom swallowed him whole as he raced toward the Balenmanor.

Turn around, return to your home, and lock your door forever. It was a beautiful thought, a dream in which Heatha did not pursue retribution for his betrayal, and the Chamberlain did not sever his contract of employment.

His reality was bondage, servitude to the Bitch of Balenmeade. Heatha owned him, and she willed his legs forward now, guiding him towards his dreadful task. She worked him like a puppet, a prop whose existence did not matter.

The Baron would punish him, someway, somehow, for his treachery and insolence. He had surely realised Barrett was escorting him for nefarious reasons. After all, Cay and Lew were his valets, his most trusted companions. Pamen and Ache were the fiercest warriors in Balenmeade, men whose purpose was to protect their lord. On the other hand, Barrett was an office clerk whose arse rarely left its chair, let alone finding itself on a saddle.

If the Baron isn't aware of his wife's machinations, he will be before long. And where would that leave Barrett then? Sure, he could confess that Heatha had employed him as her spy and profess that he did so against his will, but that didn't make him innocent of low treason.

He would be dragged back to Balenmeade and executed if the Baron did not gut him there and then.

Light rain pattered down, projecting the bleakness within his festering mind. His cloak was soaking, after being splashed by a couple of passing carriages, and being dipped into several roadside puddles. But he didn't have time to avoid the puddles or swerving vehicles. He wouldn't slow down or stop for anything.

A solitary guardsman greeted him as he reached the outer gate of the Balenmanor. He could see the man's lips moving under his hood, but the wind carried his words away. Sensing this, the man cupped his hands around his mouth and bellowed, "Well met, Mister Barrett! They're expecting you!"

Barrett's heart sank. He'd been told to present himself outside the manor before sunrise. Had the plan changed? Was the company waiting for him on the other side of the wall, cursing him for his tardiness?

Barrett didn't recognise the guardsman, but he accepted his outreached hand to shake all the same. "Thank you."

"May the sweet lady smile upon you," the guard said, displaying a gappy row of brown teeth. "Goddess speed, and may she bless your charge."

Barrett cringed. *I doubt the Goddess blesses any part of my charge. I doubt she'll bless me ever again, so long as I live.*

The sky cast heavy shadows over the Balenmanor, starving its vibrancy and grandeur. The servants would soon be stirring, and the manor would awaken with their rise, but for now, the very walls and windows slumbered. And when the collective eyes of the city's beating heart opened, Barrett would be gone.

Eight curious eyes blinked over at Barrett as he skittered across the courtyard. Four men huddled together under the veranda, falling silent as Barrett approached. Lew welcomed him with a tired smile. Cay glared at Barrett with folded arms, as he might greet an untrusted stranger. Pamen and Ache met Barrett with uninterested glances.

"Morning, I suppose," Cay groaned as Barrett reached the soggy group, all dressed in riding leathers and heavy cloaks. "Did you get any sleep? Well, me neither. Harvest was fun while it lasted, but I fear I'll be on the road for the rest of my life."

Lew placed a consoling hand on the valet's shoulder. "You and me both, lad. Ain't it a thrill?" He grinned at Barrett. "Well met, lad. That chestnut lassie over there's yours." He cocked his head toward the right corner of the yard. Barrett was relieved to discover he was referring to a horse.

A flustered stableboy attended six steeds. The Baron's white horse, Lion, caught his eye. The other horses seemed meek and innocuous beside the impressive stallion. *Like a lord among peasants.* Barrett was no husbandry expert, so identifying which of the five brown horses belonged to him was no simple task.

Lew, sensing the steward's befuddlement, leaned close and whispered, "Yours is the one to the left o' Lion." Then, standing tall, he announced, "Her name's Myra. Named the lassie meself."

Cay coughed into his hand, stifling a laugh. "*Myra?* What kind of name is that? Sounds Marrid."

Lew furrowed his brows, fresh wrinkles boring into his forehead. "If you've an issue, take it up with the Baron. I'm sure he'd be thrilled to hear you gripe about the mare I kindly named after his niece."

Cay scowled at his associate, muttering under his breath.

"Speaking of the Baron," Barrett said, scanning the courtyard. "Where is he?"

"Question the punctuality of your lord, do you?" Ache growled, breaking from his hushed conversation with Pamen.

"Last-minute preparations," Cay answered, ignoring the huge guardsman. "I reckon he's sneaking in some extra kip before we're away." He winked at Barrett before turning to face Ache's sneer. "But you didn't hear that from me."

"Watch your tongue, cur," Ache snapped, pointing a meaty finger at the valet. "Speak ill of your lord again. I'll do more than caution."

Cay shrugged, then turned to Barrett. "Would you believe I've been dealing with this grump for an hour? More fool me. I should've arrived as late as you."

Pamen placed a hand on Ache's shoulder, which seemed to calm the brute.

"He ain't late," Lew said, checking his pocket watch. "Do you see the Baron anywhere?"

Cay grumbled under his breath. "Well, you should go and drag him from his cave."

"Quiet, lad," Lew snapped. "We was told to wait, so wait, we will."

"No, the lad's right," Ache sighed before revealing a grin. "Our lord might be lost in the dark places of the manor. Someone should check on him."

The disrespect of these so-called protectors of the Baron was incredible. *Even his staunchest supporters openly jest about him.*

Ache stepped in front of Cay, his massive chest pressing into him.

"What say you slip inside and have a little look about? Call out to our sleeping lord to arouse him."

Cay's smug smile dissipated as the massive soldier glowered down at him. Then, as it appeared certain the valet was about to wet his breeches, the door to the Balenmanor opened. The four retainers moved like clockwork, falling in line beside Barrett. They stood to attention, facing the door.

The Baron stepped out into the grey morning, grimacing at his subjects. He wore a black cuirass emblazoned with the stout boar's head of his house, underneath an emerald cloak joined at the neck by a silver trinket. He'd tied his dark hair into a bun and shaved his face clean of its former shadow. His eyes were bloodshot with fatigue, but his gaze was fierce, sharp, alive and alert, piercing them, demanding answers.

This was a revitalised Hanzus, one stirred into action. The beleaguered traveller that returned from Carthane was dead. The quiet, brooding noble that had attended the Harvest feast, staring into space, his mind elsewhere, had withered away. The Baron Without Sorrow had returned to grace the world, and he was leaving his rightful seat once again, drawn away by his father's death rattle.

An intricate sheath hung from the Baron's belt. A black boar's head pommel topped the hilt of the hidden blade. A sword like that was not intended for sparring sessions or petty duels. It was a blade of war. Or rather, it was intended to appear that way, to frighten and warn potential hoodlums and brigands on the road. *Are we riding to Freestone, or are we marching into battle?* He remembered the Dogmen Lew and Cay told him they'd encountered with the Baron. He wondered if that very blade had sliced through fur and flesh, slaying monsters like the great swords of history.

Marc Kest had made Barrett pack enough clothes for a fortnight, but they had never discussed the length of his blade. And so, he'd equipped himself with the one thing his father had left before abandoning the family: a scarcely sharp short sword tucked into a battered sheath.

"Gentlemen," Hanzus said as he slipped into leather gloves, marching into the yard without looking at anyone. He snapped his fingers, and they all fell in behind him. "I pray you have made peace with your families and with the Goddess."

"The Goddess smiles upon us, milord," Lew said, helping the Baron into his saddle.

Barrett waited for the others to claim their horses. The mare that remained was the smallest of the pack. Myra's listless orbs blinked down at him, sniffing him curiously before turning away, uninterested. *Are you feeling as uninspired as I am?* Cay chuckled as Barrett struggled to jump into his saddle.

He afforded one last glance at the Balenmanor before they rode through the open gate. Dread punched him in the gut. Mother and Lerry would have to fend for themselves now. Sure, his wages from the Balenmanor would still flow into their house, but he wouldn't be there to protect them if anything went wrong. Who would comfort Lerry and read to him by the fire? Who would ward off the crooks and drunks that passed the house in search of an unlocked door?

And what about the meddling of Heatha and Vilka? Would they stop at tormenting Barrett's person, or would their spitefulness extend to the ones that shared his blood?

Bile infused his tongue.

The monotonous mornings he spent filing through reports, listening to Reymond's daily exploits, had come to an abrupt end. And his fellow accountant would turn up to work in a few hours to discover he was, again, forced to work alone. *I'm a dreadful friend, but it's all out of my control.*

As trepidation coursed through his veins, squeezing his lungs, he took in a sharp breath of air. Balenmeade air – moist, woody, the odd whiff of horse shit and rising smoke – the last he'd inhale for a while.

Balenmeade was sleeping as the party rode through its dark, damp streets. The only identifiable signs of life came in the form of solemn farmhands trudging towards the fields outside the city walls.

Barrett's thighs slapped against his saddle. His leather trousers were tight up against his arse. The realisation he would return to his bed in a few weeks buffered his resolve. How he longed to turn around and return home, but the rain pulled his mind back to the line of horses trotting ahead of him.

Balenmeade faded from view with the arrival of dawn. The rain abated, scared off by the sun.

The Old Road was nothing more than a dirt track, leading through the golden fields and plots of farmland that surrounded the city for miles. Trees bordered the road, either by accident or design, and their great overhanging branches rained wet leaves and dew down upon them.

They rode in silence for much of the morning, Barrett lagging at the rear so he could keep everyone in sight. The Baron led the procession with Pamen Ostarne at his side. The former's steed proceeded with as much guile and determination as its rider, forcing the others to play catch up.

Barrett swallowed as they passed a signpost that declared they were leaving the jurisdiction of Balenmeade. This was the farthest he'd ever ventured from home, from Mother and Lerry. Strangely, the first person who came to mind when he thought about all he'd left behind was Vilka. The girl's justification for serving Heatha was nauseating. Though he supposed he was one to talk. Indeed, he wondered whether the Baron was aware that he rode with his wife's spy.

Barrett's heart pounded at the thought, drawing sweat from his face. He had sworn an oath, not only to serve the Baron of the Krämise by virtue of his birth within the barony, but to serve as a loyal steward of the Balenmanor as well. And here he was, working against his liege lord, serving the dark interests of the Bitch of Balenmeade.

What are you doing, Barrett? As he gazed ahead at Hanzus, the honour and nobility of the man was plain in his dress and the way he held himself. He was a lord of principle, a man to inspire, a white spirit against Heatha's black soul. *And yet you betray him readily.* He dismissed that thought at once. *What choice do I have? If I return to Balenmeade with nothing to offer the Baroness, she'll have my family murdered.*

A voice barked in his ear, stirring him. "You ride like a girl."

Barrett lost his balance, almost lost control of his reins. Once he'd regained his composure and straightened his back, Cay was riding to his left.

"Well?" Cay said, his expression plain. "Do you hear me?"

Barrett shot him a glare in reply.

Cay chuckled then, revealing his sarcasm. "Seriously though, where did you learn to ride?"

"Actually, I never really did," Barrett admitted, remembering the time he rode a donkey during Harvest as a child. He'd fallen flat on his face, bruising his eyes, and almost breaking his nose. "Well, not exactly." Still, he was competent enough to ride on the road. After all, his job in the Balenmanor required him to run errands on horseback every once in a while.

"Well, you could certainly use a lesson or two." Cay bit down on his lip, then spat at the trees. "You have no idea what lies ahead of us, do you?"

Barrett glanced at Cay before returning his eyes to the road to ensure he didn't fall from his saddle. "And what do you suppose lies ahead of us?"

Cay rolled his eyes. "Oh, come off it. Do you seriously see me as some sort of dunce? I know the Baron's decision to ride out wasn't thought out or organised, but his decision to include an accountant in this foolish venture? Something else is afoot. Something strange awaits us at the end of this journey. I know it."

Barrett smiled at the valet's ignorance. "You think too much," he said, feigning disinterest. "I simply follow orders. And I was ordered to ride with the Baron."

Cay chuckled. "That's the first time I've been accused of thinking. Most claim I speak too much, but in truth, most people are bores." His smile became a frown. "Speak too much I may, but that don't stop my eyes from working. I saw the way Hans looked at you as we mounted. He don't want you here with us. So that begs the question, whose orders do you follow?"

Barrett stiffened, unable to meet the valet's invasive stare.

"I see." Cay sighed. "Well, in that case, you needn't worry about enduring your saddle for too long. You won't make it to Freestone." And with that, he stirred his mare forward, leaving Barrett alone at the rear.

Barrett felt a pang of pain as Cay joined Lew in the centre of the formation. Lew cocked his head back at Barrett and offered him a weak smile.

A time later, Barrett rode alongside Lew.

"Funny," the elder valet said. "Weren't so long ago I were thanking the Goddess I'd made it home in one piece. And though I were only home a matter of days, well..." He shook his head, his greasy hair flapping against his shoulders. "Guess what I'm trying to say is, I'm happy to be on the road again." He shot a sideways glance at Barrett. "Hey, ain't this your first time?"

"My first time, what?"

Lew offered a knowing smile. "Your first time leaving the kingdom."

"Uh, yes." Barrett couldn't meet the old man's gaze any longer. He couldn't discern whether Lew was mocking him or hearing of the steward's lack of travel pained him. Cay, in as many years as Barrett, had traversed much of Gadensland and braved the volatile waters of the Northern Sea. The Balenmanor seemed a dungeon at times, but within its walls, Barrett knew where he was. Who he was. *What* he was.

The unknown road and the foreign land it led him to were frightening prospects. Gut-wrenching. Everything he knew about the Rooksland was a sentence in a history book or an anecdote in a memoir.

"Ain't no shame in it," Lew said. "Truth be told, this is my first time travelling to the Rooksland also."

"Truly?" Barrett found that hard to believe. Lew, one of the oldest men in the Baron's service, had never journeyed west? *He's just trying to make me feel better.*

"Truly, truly." Lew reached into his saddlebag, retrieved what appeared to be an apple, leaned forward, and fed it to his horse. "Never seen the appeal, honest. Too wild. A bit like the Krämise, I guess. Funnily enough, the only time I considered visiting the Rooksfolk was when the plague spread about, and the Baron ordered the palisade wall built across the border."

"*Why?*" Barrett asked, flabbergasted.

Lew shrugged. "Call it a peculiar curiosity. I've seen the plague in the flesh many years ago. Does madder things to the mind than the body. I can tell you that."

Barrett recoiled at the thought, praying they did not encounter any plague victims across the border. "What do you know about Freestone?" he asked, hoping to forget about the plague.

"I know that's where the Baron's pa dwells. Brothers what live there belong to the Mutlen order." He glanced over his shoulder, gauging Cay's distance behind them. "And a man can't help but hear dark tidings about those brothers. Man could hear more than a few unfortunate tales of their sort."

"What tales?"

Lew shrugged his shoulders. "Oh, you know. Only that they's a bunch of old recluses with nought but the Goddess for company. Must be enough to drive a man round the bend. And some are, lad. I met a traveller once, all proper like. Brimmed hat, walking stick. You know, backpack big enough to hold an 'ole house." Lew brought his steed within reaching distance of Barrett. "So, I bought him a few ales, and his lips got going. Now, by this point, we'd drunk our share o' the cellar, and the mister loosens enough to teach me half the kingdom's secrets. We get to talking about faith. Idle chatter at first. Then he says something I don't quite understand. *I has a brother what tells me the time.* I ask him what he's on about. Don't sound sensible to me. *I know a brother what shows me a good time,* he says then, but like he's repeated himself. What you on about, I ask him again. A good time for what?" Lew looked left and right, then he leaned in toward Barrett, lowering his voice. *"I met a brother o' the church,* he says, *you know, those monks o' the mutt with their hairless scalps and their black robes.* You mean a brother o' the Mutlen order? *Maybe. Can't say I asked much on his charge. Anyway, the monk leads me to an old shack in the middle o' bleeding nowhere. Turns out it's a church o' sorts, though none as Hektor would approve."* Lew scratched his scalp. He was leaking sweat, his brows furrowed deep into his face.

"What was inside the church?" Barrett wanted to know.

Lew bit down on his lip, then he emerged with a smile. "Never mind, lad. Perhaps it's a story for another time."

———

As they rode further west, the verdant fields became wild moors, bordered by pools of stagnant marsh. More trees populated the landscape, but they weren't the rich oaks and thick ash that frequented the Balenreach. These were skinny, dead, or dying shoots of bark, thirsty despite the surrounding dampness.

The land had been abandoned by both Man and the Goddess. Barrett had never realised so much of the Krämise was uninhabitable: thick marshland, miles upon miles of desolate earth that appeared to be afflicted by some form of blight. On the maps, the barony appeared as one big open stretch of green, albeit in the shadow of the Feleric Mountains. The thought of Vilka and the Brother of Mutlen traversing this unforgiving landscape on foot, alone for weeks, was beyond comprehension.

When they finally came to rest, just off the road, Barrett couldn't straighten his legs without a flash of pain. It was as though his riding position had become his natural stance, and walking was now abnormal. He slumped himself against a tree, wiped the sweat from his face, and tried to stretch out his legs.

Just ahead of him, the terrain dipped down into a small basin, a hollow of dry, cracked earth surrounded by tufts of wild grass and fern.

The others had started a fire at the bottom of the slope. Lew was frying sausages and eggs over the flames while Cay sliced a loaf of rye bread. The Baron was marching up and down the perimeter, his eyes alternating between the dirt and the clouds. Pamen and Ache were laughing, sitting cross-legged beside the fire.

"Lad!" Lew waved over at Barrett. "Breakfast's ready, lad!"

Naming it breakfast seemed perverse. His pocket watch – which he'd adjusted as they passed the clock tower of Balenmeade Cathedral – told him it was almost midday. They had been riding for hours without passing a single soul on the road. Barrett rolled his legs down the slope, grabbed a clump of dry earth, and pulled himself to a standing. He almost fell down the hill, though he soon found his footing and stomped over to the fire.

The Baron passed him as he reached the bottom of the slope, his arms folded, muttering something under his breath without looking up.

"Suppose we should call the Baron for breakfast too," Cay said as Barrett plonked himself down between Lew and Pamen.

Lew shook his head at Cay. "Don't be a fool, lad. Did Carthane teach you nought?" He handed Barrett his food on a roll of linen – two sausages, two eggs, and a single slice of rye. "Here. Eat up, lad. I'm afraid it's light rations for now."

"You call this light?" Cay said, grinning down at his own helping. "I'll take your idea of light any day."

"I call this light," Ache groaned, grimacing at his food. "How long till we reach Kellenmoor?"

"Not long, I pray," Pamen said.

Barrett faked a smile, then gobbled down his eggs and sausages. He chewed his bread slowly, watching the Baron pace around the basin's perimeter, muttering as if he was communing with an invisible spirit. He gazed up at the trees atop the elevation where he'd been sitting before joining the others.

At first, Barrett thought he was looking at a branchless tree rooted in front of the others, but the dark form moved, pulsating. It was breathing. No, it couldn't be. As he squinted at the shape, it took form.

A person peeping their head over a clump of tall grass. A black hood shrouded their face in shadow. But Barrett knew they were watching him. He could feel their eyes gnawing into his skin.

Barrett looked at the others to gauge their reactions to this intruder, but they hadn't noticed the watcher and were still tucked into their food. The Baron didn't react either, as he continued to march up and down the basin, arguing with himself.

Barrett opened his mouth to alert them all, but Cay and Ache's jovial banter smothered him into silence. No one paid him any mind as he dropped his bread and stepped away from the fire, approaching the foot of the slope. He narrowed his eyes at the watcher, focusing on the void where a face should be, straining to discern some hint of a feature. But the stranger's face was a mask of black, their head a vague suggestion.

For a moment, he thought he was perhaps mistaken, that he was, in fact, staring at a mound of dark earth or a stump of a felled tree. But he couldn't shake the feeling of invisible eyes penetrating his flesh, invigilating his every movement.

Before he could think to act, something appeared in front of him, blocking his view of the mysterious stranger. The Baron stood in his way, his arms folded tight to his chest.

Barrett craned his neck around Hanzus, peering up at the spot where the watcher had been, but they were gone. If there had been anyone there to begin with. He glanced around, scanning the perimeter of the top of the basin. Nothing. There was no sign that any man or creature had ever been up there.

"Mister Barrett," Hanzus addressed him. "Why do you not break your fast? There will be no further respite once we take to the road. Not until the moon is upon us."

"My lord," Barrett said, attempting a bow. He couldn't remember the last time the Baron had looked him in the eyes, but here he stood, staring at him now. Facing this searing assessment, Barrett was unable to hold his gaze. "I, uh... I have no appetite, my lord."

He looked back to where the black watcher had been and wondered if he should mention it to the Baron. There was no one there now. He'd seem quite the fool with nobody to point at. Perhaps the watcher's absence was proof he'd imagined the whole thing. Yes, that was it. His mind must've been playing tricks on him, conjuring ghosts from his imagination. He was fatigued and his mind was paying the price.

"What is it?" Hanzus asked, narrowing his eyes at the steward. "What are you looking at?"

Barrett gulped down the remnants of bread stuck at the back of his dry throat.

"Nothing... nothing at all, my lord."

A Nameless Peril

Mavrian saw him everywhere she turned, painted on the walls of her chamber, smeared across the pages of her books. Käl's corpse was everywhere, watching her with invisible eyes, appearing before her even when she closed her eyes. His headless form haunted her dreams, blood oozing from his neck-stump as he chased her down an endless staircase. The ghoul caught up to her no matter how fast she descended, and though it possessed no mouth, an ear-splitting shriek hissed from its neck.

News of Käl's murder had spread through Kleäm, and the islanders were treating it like a tragedy. They detested Scarmane Trokluss for his heinous unprovoked attack. As far as they were concerned, the vassmir didn't deserve his fate. No whisper or outcry seemed to acknowledge the conspiracy that Scarmane had uncovered. Either the facts were overlooked, or the islanders denied them.

Scarmane had brought the vassmir's corruption to light in front of the courtiers of Kleäm. And the way Käl's eyes had flashed crimson before his head ceased to exist confirmed he was a fraud. Vassmirs did not possess irises. After consuming the various alchemies that allowed their bodies to become possessed by the Twins, the reds of their eyes disappeared, leaving only the pupils.

Käl had concealed his irises somehow, disguising himself as a holy man in order to steal from the temple's coffers. He was a swindler, a petty charlatan. For years, Mavrian had attended his rituals and listened to his sermons, assuming his intentions were true, his words sincere. And all along, he'd been staging his miracles, doctoring them to create a false image of holiness.

Bastard. Infidel. Scarmane's magic had ended the pretender. Gods-given power had destroyed the man that had professed to speak for them. *The irony is delicious.*

Mavrian reminded every Bloodkin who would listen that the vassmir had earned his fate, but few believed her and fewer still thought it made any difference. Scarmane was now despised by all, from the highest courtiers of Meelian to the lowest scum swabbing the dockyards. But none dared disturb him in his quarters. None dared confront him directly.

Mavrian had heard nothing more about the Veer. He'd supposedly locked himself away in his chamber, awaiting the day they would set sail for the Capital. Mavrian and the Loress would board Scarmane's ship in a few days, embarking on the long voyage to Sela'Fundor. She wouldn't miss the vulgar slab of rock that was Kleäm, but it would be strange not to have the other ladies of Vicker's Tower to turn to.

Mavrian visited the marketplace, hoping to distract her thoughts from Käl and the council she would soon attend on the mainland.

The trade district was curiously quiet. As Mavrian descended the steps and entered the marketplace square, none of the usual sounds and scents greeted her. Most of the stalls had not yet opened, and several more had been abandoned by their merchants, stripped of their signage and wares.

As she glanced around, she realised it was Bloodkin manning the few stalls that were open for business. She remembered Lucian

Grögg and Mudgar Vane's declaring at the banquet that they would rid Kleäm of its Kinsmeer.

They rounded them up! she realised. Empty tables and signposts littered the square. A few of the tables were overturned, and a blunt object had hammered one of them into several split pieces. *They rounded them up and killed them.*

She approached the stand where a lazy-eyed Kinsmeer used to sell her parchment and quills. The blue canvas roof was ripped apart, torn to pieces. As she peered over the desk, she noticed the merchant's boxes were tossed onto their sides, their contents emptied. Piles of smashed crates and torn rolls of parchment littered the ground. And blood... Dark droplets spattered the stone floor and dyed the scraps of parchment.

Somebody had attacked the merchant *here*. Perhaps they had dragged their body over to the wall and thrown it into the sea. Mavrian pictured the unknowing tradesman – a portly Kinsmeer of around forty, always smiling – stabbed and sliced as he was going about his business, hoping to open his stall for the day.

Mavrian felt sick to the stomach as she recoiled from the desk.

She wasn't sure why... or how, but she pitied the Kinsmeer. Sure, the tradesman was pig-skinned and blue-eyed...but she'd chatted with him once, exchanging idle chatter and pleasantries. And now, for the crime of being a Kinsmeer, Mudgar Vane and Lucian Grögg had murdered him.

Not murdered, she realised – after all, murder was the act of killing another Bloodkin – but it didn't sit well with her. *Käl deserved his fate, but what did this old tradesman ever do to anyone?* She hadn't even known the Kinsmeer's name, but he was humble, kind.

"Young lady?"

The voice was a punch to the gut, appearing out of nowhere. Mavrian spun on her heel to find a short, bug-eyed old woman blinking up at her. At first, she thought the woman was a Kinsmeer. She'd never seen a Bloodkin so old and ugly, but her complexion was chalk white and her irises scarlet. Her smock was similar to the dress of Kinsmeeric traders. Perhaps she was a refugee from Sylvia or the so-called Middle Kingdoms. Mavrian had heard of the small pockets of Bloodkin that, for one reason or another, inhabited Kinsmeeric cities and worked for their coin. She couldn't imagine what madness drove them to do so, but supposed it was no different to the Kinsmeer that traded in Kleäm and the southern shores of Ryne.

"You look pale, child," the woman said. Her ancient smile was somewhat reassuring. "Just as the gods made us, eh?" She winked at Mavrian, then nudged her in the arm.

Mavrian opened her mouth to speak, but the woman waved her away and snatched her by the hand.

"Come... *come!*" The woman led Mavrian across the square, weaving in and out of the empty stalls and collapsed tables. "You look like you could use a cup of something. Something strong. And it's a fine day for it, no less."

Words slipped off her tongue like blood dripping into a vial, assaulting Mavrian in quick succession.

They stopped at a stall crammed with small square and circular boxes painted in an assortment of bright colours. Shelves lined the wooden wall behind the stall, filled with potion vials and ornaments and cuttings of fabric. There was no commonality nor theme to the merchant's collection.

The woman released Mavrian's hand, scurried to the other side of the desk, then rested her elbows on the table. "You seem out of sorts, child." She stared at Mavrian for a moment, her fiery eyes boring holes into the young woman's face, then she retrieved a glass vial from under the table. "Here. Take this. This'll calm your spirits well."

"What is it?" Mavrian asked, accepting the vial, and inspecting its clear watery contents. She hoped it wasn't that vodka stuff that Kinsmeer enjoyed. She'd sipped some once from a merchant handing out samples. The horrid beverage had made her puke up her breakfast.

"Just a mild remedy, dear." The woman's smile widened. "My own recipe, no less. Won't cost you a single coin. I mean it." She sighed, scanning the empty stalls bordering her own. "As you can tell, I ain't received much custom these last few days."

Mavrian placed the vial on the table. She wasn't certain of the merchant's play, but there was some sort of mischief afoot, something that would end in her parting with too much coin. *Will this alchemy poison my mind into accepting steep prices?* She gazed over the woman's head, scanning the odd collection of ornaments populating the shelves. *What is this place?* She'd never visited this stall before, nor even glanced at it.

"Thank you, but I'm not thirsty," Mavrian said, hoping to evade the merchant's scheme without causing offence. The last thing she needed was another confrontation.

"No matter," the woman said, snatching the potion and returning it under the table. "Might I ask you a question, dear? For what reason did you come to market? Are you searching for a gift? Are you looking to treat yourself to a trinket? Or perhaps something a little more practical?"

"I... don't really know," Mavrian admitted. She offered the woman a last smile before turning to leave, but as she was about to escape, a thought crossed her mind. "May I ask you a question?" she asked, turning back to the stranger.

"Talk's cheap," the woman said, shrugging. "And I ain't in the business of cheapness."

Mavrian sighed. "I'll compensate you for your time."

The woman raised an eyebrow at that. "Very well. What answer do you seek?"

"The Kinsmeer that were here," Mavrian began, noticing the frown cracking the merchant's face. "Do you know what became of them?"

"Ah." The woman's gaze lowered to her feet. "Don't believe I can answer that, lady. In fact, I think you might've come to the wrong stall."

"Please. I'm only curious. I used to buy from a few of them, you see."

The woman sighed, then nodded to herself. She lifted her head and returned her gaze to Mavrian. Any hint of a smile was gone. "I don't know much, dear. I arrived to open my stall one morn, and most of the stalls were gone. Vandalised. The merchants had just... vanished. None showed up." She gnawed on her lip. "Look, I shouldn't have said even that much. Now, if you ain't going to browse my wares, would you kindly leave? I don't want any trouble."

"No... no, of course not." Mavrian offered a smile. The woman's position was understandable. If Grögg and Vane had slain all the Kinsmeer, they would have no trouble silencing an elderly Bloodkin. "What's inside those boxes?" She pointed at the colourful boxes scattered around the table, hoping to ease the merchant's troubled mind.

"An assortment of trinkets," the woman said, a smile returning to her lips. "Look here. Here we have a bracelet of copper and onyx, worn by a Sylvian lady of the manor, no less."

Mavrian smiled to herself as she realised what kind of stall this was. This woman had received her booty from a buccaneer. The items were black market, pilfered from Sylvian cargo vessels. Or perhaps they'd belonged to Kinsmeeric merchants that were no longer around to denounce the theft.

"That's lovely," Mavrian lied, pretending to be intrigued by the low-grade trinket. Perhaps if she built up a rapport, the woman would reveal more about the Kinsmeer.

The woman narrowed her eyes at Mavrian. "I sense you've a taste for something grander." She scanned the boxes, then retrieved a small yellow one. "Here. Here's just the thing. Take a peek and see for yourself."

Mavrian accepted the square box, running her eyes over its polished surface. The box seemed different to the others. It certainly wasn't wooden, though she couldn't quite determine the material under the paint.

"Come, dear. Do not dally. Open it up. Have a look inside."

The woman's tone had altered dramatically. Her words came not as a request or suggestion, but as a demand.

Mavrian gazed at the woman's wrinkles, hoping to learn something from her leathery features. Her smile descended into a frown, and the frown progressed to a snarl.

"Open it up. Go on. Go *on*. What are you waiting for?"

"Why? What's inside?"

"A beautiful pearl. The biggest you ever did see. Go on, girl. Open it." The woman seemed manic, her eyes wide with anticipation, her face drenched with sweat.

Mavrian lowered the box, cradling it shut in her hand.

"I told you to *open it!*" the woman shrieked, lunging across the desk, reaching for Mavrian's hand.

Mavrian staggered backwards, missing the woman's swipe by a whisker. She glanced around, searching for aid, but there was nobody in sight.

"Open it, you Morren cunt!"

Mavrian's gasped, fear winding her. Did the woman know her from somewhere? Her Morren origins were known to the courtiers of Meelian, but she didn't see how an elderly commoner could possess such knowledge.

She turned her attention to the yellow box, gripping it tightly with sweaty palms. This had all been a trick. Something awaited her inside the box, something that would hurt her.

Before she could process another thought, a dagger appeared in the woman's hand. She aimed the sharpened tip at Mavrian. "If you don't open the box this moment, I'll slice you pretty breast to pretty breast."

"Who... are you?" Mavrian wanted to drop the box, but she feared it might explode. "What do you *want* from me?" She realised that the last remark was foolish. This stranger wanted her dead.

The assassin swiped her unarmed hand across the table, pushing the boxes off the edge, scattering them to the floor. She lifted herself onto the table, crawling forward with the dagger still aimed at Mavrian's face.

Mavrian turned to escape, still clutching the box, but the woman leapt down in front of her, panting as she aimed the blade towards her heart.

"Who sent you?" Mavrian cried, hoping to alert the other merchants to her plight.

"What does it matter?" The woman scoffed. "Funny you wish for your last words to be a question. So be it." She raised the blade high above her head, ready to stab down in one swift motion.

Suddenly, the woman's eyes lit up like dancing flames, the whites of her eyes filling with the deepest red. Her arm lowered, but the dagger fell from her grasp and clattered to the stone. She clutched at her own throat, fumbling to remove the invisible fingers that strangled her. She wheezed and panted, stripped of breath.

Mavrian squinted around, terrified of what she was seeing, unsure what was occurring.

A man had appeared and was standing a few feet from Mavrian's side, chanting something under his breath. It was Scarmane, dressed in long black robes, a hood obscuring his face. His words were nonsensical, a mishmash of strange syllables, neither Nerblyss nor Sylvian.

"*Scarmane?*" Mavrian managed, but the Veer didn't seem to notice her.

To Mavrian's horror, the assassin floated up from the ground. She hovered there for a moment, her dangling legs kicking at thin air. "Wha... you..." She clawed at her own throat, desperately fighting for air. Then her fiery eyes met Scarmane. "*You?*"

The woman fell from the air, relieved of the magic that had animated her, collapsing in a heap on the ground. She did not move nor utter a sound to indicate she breathed.

"Lady Morr," Scarmane said, lowering his hood, revealing his handsome features. He appeared pained or terrified by what he'd just witnessed. "Give me that."

Mavrian handed him the box without question. He placed it on the table and made her stand well back. As he gazed at it, the box opened all on its own. A green cloud emerged from the crack, swirling upwards and spinning in a circle. Scarmane muttered more words, and the cloud dissipated, fading into nothing.

"What... just happened?" Mavrian asked him. "What *was* that?"

Scarmane inspected the yellow box, scratching his chin. "The product of foul alchemy," he said matter-of-factly, turning back to her. "What did the woman say to you? Did she tell you who sent her?"

"No... *no.*" Mavrian shook her head, trying to make sense of it all. The woman had lured her here to have her open the box, so she could inhale the poisonous fumes and die in an instant. Any other day, Mavrian might have ignored her gut and opened the box. If Scarmane hadn't shown up when he did, the assassin would have surely sunk the dagger into her chest.

Scarmane Trokluss had saved her life.

"My Veer... I... I don't know what to say."

Scarmane bowed his head. "Then say nothing. My lady, you are the only important Bloodkin on Kleäm. Such knowledge breeds undesirable attention and such births jealousy."

Was he suggesting the Loress Meels had something to do with this?

"Do not fret a moment more," he said, offering her his hand. "Come with me. I believe you have experienced enough peril for one day."

Halfbreed

G *oddess, preserve my eternal spirit. Walk with me. Join me on this journey. Guide my conscience. Hold my soul to account for good and for ill.*

Barrett placed his fortune in the hands of the Goddess now, beseeching her nightly, whispering prayers when the others weren't nearby, pleading to be saved from this living nightmare.

They had been on the road for days, perhaps even weeks. Barrett had lost count of how many times he'd witnessed the sunset.

The grey days and starless nights all melded into one. A singular world of permanent bleakness, devoid of colour, stripped of all that was pure and merry. Barrett felt nothing. He'd become nothing, an empty shell that gazed at the same lifeless oaks and overgrown fields and withered shrubberies.

They had stopped at two inns along the road – if the term *inn* could apply to such rundown shacks. The beds were nothing more than wooden benches, covered with thin, ragged, mite-infested blankets. The innkeepers fed them pungent, grey sludge that they had the audacity to call soup, and dried salty mushrooms, and ale that reeked like swamp fumes and tasted like wet dirt.

Fortunately, they camped beside the road most nights, huddled around a small fire, taking it in turns to man the night's watch.

The Baron remained silent for much of the journey, except for when they made camp, where he would sit alone or pace in circles, muttering to an invisible confidant.

Lew had elected himself camp cook. He possessed a keen eye, if nothing else, and spent the evenings foraging for mushrooms with Cay and hunting and skinning rabbits with Ache. His stews smelled revolting, but Barrett was often so exhausted from the day's ride that he couldn't taste.

After they'd guzzled down their rations, Lew told stories of the Succession Wars and the Battle That Never Was before humming tuneless songs as he gazed into the fire. His cheery optimism seemed unbreakable, meeting every frown with a beaming smile.

The evenings spent singing around the fire were a welcome distraction from the road, but every night birthed a morning of dread and aching bones.

And this morning was no exception. But something was different.

Unease flowed through Barrett, stiffening his limbs, and infusing his tongue with vomit as his head throbbed like a heartbeat. His feet were soggy in their boots and ached from ankle to toe. The riding leathers he'd slipped into seemed tighter with every passing day. They sought to squeeze the very life out of him.

As they broke camp and returned to the Old Road, Barrett realised he hadn't slept a wink. He remembered laying on his bedroll, gazing at the cool impression of the moon piercing the veil of dark clouds, but he couldn't recall drifting off. He'd watched the moon fade from existence, then the golden sun kissed the grey sky with its virgin vibrancy.

He wasn't sure how the others could sleep at night. All of them snored – the collective sound was a chorus of dry rattling and gruff groaning – and chittering insects and the distant cries of unknown animals complimented the medley of noise. Even after several swigs of Lew's mystery booze, Barrett couldn't numb his ears to the environment, nor prevent dark thoughts from pervading his mind.

I belong to Heatha now. I betray the Baron with every step. Vilka has done this to me. Without her, the Baroness wouldn't have been able to ensnare me. Vilka's charmless, tormenting face... her hypnotic, searching eyes inked the very walls of his mind. *She betrayed me... She played me like a lute.* And yet he couldn't help but pity the girl. Vilka worked for the Baroness now. Upon expending her usefulness, Heatha would thank Vilka for her service, then leave her dead in a gutter.

Barrett swallowed bile as they entered a patch of woodland, wherein the tightknit trees leaned and twisted into each other, leering over the road like wild sentries. It was the duty of all Krämisens to maintain the Old Road, but few folks inhabited this dark stretch known as the Black Lands, and it was evident by the invasive roots and overhanging branches and the weeds that grew all over the dirt path.

Hanzus Irvaye cut a beleaguered figure at the front of the procession. His eyes were red and baggy, grave and listless. Barrett couldn't imagine the horrors flowing through his mind. *His wife seeks his downfall, and his father is dying.* He only wondered which thought haunted him the most.

Barrett hadn't spoken to the Baron since the morning he'd seen that dark figure watching them atop the rise. And ever since that moment, he couldn't shake the feeling that they were being followed. Every hill they climbed, every stretch of woodland they traversed, every moor and marsh they rode around, Barrett could feel eyes upon him.

He remembered Heatha telling him Vilka had encountered Bloodkin as she travelled through the Krämise. He supposed now that those tidings had been part of the ruse to bind Barrett into her service.

Still, the thought of Bloodkin tracking them through the Black Lands ate away at him. He would have shared his fears with the others, but none other than Lew seemed interested in anything he had to say. He had tried to tell them about the mysterious watcher on several occasions, but Cay kept speaking over him, and Ache and Pamen ignored any sound that passed through his lips. So, he kept quiet.

Besides, the figure was no more than his imagination playing tricks on him. If they were being tracked, someone else would have picked up on it. Pamen and Ache had fought in countless battles, and Lew and Cay practically lived on the road.

Barrett wiped the sweat from his brows. *You're tired. Exhausted. What was it Old Drodger used to say? Tired eyes cannot see.*

"You alright there, lad?" Lew was riding beside him, he realised. How long he'd been there, he wasn't sure, but the valet was now watching Barrett with a yellow-toothed smile.

"Oh... morning," was all that Barrett could manage.

Lew's grin didn't falter. "Ain't too far from Kellenmoor now, lad. There we'll rest up, good and proper. Stock up on some bread, cured meats, selection o' cheeses. Might even drop a few silvers on fresh attire."

Barrett met Lew's smile. Kellenmoor lay, according to every map he'd ever studied, in the very centre of the Krämise. That meant the worst of the terrain was behind them.

"Do you think we'll reach Kellenmoor before nightfall?" he asked, imagining the sleep he'd enjoy resting in a proper inn bed.

Lew shrugged. "If we ride hard and true, it's possible we'd reach it before the sun drops. Seen as we're so near, we can gallop without much mind as to saving the horses' stamina. We're to stable the lads and lassies at the Man's Best Friend, you see. There they'll be watered and fed, awaiting our return for the journey home. We'll purchase new steeds to see us the rest o' the way to Freestone."

"The Baron doesn't want to risk his steeds across the border," Barrett stated. *That's the real reason, isn't it?* They'd all heard tales of horses contracting the plague.

Lew chuckled, shaking his shaggy head in disbelief. "You're a sharp lad. You see, Hans's stallion over there? It ain't no ordinary Krämisen. Lion were born from a long line o' Sylvian chargers. There's no sturdier breed in all the known world." He sighed, gazing at the dark mass of forest to his left. "Hans rode his magnificent beast all the way to Carthane and back, and it never broke a sweat. Mine and the lad's got mighty spooked when we was aboard Captain Morske's ship, but Lion over there didn't frighten once."

"What happened to Captain Morske when you were aboard the Temper?" Barrett asked. "All I heard is that he died soon after you all docked in Dyllet."

Lew loosed a slow sigh, staring off into the distance. "You'll like Kellenmoor, lad. The Man's Best Friend is the finest inn outside o' Balenmeade."

"I thought you said you'd never made this journey before."

"Not to Freestone, no. But some o' the finest sights in our kingdom lie on the Krämisen border." A widening smile crept across Lew's face. "A man could lose himself traversing the hills there. It's a beautiful place."

Barrett returned his gaze to the road ahead. Hanzus had halted at the front of the line, and the others were slowing their steeds to a stop beside him. Barrett was about to question what had caused the interruption, but then he peered into the distance and saw it for himself.

They'd reached the end of the forest. The road dipped down once it passed the last tree, leading down into a valley of low green hills.

Something was in the road at the bottom of the hill, barring passage. A gaggle of black bodies huddled together, standing eerily motionless. A few pale faces stood out from the cloud of black. They were looking up at the forest, watching the Baron and his party with quiet intrigue.

A shudder gripped Barrett's spine. A voice told him to steer his mare around and gallop back into the forest, but Hanzus and the others just stood there, as motionless as the strangers in the valley below.

Both groups were locked in a battle of wills. Who would be the first to move toward the other? Who would draw their swords? Who would flee?

Reason told him the men were soldiers of the Krämise, watchers of the road, or traders on their way to Kellenmoor. It was quite possible that they were Harvest revellers returning home from Balenmeade. There were several possibilities, but only one plagued his mind: were they the Bloodkin that Vilka spoke of?

"Are they friendly, milord?" Lew directed at Hanzus, willing his horse forward to the Baron's side.

"Bandits, by the look of them," Pamen answered, scratching his chin.

Barrett hung back from the rest, whispering calming words to Myra.

"Mayhap they're Kellenmoor riders," Ache suggested. "A greeting party, here to escort us the rest of the way. Does the alderman of Kellenmoor know of our coming?"

"Unless my kindly wife sent word ahead, Alderman Jace knows nothing." Hanzus studied the strangers, fingering the hilt of his sword. "Come." With a wave of his hand, the party eased forward. "I shall do the talking. Do not draw. But be ready to fight."

A knot twisted in Barrett's stomach. The nape of his neck pulsed with fear, a chill shot down his spine. He willed Myra forward, staying well back from the others. As they neared the black party, the urge to flee gnawed at his gut.

The strangers took form as they approached. Sickly folk, pale-skinned and clad in dark leathers. They didn't appear to be armed, but their black cloaks draped down past their ankles – space to conceal a short sword or mace or both.

Barrett glanced down at his own weapon, flapping in its sheath next to Myra's saddlebags. He wondered if it was even long enough or sharp enough to do any real damage.

"Who goes there?" Hanzus called out to the men.

Seven. Barrett counted seven men dressed in matching riding clothes. But their steeds were nowhere to be seen, nor was the nature of their business in any way plain. Their hooded cloaks obscured the upper halves of their faces. Their lips were pallid and unsmiling.

"Announce yourselves!" Ache barked, fingering the hilt of his blade. "You were just addressed by a lord!"

Hanzus shot the guardsman a silencing glare. He halted Lion a few feet away from the strangers.

One of them stepped forward from the rest, lowering his hood to reveal a shock of white hair and eyes as red as the sunset. *One eye,* Barrett realised, as he squinted at the man's pale face. His other eye was as blue as Barrett's.

"The Baron of the Krämise," the man said in a queer accent, bowing low before Lion. "Pleasure's all mine."

Hanzus stirred in his saddle, but the man's red eye didn't seem to alarm him as much as Cay and Lew, who exchanged worried glances.

"The pleasure is whose?" Hanzus retorted, glowering down at the strange man. "Introduce yourself and promptly. If I am indeed the baron that you claim, you would do well to move aside."

"Please, please..." The man raised his hands in mock surrender, then he cracked a grin, revealing brilliant white teeth. "My very last intention is to cause offence. My name is Vors Rennice, and I cannot understate how pleased I am to be meeting you."

Pamen scoffed. He urged his steed forward and wedged himself between Vors Rennice and Hanzus. "That's as far as you go, Master Rennice. Now order your men to step aside so we can be on our way. Perhaps, if the Goddess smiles upon you, my liege lord will deign to forget about this petty offence."

"Is that so?" Vors Rennice stepped to the left of Pamen's horse, glowering up at the guardsman. "I would do as you ask. I would do so without hesitation." His attention returned to Hanzus then. "But to an honourable man, his charge is his bondage."

In a flash, Rennice retrieved a curved dagger, seemingly out of nowhere, and sank it into the neck of Pamen's horse. The beast kicked out in terror, standing up on its hind legs, spilling its rider out of the saddle.

The horse staggered away in terror, swaying sideways, blood oozing from its side.

Hanzus unsheathed his glimmering blade and his servants quickly followed suit.

Vors Rennice spun towards Hanzus, panting for air, his face dripping with spattered blood. *"Now!"* he cried, drawing a short sword from under his cloak.

The assailants lowered their hoods and unsheathed their swords, charging at the horsemen, swinging their blades above their heads, yelling guttural nonsense. They all looked the same, their skin white as bone, their slick hair black as midnight. And their eyes... their eyes were crimson, like rubies glowing in the sun. These were no ordinary highwaymen.

Bloodkin.

In a flash, their blades clashed against Hanzus's long sword, Lew and Cay's short swords, and Ache's two-bladed axe. Pamen soon found his feet and charged at the assailants' backs.

Barrett had frozen on the spot. He watched as the Bloodkin parried the human attacks with ease. He fumbled with his sheath, hoping to ease out the blade. But his hands were sticky with sweat, causing the hilt to slip from his grasp.

One of the assailants broke off from the rest, charging at Barrett with madness in its eyes. Myra rose on her hind legs in fear, knocking Barrett to the hard earth.

Ear-splitting bells filled his ears. His vision was blurry, formless but for the black shape ambling toward him. As the form took shape, revealing a bloodthirsty grin, Barrett grasped the hilt of his blade and yanked it free with every last drop of strength.

The blade slashed at the lunging Bloodkin, carried by momentum. It missed the mark, but the move halted the creature in surprise.

Barrett fought against the agony as he struggled onto his feet. His head was spinning. He was about to collapse and shut his eyes forever. But something spurred him on, some hidden strength coursing through his veins. He pointed the tip of his blade at the Bloodkin, forcing his hand to grip the hilt.

The Bloodkin gripped his own sword with fresh determination, strafing slowly to the left, circling Barrett like a carnivorous beast. His gaping mouth revealed sharp incisors that appeared more arrowhead than tooth. The monster probed the air with his blade, pointing the gleaming tip at Barrett's face.

Cries of exertion and agony and the clashing of steel filled Barrett's ears. He only prayed that the gurgling screams belonged to the Bloodkin.

Barrett's opponent lunged forward, hacking wildly at the air. Barrett dodged the blade by a whisker, fired by pure instinct. Without thinking, he chopped at the man's extended grasp. The edge of his blade penetrated leather, slicing the man's forearm.

The Bloodkin recoiled backwards, clutching at the wound with his offhand.

Barrett knew not to allow the fiend time enough to react. He stabbed at the Bloodkin's chest. The blade sailed straight through, piercing the dark armour with ease. As he yanked the blade free from its burial, blood poured from the fresh gape like a shattered dam.

Barrett staggered back a few steps, almost lost his footing.

The Bloodkin fell, clutching its chest. The clean sword clattered to the dirt.

Barrett faced the ensuing battle. He was now some strides away from the nearest melee. The surrounding scene was dire: blood and gore sprayed the air; black bodies and entrails littered the road. The company was scattered, divided by their respective opponents. Some of the fighting had spilt out into the field. The Bloodkin were drawing the humans apart, backing away in different directions in order to lure and confuse.

There was more Bloodkin now, and dozens more were flocking

into the scene, wielding swords and spiked maces.

Hanzus remained seated in his saddle, overcoming his foes with ease, parrying their wayward attacks, hacking their limbs off with brutal precision. Once he'd stabbed the last of his assailants in the neck, he spun around, dizzied by this dance of death.

Somebody had unhorsed Ache, and he was spinning his two-bladed axe in an arc before a gaggle of fearless Bloodkin.

Lew was fighting on the other side of the road, hacking at the man that had named himself Vors Rennice. The apparent leader of these Red Eyes dodged each of the valet's blows with deft ease.

Barrett turned back in the direction they'd come from. A wave of figures charged at him from the tree line. Seven or more, armed with thick blades, hissing some primitive war cry.

Goddess, save me from this. Where are they coming from?

"*Back!*" Ache had appeared from nowhere. He now stood beside him, stinking of old sweat. "Get behind me!"

Barrett obeyed without hesitation. As the charging Bloodkin reached the huge warrior, his great weapon brushed them aside like a broom sweeping up spiders. His blade sliced through two of them, and they recoiled, clutching their gaping wounds.

But more Bloodkin arrived, charging at Ache and Barrett from every angle.

Barrett clutched his sword for dear life, muttering hollow prayers under his breath. This was how he would die, by the foul blade of some hideous creature, falling halfway to the destination of his fool's errand, another quest he would never complete.

Vilka was telling the truth. There *were* Bloodkin roaming around the Krämise, for what reason only the Goddess could know. But they had spawned here from somewhere. They had to have received their orders from somewhere, though their orders were clear - assassinate the Baron of the Krämise.

"We can't take them," Barrett hissed in Ache's ear.

"I'll have none of that talk," Ache grumbled. "Stay at my back. Take the fiends on *your* side, and I'll attend to mine."

Barrett spun on his heel. True enough, Bloodkin charged toward their rear. If Ache hadn't spoken, their blades would have sunk into his spine.

"There are too many!" Barrett cried. He counted five charging at him. Several more were still engaged with Cay, Lew, Pamen and Hanzus.

"These fiends are Goddessless... heathens... The Goddess will not protect them! The gracious lady is on our side!"

Barrett lifted his sword, biting down against the terror. He was going to die. That much seemed certain... but he would not close his eyes forever. He would be reborn, waking in the Gardens of the Goddess, wherein the purest spirits of Entros dwelled, basking in her company, existing forevermore in perfect harmony.

Bile filled his throat. He had never imagined that his life would end so soon. The evenings he'd wasted merrymaking and whoring flooded his mind. So much squandered time. Such a fruitless existence. There were so many places he'd wanted to visit, so many things he'd wished to achieve.

There is no hope.

Doomed though he was, he could take a few Bloodkin down with him. He was capable of that. One last act of free will. His earlier opponent had fought carelessly, without shielding himself. Maybe if he parried a few of their frenzied attacks, they'd tire, and he'd be able to cut a few of them down before succumbing to his wounds.

Barrett slashed at the approaching Bloodkin. His blow missed by a country mile, but the creatures staggered and halted, staring at him curiously. One stepped forward, probing an attack with his blade. Barrett parried with ease, but he sensed the creature was testing him.

The Bloodkin took it in turns to come at Barrett. Before he knew it, they had turned him around, and he was facing Ache once more.

Ache swatted at his opponents, swinging his axe with one hand and punching with the other. His axe imbedded itself in a fleeing Bloodkin. He leaned forward to retrieve it, struggling to loosen it from the corpse's head.

One creature slashed at Ache's back, sinking his blade into the warrior's shoulder.

"No!"

Ache roared in agony, staggering sideways as the Bloodkin pulled his sword free. But Ache dodged the creature's next swipe. He retrieved the axe and swung it at his attacker, chopping the head clean off.

Barrett parried the next attack that came his way. The blade missed him by a whisker.

He glanced over at Hanzus, who was still in Lion's saddle. He was hovering on the far side of the road, surrounded by a dozen corpses. There was something working in his eyes. Contemplation. He placed his gloveless fingers in his mouth and sounded a whistle.

Pamen fled from his opponent and jumped up onto the back of Lion, swatting at his pursuers. Cay and Lew paused from their fighting and turned to the Baron. As the Baron turned and galloped away, Cay and Lew jumped onto their respective mounts and pursued him without question.

Barrett's heart sank as he watched the horses fade into the distance, greying to tiny pinpricks before they disappeared completely. *The Baron has... abandoned us?*

A few Bloodkin chased after the fleeing party but quickly gave up on their pursuit, as they didn't possess a single horse between them. Myra and Ache's steed had vanished. He only prayed the horses escaped before these creatures could capture them.

"Stop!" a voice carried above the clashing of steel. "Lower your weapons. *Now!*"

The Bloodkin did as the voice commanded, stepping back from Ache and Barrett. The warrior didn't pay their lowered guard any mind and continued to hack away mercilessly at the defenceless Bloodkin, felling them one by one. Still, the Bloodkin did not lift a hand in defence, content with the warrior's severe judgement.

"I told you to stop!" the voice spat, addressing Ache this time.

Vors Rennice stepped into view, folded his arms, and scowled at

Barrett. His one red eye glowed like embers. His white mane was streaked pink with blood.

Ache faltered, not from the man's words but from his own exhaustion. He leaned on the handle of his great weapon, panting, fighting for air.

"Your master has abandoned you," Rennice chuckled, prompting his fellows to laugh along.

Barrett strangled his hilt as the man approached.

"We've no further quarrel with the likes of you," Rennice said, his smile fading away. "Lay your weapons down, and we shall be on our way."

Ache laughed, a bitter gurgle of disbelief and despair. "You expect me to believe the words of a half-breed?" He spat bloody saliva at the man's feet. "Your quarrel's with the Baron of the Krämise, is it not? Well, I say that man is me. So strike me down and fulfil your wretched charge."

Rennice raised an eyebrow at Ache, then he turned his attention to Barrett. "Does this brute voice the truth? *Is* he the baron of this realm?"

Barrett gulped down his fear. Ache was nodding at him, imploring him to accept this fable. He turned back to Rennice and answered, "Yes."

Rennice laboured a sigh. He glanced at one of his fellows. Then, from nowhere, an arrow hissed through the air, imbedding itself in Ache's stomach.

The warrior staggered backwards, teetering on the edge of collapsing, then he fell forward, landing on his knees. Somehow, he still gripped his axe.

"Funny," Rennice said as he sheathed his sword. "You see, I recall a memory. Oh, it was some years ago now. I was visiting the city of Dulenmeake during the Tourney of Embers." He approached Ache, looming over him with his arms folded. "I recall the names and titles of every man that lanced that day. Oh, I remember the Knight of Prunes and the Crimson Knight of Mulharrow. I seem also to recall a warrior by the name of Achen Brune. No knight, but an honourable participant by invitation of the Baron of the Krämise." His grin stretched ear-to-ear. "Do you mean to tell me you betrayed the very man that elevated you well above station? Do you mean to tell me you murdered Hanzus Irvaye and all of his descendants, usurping his seat by force?"

Blood dribbled from Ache's mouth as he lifted his head and met the man's gaze. To Barrett's surprise, he wore a sick smile. "That I did, sir. I am the..."

Rennice didn't allow the words to leave the warrior's lips. He withdrew a dagger from somewhere and sliced it across Ache's throat.

The warrior fell into Rennice. The murderer patted the corpse's back before standing tall and kicking it aside. Ache's magnificent axe clattered to the ground with a fatal thud.

Barrett realised every bone-white face was now upon him, their bloody eyes peering into his soul. Vors Rennice cleaned his dagger of Ache's gore as he set his eyes on the steward.

"And who are you?" Vors asked, frowning. "I haven't seen *you* before."

Barrett lifted his gaze to the clouds. *This is the end. I've nobody to save me. Nothing left to give.* Hanzus Irvaye was gone. He'd abandoned Barrett and Ache.

Barrett was going to die now. That was beyond any doubt. The only question that remained was *how* he would fall.

"My name is Barrett Barrett," he found himself saying, settling his gaze on Rennice's blue eye. His *human* eye. "I am of no importance."

The words wounded him. Without thinking, he'd spoken the absolute truth. The truest words he'd ever uttered. He would die a man of no importance out here in the middle of nowhere.

"Indeed," Rennice said before nodding toward one of his fellows. "Good to make your acquaintance, Barrett Barrett of no importance."

Barrett closed his eyes, readying himself for the final blow.

A woman's voice hissed through the air, the sweetest sound to grace his ears.

The Goddess.

He had reached the Gardens of the Goddess. She had saved him from experiencing the agony of the blade.

As he opened his eyes, ready to greet her, he found he was still facing Vors Rennice.

"What's going on?" he whispered, but before he could speak again, he realised the source of the woman's voice. *It was a girl's voice.*

Vilka was standing next to Rennice, dressed in full riding leathers, clutching a short sword.

"He will not be harmed," she instructed Rennice, spoken as firm as the Baroness. "Do you hear me?"

Rennice narrowed his eyes at Vilka. "Why?"

Vilka looked at Barrett, her amber eyes leaking sorrow. "Mister Barrett, I... I'm so sorry."

Vilka is working with the Bloodkin? The revelation gnawed at his heart, tearing him apart from within. First, he'd uncovered her relationship with the Baroness, and now this.

"Just do as I say," Vilka snapped at Rennice, sheathing her sword.

Rennice sighed, rolling his eyes. "Oh, very well."

Hands grabbed at Barrett from somewhere. Someone shoved something into his mouth. As he staggered back, hands gripped him and probed at his skin. Something was trickling down his throat. *Poison.* A glass vial was being held to his lips, forcing liquid into his mouth.

The world around him was blurring. Rennice's voice was softening, fading to silence. He could no longer feel his body, and yet he felt happy. Jubilant.

Blackness enveloped him. A sweet, harmonious song filled his ears. He was somewhere else, transported to another world. As he floated there, suspended in the void's embrace, the last thing he saw was Vilka's smile.

Besieged

An old woman was watching Mavrian, clutching a jewel-encrusted box with one hand and a vial of green liquid with the other, her wrinkly face impassive.

In a flash, she was gone, exploding in a puff of green smoke. The green fumes rose, gradating to black, liquefying in mid-air. The blackened droplets shot out in every direction, spraying Mavrian's face, forcing her eyes shut. She tried to blink, but the substance was heavy, sticky, hardening over her eyes.

The world had turned to blackness.

As she ripped and clawed, trying in vain to peel her mask away, she heard another explosion. Its dull aftermath pounded inside her ears like a steel stick smacking a drum.

Then, silence.

Mavrian awoke. She was in her bed. It was still the middle of the night. *I must have only slept for an hour or so.*

Sweat soaked her nightclothes, and... Sitting up, she cast her sheets aside and peered down between her legs, squinting through the darkness. A wave of relief rained over her as she saw the wet saturating her nightdress was only piss.

Groaning, she rubbed her brows in soft, soothing circles, easing the sharp throbbing in her head.

It was a terrible dream and nothing more. The realisation was comforting. The horrid woman had not been real. That deafening explosion was a mere figment of the imagination.

Or so she'd thought.

The terrible sound visited her once more, piercing her ears with its thunderous crack, forcing her to cover them. And to her horror, the room seemed to shake with the noise. *That terrible, terrible sound... will it ever stop?*

The explosion came again.

Mavrian lowered her hands, glancing towards the glass doors that led to the balcony. The panes lit up. An orange flash penetrated the curtains. Every object in the room shuffled across the floor, migrating away from the windows.

The noise was no dark conjuring of the mind. A dreadful sound boomed outside Vicker's Tower, and it kept repeating, over and over. It occurred to her that the dreadful noise could only mean one thing. *Cannon fire.*

A stampede of footsteps and anxious yelps sounded outside her chamber door. Doors slammed. Frenzied feet kicked objects over.

"*Mäga!*" Mavrian cried out, sliding off the bed and padding over to the balcony. "Mäga, where *are* you? Attend to me at *once!*"

The cannons hammered twice as she peeled back the balcony doors. Something in the room behind her fell from a shelf and smashed to the floor.

The moon's great glowing eye was blinding as she blinked through the doorway to the darkness of night. But the light did not belong to the moon, she realised, as her eyes adjusted to the gloom. As she peered over the balustrade at the street down below, she saw dark, frantic figures scurrying in both directions, barking and yapping indiscernible cries of distress.

When she lifted her chin, a flash of orange lit up the jagged rooftops and rounded towers again and again. Mavrian had to shield her eyes from the blinding light, peeking between her protective fingers to investigate the source. The orange hues that lit up the sky coincided with the deafening roars of cannon. The light pulsed like a dying heartbeat. It's accompanying thunder cracked and hissed before fading to low, soft murmurings that caused the buildings to tremble. A cloud of grey smoke rose from the other side of the buildings.

Kleäm's main docks were under attack, the bombardment aimed at the ships docked in the harbour and the buildings that peppered the dockside. *The whole Meels fleet is there.* She remembered Bënar Meels boasting about such before the Loress's fateful banquet.

A commotion caught her attention down in the street below. A gaggle of soldiers flashed past Vicker's Tower, clutching bows and spears. *As if those will help against roaring cannon fire.*

A flurry of explosions sounded from the harbour. She saw a flaming projectile whistle through the air, lighting up the night before imbedding itself in the castle's outer wall.

Mavrian's chamber door burst open. Her heart pounded in her throat as she turned back to the gloomy space.

A dark figure padded into the room, seeming to glide across the floor like a weightless banshee.

Instinct told her the stranger was a Kinsmeer. *They're assaulting Kleäm in retaliation for Lucian Grögg's purge.* And now one of them was here, in her room, about to finish the work that the old woman in the marketplace had started.

As her eyes adjusted to the dimness, the intruder's face took form. *Mäga,* she realised, noting the girl's short stature and wide crimson eyes.

"M-my lady," the girl stammered, her lips wobbling, her eyes darting around like a nervous mouse. "We're... under attack."

"By whom?" Mavrian demanded, stepping away from the balcony, shutting the glass doors behind her. "*Who* is assaulting us, Mäga?"

Mäga blubbered nonsense as she stared at the floor.

"Come," Mavrian said, padding across the cold floor and wrapping her arms around the child's trembling shoulders. "We have to get out of here."

"What do we do, my lady?" Mäga froze to the spot. "Where will we go?"

"I... I don't know," Mavrian admitted, gripping the servant's sleeve. Fear choked her lungs, squeezing out the air.

She remembered that on the other side of the island, Scarmane Trokluss had docked his ship in the small western harbour. If Kleäm's enemies had yet to reach the western side, there was a chance of escape. A slim one, but a chance. At any rate, Mäga had to be saved. The child was an innocent. And Zamrian and Cäda and Reesa...

"Where do we go?" Mäga repeated. "My lady... I know my duty is to serve you, but... but... I don't know how."

"We have to leave," Mavrian said. She crouched down to Mäga's level, forcing a smile. "We're going to have to run. You understand? Without looking back. Without stopping. Do you think you can do that, Mäga?"

The girl nodded along, sobbing quietly. "But... where do we go? There's... there's no escape. I heard soldiers talking outside... The ships are sinking in the harbour."

Mavrian bit down on her lip, nibbling the sides of her mouth as the dreadful validity of Mäga's words sank in. Even if the two of them somehow reached Scarmane's ship and fled Kleäm, thousands of Bloodkin would be left behind to face Kinsmeeric mercy, trapped on an island without escape. *Vässa only knows if the Kinsmeer will bombard Meelian into oblivion or land a ground assault.* Neither possibility was comforting.

The cannons boomed again. A bomb exploded somewhere close to Vicker's Tower. The ground trembled.

"Mäga, you're going to have to trust me," Mavrian said, holding back tears. "Now, I want you to run to your room and dress in your coat and boots and meet me back here in one moment. Can you do that?"

Mäga nodded, then scurried out of the room. Mavrian didn't waste another second, slipping out of her piss-drenched nightclothes and into thick traveller's robes. She glanced around the gloomy chamber, knowing she would never see sunlight ooze through those glass doors ever again.

Mäga scurried back into the room as Mavrian was squeezing into her boots. Once Mavrian had wrapped herself in furs and pocketed as many valuable trinkets as she could find, she snatched the servant's hand and ran from the room.

They descended the winding stairs to the level below and found the doors leading to Cäda and Zamrian's quarters were ajar. Mavrian poked her head through the doorframe and saw their chambers were ransacked. The Kamarn sisters had fled.

In Reesa's chamber, a small pot had smashed to a hundred pieces on the floor. Evidently, she too had fled the tower.

Mavrian gripped her pounding chest. *How could they?* The ladies of Vicker's Tower were her friends, allies, confidants. *How do they so readily abandon me to die?*

Mavrian glanced down at Mäga's terrified face. The servant was squeezing her hand for dear life, as though to loosen her grip meant certain death.

A commotion was ensuing as they descended to ground level. The servants of Vicker's Tower had gathered in the entrance hall and were cursing at each other.

Master Grenor, the madam's second-in-command, was standing in front of the main doors, holding his hands up in submission. The others were screeching at him, pointing accusing fingers in his face, demanding answers to the chaos.

"Calm down," Master Grenor was saying. "Calm down, I say. We'll never survive if we lose our heads."

"The Kinsmeer are coming for us!" Cäda's chambermaid cried out. "The peace is over! We'll all be slaughtered!"

"Now, now... we don't know that," Grenor returned. "For one, we do not know who those cannons belong to. For all we know..."

"For Vässa's sake, who else could it be?" Freela, the cook, hissed at him. "We're at war, Grenor! Every fool knows it. The Kinsmeer of Kleäm were purged, and now the Sylvians have come to purge the likes of us!"

Mavrian pushed her way through the seething servants. "Where is Madam Corr?" she asked Grenor, noting the tower's keeper was not among her servants.

"My lady," Genor said, his eyes widening with fear. "Please, help me speak sense to these maids."

"I asked you a question," Mavrian snapped. "*Where* is Reesa? *Where* are the Kamarn sisters?"

The master of servants visibly gulped. "Gone, my lady. The madam left with the Kamarns and tasked me with escorting yourself and the Lady Reesa to safety. But Lady Reesa has gone. I know not where."

"My lady hasn't returned to Vicker's Tower for days," spoke one of the chambermaids. It was Ola, Reesa's personal maid.

"Where is she?" Mavrian demanded, meeting the maid's nervous face. "Where has she been all this time?"

"I... I don't know."

"My lady," Master Grenor said. "We must get you to safety. We haven't much time."

"And where's safety?" Mavrian asked, turning on him. Mäga's grip was weakening, slippy from sweat.

"Why, the castle, of course."

Mavrian shook her head at the man's naivety. "The castle would protect us for a short while if the Kinsmeer do not bombard it into oblivion. But how long do you suppose the Loress would keep us alive after the food stores run low, and she has to choose between feeding her own people or the Morren lady she despises?"

"My lady," Grenor said, frowning. He had nothing more to say.

Because he knows I'm right.

Mavrian bit down on her tongue and pushed past him, leading Mäga out through the door. *I have to save Mäga, if nobody else. The* girl was innocent of every possible indiscretion. She'd served Mavrian honourably these last few years. In a way, she was the closest thing Mavrian had ever had to a sister.

They sprinted toward the castle. The road that skirted around Meelian would be their best chance at reaching the western dock.

"My lady?" Mäga squeaked at her heels. "My lady, my friends... I can't leave without them. There's Vanä and..."

"Quiet," Mavrian snapped at her. They couldn't begin to consider others. Not now. There was no time. Every single inhabitant of Kleäm deserved to live – save for the noxious courtiers of Meelian – but that didn't matter right now. They had to get themselves to safety. They had to survive.

A cannonball punched through the air overhead, shooting over Meelian's outer wall and landing somewhere out of sight, exploding like thunder. A chorus of screams rose with the smoke. *So much for the castle offering safety.*

As they reached the top of the hill, she noticed a mass of bodies had gathered outside Meelian's outer gate. The drawbridge was up, and a guardsman peered down at the crowd from the battlements above.

As they approached, Mavrian realised the Bloodkin gathered there were begging the guard to allow them entry, but their cries fell on deaf ears.

"Keep close to me," Mavrian whispered in Mäga's ear. "We'll go around."

But as soon as the words left her lips, a voice rose above the chattering crowd. "Mavrian? *Mavrian!* Over here!"

Zamrian emerged from the swarm of bodies, and Cäda came scurrying after her. "Mavrian? Thank Vässa!" Sweat drenched both Kamarn sisters, their eyes bloodshot.

Mavrian hugged them both tight. "Where is Reesa?" she asked, glancing over their shoulders towards the crowd, searching the frantic faces for familiarity.

Cäda pursed her lips. "She... she..."

"We don't know," Zamrian answered, inspecting Mavrian's face, searching it for clues. "But we can't stay here. The Loress has locked herself inside Meelian. She won't allow another soul to enter."

"Do we know what's happening?" Mavrian asked. She wasn't sure how Zamrian could remain so calm as cannonballs screeched over their heads. "Who's attacking?"

"Kinsmeer," Cäda said, her eyes mad with fear. "Has to be. But... I don't understand. How are their cannons reaching the castle? What has that sort of range?"

"They're Sylvian," a deep voice emerged from behind them. Bënar Meels stepped out from the crowd, folding his arms, shaking his head in exasperation. He clutched a short sword in one hand and played with the links of his chain mail with the other as he came to stand beside Cäda.

"*Bënar?*" Zamrian spat. "What are you... Does your mother know you're here?"

"I was attending to a great matter when the fiends assaulted the eastern harbour," Bënar chewed on his lips. "I saw them. A great fleet amassed on the horizon. And the sky lit up as their cannons roared. I saw it. I saw the Sylvian banner hoisted above their sails."

"Then it's true. The peace is really over," Zamrian said, furrowing her brows. "Bënar, you must ask your men to let these people inside. They must be given refuge."

"My fleet is sinking in the harbour," he replied, gaping at the sky as a ball of fire shot over their heads and punctured the keep, causing an explosion of timber and stone. Then, without a shred of emotion, he said, "I just don't understand. How did these Sylvians slip past our scout ships?"

Cannons rumbled in the east, and they had hit one of the keep's towers. As Mavrian turned to face the spire, fire engulfed its wooden roof. Stone debris and licks of flame rained down on the keep below, spreading the fire along the long roof of the great hall.

Screams pierced the air, rising over the outer walls. The crowd gathered outside the gate dispersed in every direction, possessed by fresh terror.

Mäga strangled Mavrian's hand, squeezing the life out.

"We need to get to the western dock," Mavrian told Zamrian. "It's possible the Veer's ship is still in the harbour there. It may be our only means of escape. We have to try."

"We must leave discretely," Bënar said, intercepting their conversation. "We must leave, and leave together, Lady Morr."

"*You're* going to flee?" Mavrian shot at him. "The Loress... your *mother* remains inside Meelian. The seat of your bloodline. Your *home!*"

Bënar scoffed, gesturing at the flames engulfing the castle's roof. "See what remains of the seat of my bloodline. I serve my family best alive." He scanned over Zamrian and Cäda, searching for support. "Each and every one of us best serves the Overlord alive. Think of your families if you cannot think of yourselves."

"There's no time for discussion," Zamrian snapped, then she jabbed a finger in Bënar's chest. "As Mavrian says, we need to reach the ship quickly, lest it leaves without us."

Bënar mumbled under his breath, words for Zamrian's ears only. Then he spun on his heel and pointed with the tip of his sword toward the left of the gatehouse. The road skirted around the outer walls, leading to the poorer districts of Kleäm. "Follow me. But keep close. I will not stop to save a single one of you."

Mavrian glanced up at the flaming castle as they jogged around its surrounding wall. Scarmane's quarters were now engulfed in black smoke. She only prayed the Veer had escaped Meelian before the Loress had barred the gates. With or without Scarmane, they would board his vessel and escape the ill-fated island. There would be a time to mourn the dead and dying, but it was not now. Her primary concern was to escort her friends to safety.

"Mavrian... *Mavrian*," Cäda blubbered, fighting for air as she caught up to jog alongside Mavrian. "We cannot leave without Reesa. She wouldn't leave us behind."

Zamrian, who had been hot on Bënar's heels, slowed down and shot Cäda a debilitating glare. "If Reesa were here now in my place, I'd pray to Vässa that the whole lot of you escaped. Now stay quiet and keep up."

"Perhaps we'll meet her at the ship," Mavrian said, offering Cäda hope, though she didn't believe her own suggestion for a second.

Bënar led them at a trot, steering them around the perimeter of Meelian. When they reached the other side of the castle, the cannons had quietened. Their booming was soft and muffled, like a distant storm. The Bloodkin here were relatively calm, more confused than anxious.

This portion of Kleäm housed sailors, dockworkers, soldiers, and labourers. Wooden shacks and decrepit towers the Loress refused to repair or replace dotted the hill that hugged the edge of Meelian before descending into the sea. The workers were emerging from their homes and alehouses, blinking sleepily at the fires that lit up the air.

"What's going on?" a skeleton of a man barked at Bënar as they descended the stone steps that led to the western dock.

"It's a sign from the gods!" a woman proclaimed, waving her hands about hysterically. "Vässa sends to us her love!"

Upon Bënar's instruction, they ignored all the claims and questions that were shot their way. As they hopped down the wide steps, pushing past drunkards and the recently awoken Mavrian imagined the wooden structures here would soon be aflame. It would take only a small spark, and the flames would spread like wildfire. If they did not perish in the flames, the workers would be cut down by Kinsmeeric swords. If the Kinsmeer spared any Bloodkin, they would enslave or torture them to death.

As they reached the final step, a plump man was waiting for them at the bottom, barring their path with a small serving boy at his side.

"Lord Bënar," the man addressed Jessa's son, bowing low before him. As he lifted his chin, his eyes scanned over Cäda and Zamrian, before falling on Mavrian and Mäga. His lips curled in disgust.

"Several queer fellows inform me that Kleäm is under attack," he said to Bënar, before turning to Cäda and chuckling at her. "Your companions appear rather spooked, my lord." Humour faded from his face as he turned back to Bënar. "My lord... please, tell me that these brigands lie."

"Lëtan," Benar said, placing a hand on the man's immense shoulder. "We haven't much time. We need to reach the western dock before our ship sails."

"Overlord be saved," Lëtan said, trotting after Bënar as he continued down the winding street. For a man so large, Lëtan was rather fleet of foot, and his small servant easily met their pace. "How many are they? And when do we plan to attack, my lord?"

Mavrian yanked Mäga by the hand, dragging her faster than she knew her short legs could travel, hurrying to keep up with Bënar's desperate pace.

"There's no time for an attack," Bënar snapped at the portly lord. "Meelian is aflame."

Lëtan covered his gaping mouth as he scanned over the ladies' faces, searching for confirmation to the lord's claim. "Gods be merciful. The hour is truly so late? Yes... yes, I shall follow you to this ship. The soul of Kleäm must be preserved."

As they raced along the narrow streets, pushing aside or dodging all who stood in their way, they passed a group of young men who called out to Bënar, asking him what the commotion was all about.

"We are under attack, sirs!" Lëtan called back to them. "Flee your homes before it's too late!"

Those nearby cursed and cried out in horror, scattering in every direction. Some latched onto Bënar's procession, looking to their new lorr for guidance and protection.

A sickening wave of relief and remorse hit Mavrian as the western dock came into view. Relief that the Veer's ship remained in the harbour. Guilt for the thousands that would perish in their wake.

"Thank Vällas the scum concentrated their assault on the eastern bay," Bënar said, halting to recover from breathlessness.

Dozens of peasants charged at the ship's loading plank, scrambling for a chance to flee Kleäm's demise. Scarmane Trokluss stood upon the quay, guarding the loading plank. He waved his hands at the oncoming peasants, imploring them to halt. But as the peasants refused to cease their charge, stampeding across the rickety quay, the Veer aimed his outstretched palm towards them, and in a flash of blinding light, the crowd flew into the air, shooting sideways and landing in the water.

"Go back!" Scarmane roared as the peasants that remained on the quay helped their drowning fellows out of the water. "There is no place for you here!"

Mavrian wasn't sure whether she was pleased or pained to see that Scarmane was alive and well. He'd already saved her from death's embrace once before. Was the debt she owed after he'd spared her from the old woman at the market stall about to increase tenfold? Would he become her saviour once again?

"My Veer!" Bënar bellowed as he stepped onto the quay. Zamrian and Cäda followed him closely as Mavrian hung back, gripping Mäga tight. "My Veer, we come seeking refuge! Kleäm is lost. We must be away!"

Sickness swelled in Mavrian's belly. This didn't feel right. *How does Bënar so readily abandon his people?* She glanced back at the streets they'd emerged from. Swarms of peasants had gathered in the shadow of the buildings facing the dock, too frightened to approach the Veer's ship.

What am I doing? How can I leave and allow these poor souls to perish? She spotted elders and small children in the crowd. *How will I be able to live with myself?*

"Bënar Meels!" Scarmane called back to Jessa's son. "Where is the Loress?"

"She burns, my Veer," Bënar stated, as if he was referring to a piece of meat. He drew his sword and aiming it at the peasants that remained on the quay. "Aside, you fools! I am the Lorr of Kleäm now. You'll do as I say!"

Scarmane bowed his head as Bënar scurried past him, climbed the loading plank, and jumped onto the ship's deck. Lëtan and his servant followed him.

"Lady Morr!" Scarmane cried out, his dark gaze falling on Mavrian. "Board my ship, and we shall leave this place!"

It's not right... it's not right. The surrounding faces were ripe with confusion and trepidation. Anxious peasants called to her for aid, imploring her to take them with her.

"Mavrian, we have to go," Zamrian snapped in her ear. "Reesa may be aboard, waiting for us."

"We don't know that," Cäda cried. "We don't know *anything*."

"Reesa is only one person," Mavrian said, swallowing bile. "Look at *them*." She gestured at the peasants facing them. "Look at their faces. Can you *honestly* tell me you'd ever sleep again if we survive this night, and we leave them all behind?"

Zamrian glared at the hundreds of Bloodkin swarming around them. They all kept their distance, fearing the Veer's magic more than the faceless enemy bombarding the other side of the island. "I see people that will die whether we intervene or not." She spun to face Mavrian, her eyes wide with rage. "Your life means more, Mavrian. So much more than anyone else here. If *you* die this night, the bloodline of Morr may well die with you. How do you think you best serve these people? Dying swiftly by their side or by surviving to fight another day? The Overlord has summoned you to Sela'Fundor. With his aid, Kleäm can be avenged!"

Mavrian closed her eyes, praying she would open them to her bedchamber. But she could still hear the soft rumble of cannons firing in the distance, tickling the insides of her ears.

Zamrian was right. Remaining in Kleäm would not aid these people. Perhaps she could comfort them for a time, but the Kinsmeer would capture and torture her, if she didn't perish from their bombardment, and in any case, she would live only a few days.

There was only one choice.

Mavrian looked down at Mäga's petrified face and offered her a smile. "Will you come with me, Mäga? Will you accompany me to Sela'Fundor?"

Mäga blinked up at her, tears streaming down her cheeks. She nodded, trembling head-to-toe.

"What about Reesa?" Cäda shrieked as Zamrian dragged her toward the loading plank. "We can't leave without her. We simply can't!"

"Good evening," Scarmane addressed Mavrian as she approached him. "I cannot begin to express my relief, as I see you are unharmed." He took her by the hand and led her across the plank, ushering her and Mäga onto the deck. "The Overlord will be pleased by all that has transpired here." He turned away from her, leaving her baffled by his statement. He announced to his crewmen, "Let us put distance between ourselves and this place, my fellows! We set sail for Sela'Fundor!"

Cäda threw her arms around Mavrian, sobbing into her shoulder. "I asked around. Reesa isn't here. Oh, Mavrian. How can this be happening?"

Mavrian held Cäda in her arms, watching as the ship drifted away from the quay.

The black horizon swallowed Kleäm whole. The island was dead, murdered by the Sylvian Empire, abandoned by its own people.

Mavrian leaned over the side and puked into the sea. *How could the gods allow this to happen?* The world would never be the same. Most of the eyes she'd ever known would soon close forever.

But Zamrian was right. They would be avenged. As soon as Mavrian inherited her uncle's fleet, she would sail them to Kleäm and gut every last Kinsmeer.

Conspiracy

Goddess, I feel it. Hektor, I feel it. Heavy in the air. Under the deepest layers of my skin. The world is dying around me. And I am destitute, useless, a mere spectator of all that decays and ends.

Hanzus could smell Jurgen on the wind, sense his spirit seeping out of his body, searching for the Gardens of the Goddess, a plane he would never find. The stench invaded his nose like fat, stinky fingers being stuck up into his nostrils.

"My lord," Pamen said, pointing into the distance. "My lord, look. At last, we made it."

Hanzus steered his steed away from the dark forest, following Pamen's finger over the moors. He squinted at the rocky hills beyond the fields. Then he saw it.

As I live and breathe.

Freestone was as he remembered it: an inconspicuous sliver of pale stone and poorly maintained timber, more akin to a ruined fortress than a notorious monastery. The series of flat walls and square towers stood sentinel atop the tallest hill, presiding over the heather-brushed moors and the pockets of the grey forest.

Hanzus knew that despair and misery lay beyond those hills, stretches of blighted land and towns and hamlets crippled by plague.

He realised there was no way of knowing that the brothers within Freestone were untouched by that foul disease. Supposedly, the monks kept away from the plagued cities, but Hanzus knew well that policy and practice were often fickle friends. His own borders were testament to that: in theory, the Krämisen guards watched and patrolled every inch of the Rooksland border, but Brother Edennel and that vagrant Vilka managed to enter the barony, seemingly without conflict.

And perhaps so too did those Bloodkin. He wasn't sure where else they would have come from unless the Marridan lords had allowed them safe passage or they had slipped past the Gunnic tribes to the south. Hanzus had questioned the guards they'd met on the border, but the men stationed there had neither seen nor heard tell of any red-eyed monsters.

They'd ridden for three days after crossing the border. Hanzus did not trust the Rookish inns, nor did he wish to encounter any degenerates on the road, so they strayed from the Old Road, traversing the wild woodland and moors. The new mount he'd purchased in Kellenmoor was no Lion, and so their pace upon this hard terrain had slowed.

But they'd made it.

Freestone, the holy site upon which Sage Curthus once tread, was calling out to him, beckoning him forth with its wicked song. The waking sun kissed the walls with its hues of amber and rose pink. The isolated monastery almost appeared welcoming.

The bitter taste of Rooksbrew still infused his tongue from the night before. A knot formed in his stomach. In a few moments, he would look upon his dying father.

"What a sight," Pamen said. Hanzus couldn't tell whether he jested.

Hanzus halted in the middle of the road. Following the track with his eye, he gazed up at the pinprick that was Freestone's only gatehouse.

Cay and Lew stopped at either side of their lord, frowning at the sun-kissed monastery.

"Hektor almighty. That Freestone?" Lew said, doubt etched into his wrinkles.

Cay sighed, hunched over his saddle. "I have to say, I expected something more... impressive."

"Hush, lad," Lew snapped. "This here's home to true devotion and holy servitude. Folk here are true servants o' the Goddess. They deserve your respect."

Cay raised a questioning eyebrow. "As you say."

Hanzus ignored their squabble and turned back to Pamen, but as he opened his mouth to speak, the soldier trotted over to Cay.

"You'd do well to mind your tongue, boy," Pamen hissed, jabbing an accusing finger into his chest. "Freestone were built to protect the good and the righteous from Goddessless yelps like you. You'd do well to think on that as you tread its hallowed ground."

"I will be entering Freestone alone," Hanzus spoke over them, drawing Pamen's scowl in his direction. The soldier remained loyal, but Hanzus knew that Pamen Ostarne despised his master for abandoning Ache to those Bloodkin highwaymen. "I want you to set up camp upon these moors. We shall break our fast upon my return."

"My lord," Pamen said, yanking his horse around to face his lord. "I know well that Freestone's sacred ground, but please, for nought more than precaution, take me with you."

Hanzus managed a smile. "Believe that I have the means to protect myself from clerics, Mister Ostarne. You see, I've fought several monks in my time. These Mutlen brothers will be easy pickings." Then, after noting Pamen's confusion, he said, "I have fought them in a war of *words*."

Pamen still appeared baffled. "As you say, my lord. But if, for whatever reason, the stew sours, you need only send a sign."

"And how do you suppose I do that?"

Pamen rummaged around in his saddlebag and retrieved a thin strip of red fabric. He bowed as he handed it over. "I've a keen eye, lord. I'll keep that eye stuck to those walls up there. Should you need me, wave this flag and I'll come."

Hanzus neatly folded the fabric and tucked the square into his belt. "That breakfast," he said, turning to Lew. "Make it meaty if you can."

"We ain't got none, milord," Lew said. "Think we've some biscuits and a stick o' cheese. No more."

Hanzus scoffed at that. "This is wild land. For Hektor's sake, kill something."

He didn't wait for a reply. He urged his mount forward. As he climbed the hill and neared Freestone, he realised the walls were in disrepair. The white paint slapped over the surface showed cracks and peeled in places. Wild, yellow grass surrounded the walls, entangled with weeds.

The gates were wide open and unguarded. *Are they expecting visitors?* That didn't sit well with him. He squinted through the gateway. Inside, a trimmed hedge bordered a stretch of pale lawn, and beyond that, a courtyard of paved stone was adorned with potted plants.

Hanzus ducked his head as he passed under the low, curved archway. He dismounted and tied his unnamed steed to the hook by the gate. It was unusual for there to be no guardsman to do it for him. As he peered around at the empty complex, unease gnawed at his insides.

It's too quiet. Yet there were no signs of forced entry, no blood spattering the pavement, no corpses littering the scene. He sensed no foul play afoot, and yet the place appeared uninhabited.

Perhaps the monks are at prayer, he reasoned as he stepped into the courtyard. A statue stood in the centre of the yard: a bearded, muscular figure with well-cropped hair and maddened eyes. It was the Prophet Hektor, no doubt the crudest depiction he'd ever witnessed.

A stone building loomed over the statue's shoulder. Stained-glass windows bordered its immense wooden door, a small Cross of Hektor perched atop the arched roof. It was an underwhelming structure, bland and unimposing, the antithesis of the grand cathedrals that populated the Empire-proper.

Suddenly, somewhere, a door burst open.

As Hanzus searched for the sound's source, he noticed a single-storeyed building to his left. The middle door was wide open, and a short, disgruntled figure was pacing across the yard toward him, shaking their bald head and muttering under their breath. The man wore the simple black habit of a Mutlen brother and had a silver Cross of Hektor dangling around his neck.

"No, no, *no*. This simply will not do. No, no, not at all. There will be no admittance today, young man. There will be no handouts, no free confessions bestowed upon your person." The monk halted inches from Hanzus and placed a firm hand on his shoulder. "I told Brother Harper over and over. Over and over and over, I told him. Shut the gate. *Shut the gate.* And does the man listen?" He grimaced toward the gatehouse. "Evidently not." His breath reeked of garlic, his clothes of soap and sweat. "Now then, back outside you go. Quickly now, if you please." His eyes narrowed. "*Well?* I haven't got all morning."

When Hanzus didn't answer, the monk grabbed him by the shoulders in a feeble attempt to direct him towards the gatehouse.

"I'm not going anywhere." Hanzus dug his heels into the pavement. Try as he might, the monk was unable to shift him an inch. "I'm here to see... for fuck's sake, man, remove your hands from me at once."

The monk stumbled backwards, his eyes widening in horror. "How *dare* you espouse such profanity here! Freestone is built upon sacred ground. You will... you will..."

"I'm here to see Jurgen Irvaye," Hanzus spoke over him, gritting his teeth.

The monk opened his mouth to speak, but surprise or horror stole the words from his tongue.

"I'm here to see Brother Jurgen," Hanzus amended himself.

"You... that is... *what?*"

"Brother Jurgen. He joined your order many years ago."

The monk made the sign of the cross over his chest. "Bless her holy name. Yes... *yes*, Brother Jurgen is here. And... and... who can I say is... that is to say... who... who are you?"

"I am his son." Hanzus swallowed the knot in his throat. It all came down to this one dreadful moment. "Is he still with us?"

The monk paled. He nodded slowly, his blue eyes unblinking. "Forgive me, my lord. We have been inundated with undesirables as of late. My name is Brother Namus. Come, I shall take you to Brother Jurgen. Though I must forewarn you, the man holds onto life with weakening resolve. This way, my lord. Follow me, if you please."

The monk led Hanzus toward the building he'd emerged from, scuttling across the pavement like a cautious rat.

"May I ask, my lord, do you ride with Brother Edennel? We lost contact with him just before he reached Balenmeade. The leader of our order is most troubled by this."

Hanzus sighed. "Your brother is dead." *And it's all because of my malicious wife.*

The monk's frown deepened. "Then it is as we feared. Brother Edennel was a good man. A pious man. He knew the scriptures well, far better than most. His knowledge exceeded my own, in fact. Alas, he is with the Goddess now." As he reached the building, he held the door open for Hanzus. "Please."

Inside, the aroma of garlic and soap was everywhere. Paintings of sages and great monks filled the corridor from floor to ceiling. The oil-eyes of these old men watched Hanzus with suspicious intrigue. The knowledge that Jurgen had once gazed upon these artworks filled his throat with sick.

"You should know, my lord," Namus said as he led Hanzus down the dark corridor. "The state of Brother Jurgen's person is not a sight pleasing to behold." He halted at the end of the passage, where a set of double doors barred the way. "Brother Jurgen expects you, my lord, but you should know... you are not the first to call upon him this day." He cocked his head toward the door.

Hanzus hesitated. "What do you mean?"

The brother wore a nervous smile. "My lord, I cannot say. The man was frightfully insistent he remain anonymous." He now could not meet Hanzus's gaze. "I *can* tell you, however, that this man has scarcely left your father's side. Enter, my lord. Your father awaits you."

Hanzus swallowed sick as he turned the handle and pushed the doors open. A rotten stench oozed through the gap, causing him to gag. He covered his mouth with his sleeve, but it offered no reprieve. The pong was everywhere, defiling his nostrils, stinging his eyes.

"I'll be here, should you need me," the brother said, backing away from the doors. His words faded away as Hanzus stepped inside.

The room was lit by a few small candles. The thick curtains were drawn. As Hanzus adjusted to the gloom, the doors behind him shut.

In the centre of the room, the narrow bed reminded Hanzus of an open coffin, its mustard sheets spattered with brown stains. The smell of sweat and piss filtered through the unmistakable stench of something – or someone – rotting. A skeletal form poked out of the bedsheets. It was Jurgen. Even close to death, his frown was all too familiar.

But Hanzus could not name the shadowy figure seated beside the bed. The person hid their face under a large, dark hood. Their pale, slender hands fumbled with a vial of pink liquid as they gazed at Hanzus through the gloom, watching him with invisible eyes.

Turning back to the bed, Hanzus squinted at Jurgen, trying to make sense of the pitiful scene. Sweat saturated his father's pallid face. His grey, lifeless eyes were mere shadows of their former vigour. Those eyes had once been blue. They had commanded fear and respect in equal measure. His stare was captivating, a look of undeniable potency. But those dark, sunken sockets gazed warily at him now, desolate and defeated.

"Who's there?" Jurgen croaked. "I see you... though I know not your face. Name yourself."

Sick filled Hanzus's throat, infusing his tongue with bile. He swallowed it down as he approached the bedside.

Jurgen's voice was as feeble as his appearance, a faint echo of its former greatness. During the height of his reign, Jurgen had delivered great speeches, conquering the world with mere words. And now those lips were bloody, cracked. His speeches were no more than dead thoughts.

"I am your son."

"*Hans?*" Jurgen croaked, spluttering into his hand, coughing from deep within his chest. "Is it really you?"

"It is," the hooded stranger hissed into the dying man's ear, just loud enough for Hanzus to hear.

"It is... It really is you," Jurgen blubbered, his listless eyes filling with tears. "I knew you would come. Brother Namus warned me against harbouring such blind faith. But in my heart, I knew. As soon as I dispatched Brother Edennel with my message, I knew you would answer my call." He stopped to catch his breath. "Come close. Let a father look upon his son one last time."

Hanzus obeyed, waddling over to the edge of the bed. As he accepted his father's outstretched hand, he sensed the true enormity of the man's deterioration. He was holding hands with a skeleton, a shadow. The fact he could still breathe was a miracle.

"*See.* See, I told you he would come," Jurgen said to the hooded stranger. Even up close, Hanzus could not get a good look at the man's shrouded features. "And here he is in the flesh. My son." A smile crept over his cracked lips, but it faded as soon as it had arrived. His eyes gaped wide with terror. Then he clamped them shut, gripping Hanzus's hand for dear life.

"Father?"

Jurgen's grip loosened. His eyes reopened, focusing weakly on Hanzus.

"How long does he have?" Hanzus directed at the hooded man.

"It's difficult to judge."

"Then, by the Goddess, what is your prediction?"

"I am no healer, my lord. Brother Jurgen has thus far endured. An astounding feat, all things considered."

"What happened?" Hanzus returned his gaze to Jurgen. Those grey, listless orbs blinked up at him. "What manner of poison are we dealing with?"

"If I were to guess," the hooded man said, "Deadroot, winwort and kenolotus."

"Old Man's Misery." Hanzus was familiar with the concoction, but kenolotus was uncommon in the Rooksland, and winwort even more so. Deadroot was almost impossible to find and, if the legends were true, harvesting could only be during a full moon.

"The slowest poison known to man," Jurgen said through clenched teeth. "I've dealt with some... vicious enemies in my time... but none living would I wish this fate upon."

"It rots you from the inside out," the hooded man explained. "And once the rot has started, there is no stopping it."

"Which is now purely academic," Jurgen said. "I have made my peace with Hektor and the Sages. The Goddess now awaits me. The Sages are calling my name." He closed his eyes, a smile gracing his face. Then his eyes snapped open, and he stared at Hanzus. "Why have you come, Hans? Why are you here?"

Hanzus opened his mouth to speak but found no words to express his bemusement. Jurgen's eyes flickered about his face, evaluating every fibre of his son's being.

"Come to watch an old man wither away in agony, have you? Come to watch your father crumble before your own eyes?"

Hanzus snatched his hand away. He'd risked it all, leaving his barony once again to Heatha's mercy. He'd flown across the border as fast as Lion and his Kellenmoor stallion could carry him. He'd abandoned Barrett and Ache to die. *And all for this?*

Spit bubbled through Jurgen's teeth. "I suppose you consider this a fitting end to the chapter of my life. The *true* Baron of the Krämise, rotting slowly before your very eyes. *I* made you baron, Hans. What more could you ask of me? What more can you take?"

"*You* summoned me here," Hanzus retorted, but he stopped himself from saying more.

He's not thinking clearly. The rot has reached his brain, sullied his mind. He wanted to believe it was the poison talking, but deep down, he knew the old man spoke true. His truth. The hatred Jurgen harboured for his son was undiminished. And perhaps, in some sordid way, he was right. Perhaps Hanzus *had* travelled to Freestone to close a chapter, to witness this miserable being choked and fade to Oblivion.

"I seem to remember you naming me your heir." As the words left Hanzus, tears stung his eyes. "I ask for nothing."

Jurgen's eyes narrowed again. "That I did. And yet you treated me like an ungrateful swine. You always did. You always will be ungrateful to me. Ungrateful to all. Shit, I'd have named your mother my heir if she'd still been alive. But there is such a thing as tradition, Hans. Such an unfortunate thing as the law. And where, Hans, would we be without the rule of law? We would be no better than these confounded Rooksfolk. No purer than those fucking red-eyed bastards." As soon as the words left his lips, Jurgen's head fell flat against the pillow. His eyes were fixated on the ceiling, sweat oozing from his forehead. When he'd regained his senses, he was panting for breath. "Like my father before me, I fade into the frayed pages of history. And I fear that history will not judge me kindly." His eyes snapped toward Hanzus. "How *you* are remembered is yet to be decided."

The hooded man coughed into his hand, stealing Jurgen's attention. "The toxin is ready, my lord."

My lord? Jurgen had forfeited that address the day he exiled himself to Freestone. He glimpsed the shrouded man's crooked nose. A lock of red hair flopped over his face.

"What is this toxin?" Hanzus asked. "You said there was no cure."

Jurgen accepted the vial and pulled off the stopper. "Hans, you must understand. I accepted my fate many days ago, in this very chamber." He strained a slow exhalation, then shut his eyes, breathing in the potion's odour. When he opened them again, he lowered the vial and narrowed his eyes at Hanzus. "I don't know who was behind this, Hans, but they did this to hurt *you*."

Hanzus stared at the man. If the poisoner wished to hurt Hanzus, they'd have known where to find him.

Jurgen continued: "Mayhap, my methods as baron were harsh. But I acted with my conscience. The way I deemed right. All I ever wanted was the best for you. As did your mother. The legacy I leave will live on in your name. Whether you distance yourself from it or embrace it entirely, I will remain a part of you still. The Barons of the Krämise will continue to be mocked and scorned throughout Gadensland, as they've always been. It matters not who seats himself upon that throne of fallacies in Vinerheim. We are Krämisens first and Krämisens till our last breath." He spluttered bile into his hand. "You must understand, Hans, an attack on me is an insult to the very name of Irvaye. The Krämise has been poisoned. Whatever you think of me, Hans, that is all that matters now."

"I don't understand," Hanzus said, holding back tears. "This poisoner... why would they not come for me directly?"

"Perhaps they wish for you to live. To live and suffer."

"Who could have done this?"

"A group of strangers visited the monastery just before... before I became *this*," Jurgen said before erupting in a coughing fit.

Hanzus's heart sank. "Who were these strangers? Where did they come from?"

"I know not," Jurgen said, clutching the vial to his breast. "All that matters now is that you keep your family safe. Return to them with Goddess speed. Protect them. Do not stray from the path. My time here has expired." He held the vial to his lips. "While I understand you'll never forgive me, son... know that my love for you never died."

Jurgen swallowed the pink medicine in two short gulps. He handed the empty vial back to the hooded man and wiped the thick residue from his lips. His eyes fixed on the ceiling. He was whispering something, muttering incoherent babble under his breath.

"What's happening?" Hanzus demanded, turning to the hooded stranger. "What did you feed him? Answer me!"

"I fed him that which he asked for," the man replied. "A release."

Jurgen's pupils were dilating. He spluttered once more. His breath caught in his throat. His final breath. A gurgle of air exhaled from him slowly. His eyes stared up at the ceiling, lifeless.

Jurgen Irvaye, the Baron Without Sorrow, was dead.

Hanzus turned to the stranger, his lip quivering. "You... you *killed* him."

"The poison killed him," the man retorted, closing the corpse's eyelids. "Jurgen was waiting for you. He knew you would come. To that end, he never lost hope. And so, his orders were for me to administer the toxin as soon as you arrived. I owed your father that one last courtesy."

Jurgen had been holding on for days, weeks, writhing in agony as he awaited his son. How much pain and mental torture had Hanzus condemned him to endure by stopping at roadside inns and restocking his provisions in Kellenmoor?

"Now he is at peace," the stranger said, intercepting Hanzus's thoughts. "That is all that matters now."

"Hektor guide you through the darkness." Hanzus clasped his hands together in prayer. If there was even a slim chance that he could convince the Goddess to accept the man's black spirit, he would take it. "Dear Goddess who rules above, accept this man. Hold him close to your bosom. For this man comes to you a sinner. Born of flesh, blood, and bone, corrupted by the ways of Man. Forgive his trespasses, I beseech you. Forgive him and allow me to repent on his behalf."

"Really, there is no need for that." The stranger's voice changed. No longer did he use the soothing speech of a Rookish monk. There was no mistaking his accent now: Gadian, but he was not Krämisen.

Hanzus squinted at the man's shadowy face. "Who are you?"

"You mean you do not know? Really, Hans. Do you know me so little?" He pulled his hood down around his neck. It was no Brother of Mutlen that met his eyes, no bald head and humble face that emerged from the cloth. The man possessed a mane of ginger curls and a handsome face of chiselled features.

"It... it can't be."

The man frowned. His gaze was piercing. His eyes were blue flames. "Oh, that it can, Hans. That it *is*."

"Arwel."

Years had passed since he last gazed upon Arwel Nate. The Baron of the Tyldar was an elusive figure, appearing at the Council of Barons one week and in the brothels of Dyllet the next. Hanzus had issued the man's summons a dozen times or more and never were they answered. But here he was in the flesh, grimacing down at the corpse laid out before him.

Arwel returned his gaze to Hanzus. "Quite so. And a long time it has been, my old friend. Too long. I regret that we should meet in such a rotten place and time as this, Hans. It is most regrettable."

The monks of Freestone had isolated their gardens from the rest of the monastery, populating it with herbs and vegetables and less functional plants flowering every colour of the rainbow. A pebble path twisted in and out of the beds, meeting an abrupt end at the edge of the cliff. The disparity between Freestone and the land surrounding it was stark – wild forest stretched as far as the horizon, moors filled the foreground, a sea of thick grass, thorns, and heather.

Out there somewhere, Pamen, Lew and Cay awaited him. Soon they would begin the treacherous march back to Balenmeade. It would be slow and uncomfortable with Jurgen's corpse in tow. He would have to hire a wagon. They would take the main roads and pray that those Bloodkin highwaymen did not find them. The ghost of his father would haunt him every step of the way, from the second he peeled him from his bed to the moment Hanzus buried him under the oak of his name.

Arwel watched him in contemplative silence, his hands clasped behind his back. They had been standing here for some time, saying nothing.

"I don't understand," Hanzus broke the quiet. "What are you doing here?"

Arwel considered his words, inspecting a white petal with his fingertips. "Not two weeks ago, I was celebrating Harvest with my folk. Making merry with games and fireworks and enough wine to drown every courtier in the King's palace." He snatched his hand away from the flower as if the plant had threatened to bite his fingers off. "Then a messenger came to me with a frightful report." He returned his gaze to Hanzus, alternating focus between each eye. "A tale of assassination, slow and cruel. I made haste without delay, with the poison that would end your father's suffering in hand. The road was hard. The rains had swamped much of the Tyldar. But I stopped for no man. I rode alone, disguising myself as a plain traveller so as not to warrant unwelcome attention." Turning toward the church, he gestured for Hanzus to step ahead of him, following him closely as they treaded back down the path. "The day I arrived, the monastery was in uproar. A strange group had recently departed Freestone. Hoodlum travellers, quiet in manner. Quiet but disruptive. The brothers were in disarray, fretting like frightened chickens. But my presence calmed them."

"These travellers, who were they?" *I don't suppose my Bloodkin had a part in this?*

"I wish I could say, but these monks speak in riddles. They quote the holy book at every opportunity, uttering no real sense. You'd sooner hear wisdom from these plants than you would from the Brothers of Mutlen. But whoever these disrupters were, their visitation certainly coincides with your father's poisoning."

"You say they departed not long before your arrival?"

Arwel nodded. "The heathens disguised themselves as lowly wayfarers. The monks gave them shelter for weeks. They broke bread together, shared songs, and the bastards even joined the monks in prayer. And though the brothers suspected the travellers of poisoning Jurgen's soup, they thought to keep them here as long as possible, to gather evidence of their crime. But the travellers left suddenly in the night. Mayhap they were forewarned of my coming."

Hanzus swallowed a hard lump. "I need to speak with the brothers. Every one of them."

"Believe me, I've exhausted the brothers of all they know." Arwel sighed. "All I could I discern was that the men in question kept their faces shrouded at all times. They arrived with one true intention in mind, but even after your father's fate was confirmed, they lingered. Like they were waiting or searching for something. The brothers do not know what their secondary purpose could have been. Perhaps they wanted to ensure the poison was working as intended. Either way, they are gone now. There is not much we can do about faceless men with questionable intentions." He sucked in his breath. "What will you do now?"

Hanzus halted in the middle of the path. His body was tingling all over.

Jurgen's pale face and bloody, bulging eyes had inscribed themselves in Hanzus's mind. And the way Jurgen had twisted into a smile, knowing he was moments from death.

Turning to the church window that overlooked the garden, he glimpsed his own reflection. A handsome, confident man blinked back at him, seemingly unperturbed by the grave matters at hand.

He turned back to Arwel. "I came here to return Jurgen to

Balenmeade, where he'll be buried under the oak of his name. That is my duty now."

"Will you not investigate the peculiarities surrounding your father's death?"

"You've given me nothing to go off. You told me you questioned the monks, and they told you nought of these strange travellers."

Arwel sighed. "Well, they did tell me something that might be of worth."

A shiver ran down Hanzus's spine. "What is it? Tell me."

"The evening before they disappeared, Brother Namus confronted the travellers. He demanded they make their intentions plain, that they reveal the purpose of their stay in Freestone, that they declare the true nature of their journey." Arwel paused, bending down to inspect the petals of a purple flower. "They would not declare their intentions, though they did not appear ruffled by the brother's interrogation. But they did reveal one thing. One snippet of information I believe they did not mean to reveal."

Hanzus swallowed the bile rising in his throat. "Go on."

"The brother asked them where they would ride to after Freestone, and one of their number replied." He rose from the flower, lifting his eyes to Hanzus's level. "The Black Rook Inn. A small, unassuming shack not far from the Krämisen border. You have heard of this place, I presume?"

Hanzus searched the deepest chasms of his mind, hunting for a memory, a whisper, or a suggestion of that name. He did not recall where he'd heard of this Black Rook, but it rang a bell somewhere, long forgotten in the back of his mind.

A cool breeze swept Arwel's red locks over his face. "I am sorry we should meet like this, Hans. I am sorry for all that has happened."

"As am I." Hanzus turned back to the cliff's edge, glancing at the shrouded woodland on the horizon. Soon he would traverse that ominous landscape, venturing southeast to the Krämisen border.

But *how* soon?

He'd promised to return Jurgen to Balenmeade, where his corpse rightly belonged. He'd made that promise to the Goddess. He'd made the promise to himself. But these clumsy poisoners had revealed an invaluable clue as to their potential whereabouts. If they rode to the Black Rook Inn with haste, there was a chance they would intercept the murderers.

"What is your plan?" Arwel asked. "Will you rest in Freestone awhile?"

"You say these travellers are headed to the Black Rook Inn?"

Arwel inclined his head.

"And you know how to get there?"

Arwel nodded once more. "I do. But your plans to return your father..."

Hanzus waved him into silence, gazing at the sun's warmth beaming down on the bleak moors. "Jurgen was right. These strangers poisoned his soup to hurt me. I will not sleep until I learn why."

Captain Morske visits my cabin with a knife... Bloodkin marauders await me on the Old Road... and now my father is dead. Somebody wanted Hanzus dead. They sought to torment him every step of the way on the journey to his demise. They had worked within the shadows, making him believe the Despot and Heatha were behind all of their schemes. *And perhaps they are, but there's only one way I'll ever learn the truth.*

"You have lived with these monks," Hanzus said. "Do you believe that an arrangement could be made to keep Jurgen here for a short time?"

Arwel considered him through narrowed eyes. "You mean to follow these faceless travellers?"

"I asked you a question."

Arwel sighed. "I could persuade them not to bury Jurgen, yes. They keep a space in the catacombs below the church, where bodies are left to rot. Though, seen as Jurgen was a Brother of Mutlen, they would ask for my assurance that your father will one day be buried."

"Oh, Jurgen shall be buried. In Balenmeade, under the oak of his name. Where he belongs." Hanzus turned away from Arwel, unable to hold back from tears. "But first, we must ride to this Black Rook." He met the baron's gaze, revealing his sorrow, revealing his weakness. "Will you join me, Arwel? I do not implore you to do so, but it would please me greatly if you should accept."

Arwel placed a firm hand on his shoulder, offering something of a smile. "I will do as you ask. The enemies of the Krämise are my enemies also. I will help you find these cowardly fiends and uncover the purpose of their plot." He leaned in close, touching Hanzus's forehead with his own. "I will help you find retribution."

Prisoner

"Mister Barrett? Mister Barrett, do you hear me?"

The voice floated around his head like the morning song of a beautiful bird. Sweet vibrations weaved through his very fabric, touching him with kindness, serenity, with its eternal blessings. The Goddess was kissing his soul, granting him life, feeding him undying love.

But he did not see her. He could see nothing. At least, he thought he was looking at nothing, but as his eyes adjusted, the blurry form before him started to gain features. He was staring at a face.

Vilka's face.

The girl was blinking down at him from far above. He could not feel his legs, but he surmised he was sitting. Vilka was standing, leaning over him, unblinking, pursing her lips in thought.

"You're alive, in case you're wondering," she said before standing tall and glancing over his head.

He couldn't feel a thing. Even as he blinked, he couldn't feel his eyelids twitch. He tried to turn his head, but all he could do was roll his eyes.

"Where am I?" he tried to say, but the words came as pure nonsense, a collection of meaningless sounds and sprayed spittle.

Vilka knelt before him, fixing him with a glare.

"Where am I?" he reattempted, but the words seemed to confuse the girl further.

He could hear other voices behind his back, indiscernible grunts and intelligible speech that had to belong to some foreign tongue.

He glanced over her shoulder and out the vague impressions of trees. An orange light flickered over the ground, casting dark shadows from the trees.

"Listen," Vilka said under her breath, stealing his attention. "Just keep quiet, will you? Don't make any sudden movements, and you'll live to see another day. Don't make me regret sparing you."

She narrowed her eyes at him. Green eyes, not the brown he'd known in Balenmeade. *Green eyes... Why are they green?* Hers had been green eyes all along. Something told him that was significant, but his mind was foggy. He could not make sense of his thoughts.

"Keep your mouth shut," she spoke slowly through her teeth. "Do *nothing* else."

A gruff voice filled the air, echoing from everywhere.

Vilka rose and peered over Barrett's head. "I'm feeding him!" she barked into the darkness. "I said to leave me the *fuck* alone!"

"Then get on with it!" the voice replied. It was deep, deeper than any sound he'd ever heard. It wasn't pleasing. He wanted to escape it, to flee from its owner. He wasn't sure how, but he knew the voice wanted to hurt him, to torture him slowly, to hang him upside down from the nearest tree, poking him with a thousand spears.

"Listen to me," Vilka said under her breath, bringing her face close to Barrett.

He could smell her breath. *Dear Goddess, I can smell.* And the fragrance was the sweetest, the most beautiful thing he'd ever experienced.

"Listen to me," she repeated. "If you hear nothing else, then hear this. I didn't mean for it to go this far. I didn't ask for *any* of this. But life don't always play out the way we want. *You* can appreciate that."

Vilka left him, left him wallowing in the sea of his own pitiful darkness. He was alone, truly alone, for the first time in his life. For the Goddess had deserted him. He was her servant no longer, her child no more.

The last thing Barrett heard echoed in his mind over and over:

"They're headed to the Black Rook... inn?"

"They're headed to the Black Rook *Inn*."

"They're *headed* to the... Black Rook Inn."

Silver tongue

"You blame me for Ache's death," Hanzus stated.

Pamen uttered no response. He didn't have to. Silently, he frowned at the black blanket of trees that surrounded them on all sides, his eyes aglow with the dancing flames of the campfire. Hanzus only wondered if the fire in Pamen's eyes projected a hidden desire festering within his heart. The desire to avenge Ache's death. The desire to desert the lord that had condemned his friend to die.

"I would not blame you," Hanzus admitted.

Arwel, Cay and Lew were sat in the middle of the clearing, sharing booze and stories, huddled around the fire.

Something didn't sit right with Hanzus. Arwel had displayed a scant interest in their friendship over the past few years. Sure, they exchanged regular letters, but Arwel had turned down or ignored all of Hanzus's suggestions to meet. And yet he'd felt compelled to ride to Freestone and relieve Jurgen's suffering. And yet here he now was, making merry with Hanzus's servants.

"I am your man, lord," Pamen muttered under his breath, not trusting the words to be spoken at volume. "If Ache fell, he did so honourably. Fighting till the last. It's the end he would've chosen. Ache was your loyal servant, my lord. As am I."

And with that, the warrior stomped over to the campfire, plonking himself down beside Cay and accepting the valet's offered flask.

Hanzus lingered on the edge of the clearing, seating himself on a flat, smooth rock that bordered the shadow of the trees.

They had set up camp hidden well from the road. They'd been riding for three days, veering southwards, venturing deeper and deeper into the plagued heartlands of the Rooksfolk. Fortunately, they'd encountered few travellers on the road, and whenever their path steered them toward a village or hamlet, they'd managed to skirt around undetected.

The party assumed the guise of wandering merchants, heeding Arwel's advice, crafting a tale of a lowly station for all they encountered. But the few strangers they passed did little more than wish them a good day or grunt in their direction.

Hanzus instructed the servants to address him by the name Grathan, which Arwel assured him was a believable name for a merchant. Hanzus had left his cuirass and emerald cloak in Freestone, as the emblazoned attire would expose his true identity. The Mutlen brothers had provided them all with fresh riding clothes, as well as a week's worth of food provisions.

On the face of it, Hanzus and his party were commoners who happened to own horses – a sight not uncommon in the Krämise, but Hanzus imagined few in these parts could afford steeds. Considering such – and seen as how their accents would surely give away their outlander status – they agreed to pose as Algen tradesmen, for Rooklanders were known to distrust men from outside the Empire. Much like the Rooksland, Algeny was a vassal state of the Sylvian Empire. Hanzus and Arwel reasoned that no Rooklander would be travelled enough to distinguish between the accents of Gadensland and Algeny.

In line with their ludicrous disguise, Hanzus was not feeling himself. A part of him was missing. Jurgen's demise meant a slice of his soul had withered away.

And so, when they made camp, Hanzus kept himself isolated from the others, watching his men make merry from a distance. He yearned for the fire's warmth, for the swell of wine in his belly, but he didn't wish to speak. Above all, he craved solitude, to be alone until all of this was over.

But it would never be over. Above all else, that ugly truth was clear. *Jurgen is no more. Jurgen is dead.* The thought seemed unreal, even as he pictured his father's lifeless face gawking at the ceiling of his putrid monastery chamber.

Hanzus had been anticipating Jurgen's death for years. And yet, the realisation he was gone filled him with as much dread as relief. His father had been a menace, an uncompromising zealot of his own greatness. But Jurgen's death signified the end of an era, a shift in the balance of power. And an unknown shift at that.

Hanzus could never repeal nor repent for Jurgen's past actions. Hanzus would never cure himself of those memories, of the horrors he'd witnessed.

Father, how could you do this to me? How could you leave me here, alone, with all this knowledge? I cannot undo all you have done. I'll never make right the crimes you committed against your people... against the Goddess.

The fate of Jurgen's spirit was out of his hands. Hanzus had done his part, whispered his prayers and lit his candles. Jurgen's chance for absolution may have passed, but the fate of his own soul remained uncertain.

Leaving Jurgen's corpse in Freestone had been a difficult decision to make. Above all else, his task remained to return the body to Balenmeade. He had to bury Jurgen under the oak of his name, to provide him with the one slim chance his spirit had of reaching the Goddess.

But first Hanzus had to find answers, to learn why someone had poisoned Jurgen. And the rumour that these allusive murderers marched toward the Black Rook Inn was his only lead.

Father... whose hands tipped poison into your soup? How was it that your fellow monks failed to discern their true identity?

He played the scenario over and over in his mind. His thoughts lingered on Jurgen's faceless poisoners as he tried to make sense of the events that had transpired over the past months.

The Bloodkin they encountered on the Old Road had been no ordinary highwaymen. How they'd come to be in the Krämise baffled him the most. Bloodkin were forbidden from entering most baronies within Gadensland, the Krämise chief among them. How a band of Bloodkin had traversed the Krämisen roads undetected was beyond him.

Though, not entirely undetected... He recalled Heatha's tale that Vilka – that wretched vagrant she'd stowed away in the Balenmanor – had encountered Bloodkin on her journey to Balenmeade. The nearest location to the Krämise that permitted Bloodkin was Vinerheim, many days to the north. Although, the Red Eyes there were no more than lowly wretches. And the marauders they'd encountered on the Old Road were no slaves or serfs. They had equipped themselves well, dressed in uniform armour and matching cloaks.

And the way they fought... The Bloodkin had held back, parrying the human attacks without mounting any real offence of their own. *But why?* The wretches were without horse. Their intention mustn't have been to pursue Hanzus. *Who sent them?* Only Heatha and a select few within the Balenmanor knew of Hanzus's true purpose for riding out of Balenmeade.

Heatha is behind this. She had to be.

But from what dark corner of the world had she found Bloodkin willing to do her bidding? *What bargains have you made, beloved wife? Did you whore yourself out to that halfbreed like you did my father?* The creature's name echoed in the deepest chasms of his mind. *Vors Rennice... Vors Rennice...* He'd never heard of such a being. The forename sounded like some gutter spawn of Ryne, but the surname belonged to Sylvia.

His head ached from thinking.

When he returned to Balenmeade, he would hold Heatha accountable for all she'd done. For all that she'd put his servants through. Heatha had placed Barrett Barrett amongst Hanzus's company. Barrett was a feeble accountant who possessed neither the ability nor courage to defend himself. She had doomed the boy the moment she ordered him to act as her spy.

Spy or not, the guilt ate into Hanzus. *His* orders had condemned Barrett and Ache to death. If he hadn't sounded the retreat... if he'd fought on against Rennice and his hideous henchmen, Mister Barrett would still be alive.

His thoughts were interrupted by approaching footsteps crunching into grass and stone. Arwel stood over him, holding out his wineskin like a votive offering.

"Here," the Baron of the Tyldar said, seating himself beside Hanzus. "Thought I'd save you some Lerthian before your men devoured the lot."

Hanzus sipped the sweet beverage. Undiluted pleasure greeted his tongue. The Lerthian wine was arguably the most generous provision Brother Namus had presented them with. The Mutlen brothers had treated Hanzus with a suspicious amount of kindness. Did they believe themselves indebted to the son of *Brother* Jurgen? Or was there something sinister at play?

"You've some fine men in your company," Arwel said, accepting the skin back from Hanzus. He swayed side-to-side, struggling to maintain eye contact as he swigged the wine.

Of course, he's fucking drunk. Some things never change. Hanzus grimaced at the dark forest around him. According to Arwel, they were now deep within the Horthian Woods, a stone's throw from the Rookish city of Camensrot.

Lew was roasting rats on a spit over the fire. They weren't the most appetising of creatures, but these lands belonged to the Earl of

Camensrot, and though the lord would never learn of Hanzus's presence within the Horthian Woods, Hanzus would not dishonour the noble's laws by hunting his game. Rats, however, were exempt from such laws, and they infested this damp forest at every turn.

"They're loyal men," Hanzus said, taking another sip of wine. The bitter aftertaste clawed at his throat. "A trait I've found to be rare as of late."

Arwel considered him with cold eyes. "In truth, I believed you to be jesting when your letters spoke of Heatha's dark machinations."

Hanzus sighed. He supposed Arwel would forget most of this conversation come the morn. "I fear my wife does more than merely machinate, Arwel."

"Do you suspect Heatha had something to do with the happenings in Freestone?" Arwel asked, holding the wineskin to his lips. His eyes were wide as saucers. "Surely that cannot be."

"Oh, it can."

"What makes you so sure?"

Hanzus thought about that. In truth, he wasn't sure of anything. But his gut told him Heatha had a hand in this. One way or another. She'd murdered Brother Edennel before Hanzus could hear his story in full. She'd conscripted Mister Barrett to spy on her behalf. In all probability, she'd ordered those Bloodkin to stall him on the road.

"I pray that when we reach the Black Rook, we find my father's poisoners sleeping in their beds," Hanzus said, scratching at his knuckles. His hands itched for combat, eager to wrap themselves around the murderers' throats.

"We should reach the Rook by tomorrow evening, Goddess willing."

Hanzus took a long swig of wine. "What do you know of this inn?"

"Only that it's owned by a woman. A widow whose inheritance was enough to save the Rook from ruin. As you can imagine, the inns and alehouses close to the Krämisen border do not prosper as they once did."

Hanzus denoted bitterness in the baron's tone. "I closed my borders under the King's instructions. The Rooksland is stricken with plague."

"Yes, yes." Arwel waved him away. "Halmond closed my borders too. And as a result, the Rooksland's suffering grows and festers by the day. The Rooksfolk are subjects of the imperial crown. That much is true. But the Sylvian king does not offer them aid. On the contrary, the Rooks are taxed more than they were *before* the plague. Most families are incapable of providing for themselves, and yet they are expected to relinquish two-thirds of their wealth to fill imperial coffers. Most cannot afford this mad sum, and those that could refuse to pay it. King Halmond fears the Sylvian army will march into the Rooksland and overthrow its leaders, snatching the last echoes of freedom this Goddessless realm still clings to."

Hanzus sighed. "The plight of this realm does not concern me. I fear my own realm will fall to ruin before this backwater does."

Arwel raised an eyebrow at that. "What makes you say that?"

Hanzus had yet to inform Arwel of his encounter with Vors Rennice's Bloodkin. He inhaled a deep breath, then he explained all that had occurred in the last few weeks. Captain Morske's foiled assassination attempt after appearing in his cabin, brandishing Arwel's note. Vilka's appearance in the Balenmanor and how Heatha seemed content in hiding the vagrant away in the manor's attic; Brother Edennel's appearance at his feast, and how Heatha had ordered some crook to poison the messenger in his cell. And how Heatha had instructed Barrett Barrett to act as her spy.

When Hanzus finished his tale, Arwel met him with a frown. "These are dark tidings indeed. Though, I fail to understand how you came to receive word from me while aboard the HMS Temper."

Hanzus didn't take the man's meaning. *Has the wine filled his brain with utter nonsense?* "How do you mean?"

Arwel grinned over the wineskin. "I've crafted you many letters, dear Hans. Well wishes and idle chatter. But I don't recall sending you any warnings." He swigged a mouthful of wine, swirling it around his mouth before swallowing in one. "Also, how would I have known you were aboard the HMS Temper? True, I knew you were travelling to Carthane for the negotiations, but how would I have known what ship you'd boarded? And... and... do you have any idea how complicated it is to send messages across the sea?"

Hanzus wasn't sure if this was just another of Arwel's inappropriate jests. "The note... it bore the seal of your house. The Owl of Nate. The parchment was inked with your handwriting. For Hektor's sake, I saw it with my own two eyes."

The note had been genuine. He was sure of it. He remembered inspecting its seal, proving its authenticity. If the letter was a forgery, it had been a convincing one indeed.

But if Arwel hadn't sent the warning, who had? And why would they pretend to be the Baron of the Tyldar? Had they reasoned that Hanzus would only take heed of their message if it came from Arwel? Or was their claim bogus, a means to divert him from the true culprit, the real puppeteer that had sent Morske to his cabin?

Arwel was shaking his head. "Believe me, Hans, I sent you no such note. What did it say, exactly?"

Hanzus searched the catacombs of his mind, straining to remember the exact words. "It said *the Despot is everywhere.*"

Arwel scratched his chin. "At present, Prince Perryn is the least of our concerns. Last I heard, the Despot had taken ill and retired to his estate in the Counties."

Hanzus shuddered. Ordinarily, news of Crown Prince Perryn's sickness would have warmed his heart, allowing him to rest easier in his bed. The Despot was the clear enemy – the adversary of every baron with a shred of honour and decency – but this new foe worked deep within the shadows.

"You are certain you did not write that note?"

Arwel shook his head. "It seems to me that whoever sent this note did so to confuse, to divert you from their trail. Evidently, it worked."

Bile rose in Hanzus's throat. He was a fool not to question the note's authenticity. Come to think of it, perhaps he'd been so engrossed in the impending melee with Morske, he hadn't inspected the letter close enough.

Someone had forged Arwel's handwriting and imitated his seal. But why would they go to all that effort when their aim was to have Hanzus killed?

Heatha must *be behind this*. No one else possessed the guile and wits to manufacture these events. She had poisoned Jurgen, just as she had poisoned Brother Edennel... Perhaps she'd done so just to lure Hanzus away from Balenmeade. *But to what end?* It was possible she *expected* Morske to fail in his attempt to murder Hanzus, and she had sent the fraudulent Arwel note to aim his suspicions in the wrong direction.

"I don't like the sound of this," Arwel said, handing the wineskin back to Hanzus. "We must tread carefully. It's possible we are walking headfirst into a trap."

Hanzus swallowed, relishing the bitter aftertaste that stung the walls of his mouth. Something told him this Black Rook Inn would not stock fine Lerthian wines. He would have to savour this taste while he still could.

"I know," Hanzus admitted. Unless Jurgen's murderers were mindless fools, they had told the Mutlen monks of their plans to reach the Black Rook for a reason.

Arwel gulped. "Hans, are you sure you want to do this? We could return to Freestone at first light and..."

"I will not turn back, Arwel," Hanzus spoke over him. "Whether it is by their design or not, I *will* catch up to these poisoners. I *will* learn the true identity of my enemy." He took one last sip of wine. "You may return to Freestone at first light if you wish. I will not stop you. As for me, there can be no turning back."

Arwel met him with a smile. "Now, what did I tell you? The enemies of the Krämise are the enemies of the Tyldar." He wrapped his arm around Hanzus. "We shall learn the truth together. It's what Jurgen would have wanted."

Torment

"Your name is Barrett Barrett?" the voice asked. It came from nowhere and everywhere all at once, tickling the insides of his ears, probing his brain, touching his mind.

Barrett opened his eyes. They widened no more than a crack.

One blue eye and one red eye greeted him. The unsmiling face belonged to Vors Rennice, the Sylvian-tongued halfbreed that commanded the band of Bloodkin.

"I asked you a question, boy," he spoke plainly, his odd eyes sinking into Barrett's flesh. "And you will answer."

Barrett blinked around. Darkness surrounded him. An engulfing abyss filled only by Rennice's face. He didn't know where he was or if he was truly anywhere. He supposed he was sleeping. If he wasn't sleeping, he was dead. If the latter was true, this Vors Rennice was no more than a dark spirit sent to torment him. But that would mean the Goddess had rejected his soul, declaring it black and unworthy of her blessed realm.

He resided in Oblivion, condemned to suffer here for all eternity.

"Your name," spoke the spirit that looked like Vors Rennice. "The girl tells me you have worth. I am not disbelieving her, but I would hear the truth for myself."

Rennice seemed real enough, formed of flesh and sinew, but black spirits had the ability to deceive. This was likely some ruse, some attempt to coax him into condemning his soul further. He would not fall for it. He would not allow this spectre to torture him.

"Vilka tells me that the Baroness of the Krämise placed you here. I am not disputing this. I would, though, hear it from your mouth."

Barrett parted his lips to speak, to express his scorn, his defiance. But as he strained to utter a sound, only saliva spouted from his lips.

"I see that the poison cripples you still," the spirit said. "Fear not. It will not claim your life. The gods have carved a path for you, so I'm told. Your miserable existence will continue, Mister Barrett. For now." He peered over Barrett's head, focusing off into the distance. "Hopgar, the poison is sullying his mind still. Keep an eye on him and inform me if his state alters."

Barrett's eyes were closing. Blackness claimed him once more, wrapping him in its blanket.

But words punctured his ears before he could escape the mocking spirit: "We are close now, my brothers! Soon, the baron will *meet* his sorrow!"

The Black Rook

The Black Rook Inn. That was what they called it, though its very name was an act of pure mockery. This *inn* was no more than a shack in the middle of a small glade.

Twisted branches loomed over the road leading into the glade, reaching for Hanzus like grasping fingers. They'd delved deep into the Horthian Woods, the heart of the Rookish wilds. The trees here were like skeletons, withered and meek, starved of all sustenance. And yet, cool moisture hung heavy in the air, slipping down his throat, filling his lungs with putridity.

The sun was setting above them, announcing the arrival of the Goddess. Though, glancing around, it was evident the Holy Mother had deserted this bleak place.

The Black Rook was a ruin of wood and plaster, a shipwreck left to fester and rot. And like a ship, it reached taller than the trees, consisting of five or six levels – though the rows of windows were so uneven it was hard to tell where one level finished and the next began. Such crude structures existed in the lower marshlands of the Krämise, though none on this scale. *Such degeneracy.* The fact they'd hidden this building deep within the forest was its only redeeming quality.

Hanzus approached the inn at a trot, scanning around the clearing. He spotted a man tending to a horse outside the entrance. Unless the shadows were hiding more faces, the stranger was alone.

Hanzus halted. "We stick to our tale," he said, turning back to his servants. "My name is Grathan. Remember it well. At no point will you address me as your lord. I am an Algen tradesman passing through on my journey home. You are Algen men I have recruited with the promise of coin. Our relationship extends no further than that."

"Though *I* am your brother," Arwel reminded Hanzus, flashing a smile his way. "My name is Hophan," he explained to the servants. "Cay, you are Lathus. Lew, you are Facop. Pamen, you are Gethop."

"You are *brothers?*" Cay frowned at Arwel's shock of red hair. "Also, how am I supposed to act like an Algen if I've never even heard one speak?"

"If you keep your mouth shut," Hanzus hissed through his teeth. "These simpletons will suspect nothing. That goes for the lot of you. We have ridden here for one purpose and one purpose only. I demand the silence of each of you. Should any fool ask for it, you will provide your false names and utter no more."

"Look," Arwel said, gesturing at a signpost that was staked into the road beside him. Four crooked arrows branched off from the sign. The only words Hanzus could discern read, *Camensrot, twelve miles.*

Hanzus scoffed at that. *How many Rooklanders do they suppose can read?*

"We're a stone's throw from Cookenstown in the south and Medrow in the west," Arwel said, inspecting the sign. "If our friends have departed the Black Rook already, we'll turn our attention to Medrow, then Cookenstown."

"One thing at a time," Hanzus said. *Who's to say my father's friends do not await me on the other side of that inn door?*

The more he thought about it, the more he believed the poisoners had wished for Hanzus to follow them to the Black Rook. *Why else would they divulge their destination to those useless monks?*

"Hail, friend!" Hanzus called out, trotting toward the gaunt fellow outside the entrance. "Do you work at this here establishment?" The wretch turned to face him but said nothing. "Is this not the Black Rook Inn?"

"Depends on who's asking," the stranger croaked. Their voice was shrill, feminine. They'd stuffed their long, dark hair into a bun and made a crude attempt to shadow their eyelids and rouge their lips. It was a young woman, Hanzus realised, as he reined his steed to a halt in front of her. She had the look of a whore about her.

"My name is Grathan." Hanzus raised his hand in greeting. "My men and I seek shelter for the eve. And perhaps the next." Then, when the girl gawked up at him, he asked, "Are there no rooms available?"

Turning back to her horse, the girl dragged a brush over its mottled coat. "For a price." She snapped her scrawny neck back toward him, running her dark gaze over his party. Her eyes lingered on Arwel as he trotted to a halt beside Hanzus. "By your look, you's fine folk for the likes of these parts."

Hanzus had prepared for such an observation. "We have ridden for many days." He dismounted. His boots thudded into the soft dirt. He led his steed over to the woman and handed over the reins.

The girl's whiff greeted him before her gappy smile revealed a few mustard-brown teeth. She reeked of stale piss and something rotten. Dirt mottled her pale skin and spoiled the fraying rags draped over her skeletal frame. By the look and whiff of her, she hadn't bathed since the day she was born.

"I don't suppose many Algens visit your inn," Hanzus said, nibbling on his lip as the sickly stink filled his mouth.

The girl's dark eyes considered him. "The Rook ain't mine, mister. Tis my ma what keeps the inn." She raised a ruffled brow. "So you's Algen then? Can't say we welcome in much southern folk."

Hanzus stifled a sigh of relief. *Thank the Goddess for that.* She believed him, for now.

"Good evening, young lass," Arwel said, dismounting. He handed his reins to Lew and marched over to Hanzus's side. "Tell me your name, and I shall give you mine."

"Viola." She spat brown saliva at her horse's hooves.

"Hophan," Arwel introduced himself, wearing a thin smile. "Pleasure's mine."

Viola stared at him, dumbfounded. Evidently, the wretch had never heard such a phrase. She turned back to Hanzus and said, "Ma cooks the best stew in all Horthia. If you seek full bellies and a warm hole to rest, you's have come to the right place."

"I'm gladdened to hear it," Hanzus said, inclining his head.

"Leave your mounts with me. I'll tend to the beasts awhile, as you make yourselves at home. Ma will see you's are taken care of." She inspected Hanzus's stallion with her bony fingers. "You's in luck for stopping this eve. Our Rook's now home to the finest bard this side of the Middle Kingdoms. And it can't go unstated, ma offers the stoutest brew in all Rookland. Or, if you's preferring stronger brew, we stock mead from Layland. And Dascony wine, if you's a taste for the foreign." She paused, biting down on chapped lips. "Yeah, we've some rooms to fill. A few, mind. Some fellas rode in a few eves back, and we still ain't rid of them."

A shiver rippled down Hanzus's spine. *Does she refer to Jurgen's poisoners? Or perhaps the Bloodkin from the Old Road?* No, surely a Rookish establishment would not shelter Red Eyes.

Viola was staring at him, chewing some dark substance with her mouth gaped open, flicking it between tooth and tongue.

"Fine place," Cay said, grimacing at Viola as he came to stand between the two barons. "Why'd you call it the *Black Rook*?" Then, when she didn't answer, he scoffed and said to Hanzus, "Don't these folk realise *all* rooks are black?"

Viola glowered at the valet. "I don't take kind to your meaning, mister."

"Do not listen to my friend," Hanzus said, shooting Cay a silencing glare. "He is weary from the road. As we all are." He snatched Cay by the wrist and dragged him over to the door, well out of the girl's earshot. "What did I say? Keep your mouth *shut*."

Cay scowled at him. "Yes, *my lord*," he muttered under his breath.

Hanzus swallowed bile. Cay's insolence had grown louder and louder since Freestone. He'd lost all respect for his lord, and his sense of duty. The valet hadn't openly declared his dissent, but he spoke to Hanzus as if they were now peers. Hanzus had too much on his mind to correct the boy's behaviour. *But you can rest assured, a day will come when I remind you of your place.*

Cay muttered something under his breath before approaching the door and yanking it open. Sweat and ale infiltrated Hanzus's nostrils as the door swung shut behind him.

Hanzus glanced back at Lew and Pamen, who were handing their steeds over to Viola.

"I like her," Arwel said, approaching Hanzus and wrapping his arm around his shoulder. "Do you think the bitch likes me in return?"

Hanzus pushed the fool's comment aside, grinding down on his teeth. *Jurgen's poisoners are here, somewhere.* He could feel it in his bones. He fingered the hilt of his sword, running his fingertips over the scabbard.

Arwel's smile faded as he noticed the placement of Hanzus's hand. "Now, now, Hans. Stop your fretting. There's only one way to discover if we're walking into a trap."

The Black Rook was, more or less, an extension of the land outside it. Shoddy woodwork plastered with hoary paint. As he ran his eyes over the wonky timber and misshapen boards, he made out every wild brushstroke. Where the fireplace touched the walls with its orange glow, the surface reminded him of melting cheese. Damp skirted the ceiling. Patches of spilt ale and vomit stained the floorboards. Crooked beams held everything together, but only just.

There had been no hoodlum warriors awaiting them as they'd entered the drinking hall and found a table by the fireplace in the corner. The Rooksfolk seated around them did no more than whisper and gawk at Hanzus and his crew. Every man was unshaven, unwashed, and unkempt, clad in stained tunics and tight coifs. If Jurgen's poisoners sat amongst them, they hid themselves well.

Hanzus had half a mind to stand up and announce his name and purpose for all to hear. Even if the poisoners weren't here, the Rooksfolk would soon spread word that the Baron of the Krämise had made a home of the Black Rook Inn.

But exposing himself would do more than simply summon his foes. He would make an enemy of every wretch gathered here. These poor Rookish bastards were unable to cross the border and escape their plagued realm upon the pain of death. To reveal he'd crossed the border into the Rooksland, doing in reverse that which they could only dream of would enrage them with jealousy. And, upon realising he was a nobleman, they would strip him of his coin and the cloth under his leathers. If they didn't slit his throat, perhaps they would ransom him to the King of Gadensland. A ransom he was unsure Halmond would be willing to pay.

"More ale?" Viola asked. Hanzus lowered his gaze from the ceiling to find the girl hovering over his table, carrying a tray of mugs overflowing with booze. A dog-faced man from the neighbouring table smacked her on the arse, prompting a chorus of chuckles from his fellows. But the poor girl seemed too afraid or embarrassed to pay it any mind.

"Thank you, lass," Arwel said, accepting five mugs from her tray and passing them around the table.

"Something wrong with your brother?" Viola asked him, cocking her head in Hanzus's direction.

"We are each of us weary from the road, my dear," Arwel said. With his eyes, he pleaded for Hanzus to sip from his cup.

Hanzus had yet to finish the last pint of Rooksbrew that Arwel had retrieved from the bar. He had no appetite, especially for Rookish ale. And he couldn't get drunk. He had to stay focused, alert to danger. He couldn't dumb his mind in such uncertain company.

"Don't trouble yourself, my dear," Arwel said, smiling up at her. When Viola turned her attention to another table, he frowned at Hanzus. "Sip some ale, Hans. It'll calm your nerves."

"Calm my nerves?" Hanzus laughed in disbelief. "My father's murderer may well sit among us." He met Arwel's gaze, grinding his teeth.

Arwel sighed before glugging a mouthful of ale. "Have a couple of pints, at least. Enough to calm and no more."

Arwel didn't understand. *He'll never understand.* The Baron of the Tyldar had known Jurgen Irvaye, known him well. He'd respected him enough to ride recklessly to Freestone and help ease his suffering. *Delivering the final blow that Jurgen so desperately craved.* But Arwel's was not the same blood that had flowed through Jurgen's veins.

The sins of Jurgen belonged to Hanzus now. Unlike Arwel, who could return to his home and forget all that had transpired here, Hanzus could not escape from the ghost of his father, nor the memories they'd shared.

Father, how could you? At the hand of Jurgen... at the hand of the Baron Without Sorrow, Hanzus had witnessed the cruellest of tortures. Trials of immense suffering. He had forced a young Hanzus to participate...

Hanzus brought the first cup of Rooksbrew to his lips, allowing the bitter liquid to slide down his throat. The brown beverage was vile, but everything was sweeter than those sordid memories.

"Do you remember that careening we witnessed along Marlin Bay?" Arwel asked him, smiling to himself. Lew and Cay eyed Hanzus over their mugs, awaiting their baron's answer. Pamen was staring at the wall, uninterested in everything around him.

"I..." Hanzus strained to remember what Arwel was referring to, but then the image came to him. A crew of sailors had dragged one of the King's warships onto the sands close to Dyllet, lowered it onto its side, and then scraped its underneath. The thought was a welcoming distraction from that of Jurgen. "Yes. Yes, I remember."

"The captain chose an absurd time to careen his vessel," Arwel explained to the intrigued valets. "The skies were black with the worst storm I ever did see. Still, the captain's men didn't falter. In spite of the rain and the thunder and the approaching tide, they did not abandon their task. Goddess, those were hard folk." He finished his ale and wiped his lips clean of froth. "Some of those barnacles were as big as this table."

As Arwel continued his dramatic tale, stealing Cay and Lew's rapt attention, Hanzus found his mind wandering as he scanned over the hall.

At the far end of the long room, a plump woman stood behind the bar, zealously scrubbing the surface with a wet rag as barmaids served the surrounding punters. The hall was filling with low wretches, and most seemed content to stand and drink, filling every corner of this damp coffin with their harsh voices and musty stench. He assumed these regulars were the inhabitants of the nearby towns Arwel mentioned. They were all skinny and appeared sickly. He only prayed none carried the plague.

The woman behind the bar stood out from this sea of skeletons. She was the only wretch in sight to possess droopy cheeks and a rounded belly. She had to be the innkeeper. This *ma* Viola had spoken of. He only wondered – if this portly woman was indeed Viola's mother – why she stuffed her own face but did not feed her daughter.

Hanzus rose from the table, prompting Arwel to pause from his story.

"Where are you going?" the Tyldar baron asked, disconcerted. "You told us to sit and wait."

"Has the plan changed?" Pamen hissed, glancing up from his cup, resentment flooding his eyes.

"Nothing has changed," Hanzus snapped, kicking his chair under the table. A Rooklander scurried over and asked if he had finished with the chair, but Hanzus waved the wretch away. "You *will* sit and wait," he said to his men. "All of you."

Without awaiting a response, he stormed away from the table, pushing through the sweating crowd, fixing his eye on the innkeeper. As he reached the bar, the plump woman turned her eyes on him.

"Are you the innkeeper?" he asked her.

Wordlessly, the woman dropped her rag somewhere behind the bar and raised an eyebrow at him. She spat brown saliva onto the floor and stomped away from him, disappearing through a door behind the bar.

"Don't mind my ma," Viola said. She'd appeared next to him, birthed from the sweltering crowd. "She don't take too kind to new faces. But I assure you, so long as you've coin in your purse, your men are welcome here."

Hanzus turned to face her. In the firelight, he realised her eyes were not brown, as they'd appeared in the gloom outside. There was a hint of green in the middle of her irises, but they were dark, muddy, like dull emeralds caked in dirt. That had to be rare in these parts. There had to be a drop of Marridan in her blood.

"The stew'll be ready soon," she said before he could open his mouth. She narrowed her eyes at him. "You want something a tad heavier than ale? Mead or vodka, perhaps?"

"The ale is most satisfactory." He pursed his lips, wondering whether to proceed. "Viola, might I ask you something?"

She raised an eyebrow at that. "Depends what it's worth."

Hanzus sighed. "I would compensate you for your answer, of course." After he dodged the flailing arm of a passing drunk, he invited Viola to follow him over to the wall, where the crowd was sparser. Praying they were out of drunken earshot, he retrieved a silver coin and placed it in her hands. "Viola, when we spoke outside, you mentioned that you'd recently welcomed another group of travellers into your inn. Could you describe them to me?"

Viola sighed, rolling her eyes away from him, searching for an escape. Failing at that, she inhaled a sharp breath and met him with a glower. "Queer folk pass nightly through our doors. You expect me to remember them all?"

"You mentioned you were unable to be rid of these travellers," Hanzus said, retrieving a second coin and hovering it over her hands. "Tell me what they look like. I'll ask no more of you."

She exhaled slowly, accepting his silver. "I mentioned travellers to make you think we'd few rooms to spare. It was a trick, mister. A ploy to make you part with your coin and quick. Truthfully, we ain't been filling our beds of late." She smiled, flashing her brown teeth. "You know, we ain't seen no foreign folk for some time. Sure, a few Algens stop from time to time, but I ain't ever welcomed folk from the Krämise."

Hanzus skimmed over her smirk, questioning her meaning. Then it hit him. Fear trickled down his spine, taking hold of his entire body. He staggered back from her. She wasn't bluffing. Somehow, she'd seen through his ruse.

"Look," she whispered, her smile fading. "Your secret's safe with me. Ma don't take too kind to your breed, but it don't make me fret none. So long as you keep the coin flowing, I'll keep the ale flowing. And I won't ask what a gang of Krämisens is doing sneaking about the Horthian Woods. If all you mean's to sip our brew and sleep in our beds, your business will remain your business."

"I don't know what you're talking about," he said, though he knew his words were senseless. She'd rumbled him. This Viola was not the common fool she appeared. She must've recognised his accent the moment he'd first opened his mouth.

"Nor me," Viola said, smiling once again. "So long as you men keep to yourselves, no man here'll trouble you. For now, you remain Algen to these folk. You've my word on that."

Hanzus could feel the sweat trickling down the nape of his neck. "We will do no more than eat and sleep here. You have *my* word on that. On the morrow, we shall return to the road."

Though doing so might allow Jurgen's poisoners to slip away, Hanzus realised he might have to abandon his search of the Black Rook in order to leave with his life.

"Very well," she said, looking him up and down. "But before you walk away, you'll have to kiss me."

"*What?*" He stared at her, waiting for her to reveal she was jesting.

"Do not turn, but several eyes are now upon us." She leaned in close to him. Her rotten breath filled his nostrils. "Folk will wonder why you pulled me aside. Kiss me now and let them wonder no more."

As her lips brushed against his, he wanted to be sick. He daren't turn to the crowd to see if she was telling the truth.

When she pulled away, she greeted him with a smirk. "Your beds are ready. The five rooms on the top floor are yours. Should you find yourself cold or lonely in the night, Mister Algen, you know where to find me." And with that, she padded away from him. She turned back to face him before joining the crowd. "Eat and drink up, Grathan. If you mean to depart on the morrow, you'll be needing your strength."

Sickness swirled in his belly as he gulped down the last of the stodgy stew. He wasn't sure what the insipid sludge comprised. He didn't dare ask. When Viola had brought the tray of bowls over to them, she'd addressed Arwel only.

Indeed, the innkeeper's daughter avoided Hanzus's eyes every time she passed his way. He wasn't sure if it was shame for kissing him in front of these drunks, or his Krämisen lips had left a foul taste in her mouth.

If you only knew I was the lord of that realm, the realm that you no doubt despise. Upon learning his title, he wondered if the girl would drag him to her bedchamber or ask her punters to seize him. There was a time when such a thought would have amused him.

As he stared into his cup, he was uncertain he'd ever laugh again. If Jurgen's poisoners did not make themselves known soon, Hanzus would have to leave without a single clue as to their whereabouts.

As the night dragged on, fresh swarms of Rooklanders packed into the hall, squirming for a taste of ale and the innkeeper's tasteless stew. If the evening turned sour, Hanzus and his men would have to swim through a sea of bodies to escape into the night. But he pushed that thought aside, scanning over the library of faces, searching for anything that stood out.

Music was playing from somewhere, humming over the crowd.

From his chair, he could still just about spot the innkeeper. On more than one occasion, as he scanned over the bar, he was certain her eyes flashed toward him, but every time he squinted at her face, she aimed her eyes elsewhere.

"You know what?" Arwel said, swaying in his seat. "This place is growing on me." He glugged down what had to be his seventh or eighth pint. A graveyard of empty mugs now littered their table. "I fear I might even like it here." He blinked up at the ceiling and almost lost his balance. "How much forest do you suppose they felled in order to build this... this *place?*"

Hanzus sighed, inhaling the sticky warmth. "Who knows?" *Who cares?* Unlike Arwel, he remained sober. He'd paced his consumption of ale perfectly, pausing whenever he felt a wave of dizziness. Arwel, Lew and Cay had displayed no such restraint. Pamen, however, had retired for the evening.

Hanzus postponed his own retirement, dreading the piss-stained, mite-infested sheets that no doubt awaited him at the top of the stairs. And still, he couldn't shake the fear that the poisoners sat amongst him, whether alert to his presence or not. He felt their invisible eyes scanning over him. Unease crippled his gut. The food in his belly swirled and bubbled like a witch's cauldron. Drunks peppered him with frowns and wary glances. Often, their eyes lingered for minutes at a time.

As Hanzus lifted his mug to his lips, he realised the hall was falling silent. The chorus of gruff, merry voices faded to an echo, then a whisper.

The crowd filling the space between the tables and bar was shifting, splitting in half. As the sides parted ways, the gap revealed a small stage to the left of the bar. A bard stood upon the stage. He had paused from his song, bowing low before the crowd. He was a handsome fellow, with wavy blond locks and a pink face.

The Rooksfolk cheered and whistled at the bard, slapping their clammy hands together in applause.

"Thank you, thank you," the bard cried out, waving graciously as the crowd simmered down. He spoke with an accent not of this realm – Sylvian, if Hanzus wasn't mistaken. "Friends! As always, I am indebted to your kindness. Now, with your leave, I shall deliver a slower piece. 'Tis sombre in nature, but I'm sure it will come as a treat to your ears."

The hall fell silent as the bard commenced a slow melody. The strings sang gracefully with every stroke. But rather than harmonise the sweet instrument with his own voice, someone else stepped up onto the stage, stood beside him, and began to sing.

It was Viola.

Her voice was like silk caressing skin. Her harsh accent dissipated entirely as her humming harmonised with the soft strumming of the strings. Words whispered from her tongue. It was beautiful, like a robin's morning song.

The weight of time upon my face,
I see the light, I feel the taste,
The hurt that once became my soul,
I don't remember life at all,
The lord of steel is strong before,
The gates of iron there before,
My parted soul forms wisps of grey,
Becomes the forest of decay,

Lift me up above the clouds,
The mottled leaves of trees of brown,
I keep my soul for none to claim,
I left my claim forgotten,
The whisper passing from my lips,
Fades with prayer I long to share,
But too I have forsaken oaths,
The land I loved once before.

As the bard completed his final strum, the room erupted in frenzied applause. He saw grown men wiping away tears, hiding their shame and sorrow in their cups.

Hanzus fought the tears threatening to leak from his eyes. Viola's words had touched him, triggering something he'd kept locked in the dungeons of his mind.

Arwel was shaking his head as Hanzus returned his gaze to the table. "Shut your eyes, and you might just forget the number of cocks she's sucked."

Cay and Lew chuckled.

Hanzus scoffed, unamused by the baron's crudeness. "What do *you* know of music?" Hanzus wasn't sure Viola was the whore Arwel painted her out to be. *There may well be more to this girl than meets the eye.* "Hlus Gaam said that the ugly soul is capable of producing beauty."

Arwel's eyes widened with surprise. "Goddess above, don't tell me *you've* become a poet now. The world is already plagued with wordsmiths that speak of hidden beauty in every withering flower."

Hanzus waved the man's tomfoolery away. He turned back to Viola. Her brown smile beamed at the approving crowd.

"I shall retire," he said, rising from his chair. The hunt for the poisoners would continue tomorrow. Arwel was right when he suggested they investigate the towns close to the Black Rook. The wretches he sought were not here.

Arwel stared at him. "What happened to sitting and waiting?"

"You're welcome to sit and wait all eve if it suits you," Hanzus groaned, turning to the staircase. *Riding here was a waste of time.*

His bed for the night was calling his name. He needed rest, reprieve. He needed to escape from the stench of this hall, and the horrid faces inhabiting it. He had to flee from his own mind, from the doors that Viola's song had unlocked.

Judgement

Primitive music was playing. A low rumble punctured by the occasional resonating shrill note. A droning voice howled over the instrumentals like an injured dog.

Hanzus's pillow was no more than a slice of unstuffed coarse fabric. But it embraced him like soft hands, caressing him, gentle, willing him to slumber. Vors Rennice's Bloodkin and Jurgen's faceless poisoners besieged the walls of his mind, demanding he stay awake, alert.

But he was tired... so very tired...

The music had stopped.

The silence didn't last for long. Frantic voices filled the halls below.

Hanzus waited, praying the bard was breaking to tighten his strings and down some ale. But as the lute's silence dragged on, the voices grew in volume and ferocity.

Hanzus eased an eye open. The candle beside the bed was still burning. The wax had barely melted.

A piercing scream rose above the flurry of sound – terrified, desperate, bordering on the inhuman. Shouts followed, a medley of rage and anguish.

Hanzus lifted his head from the hard pillow. Every hair on his body stood to attention. His cheeks were hot to the touch. His lungs felt constricted, as though penetrative hands squeezed them.

He sprang from the bed and scurried over to the window.

The full moon offered no guidance. He squinted down at the clearing below but saw only darkness.

Below the floorboards, the screams grew louder. Outside his door, a stampede of boots slammed in the corridor. Madness had possessed the Black Rook, such madness as existed on the battlefield. War left a man hollow, soulless, stripped of his humanity. Had war found him here? He couldn't think straight. *The Bloodkin... have they followed me to this place?* Or perhaps the poisoners had been here all along and were now revealing their hand. *Have I walked into a trap?*

A knock came at his door.

The moon's mesmerising glow rooted Hanzus to the spot. *The Goddess is radiant.* She was talking to him. *You will survive this night, Hanzus Irvaye. Now nothing can harm you.*

"Milord? *Milord?*" a muffled voice croaked from the other side of the door.

So, they are *here. The time of judgement is upon me.*

He didn't hear the door open, but there was now a man beside him. A crooked nose danced around the corner of his vision. Crazed eyes swam all around him. The man's mouth was opening and closing, but he emitted no sound. A barrier existed between them.

A cool hand touched his wrist. Then, clarity returned.

"Milord? We have to leave... at once."

"Lew."

It *was* him. The old valet was panting, his sharp features dripping with sweat. Behind him, the door was open. Bodies flew past the doorframe, shoving each other as they raced across their corridor.

"Milord, we have to get out of here!"

Ale was heavy in Lew's breath, but his gaze was sober. "The Rooksfolk, milord... they're... they're crazed."

Hanzus blinked at Lew, trying to make sense of his words. The man's reddened eyes were about to pop out of their sockets.

"The inn's under attack, milord. We cannot fight them. They're too many. We have to get you to safety. We need to go *now*."

Lew snatched Hanzus by the wrist and led him into the corridor. Bodies smacked into Hanzus, punching him in the ribs. As they descended the staircase, folk were falling over each other, flying down the steps like rats fleeing a sinking ship.

Hanzus tried his best to keep up, but Lew was nimble. He danced around these rascals with ease. As they reached the next floor, a punch to the shoulder threw Hanzus backwards, and once he'd regained his footing, Lew was nowhere to be seen.

The crowd had taken him.

"Out of my way!" Hanzus barked ahead. A pile of bodies filled the corridor. He pushed the buttocks of the man in front of him, but it was in vain. The procession was moving, but slowly, like a turbulent river of flesh and sweat-drenched wool.

Where the corridor forked in two directions, the crowd dragged him to the left. The river's flow had taken him. The frenzied swarm moved as one.

They reached the final staircase leading to the ground.

Screams filled his ears as the swarm dragged him down the steps. Fists smacked into his shoulders. Boots kicked at his shins. Raw strength alone helped him keep his footing.

The drinking hall was a sea of anguish. Maddened faces were everywhere. Intelligible nonsense spewed from their frothing lips. Cries for aid, calls to retreat. The drunks that had previously been laughing and drinking together were friends no more. It was every man for himself. They went punching and kicking as they scrambled for the exit.

As Hanzus reached the final step, he searched for the source of their panic, but the crowd shifted in every direction like the waves of a stormy sea. And he was the ship caught in its waters, his sail broken, his crew having deserted him.

"What is... *happening*?" he cried into the air. "Why do you *flee*?" Was every Rooklander spineless? Had a few Bloodkin spooked all of these men?

He couldn't see any Red Eyes. He couldn't see anything.

Then he spotted Lew.

"Lew! *Lew!*" he yelled, but the ambience of noise swallowed his voice. "Lew, I'm over here!"

The valet's face vanished, swallowed by the sea of strangers.

A tall brute stormed past Hanzus, swatting men aside as he bellowed in their ears. Most jumped out of his way, and those that didn't he knocked onto their backs.

Hanzus seized the opportunity, making for the gap the man had left, ducking under flailing arms and butting heads. As he lost sight of the tall brute, so too did he lose his bearing. He scanned the hall, but he couldn't spot the exit.

Lew's face emerged from the swirling mass, pressing up against him. "Milord!"

Lew snatched him by the arm, leading him through the sea of despair. They reached a wall. To their left, men were flinging themselves off the staircase, splatting onto the floorboards below. To their right, a mass of bodies gathered around the door, slowly filtering through it, escaping into the night.

"What's going on?" Hanzus barked in Lew's ear. The valet gaped at him as if the words hadn't made sense. "Why do these curs flee? What sparked this terror?"

Lew gaped at him.

Hanzus returned his gaze to the crowd, scanning over their heads.

Then he spotted it.

To the left of the bar, upon the stage, a dark figure stood. Blood oozed from the man's hairline, dripping from his nose and chin, plastering his black robe. His skin was white as bone. *Could it be?* He squinted at the creature's eyes, which were red as the blood that dripped off them.

They have come.

A pile of lifeless bodies surrounded the creature's feet. A pale grin stretched across its face. The Bloodkin lifted a red dagger high above its head.

"Scatter! Scatter you cravens!" the Bloodkin shrieked, pointing the tip of his blade at the sea of terror swirling around him. "Be gone, vermin! Leave this place while you can!"

Hanzus fingered his scabbard. "Goddess, damn you!" he barked at the fleeing crowd. The legends were true, after all. *The Rooks are all craven... meek fools... Goddessless bastards.* Unworthy of the lowest form of pity.

Hanzus kicked at every fool that passed him. "Stand your ground, coward! Stand against this heathen! We are kinsmen. Stand with me, and we'll send this creature to the Oblivion!"

But the Rooksfolk didn't share his courage. They retaliated by punching him in the gut and barging him with their shoulders as they ran past. They would sooner fight a Krämisen than stand against this Bloodkin.

"Come on," Hanzus hissed in Lew's ear. "Come on... we have to do something. The Bloodkin's here for me." *To finish the job, they started on the Old Road.* He glanced around, but he couldn't see any Red Eye other than the one upon the stage. *But they're here somewhere.* Perhaps they were surrounding the inn.

Most of the drunks had filtered out through the door. The sea of bodies had grown sparse. Hanzus pushed his way toward the stage. Broken bodies littered the floor. Some were crawling away, but most were unconscious or dead.

A second Bloodkin had appeared upon the stage. He was carrying a lute in one hand – the same instrument the bard had used to accompany Viola's song – and a curved dagger in the other. A shaggy mop of black hair brushed his shoulders. His crimson eyes found Hanzus.

"This baron of sorrow," he said, inclining his head in a mocking bow. He stumbled over the words. The Sylvian tongue was new to him. "This pleasure is belonging to this one."

Hanzus unsheathed his sword without a second thought. "Your words are poison! Your speech betrays you as vermin! A foreign invader! A stain upon this earth!"

"You will not be taking another step." A third man had stepped onto the stage. He was... *human.* His skin was pink, one of his eyes blue, but the other eye was as red as a Bloodkin's.

It was the wretched halfbreed he'd encountered on the Old Road. *Vors Rennice.* He'd never forget that name. The mongrel's eyes were hypnotic, so much so that he almost missed the child that was standing in front Rennice.

A girl much younger than Viola, tears rolling down her cheeks. As Hanzus approached the stage, Vors Rennice lifted a knife to her throat.

"You will not be taking another step," Rennice repeated. "One more, and this girl will be dead. You have my word on that, *my lord.*" He flashed a cloy smile. "Oh, and please do forgive my men. Most are unaccustomed to your tongue." He turned to the Bloodkin that had spoken before him. "You heard the Baron of the Krämise, Gruplin. Your speech is impure. Your accent offends him."

The two Bloodkin beside Rennice chuckled under their breath.

Hanzus's heart rattled in its cage. *He* had caused this. No deaths would have occurred if Hanzus hadn't stopped here. The Bloodkin had followed Hanzus all the way here from the Krämise. *Who knows how many innocent lives they've slain on the way.*

Hanzus could not move. He couldn't peel his gaze from the poor child Rennice had captured. She was fifteen or sixteen, perhaps. Rookish or not, the poor wretch was too young to die. To die like this, at any rate. Her people had abandoned her, fleeing to save themselves. *Only I can save her now. I am the only thing that stands between the dagger and her throat.*

"Oh, wait," Rennice said. "Now I am remembering. Sylvian is

not the true tongue of your kin either, is it, my lord? As a matter of fact, I am recalling reading that the Sylvians butchered the last speakers of the Krämisen tongue. Is this true?" He twisted into a scowl. "Have you ever pondered on why the name of your barony sounds so... so... inhuman? *Krämise*... it is almost sounding like it belongs to the Bloodkin. Do you agree?"

Something caught Hanzus's attention in the corner of his eye. Turning to the bar, he realised the innkeeper was hiding behind it, her nose peeking over the counter. Viola was beside her, gaping at the stage in horror.

"Milord," Lew hissed over his shoulder. "Milord, we have to leave. *Now.*" The valet had appeared beside him.

Hanzus nibbled on his lips. "We cannot abandon the girl. Ready yourself for a fight. The halfbreed is mine."

The hall was empty now. Floorboards glimmering in the firelight – a sticky sheen of blood and vomit.

"Let the child go," Hanzus said, turning back to the stage. Vors Rennice's grin widened. "Your quarrel is with me. Let her go, or I swear in the name of Hektor your death will be slow."

"The name of Hektor is meaning nothing to these men, my lord." Rennice frowned. "Your swearing on it means less than nothing. We may begin this merry dance, my lord, but only after you have relinquished your blade. Surrender to my kin, and you have my word, I will not harm a single hair on this pretty child's head."

Lew was trembling beside Hanzus. *Where are the others?* Pamen and Cay would not have abandoned him, and Arwel Nate was many things, but he was no coward.

Rennice brushed the girl's neck with the flat of his blade. He kneed her lightly on the hip, muffling her groans with his gloved hand.

"I am not the bluffing sort," he stated. "I am inviting you, my lord, to lower your blade."

The odds were not in Hanzus's favour. He reckoned that either Bloodkin upon the stage could take Lew with ease. When they'd encountered these creatures on the Old Road, the Bloodkin hadn't been aiming to kill them. But the heaps of bodies upon the stage told him their strategy had changed.

But I can't surrender to these heathens without at least trying.

Somewhere behind him, a door creaked open. Boots crunched. Floorboards squeaked.

"Lew, what's happening?" he whispered. He daren't peel his gaze from the stage.

"They surround us, milord."

"How many have entered?"

"Three more."

Rennice's gaze flashed over Hanzus's head. His lips curled into a smirk.

Hanzus swallowed bile. He'd fight, but he wouldn't allow this innocent girl to be cut down in the process. As he loosened his grip on the hilt, his sword slipped from his grasp, clattering to the floorboards.

"How very much disappointing," Rennice said, pouting dramatically. "The *Baron Without Sorrow*. They are calling you that, are they not? Funny. See what sorrow we bring." He removed his dagger from the girl's throat, allowing her to hop off the stage and scurry over to the bar, where she found refuge with Viola and her mother.

"And what are they *calling* you?" Hanzus hissed up at the halfbreed. "Butcher of the innocent? Traitor to one's kin? Oh, but you are kinless, are you not? I see the freakish anomaly of your eyes. You are born of the Oblivion. Doomed and accursed. Neither human nor Bloodkin."

Rennice merely chuckled at that. "*Me*, my lord? I thank you for promoting me to such lofty heights. Accursed, am I? I'll admit, I am liking the sound of that." He sighed, running his fingers over the flat of his blade. "No, my lord. I am nothing more than vagrant scum. This is what your folk would call me." He aimed the tip of his blade toward Hanzus. "But *you*, my lord, now you are having a tale worth sharing. You prevented a war, so I hear. A war that would have devastated the entire world of Bloodkin and Men. And so, I am thanking you, my lord. Thanking you that I exist in an undevastated world." He lowered his neck in something of a bow. "Strangely, though, I have heard varying accounts of what transpired during the Battle That Never Was. Some are speaking your name like it is a curse, and others like it is belonging to a saviour. Throughout these parts, the tale of your heroism is tossed around like a bag of mystery meat. Though I am yet to decide what sort of meat you really are."

"Mutton?" the Bloodkin to his left suggested.

Vors Rennice frowned at that. "Perhaps. I am undecided." He leaned forward, resting his dagger on his kneecap. "I *can* say, however, that we are having in our possession an assortment of meat." He stood tall and clapped his hands together, peering over Hanzus's head. "Bring him in!"

The door creaked open once more. Hanzus couldn't hide his curiosity this time. He turned to find two Bloodkin dragging a limp body across the floor, a mottled bag tied over its head. Around the mouth, the fabric expanded and contracted as the poor wretch fought for air.

Hanzus eyed his sword on the ground, inches away from his feet. Lew's sword, too, sat beside it. *If I could only reach out and...*

"It may relieve you to be learning of your man's safe arrival," Rennice said, stealing Hanzus's attention. The halfbreed pointed at the masked captive with the tip of his dagger.

One of the Bloodkin holding the captive ripped the bag off his head.

Holy Mother... he's alive.

There knelt before him was Barrett Barrett. His hair was tangled and knotted, his eyes bulging and bloodshot. The two Bloodkin captors grasped his shoulders, forcing him to stay low on the ground.

The lad was muttering something. "The woman with the green eyes... the green eyes." He groaned and spluttered, blinking absently around the room. *He's possessed.* His eyes fixated on the ceiling, trembling in their sockets, about to burst.

"What's wrong with him?" Hanzus demanded, turning back to Rennice.

"Green eyes... green eyes," Barrett's voice echoed. "Green eyes... the green eyes..."

"*Silence!*" Rennice boomed, spraying spittle in an arc. Once Barrett had fallen quiet, the halfbreed cracked a smile. "Now that I have your full attention, my lord, I would like very much to return to the matter at hand." His eyes searched the room. "My lady? My lady, where are you? Must I begin without you?"

"I'm here."

The innkeeper had abandoned her hiding place. She patted down her apron and padded over to Rennice, halting by the foot of the stage.

Rennice bowed to her. "The stage is yours, as it were, my lady."

"What in Hektor's name is going on here?" Hanzus hissed. *What low treachery is this?* Had the fat innkeeper been serving these creatures all along?

"Come here, children," the innkeeper cooed, waving her hands as though she was summoning puppies. "Come now, don't be shy."

Reluctantly, Viola and the urchin Rennice had threatened to end emerged from the bar, scurrying over to the plump woman.

Something sharp dug into Hanzus's spine – a blade held to his back, its tip piercing his leathers. A hand emerged from behind him, dragging his fallen sword across the floor and out of view.

Fuck. His heart sank. How could he have been so foolish? How could he have allowed these creatures to distract him? They had defeated him before he could draw a single droplet of heathen blood.

The innkeeper embraced the two girls, patting them both on the head. "The night is almost over, my lovely girls." Her hands were trembling. She smiled down at the nameless child. "You did well, my darling. So very, very well. I could not have asked for more." She withdrew from her apron what appeared to be a biscuit and handed it to the girl. "Here you are, my dear. You deserve a good rest now. Your mother loves you very much."

"What madness is this?" Hanzus spat, unable to hide his disgust a moment longer.

The innkeeper turned on Hanzus, malice oozing from her bulbous face. "There you are," she spoke through her teeth. A droplet of sorrow trickled down her pink cheek. "Baron Irvaye of the Krämise. When first you entered my beloved Black Rook with your band of merry men, I hardly believed my eyes. I daren't hope. You see, too often have I held vengeance in my grasp, only for it to... slip away." She smiled at Viola, then at her other daughter. "I will never doubt again, and it is all thanks to you, my darling."

"*Vilka!*"

The innkeeper scowled past Hanzus. The voice, he realised, had come from Barrett.

Hanzus squinted at the young girl's face. *Surely not?* What were the chances that *this* girl – the girl he'd relinquished his sword in order to save – was the same Rookish vagrant that Heatha had kept as a pet in the Balenmanor?

The girl in question was blinking in Barrett's direction, chewing merrily on her biscuit. Her eyes were green, as green as summer leaves.

"*Vilka?*" the innkeeper spat, holding her belly as she laughed. "Ah, yes. We couldn't have you skipping around Balenmeade with your actual name now, could we, my darling?" Her smile died as her gaze returned to Hanzus. "*Vilka.* Slips off the tongue, does it not? I heard the Rooksfolk speak of a legend. Vilka, the wanderer that never slept." She smiled down at her youngest daughter. "And sleep, you did not. My dear, you have made your mother most happy. Your father smiles down upon you."

"*Vilka?*" Hanzus directed at the girl. "Are you the child that my wife sheltered?"

He'd sensed deviousness afoot when Heatha had informed him of Vilka's presence in Balenmeade, but thoughts of Harvest,

Carthane, and Jurgen's impending death had distracted him. And Vilka had been serving a dark purpose all the while, spying for this innkeeper, serving Rennice and his Bloodkin.

"Her name ain't Vilka, you pig," Viola spat, aiming a trembling finger at Hanzus. "You got no ears?"

Hanzus swallowed vomit. The Bloodkin's blade pressed into his back.

He should have left the Black Rook as soon as Viola became aware of his Krämisen accent. That had been a sign, a message from the Goddess to escape.

He ran his eyes over Vilka. She had infiltrated the Balenmanor, and now she was here. The innkeeper of the Black Rook Inn was her mother. *Goddess, how can this be so?*

"Calmly, my dear." The innkeeper placed a hand on Viola's shoulder. Then she scowled at Hanzus. "I thank you for allowing my child to sleep in your home. Your wife was a most gracious host. Though, let us not let that distract us from the matter at hand."

"Who are you?" Hanzus wanted to know. This game had dragged on for long enough.

"Really, my lord." The innkeeper stepped forward, her rosy cheeks wobbling with every step. "I look upon your face now as if it were the last time I beheld it. To tell you the truth, I have thought of little else. For seven years, I have been closing my eyes to find you staring back at me. For seven years, the Baron Without Sorrow remained my companion. My tormentor. But no longer." She stopped a few inches from him. She reeked of sweat. "I believe that if I were to close my eyes right now, I would see only darkness."

"I'll have your name, woman," Hanzus spat through his teeth. Something about her did seem familiar. It was the eyes he recognised, though he couldn't recall the face they belonged to.

The woman edged closer, her eyes widening with every step. "I was there, my lord. I was there that day on the battlefield, watching you from a distance. I was there the day they took him away in chains... beating him to a pulp."

Hanzus stared at her, unpacking her features. *The eyes... it's the eyes that are familiar.* Green eyes, polished emeralds. But the rest of the face could have belonged to anyone... a chambermaid, an old whore.

"High treason was the verdict." A tear rolled down her cheek. "*Verdict* I say. As if he received a fair trial. Have you ever, in fact, heard of a *fair* trial, my lord?" Tears were pouring down her face now. "Yes... in many ways, he *was* a guilty man. Guilty of many a sin, but no sin so great as to warrant..." She faltered, choking on her tears.

Vors Rennice stepped down from the stage and placed a caring hand on her back. "Slow, my dear. There is no need to be rushing this. The Lord Irvaye is going nowhere."

"You still don't remember me, do you?" she snarled at Hanzus, sucking up the tears. "You just stood there staring at me, without a drop of remorse in your blackened heart. And all you could say to me... all you could bring your forked tongue to hiss at a grieving widow was... *Take care of those children, Lady Lockett.*"

Hanzus gaped at her, trying to make sense of the words. Then the realisation surged through his body, clenching his gut, strangling his veins, turning his blood to ice. Could it be that under those wobbly cheeks and greasy hair was... was... *Sir Henry Lockett's widow?*

"*Tamara?*" The name turned to ashes on the tip of his tongue. He felt weak, as though poison coursed through his veins. He felt dizzy. He was losing his footing.

The last thing he saw as he fell to the floor was Tamara Lockett's smile.

The sun was hiding. A single beam of light broke through the charcoal clouds, kissing the courtyard with its soft illumination as the rain pattered the cobbles.

From the dark battlements above, the Royal Guard, in their cloaks of gold-and-blue, watched the scene below like deadpan sentinels. They reminded Hans of the gargoyles that sat above the Chapel of Sage Mannus.

"Over here, my love!" Heatha called to Hans as he entered the courtyard, wearing that girlish smile of hers as she floated in this sea of lords and ladies.

After he'd swam through the horde of gossiping nobles, Hans approached his wife and kissed her on the cheek. "What did I miss, my dear?"

"Henry Lockett is no more, my lord," Baron Burnice spoke up. He'd been watching Hans closely as he came to stand beside his wife. "I'm afraid you missed quite the spectacle."

Henry Lockett, the King's own secretary, a traitor of the highest order, had been drawn and quartered. And Hans had missed it all for an additional hour of pleasure in the inn. But he could hardly have helped himself. Mister Kaswick served the finest wines in Vinerheim, and that Mistress Betty's bosom...

"It was strange," Heatha said, addressing no one in particular. "I tried to watch the execution, but I couldn't. I found myself entranced by his wife as she scrambled to reach the stage. Her grief, her sorrow... Hans, I have never seen anything like it."

Hans hadn't quite heard her. "What's that you say, my dear? Whose wife?"

King Halmond Verstecian was watching the stage from his balcony above, silent and motionless. He reminded Hans of the statue in the palace gardens that depicted Hektor awaiting his final judgement before the Goddess. Only, this statue was exacting his own form of judgement.

"Never mind," Heatha muttered under her breath.

The commoners started jeering like wild beasts, throwing their rotten fruits and vegetables at the corpse sprawled over the podium. The guards were barely able to contain the braying mob.

A procession pushed its way through the crowd – Jesmond Verstecian, flanked by a dozen or so guards. The commoners' wrath was diverted in the prince's direction.

"He would have been our king," Heatha said under her breath.

Hans scanned over the faces gathered around them. Convinced that none had heard her, he nudged his wife gently in the ribs. "Careful, my love. We wouldn't want you to join the good prince."

The executioner made no attempt to remove the pieces of Henry Lockett that lay strewn across the podium. Black flies swarmed around the scene, hungry for the dead, and hungrier for the almost-dead.

The law favoured Jesmond as it forbade royalty from experiencing the gruesome form of execution Lockett had endured. Halmond would not have protested this regardless, as a hurried performance meant his brother's swift removal from the world.

Jesmond made the sign of the cross as he approached the block. The executioner had severed several heads there that morning: minor accomplices, servants found guilty of aiding their would-be king. A sham trial had revealed Lockett and Jesmond to be the only noble conspirators of this foiled overthrow. Hans knew otherwise.

"May I speak a few words?" Jesmond asked his executioner, but the leather-masked man shook his head. Jesmond knelt before the block.

Hans found himself staring into the man's eyes. Jesmond muttered something under his breath, no doubt begging for his entrance to the Gardens.

The axe fell swiftly, slicing the prince's head off in one swoop.

The executioner held up the dripping head for all to see. "All 'ail King 'almond! All 'ail the King o' Diamonds!"

And the crowd responded in kind, punching the air, cheering madly. The executioner had sated their appetite for now.

As the commoners dispersed from the courtyard, the rains fell harder, beating down on the stage, washing away the blood and gore.

King Halmond retreated from his balcony, disappearing into the palace. Heatha, too, had vanished when Hans turned around. The barons were filing into the palace for shelter.

Hans found himself unable to follow them. He stood alone in this courtyard of blood and rain, watching as the servants cleaned the mess and the executioner wiped blood from his axe.

"Hanzus Irvaye," a voice spoke. He turned to find a woman, perhaps no older than twenty, clutching a babe in her arms. Black makeup ran down her gaunt face. A child of three or four was tottering alongside her, sucking at their thumb.

Hans squared his eyes at the woman. "I beg your pardon?" He couldn't place the woman. Though she dressed modestly, she looked upon him as an equal. "Who are you? Why do you not address me according to my station?"

"How can you live with yourself?" she croaked, her body trembling. "My husband had no choice. Jesmond threatened him... threatened us all. He didn't deserve... *that*."

So, it was the late Henry Lockett's wife, Tamara. A common wretch birthed off the gutter.

"Your husband was a traitor of the realm," Hans assured her. "If I were you, I would pray for his soul."

"You murdered his soul." Rage reddened her face. "You'll pay for this. Mark my words, lord. The Goddess'll strike you down, or I'll wield the knife myself."

"I beg your pardon..." But before Hans could conduct his thoughts, Tamara Lockett and her daughter were scurrying away. He took a deep breath, then called after her, "Take care of those children, Lady Lockett!"

"Wake up."

Something slapped his face, stirring his senses. He sat in a chair. A sword pricked his shoulder. Six pairs of red eyes were upon him. In the middle of them, Vors Rennice stood with his arms folded, watching Hanzus with smug curiosity. The innkeeper was beside him, and under her arm, Vilka chewed on a biscuit. They were still inside the Black Rook.

"So now you see it," the plump woman said matter-of-factly. He knew now she was no ordinary innkeeper. "You remember my face. You remember what you did. I can see it in your eyes."

"Tamara Lockett," Hanzus said, half-believing his own words. "And Vilka and Viola... The two children I saw that day. The day their father died."

"The day their father was *butchered!*" Tamara screamed, spraying him with spittle. Vilka dropped her biscuit and scurried away from sight. "*Torn* from us! Eviscerated before our very eyes! Because of you, my lord. *You!*" She aimed a trembling finger at him, her emerald eyes bulging with rage.

"Henry Lockett committed high treason," Hanzus reminded her. He was unsure how he would escape from these heathens. He supposed his only hope was to stall them and pray Arwel hadn't abandoned him. "Your husband's fate was in his own hands, and he decided to back the wrong man. Jesmond had no right to usurp the crown from Halmond. None at all. He had no right to drag our kingdom into a war we could not win. Henry Lockett's suffering was *just*. A consequence of his own treachery." His words, it seemed, were like arrows deflecting off plate armour, serving only to irritate.

"*You* stood as a witness before the King's jury," Tamara retorted. "It was on *your* final word that the verdict was passed. I was there, my lord. The jury was leaning toward a quick, painless death for my dear, dear Henry. There were even whispers he would be saved from the headman's block... that he might live out the remainder of his days imprisoned. But you... *you...*" Her accusing finger waggled at him once more. "*You* brought your venomous tongue before the jury. You *implored* them to inflict vicious, unimaginable torture upon my husband." She broke down in tears. "And they *agreed* with you."

Vors Rennice wrapped a soothing arm around her shoulder as he appraised Hanzus.

"So, you see, all's fair." A new voice entered the fray. The brown smile of Viola pushed its way into view. She stood beside her mother. "You took something from us, so we took something from you."

Hanzus wanted nothing more than to lunge at the girl, to wrap his fingers around her neck and squeeze... squeeze until her worthless life was spent. But the cold tip of a Bloodkin's sword pressed into his neck. Instead, he said, "What folly do you speak of?"

Viola's smile widened. "You don't think your old pa poisoned himself now, do you? We sent Vilka here to bait you out of your little hiding place. But you were gone when she arrived in Balenmeade. So, we improvised."

"Yes, my dear, you did," Vors Rennice said, sighing. "I want you to know, Lord Irvaye, the murder of your father was not of my doing. *I* sent young Vilka to Balenmeade to lure you here to the Black Rook. During which time, my associates here took it upon themselves to visit Freestone." He rolled his eyes at Tamara. "Things did not go as planned."

"I told you," Tamara snapped at Rennice. "The debt will be paid as soon as the House of Irvaye is eradicated. They *all* must die. Jurgen had to go regardless."

Hanzus's heart was pounding. *Francessa... Hessan...* The monsters were threatening his children now. And he was unable to protect them.

Rennice inclined his head. "Indeed, lady."

"I knew I had to hit you where it *really* hurt," Tamara said, returning her gaze to Hanzus. "As we speak, assassins crawl softly into your children's chambers. It won't be long until the process is complete. And just as you eradicated the name of Lockett, the House of Irvaye shall vanish from history." She cut through the air with her hand, emulating an axe.

Hanzus spat at her. "Then why not murder me in Balenmeade? Why lure me here?"

Tamara chuckled. "And miss the opportunity to hear you scream with my own two ears? No, my lord. No, I don't think so."

"Then why employ Captain Morske to murder me aboard the Temper?"

Tamara appeared perplexed at that.

"Yes, we heard of such a happening," Rennice sighed. "But alas, my lord, that act was not of my doing." He bore a smile. "You are a popular man, it seems."

Not their doing? So, Captain Morske's blade and Tamara's poison aren't connected... at all?

"You should know," Tamara said. "I've yearned for this moment for as long as I can remember. You'll forgive me if I take the time to savour it."

Vors Rennice bowed his head. "It has been an honour to follow your movements over these past weeks, my lord. But alas, our time together is nearing its conclusion." He gazed up at the ceiling, searching for the right words. "But before we proceed, my lord, I am wishing for you to know a thing. Although the Lady Lockett's grudge toward you is personal, I myself am holding none."

Hanzus spat at the creature's feet. "You fucking pigs! I'll gut you like the gutter-shits you are!"

"Though amusing that would be, I cannot warrant it," Rennice said, waving him away. He nodded toward the Red Eye aiming their blade at Hanzus. "I am believing that now is the time."

"No... *wait.*" Tamara scurried to Hanzus's side, bringing her face close to his. Her breath reeked of garlic and stale bread. "I want you to know, my lord, I hold you personally responsible for the fate of my husband. You alone. Henry was loyal to the King until his dying breath. You, on the other hand, have serviced yourself and no other. You would not know loyalty if it was fed to you by force."

"There are those that remain loyal to me," Hanzus hissed. *I pray they know I'm here.* "Do you think that by killing me, you will bring peace and security to your children? The King, for one..."

"The King is a halfwit," she spoke over him. "And your threats are baseless. None will learn what transpires here tonight. There will be nothing left of you to learn from." She paused to catch her breath. "I want you to understand the suffering I've endured these past years. I want you to *feel* the suffering of Henry." She exchanged a dark look with Rennice before turning back to Hanzus and swallowing. "What *you* had him endure. Prepare to be hanged, drawn, and quartered."

"You heard her!" Rennice boomed, holding his arms out like a preacher. "The lady is demanding a hanging, drawing, and quartering!"

As their words seeped into his mind, arms seized Hanzus from every angle, dragging him out of the chair.

"Then, and only then, will the debt be paid," Tamara said to Rennice. She whispered something else in his ear, then added for all to hear, "I promise you that."

The last thing Hanzus saw before they dragged him through the doorway was Vilka staring at him, her emotionless face carved out of stone.

Deliverance

Barrett was conscious. He could twitch his fingers, but they were stiff. He could flutter his eyelids, but they would not fully open.

Boots crunched into dry earth, dull thuds that vibrated his eardrum. Then a piercing cry grew louder and louder, like a blade scratching glass. Someone or some*thing* was screaming.

Vigour surged through Barrett's veins. His eyes snapped open. Light blinded him. When his eyes adjusted, the sight they beheld didn't seem real. Was he suspended in a macabre dream? Was he dead? Had the Goddess abandoned him?

Hanzus Irvaye leaned against a tree as milk-skinned men grasped and punched and smacked him. The Baron lacked the strength to resist. He was lifeless save for the groans he emitted. Two Bloodkin held him in place while another stood by uttering a low, ominous chant. A third Red Eye was looping a noose over the Baron's neck.

He glanced around and saw only Bloodkin. They were everywhere, but none had noticed Barrett's consciousness in the corner of the clearing. He willed his body to crawl, to escape, but his limbs were rigid. Everything ached.

Vilka betrayed us. She's one of Henry Lockett's daughters... She was sent to lure us into her mother's trap.

It was all flooding back. Vilka was not Vilka at all, but Wilkoria Lockett. Her mother, Tamara, was the fat innkeeper of the Black Rook. The sickly barmaid, Viola, was Vilka's sister. The Locketts were behind it all: Vilka's appearance in Balenmeade, the Bloodkin, Jurgen Irvaye's assassination...

Hanzus yelped and thrashed, but his resistance was futile. Four pairs of hands now pinned him up against the tree. One cupped Hanzus's jaw like a goblet, forcing him to face the sky. Then the other three retreated several paces, bowing their heads and holding their hands in prayer. The one who remained with him grasped Hanzus like a prize, dominating with ease.

Barrett struggled onto his feet, then faltered and fell back against what had to be a tree. No one seemed to notice him. He sat back, propped up by the obstacle. From what he could tell, his body was unharmed, but it was sapped of all energy. His head throbbed incessantly. His vision was blurry. He was going to faint.

"Wait!" a shrill voice cut through the air, stirring Barrett's senses.

The Bloodkin holding Hanzus's face paused, his scarlet eyes searching the black blanket of trees.

A plump figure swept into the scene. Tamara Lockett, the woman who'd revealed herself to be Vilka's mother. From somewhere, yellow light illuminated her against the dark woodland backdrop. Barrett blinked several times before he realised she was carrying a lamp.

"Before we part, my lord, I must know something." Tamara held the lamp up to the Baron's face. "I need to know if you repent for your actions. I would hear it from your own lips. Tell me now whether you feel remorse or sorrow. Tell me now whether you regret what you did to my Henry."

Tamara nodded at the Bloodkin holding Hanzus, who then weakened his gasp. Hanzus's head drooped down. He coughed several times before lifting his chin and meeting the innkeeper's face.

"Repent, you say? *Remorse?*" Hanzus croaked, red spittle bubbling from his lips. He almost sounded amused. Blood oozed from his hairline, trickling down his forehead. "Remorse for what? Your husband was a traitor."

Tamara straightened. "Think carefully, my lord. Repentance will be met with forgiveness."

"He ain't yours to forgive," the Bloodkin hissed at her.

"Indeed. But we can offer a quick death, can we not? That which was never afforded to my dear Henry."

The Bloodkin scoffed at the idea, but he turned to Hanzus and said, "Well, what d'you say?" Then, when the Baron did not reply, he turned back to Tamara. "So you see, your baron don't want no mercy. A quick death he won't receive from me. Vors wants him to die slow."

Before any of them could react, Hanzus gargled and spat in the plump woman's face. "Your bastard husband would have had our kingdom down on its knees! Slaves to the Sylvian Empire, no better than the fucking Rooksland! Jesmond planned to cede the kingdom's power to the Empire! Don't you see, you stupid bitch? Your Henry is rotting in oblivion as we speak."

Tamara's hand was trembling as she wiped pink spittle from her face. "It is as I feared then. There can be no forgiveness without repentance, my lord. Henry held no grudges. Even at the very end, he forgave the False King for the unjust punishment delivered upon him." She slapped the Baron across the cheek, her eyes aglow with rage. "As for *you* and that snake, Arwel Nate, there can be no mercy."

Baron Arwel... does she mean he's here? Barrett squinted around the darkness. Bloodkin lurked on the edge of the clearing, their milk-white faces glowing in the light of their torches. *Like ghosts waiting to snatch the Baron's spirit.*

"Where *is* Nate?" the Bloodkin holding Hanzus snapped at Tamara.

She shrugged. "How should I know? Bastard slipped away when the inn was busy. It was like he sensed something. Perhaps he caught a whiff of your stench."

"Fear not, lady." Vors Rennice stepped out of the shadows, clutching a curved dagger that glimmered in the torchlight. "We are knowing the location of Silvertongue." His attention turned to Hanzus then. "It would appear your friend has abandoned you, my lord."

Barrett's heart sank. *Then there's no hope for any of us.*

"Proceed," Tamara barked at Vors. "Do it now. Let Vässa judge his wretched soul."

Barrett fingered his belt, searching. His scabbard was empty. *Shit.*

"*Vässa?*" Hanzus spat. "Don't tell me you worship the Twins now? You miserable, blasphemous cunt."

Tamara giggled like a child. "Oh, that *is* rich coming from you, my lord. What do you know of gods and goddesses? What do you know of morality? I question the morals of any man that breaks bread with Arwel Nate. Just see where that friendship got you." She thrust her head back and cackled at the night's sky. "You chide me for my worship of the True Gods, and yet it was *you* that turned me away from that unfaithful whore of a goddess. *You* that caused my fall from grace. I lost everything. *Everything.*" She pushed her face so close to Hanzus their noses touched. "But *they* found me in my hour of desperate need. *They* lifted me up out of the gutter." She stepped back several paces, her eyes hypnotically glued to the Baron. "And here I am, because of the Twins. *They* gave me the strength to carry on. *They* gave me a chance to redeem myself. Vengeance. But such kindness demands something in return." She nodded along with her own words, peering up at the sky. "You will weep long before this night is through, my lord. You will suffer as my dear Henry suffered."

"And *you* will join him in Oblivion," Hanzus spat through his teeth. He struggled against the Bloodkin's grip, but his flailing was useless. "With the Goddess as my witness, I curse you now..."

"There is no need to prolong these formalities," Tamara spoke over him. "Gods forbid, my Henry was not afforded any such courtesy." She nodded at Vors. "Master Rennice, you may proceed."

"Indeed," Vors said, inclining his head. "Apologises, my lord, but we are not having the means to draw you. We must, therefore, improvise." He cleared his throat, then clutched his dagger with both hands. He appeared to close his eyes as if to pray. "Under the watchful eyes of Vällas and Vässa, I, Vors Rennice of the Plargross, do sentence you, Hanzus Irvaye of the Gadensland, to die."

Barrett had failed his lord in every conceivable way. The end was now. The end of Hanzus, the end of Barrett, the end of their world. The Bloodkin would gut Barrett once they had disposed of the Baron. But right now, every red eye in the clearing scrutinised Hanzus, transfixed. If Barrett moved now, he could sneak away and...

No.

He couldn't just abandon his lord, as Arwel had done. He'd betrayed Hanzus once already. *Never again.* He would stand and fight, no matter the hopelessness. He would lie down his life in service to his liege lord, the way a true Krämisen would.

But it was too late.

The noose tightened around the Baron's neck. He was being lifted off the ground. Hanzus clawed at his own neck, his legs kicked out at nothing. Vors and his Bloodkin stood back to watch the macabre scene unfold, but Tamara remained close to the Baron's wriggling feet.

Then Hanzus's movements slowed. His legs stopped squirming. His arms dropped to his sides.

Rennice waved his hand, and the Bloodkin stationed behind the tree cut the rope, sending Hanzus crashing to the earth below. Two Bloodkin rushed forward and propped him up. He was just about conscious, gurgling for breath.

"Vällas, bless this blade," Rennice said, lifting his dagger high above his head. His eyes closed in thought. He breathed in slowly through his nose, smelling the fear in the air. Then his eyes snapped open. The odd orbs were aglow with malice. He aimed the tip of his blade at Hanzus's chest.

Bone crunched. Flesh ripped. The blade entered over and over, penetrating like a violent lover, the blows alternating between chest and stomach. Then, like a practised butcher, Rennice dragged the blade up along the sternum, shredding the Baron's tunic, dark blood oozing from the rip.

And then it started. One by one, fingers extracted entrails from the gaping wound, gore-soaked elements pulsating in Vors's bloody hands. Barrett tried to look away, tried to shield his eyes from the horror, but the senseless violence gripped him as though invisible fingers wrenched his eyelids open and held him down in place.

Blood sprayed over every face as the Bloodkin surrounding the clearing began to close in on the Baron. Tamara didn't recoil from the gore plastering her lips.

"Stop... *stop*... just make it stop!" Barrett tried to yell, but he hadn't the strength and the words caught in his throat. "S-s-st-op." He spluttered, his tongue sluggish. He was nothing more than his eyes and ears now. The last drop of humanity he possessed screamed for the madness to end, but the sound remained hidden and locked inside his head.

Finally, Rennice ripped the Baron's beating heart from his chest. He held it above his head like a trophy for all to see. The Bloodkin cheered and hooted as Rennice tossed the organ aside like a scrap of unwanted food.

One of the Red Eyes handed a sword to Vors. The halfbreed held the blade above his head, muttered something, then, in one fell swoop, hacked Hanzus's head clean off. Blood sprayed in an arc as the lifeless corpse crumpled to the ground.

A scream hissed from Barrett's lips. His voice had returned at the least opportune moment. Every face in the clearing turned in his direction.

Tamara squealed in delight, clapping her hands together like an excited child. Gore painted her face red. "My dear Henry! In *her* eyes, you are avenged!"

Rennice grimaced toward Barrett, then he furrowed his brows and turned back to Tamara. "*Her?* Who is *her?*"

Tamara hadn't heard him. She skipped over to Hanzus's corpse and served it several feeble kicks.

Every red eye had returned its attention to the innkeeper.

"My dear, dear, *beautiful* Henry!" Tamara spoke manically to herself, grinning up at the sky. "I see you now smiling down at me. The process is complete! You may rest in peace now. But wait for me, my love. When I join you, we shall wander the Gardens together for all eternity."

"What is this garden you are speaking of?" Vors asked, wiping his blade clean of gore.

Tamara's bulging eyes fell on Rennice. Her smile faded as she wiped the wet blood off her face with her sleeve. "It would appear our bargain is complete, Mister Rennice. I thank you profusely for assisting me in this great task."

"I asked you a question," Rennice said coolly. "You mentioned that you would wander a garden eternally. What is your meaning with this?"

Tamara whitened. Her eyes alternated between Rennice and his red-eyed thugs. "What... what do you mean? The garden... ah yes, that is a simple expression that..."

"And he who lived a pious life, rejoice, for he shall wander the gardens green for an eternity, wrapped in the grace of his lady." Rennice's words were a direct quote from the holy books of Hektor. But Barrett doubted this filthy halfbreed was a devout follower of the Prophet.

Rennice smiled as the woman frowned.

"The Gardens of the Goddess," Rennice said, seeming satisfied. "Is this the garden you are referring to?"

"No." Tamara was backing away from him now. "No... no. I would never speak of that fictional goddess. You have to believe me, Vors, I would never... I am true to..."

"*Yes?*" Rennice hissed over her, furrowing his brows in a snarl. He lifted his blade, aiming the tip at her neck. "You swore an oath. An oath to the Twins of Blood. An oath to *him*! Are words meaning nothing to you?" He gestured at the Baron's ruined body. "Is *this* meaning nothing to you?"

"No... I mean yes... that is to say *no*..." Her eyes were a mix of terror and confusion. "*No.*"

It was too late.

Vors lunged forward with his sword, slashing at the woman's neck. She recoiled backwards, clutching her wound, and as she reeled beside Hanzus's corpse, Rennice slashed once more, slicing her head from her shoulders. It rolled across the earth, stopping beside Hanzus's severed head. For a split second, Barrett swore the woman's eyes were blinking at the Baron's face.

"Our purpose is done!" Rennice announced, wiping his blade once more. "Make ready to move!"

"What of the Kinsmeer?" One of the Bloodkin nodded in Barrett's direction.

Rennice straightened. He didn't so much as glance Barrett's way. "According to Vilka, the man is worth something. If that was true, such a worth is valid no longer. Dispose of him, Bevrian." Rennice walked away from the clearing, slipping out of his gloves. "We move out!"

The Bloodkin called Bevrian lingered in the clearing as the others followed Vors Rennice out of view. His crimson eyes scanned over Barrett like a beast calculating its prey. He unsheathed his dagger and padded toward him.

Barrett patted the surrounding earth, searching for a sword, a weapon, anything.

He found nothing. *Goddess, save me.*

No divine force would protect him now. Bevrian aimed his blade at Barrett's face. He was inches away from hitting the mark.

As Barrett's hand ran along the underside of his belt, searching, he felt something protruding from his back pocket. A small shape, not usual in the slightest. Without thinking, he slipped his fingers inside the pocket. His nails brushed against what felt like leather.

Save me... save me...

"Eh?" Bevrian had stopped in his tracks, blinking dumbly at the tree behind Barrett. "Where'd you go?"

The Bloodkin was toying with him now, using him as a plaything.

Barrett was shaking all over. He withdrew the object from his pocket and gripped it tight in his hand. It felt like a small book, small enough to fit in his palm.

"This some sort of trick?" Bevrian was looking straight into Barrett's eyes... or was he? He was staring straight through him.

"Sorcery!" the Bloodkin declared, staggering back several steps, his scarlet eyes wide with fear. "Witchery!"

Barrett stared at the creature in disbelief. The Bloodkin was playing a trick, though to what end it wasn't clear. Barrett edged himself away from the tree, seizing the opportunity regardless. A sting shot up his spine. Relentless agony. Pushing the pain aside, he slid forward onto his elbows and shuffled sideways, gripping the book for dear life. This tiny object had breathed new life into his body, ordering him to survive.

Bevrian stood facing the tree still, dumbstruck, terrified. His grip on his dagger was weakening. The hilt slid down to the tips of his fingers. "I know you're still there, Kinsmeer. Despite your witchery, I'll... I'll find you!"

Barrett slid across the moist earth with surprising ease. His arms did most of the work, dragging his rigid legs forward. His chin bumped against hard mounds of earth. Dirt spattered his cheeks. He passed a dark fleshy clump suspended in a pool of blood – the Baron's heart if he wasn't mistaken.

I am so sorry, my lord. I failed you.

But he didn't linger on the thought. All he had now was the willingness to survive, the compulsion to escape.

He reached another tree. Turning painfully back toward Bevrian, he discovered the Bloodkin had dropped his dagger and was scratching his head with uncertainty.

"Pox on you!" the Bloodkin wailed before scurrying away from the clearing in search of his master.

With the immediate threat gone, the last remnants of Barrett's energy dissipated. His head was heavy as iron, his sight blurry. He found himself fading... fading from the world.

The Call of Oblivion

Hanzus Irvaye was standing in front of Barrett, smiling as he took his hand.

"Welcome, welcome," the Baron said, ushering his loyal steward into a chair. The second-largest seat at his table. His pride of place. "Now, you will feast with your baron. And tonight, we shall make merry."

Hanzus gestured down at the long table. Past all the seated courtiers eagerly awaiting the feast, a jolly jester was performing a merry jig. As soon as Barrett looked at him, the jester paused from his dance and bowed dramatically low, and when he rose, a lute had appeared in his hands.

"My lords!" the fool boomed for all to hear. "My lords, pray allow me the great honour of serenading these fellows."

Hanzus raised a playful eyebrow Barrett's way. "Well, what do you say? After all, this is *your* feast."

Barrett chuckled at that. "Have you ever known me to refuse a happy fool?"

Hanzus clapped his hands together and sank into his chair. "Make us jolly, dear fool! Sing us a happy tune!"

The jester skipped up and down the banquet table, strumming away on his instrument with cheery abandon. Barrett recognised the tune at once. It was his favourite. The fool's voice was easy on the ears, and the courtiers all sang along.

Balenmeade, Balenmeade,
What have you done?
You served me your riches, and now I am glum.

Balenmeade, Balenmeade,
How could you paint?
Your beautiful picture for my mind to taint.

You lifted me, gifted me,
Mended my sorrow,
You kept good your promise to greet me tomorrow.

You made me your lover, a love without end.
And now I'm indebted to keep as your friend.

Balenmeade, Balenmeade,
How could you keep?
My heart that was gave you to never mistreat.

Balenmeade, Balenmeade,
I shan't ever find,
A town of your richness and folk of your kind.

You lifted me, gifted me,
Mended my sorrow,
You kept good your promise to greet me tomorrow.

You made me a part of you,
Made me a home,
And never I'll leave you,
Should I ever roam.

Barrett was humming the tune as he awoke. The song turned to ashes on his tongue, graduating into an agonising scream. He was yelling, as loud as his feeble body would allow. Every last drop of raw strength concentrated in his throat as the screech hissed from his lips.

"You're alive," a calm voice spoke to him, originating from nearby.

Barrett fell silent. His eyes creaked open. The shape that greeted him didn't belong to a person but a wall of mud-brown. He was staring at wood, he realised – a dark, knotted wall riddled with splinters.

But walls can't speak.

He tried to shift his gaze from the wall, but his head was stiff, clamped down in place. His body was unmovable. A thick sheet of ice had frozen over him.

Moments later, he gained the strength to crane his neck. He was lying on a bed, its mottled sheets covering his sternum.

Someone was sitting beside him, perched on a stool. A wrinkly, neckless face slotted underneath a green felt hat. An elderly woman. There was a softness to her aged features, a kindness to her dark brown eyes.

"I'm pleased to see you waken," she croaked. He didn't recognise her face or voice, but her presence was soothing. Something told him she'd been sitting there for hours, if not days.

"Where am I?" Barrett squinted up at the ceiling, but the damp wood offered as many clues as the walls. Perhaps this kindly hag found him in the woods and escorted him to her shack, though he doubted she'd have been able to carry him.

"You're safe, dear. You needn't despair a moment more. I'll take care of you now."

Barrett retrieved his left arm from the sheets, ran the tips of his fingers over his forehead. He didn't feel pain. He didn't feel anything.

"The Bloodkin," he said. The woman's features creased, revealing dozens of new wrinkles. He opened his mouth to speak more, but no more than primitive rasps and squeals passed through his lips.

The woman's eyes widened with fright. "Don't dwell on unhappy thoughts, love. Threat's gone now. You're safe. All's to be done's for you to mend, and it'll happen in good time."

Safe... The word echoed in the deepest, darkest depths of his mind, stagnating like a foul stench. *I'm safe... but at what cost? What expense?* Who had Barrett made unsafe so he could rest in this bed?

Barrett held his head, rubbing his temples. His thoughts were dark. He couldn't make sense of them. He wanted it all to end. He wanted the dreadful images to burn out and turn to ash on the wind.

Hanzus Irvaye... the Bloodkin... Vilka. Had it all been a dream?

"Where am I?"

The woman knitted her grey brows, ruminating on his question. "You need rest now. Rest your bones, rest your noggin. Both's weary."

"Where am I?" Barrett repeated. Tears welled above his cheeks. He feared he already knew the answer.

"You been brought to the Black Rook Inn. Here you'll mend, but only if you let yourself rest."

Bitter droplets streamed down his cheeks, forming wells of despair in the creases of his face. *The Black Rook Inn.* That was the place the Bloodkin spoke of. Had they somehow lured the Baron here?

"He's dead because of me," Barrett admitted. Ashamed, he turned away from the healer's ancient eyes. There was wisdom behind her reticent gaze. A look of innate knowledge as to the meaning of his words. He didn't wish to be judged by this strange hag for a moment longer. "I'm to blame," he whispered, sobbing into the sheets.

"A poison dwells in your belly," the woman stated matter-of-factly. "It sullies your mind. Don't pay mind to such dark thoughts. Think only of your mend."

Poison? Yes, the Bloodkin had fed him with a mysterious liquid when they'd captured him on the Old Road. It was that very potion that had lulled him into a deep sleep, the sleep that had given birth to this nightmare.

Vors Rennice had ripped Hanzus Irvaye's heart out before Barrett's very eyes.

Goddess, have mercy on my tainted soul.

That harrowing image would haunt him forever. He would never be free of its grasp. He'd never atone for the sins that led him to the Bloodkin. *The Baron's death is my fault. I betrayed him. I turned my back on him the moment I chose to follow Heatha's instructions.*

"I will never recover," he told the hag, turning back to her. "I will never forget what I saw."

The woman frowned at that. "You're sturdier than that. Can see it in your eyes. You'll recover, lad. Hear me, you will." She narrowed her dark eyes at him. "You won't be giving up easy. This old bat won't let you. You'll lay in this bed, and you'll sip the stews I bring. With Goddess on our side, the poison'll pass from your body before long."

She rose from the stool and shuffled away from the bed. "We'll speak on the morrow, love. There're others I must attend to."

Others? Bile filled Barrett's mouth. How many more had the Bloodkin maimed?

"Please... don't leave me." *Don't leave me alone with my thoughts.* Thoughts would consume him long before any poison did.

By some twist of fate, he'd survived his Bloodkin captors. And yet, they would remain a part of him, his tormentors forevermore. He'd never forget their horrid speech, their bestial eyes, the sickening ease with which they'd extracted Hanzus's organs.

"How am I alive?" he cried out, tears stinging his eyes. "How did I survive?"

Bloodkin had destroyed the Baron Without Sorrow with ease. And yet, Barrett Barrett, an accountant of the Balenmanor, had evaded all their daggers.

"You breathe 'cause the Holy Lady wills it," the old woman stated. "Now honour her mercy by letting me mend you."

Barrett knew no godly intervention had spared him.

The memory didn't make sense, but it was there all the same, clear in his mind.

A small book had saved his life, a thin scrap of leather and parchment. He'd discovered the object slotted in his pocket as the Bloodkin named Bevrian approached him with a dagger. The act of clutching the book had turned Barrett invisible to Bevrian's eyes, enabling him to crawl to safety.

But how was that possible?

What black sorcery could have enchanted a book to render its wielder invisible? And how had such a thing found itself in his pocket?

None of it made sense. The memory was untrue, a corruption of the mind. The poison's doing, no doubt.

But he *had* escaped. However, it had occurred, he'd survived the Bloodkin.

The woman's sigh interrupted his thoughts. "Rest now. I'm needed elsewhere."

"Wait! What is your name? I would know the name of my healer."

"Solka," was the reply before the door closed.

Every few hours, Solka brought bowls of grey, tasteless soup and mugs of greenish, pungent tea to his bed, claiming the liquids would help him sweat and piss the poison out.

Barrett was unaware of the passing of time, but he rarely saw daylight. When he awoke from his nightmares, the moon leaked through his window, serving as his constant guardian.

One evening, as Barrett sipped his tea, he watched the bedroom door creak open, and a hunched figure shuffled into the room, shrouded by the shadow. Their hair was much darker than Solka's.

A shiver rippled down Barrett's spine as the stranger stomped through the gloom and halted at the foot of his bed. Fear told him the Bloodkin had returned to finish him off, but as the moonlight brushed the stranger's face, he realised they were no stranger at all.

"*Cay?*" he croaked, unsure that he could trust his eyes. "Cay, is that... you?"

He had to be dreaming, or else the poison had consumed his brain. He squinted through the gloom, studying the man's features. They appeared to be Cay, unless a demon had taken his form.

"Barrett," Cay said, scarcely louder than a whisper. He was gazing at the floor. "Forgive me... I was too ashamed to visit you."

Barrett struggled to discern the valet's shrouded features. "Cay, thank the Goddess you're alive. Where... where are the others?"

Wordlessly, Cay turned back to the door and patted it closed. He padded over to the stool, seating himself beside the bed. He seemed incapable of meeting Barrett's gaze.

"Barrett, will you ever forgive me?"

Barrett squinted at the valet's face, trying to make sense of the question. "What do you mean?"

"Please... I'll explain." Cay blinked down at his hands. "When we were confronted with Bloodkin on the Old Road, the Baron ordered us to retreat, to continue on to Freestone without fighting on. So, I ran with the others, without issue or complaint. I didn't realise that you and Ache weren't with us until it was too late." He paused, pursing his lips in thought. "I never forgave the Baron for abandoning the two of you to die, but I didn't consider at the time that I too was to blame."

"What? No." Barrett recalled the event clearly: Hanzus seated in Lion's saddle, barking at his servants to retreat from the Bloodkin. Barrett had watched their horses fade into the distance before Ache was slaughtered before his eyes.

But it wasn't Cay's fault. The valet had been following orders. *We've both been following orders... bad orders. And see where they've led us.*

"I never spoke against it," Cay explained. "We arrived in Kellenmoor the eve after that battle. I slept well in the inn that night, thanking the Goddess for sparing me." He lifted his chin, meeting Barrett with his teary eyes. "I promise, I never imagined in my wildest dreams that you were alive. That those beasts hadn't gutted you as soon as we fled. When I heard you were here in the Black Rook, I realised those creatures had dragged you all the way here to act as their hostage. Barrett, I'm... I'm so sorry." He wiped the tears dribbling down his cheeks. "Tell me, please... did the Red Eyes spare Ache also?"

Sick filled Barrett's throat. He had no choice but to swallow it. "Ache... he... fell protecting me."

It was true. There may have been whispers throughout the Balenmanor that Ache was loyal to the Baroness only, but the fierce warrior had died with honour, fighting the Bloodkin to the very end. He'd attempted to impersonate Hanzus, to take the blade on his behalf. Ache died a hero.

"Where are the others?" Barrett asked, sucking up the tears that threatened. "Lew... Pamen... Tell me they're alive."

"I'm sorry," Cay said, hanging his head in shame. "The Lord Nate and I were able to..." He faltered, choking on his words. He held his head in his hands, sobbing into his palms.

Lord Nate? Barrett recalled the Bloodkin mentioning the Baron of the Tyldar. But his mind was foggy. The memory was weak.

"After Kellenmoor, Hanzus led us to Freestone," Cay continued, lifting his head. "When we arrived, the Lord Nate was there already, waiting for us, tending to Hanzus's father. After Jurgen passed, a monk told us that his poisoner was headed to the Black Rook, so we travelled here." He shook his head in disbelief, spraying tears in an arc. "*They* caused this, Barrett. The monks. Without their information, we'd never have come here."

This was the fault of the Mutlen brothers? No, surely, they weren't behind this. Barrett remembered the fat woman who'd stood in front of Hanzus, taunting him before the Bloodkin murdered him. She was human. The more he thought on it, the more he recalled. The Bloodkin had dragged Barrett into this inn... dragged him before Hanzus and Lew, who were captives as well. The fat human had stood there, beside Vors Rennice, and claimed to be Vilka's mother.

They were behind this. Vilka and her mother were the traitors. All along, Vilka's true purpose had been to lure the Baron of the Krämise to his death. And the innkeeper's other daughter had revealed herself to be Jurgen's poisoner. The whole wretched family had been working with the Bloodkin all along.

Bile filled Barrett's mouth. He remembered Vors Rennice slaying the fat innkeeper, though he couldn't recall why. *Damn my mind.* The memory was hazy, unclear. Though, if the Bloodkin so readily turned on the innkeeper, who was to say they didn't slit Vilka's throat also?

"Did they find a girl after the Bloodkin fled? She had brown eyes. Or they could have been green." Something told him they were, in fact, green. He recalled the oracle's words in Balenmeade before the

Feast of Harvest: *The woman with the green eyes is your future. You will not escape her. You cannot. Your path is set out before you, and it cannot be rejected.* Even now, he remembered the crone's words clearly. They lived within him.

Cay raised an eyebrow. His eyes had dried up. "Yes, a girl was found. The innkeeper's daughter."

Barrett shuddered. *That has to be her.*

"Her name was Viola," Cay said, dispelling Barrett's notion. "She served ale and stew to the barons and me, here in the Black Rook before things turned sour. But Viola was found with her throat slit. It seems the Bloodkin spared no one. None but you." He narrowed his eyes at Barrett. "How *did* you escape? You were found unconscious under a tree, a stone's throw from Hanzus... or what remained of him. What did you do to survive? Play dead?"

Barrett turned his gaze to the ceiling. Still, his mind convinced him that a small book had saved his life. *Madness... the poison plays tricks on you.*

"I'm not sure," Barrett lied. He couldn't tell Cay about the book – he would sound ridiculous. "I saw the Baron... I saw his life taken in front of my own two eyes. Then I awoke in this bed."

Cay nodded, seemingly convinced. "All that matters is you're safe. Barrett, will you ever forgive me for leaving you? If I'd have only known you were alive..."

"There's nothing to forgive," Barrett said, offering a weak smile. "How did *you* survive the Bloodkin?"

Cay sucked in the crisp night's air as he gazed out the window. "From Freestone, the Lord Nate guided us here to the Black Rook. Hanzus and Nate were convinced they could sniff out Jurgen's poisoner. So, we sat in the drinking hall below this room, and we waited. But nothing happened. No doubt, Hanzus took that to mean we hadn't stepped into a trap. He retired to one of these rooms for the eve, and not long after, something happened... I don't know how, but the bard that'd been playing on the stage... one moment he was smiling out at the crowd, the next his head was gone from his shoulders. A Bloodkin stepped up onto the stage, and flames spawned from his hands. He was a sorcerer, Barrett... a... a fucking sorcerer." His gaze returned to Barrett. His eyes were wide with anguish. "The Rooksfolk turned to madness... turned wild. The bastards fled for their lives. Not one of the cowards stood to fight. The crowd dragged Nate, Pamen, and me out into the night. Bloodkin were everywhere. Goddess above, there were hundreds of them. We fought bravely, felling handfuls of the creatures. But Pamen fell. He... he was stabbed through the chest. The Lord Nate and me fought for what seemed hours, but the Bloodkin... it was like they weren't truly fighting us back. Their aim must've been to distract us, to lure us away from Hanzus. Eventually, they sheathed their weapons and fled from us. Rookish soldiers arrived at the Black Rook not long after, but it was too late. The sun was rising when we found you, and... what remained of our baron."

Barrett's eyes were filling with tears. "I failed him."

"*We* failed him," Cay said through gritted teeth, anger overtaking sorrow. "The Lord Nate remains here still in the Black Rook. On the morrow, he means to ride for Freestone with the remains of Hanzus in tow. There, he'll gather Jurgen's corpse and transport both father and son to Balenmeade. To return them to their rightful place." His face hardened. He gulped. "I mean to ride with him."

Barrett tried to lift himself up from the bed, but a sharp pain pulsed in his shoulders. Strength failed him. He collapsed. His brittle bones smacked hard against the wooden surface. He turned back to Cay, panting, sweat trickling down his face.

"You're too weak to ride alongside us," Cay said. "But I won't leave you here." He rose from the stool, frowning down at Barrett. "Healer Solka tells me the poison has all but drained from your body. You'll ride with me." He drew a deep sigh, turning to face the moon. "We'll return our master's body to Balenmeade. After that, we will plot our revenge."

Cay stomped out of the room before Barrett could murmur a word in response.

Barrett remained under his sheets, drenched in sweat and tears, fighting for air as he fought the call of Oblivion.

Cay was right. They could avenge the Baron's death.

The Bloodkin were still out there, hiding somewhere in the Rooksland or the Krämise. And Vilka was with them. If she hadn't shared her mother and sister's fate.

He had to learn the truth. Why had the Bloodkin hunted Hanzus in the first place? And who did they work for? The innkeeper had played a part in the Baron's demise, but Vors Rennice had disposed of her like she was nothing. Rennice had to be following instructions from someone else.

The Baroness?

With Hanzus now dead, Heatha could rule the Krämise unopposed. The Baron's heir, Hessan, wasn't of age. His mother would have to govern in his stead.

But then he remembered the claim the fat innkeeper had used to torment Hanzus before his execution. *As we speak, assassins crawl softly into your children's chambers.* Those were her words. Was the claim some heinous lie, designed purely to torture? Or was there substance to her monstrous bile?

Barrett's head throbbed.

If only he could remember all that had transpired. But the poison infused his brain, and he was so very tired...

Then he remembered. The dam burst within his mind, drowning him with terrible memories.

The Black Rook's innkeeper had been Tamara Lockett, the widow of Henry Lockett – a man who'd supported Prince Jesmond's attempt to usurp his brother's throne. Hanzus and Arwel had uncovered this plot moments before the Battle That Never Was, thus preventing the conflict from going ahead.

Of course.

That was the reason for all of this. The Bloodkin had lured Hanzus to the Black Rook for the widow to exact revenge upon him. But there was more to it than that. Vors Rennice had apologised to

Hanzus before his execution, claiming he didn't share Tamara's grudge. He was a hired mercenary, and yet he murdered Tamara before she could reward him for his service. Tamara wasn't Rennice's true employer, and if he had truly sent Bloodkin to assassinate Hessan and Francessa, Heatha wasn't behind his orders either.

By the Goddess.

Vilka was the daughter of Henry Lockett, and now she belonged to Vors Rennice. If he didn't slaughter her first, he would use the girl for some dark purpose.

Barrett rolled over to the side of the bed and puked onto the floor.

Tamara Lockett's fatal words echoed in his mind: *As we speak, assassins crawl softly into your children's chambers.*

Vors Rennice's diabolical plot did not end with Hanzus.

"*Cay!*" Barrett shrieked, struggling to lift himself from the bed. "Cay, come back! I remember! I remember everything!"

The Message

"Lady Morr?"

The voice startled Mavrian, almost causing her to lose her balance. She'd been leaning over the balustrade up on deck, mesmerised by the calm waters around her.

She turned to find Scarmane Trokluss smiling at her side. His milky skin glowed like an iridescent moonstone in the morning sun. He'd slicked back his black hair and tied it into a small bun.

"My Veer," she said, bowing as she attempted to match his smile. "I was just watching..."

"It's peaceful, is it not?" he spoke over her, his lips straightening as he gazed at the azure horizon. "One can find oneself lost in thought at sea."

Mavrian nibbled on the walls of her mouth. "I must confess, I am not at peace."

How could she be? They'd forsaken the people of Kleäm, left them behind to endure a short life of rape and ruin. Reesa was among them, dead or enslaved. Mavrian would never see her friend again. She'd never see Kleäm again.

"Nor I," Scarmane admitted. His vacant expression didn't suggest a lie. "If I have learned one thing and one thing only, it is that I shall never be at peace. As Bloodkin, I fear our lives may never be peaceful."

Mavrian feared he was right, but she didn't dare voice it.

"My Veer," a third voice spoke. A man had appeared next to Scarmane, panting, short of breath. "My Veer... I've news. I came as soon as I... heard it."

"*News?*" Scarmane echoed. He spun on his heel and appraised the intruder with a raised eyebrow. "Seen as how this news caused you to interrupt the Lady Morr and I, it had better be worth it."

The man widened his eyes at Mavrian. "My lady, forgive me..."

"Out with your message, Lers," Scarmane snapped over him. "Speak it now, then be on your way."

"My Veer," the man blubbered, blinking fearfully at his master. "A raven landed aboard. Just now, that is. The message speaks of..." He paused, rolling his eyes over Mavrian. "It pertains to the matter across the sea, my Veer."

Scarmane stiffened at that, his eyes narrowing at the man. "Go on."

"The boar is no more," the man uttered before bowing his head low. "The message comes from Vors Rennice."

Scarmane's eyes widened with surprise before he settled on a smile. "Thank you, Lers. You will hold the raven and await my response. Now go."

"My Veer," the man said, bowing low to Scarmane and Mavrian before scurrying away from sight.

Mavrian turned to Scarmane, trying to gauge his reaction. He looked pleased and troubled at the same time. It was as if the cryptic message was a cause to both celebrate and mourn. She made no sense of it. *Boar is no more?* Who or what did that refer to? There were no boars in Plargross other than those imported from the Kinsmeeric realms.

"Who is Vors Rennice?" she asked.

The Veer turned back to her. His unsmiling face was impossible to read. "Oh, a mere nobody, my dear. His message, however, will please my master greatly."

About the Author

Davey Cobb is a writer of fantasy, horror, and all things weird. Hailing from Manchester, England, he draws inspiration from everyday madness and mundanity.

Printed in Great Britain
by Amazon

24575513R00228